LIE BESIDE ME

A British Murder Mystery

THE WILD FENS MURDER MYSTERY SERIES

JACK CARTWRIGHT

PROLOGUE

The place was perfect. Exactly how she had imagined. There was silence, save for the wind rushing through the wild, tall grass. Her life was about to change forever, and the thought of what might be pulsed through her body.

The summer sun bore down on the ruins of Tupholme Abbey, lighting the old stone in hues of red and orange, and warming her naked skin. Her body tensed in the heat, and she arched her back against the old, tartan blanket, savouring the gentle breath of air and the touch of the cool grass between her toes, imagining his surprise when he found her. The thought of seeing him, of being alone with him with nobody to tell them it was wrong, or to stop them somehow, sent a wave of heat that coursed through her like electricity.

His footsteps swishing through the long grass around the old ruins were the delicate percussion to the thudding beat of her heart, and his silhouette against the sun as he stood before her was the shape of her dreams, her hopes, and of things to come.

"I see you started without me," he said. His voice was songlike, soft and silky, yet effortlessly masculine.

With the sun behind him, his details were obscured, shaded. But she knew them, and if she closed her eyes, she could see them in her mind's eye. He bent to place the hamper down.

"I was keeping the blanket warm," she said. "What kept you?"

"I was chilling the wine."

"Wine? Really?"

"It's a picnic. We can't have a picnic without wine."

She shoved herself up onto her elbow, but stilled when he raised his hand.

"Stay. Don't move. Not a muscle, you hear?"

She nodded and lay back, leaning on one elbow.

"What else is in there?"

"A surprise," he said, and she heard the smile in his voice.

He dropped to his knees at her feet, allowing the sunlight to blind her once more.

"Close your eyes," he whispered, so she did, without even thinking.

Then she felt him close to her. His scent was the wildflowers and the air, and his breath the breeze. And his gift, the surprise he had promised, was the cool, soft touch of a tender strawberry on her lips. She bit down, carefree, and childlike, letting the juice cling to her dry lips.

He straddled her now, and she lay back as he poured the wine. The chink of glass on glass teasing her with what was to come. These delays. That was what he did. That was her opiate, and she found her hands clammy as she lay in wait.

But things were to be done properly. There was a way to do things, and those traditions should be followed. That was his way. When the time came, he would deliver, and she knew it. But by God she wished somebody would tell her body that. The ache beneath her stomach, the way one foot caressed the other involuntarily, and the way her mind wandered to how things might play out were all signs her early exploration had yet to wane.

She was ready for him. She'd been ready for hours. Since he'd first messaged her, in fact.

"To freedom," he said, holding a glass out for her to take.

"In a moment," she told him, and he set the glass down beside the hamper.

She rolled onto her elbow again to watch him with a glee that was growing harder to conceal.

"I thought about you today," he said, resting his glass in the grass beside the blanket.

"I thought about you too," she replied, and found herself biting down on her lower lip again.

"I'm serious. I thought about us. You know? If it could work."

"You've got doubts?" she said, and the heat that twitched her toes and wet her palms dissipated, leaving only winter where summer had shone. "You have, haven't you? You're not going to go through with it."

"No. No, I am. I am," he said, and his touch ignited a candle flame, where only moments before, a fire had raged. "Forget I said anything."

"Forget? What's wrong?" she said, reaching for her clothes, but he stopped her, his hard grip clamping down on her wrist.

"I said forget it," he said, that silky tone replaced with a baritone rumble.

"You're going to do it? You're going to leave her?"

"Of course," he replied, and with a nudge, she was on her back once more, this time with him over her, smothering her. Possessive. "I made you a promise, didn't I?"

"You did."

"I won't let you down."

"Promise."

"I already did–"

"Say it again. Tell me. I'm not sure if I can go back now. Promise me. Promise me we can be together."

He lingered there above her, searching her eyes for some kind of truth. But there were no lies. She had herself bare in every sense of the word, and now she needed him to do the same.

In every sense of the word.

"Promise me," she said, growing impatient. She just needed to hear him say it. It had been a week since they had spoken, long enough for his mind to be changed.

"Shh," he whispered, leaning in to nuzzle her earlobe the way she had imagined him to. "Relax."

"Tell me," she breathed, and she felt herself succumbing to his spell. Her legs, with a mind of their own, wrapped around him, pulling him into her. And she clung to him, feeling the tight muscles beneath his shirt.

It was all so familiar. It was as her dreams had been. His silhouette, his strength, his voice, and his smell were exactly how they would have been had she, by some divine will, created him herself.

He kissed her, and she was lost to his powers, with all thoughts of promises and the future cast away in an instant. And boy, could he kiss. Soft at first, and slow, as if he was simply preparing her.

But nothing could prepare her for the irony taste that followed, or the way his strength seemed to wane, and his weight pinned her to the blanket.

And the way his heavy breaths faltered and stuttered, which only moments before had been in harmony with her own. A duet. A chorus of passion that climaxed before the crescendo.

"John?" she whispered, her fingers groping his back for the source of the wet, sticky blood she felt. "John, talk to me. You're scaring me."

But he didn't move.

A breath came. An exhale, long and protracted. Final.

"John?" she said, panic taking over her senses. "John, get off. Please..."

But the only reply she heard was the ruins of the abbey, echoing her screams.

Then there was silence, save for the wind rushing through the long grass. And she was blinded by the sun, save for a few scant clouds hanging far above them. With his weight pinning her to the ground, she reached around him in a tentative embrace. But the sentiment was short-lived. Her fingers found something warm, wet, and yet tacky.

And she screamed once more, knowing that, just as she had thought, her life would never be the same.

CHAPTER ONE

Detective Inspector Freya Bloom surveyed her team from her place beside the whiteboard. She paused for a moment, considering how she would begin the briefing. They made her feel proud. Each and every one of them had proved themselves invaluable over the past seven or eight months, since she had transferred from London's Metropolitan Police to the small, rural Major Investigations Team in Lincolnshire.

"Some changes," she said, and tapped the whiteboard with the end of the marker. "DC Cruz and DS Gillespie. Consider yourselves joined at the hip. Where one of you goes, the other goes with you."

"Like work-wives?" Nillson said, clearly hoping to stir up some kind of retort from one of them.

"Just colleagues," Gillespie said. "I'll thank you very much."

"Who would be the wife?" Gold asked. "If you were married?"

"I thought that much would be obvious," Gillespie said. "Him. I'm six foot two, and he's—"

"I'm what?" Cruz said, his voice more than a full octave higher than Gillespie's, and even with them both sitting down, he was more than a foot shorter in height.

"You're just you, sweetheart," Gillespie said, and he blew Cruz a kiss, then winked at Gold.

"Ah, come on," Cruz complained. "Boss, do I really have to be joined to the hip with him? Can't you pair me with..."

He looked around the room at each member of the team.

DC Anna Nillson was the only female sibling of five, and, as a result, had little patience and was always keen to bring down a runner. She eyeballed him with evident distaste, and Cruz moved to the next person.

DC Jackie Gold was a single mother with more patience and empathy than any of the team, and as a result had recently elected to be the team's dedicated Family Liaison Officer. People opened up to her. She had a way about her that none of the force's development courses could teach. Cruz moved on.

DC Denise Chapman's strengths lay in research. She could dig details out on any suspect before anybody else had even turned their computers on. That was in part due to the laptops being far from suitable for the jobs they had to do. She enjoyed wearing knitted cardigans to keep her warm, kept her haircut short and plain, and was as mild-mannered as everybody's favourite aunt. Rarely did Chapman venture from the office, where she coordinated the team with precision and attention to detail.

Which left Cruz only one further option.

DS Ben Savage was Freya's right-hand man. There was no way she would lumber him with Cruz, who was often childlike in his mannerisms, and somehow always managed to hurt himself. There had also been more than one occasion when he had actually wet himself. Ben was too good for that. Ben was being lined up for Freya's job when the time was right. Pairing him with Cruz would only undermine his chances of making the next rung up the ladder.

"Ah, forget it," Cruz said, eyeing Gillespie and shaking his head.

"You are officially my new coffee-boy," Gillespie said with a smile.

"Is that how you mentor younger officers, Gillespie?" Freya asked.

"No, boss. It's how I keep them in check. Let them know who's boss. I'll have him whipped into shape in no time. I might even be able to help him stop wetting himself."

"I'm sitting right here," Cruz said.

"Chapman. No changes for you, I'm afraid."

"Fine by me, ma'am."

"Same for you, Ben. You're stuck with me, I'm afraid."

"I'll save my comments for the pub," he replied. "You can't sack me there."

"Speaking of which. It's nearly time," Gillespie said, with a quick look at his watch. "It's Friday night. If you could make this briefing last another twenty-one minutes, boss, I'll send Cruz down there to get the drinks in."

"You do realise that as DC Cruz's superior, you'll be expected to go through his statements and reports?"

"Eh?"

"It's true, Jim," Ben added. "Unless, of course, you want to hand them into DCI Granger without checking them first."

"Granger?"

"He reads them all. Doesn't want HQ thinking we're a bunch of misfits and outcasts. As long as you trust Cruz's abilities as a police officer, you'll be just fine."

"His abilities?" Gillespie repeated. "He doesn't have any bloody abilities."

"Oy," Cruz said, but his objection went mostly unnoticed.

"I suggest you get reading then," Freya said. "DCI Granger likes to read them all over the course of the weekend."

"Eh?"

"I make that twenty minutes," Ben said, smiling.

"Ah, for God's sake," Gillespie said.

"We'll get a beer in for you," Nillson said. "What about me, boss? Am I still on my own?"

"No," Freya said, and she waited for the team to digest the information.

"I'm not on my own?" Nillson said. "But Gold is FLO now, right?"

"Yes, that's right. Gold will be working alone, mostly. She may even be seconded to other teams on the occasion."

"So, who am I with?"

"We have a new team member," Freya said with a smile.

"Eh?" Gillespie said. "Someone new?"

"Yes, Gillespie."

"You mean, I could have had someone other than this idiot?"

"No. No, you couldn't," Freya said. "I think the two of you will be very happy together. You make a lovely couple."

"So, who do we have?" Ben asked.

"And why do we need someone new?" Nillson asked.

"Because just like every DI needs a solid DS behind them, every detective sergeant needs a solid DC behind them."

"I don't get it. I'm not a…" She paused, and for the first time since Freya had met the young officer, she saw true emotion. "Oh my God."

"Congratulations, Detective Sergeant Nillson," Freya said, with a smile. "You passed your exam."

CHAPTER TWO

For the end of week drinks, it was typical for the team to walk along the high street to the local pub, which was so very different from the swanky bars Freya had enjoyed in London. On occasion, she was surprised, charmed even, by the quaintness of the little pubs that dotted the Lincolnshire countryside. Thankfully, the pub closest to the station oozed character, unlike some of the places Ben had taken her, which smelled worse than they looked, and were often filled with unsavoury characters with very little in the way of etiquette and manners.

From day one in Lincolnshire, Freya was determined to instil a little class and dignity into her team, and she had done so to a degree. Should the need arise, Gillespie now visited the washrooms to break wind. Cruz had been made aware of his nose picking. And Nillson no longer put her feet up on the desk.

There was still a long way to go, and she hoped the addition of the new team member would help them on that journey.

It was Ben who ordered the drinks, while Freya scanned the pub for a familiar face. An old man sat at the bar on his own nursing a pint of ale. Two women were sitting in a booth, each of them with a glass of wine. They sat close, one of them smiling as the other recited an anecdote. Another man sat alone. He was what her father would have called heavyset, with broad shoulders and not much in the way of a neck, like a rugby player. She spotted her new team member in the corner sitting near a young man who was flicking through the pages of an old Lincolnshire Echo, and she gave a nod, discreetly signing for them to stay there for a moment.

"So?" Nillson said. "Are they here?"

"They are," Freya replied, grinning. "See if you can spot them."

Giving them a guessing game hadn't been the plan, but it felt like a fun way of starting the evening.

"I think I know," Gold said, as the barman handed her a glass of wine.

"Yep, me too," Nillson added.

"Chapman?" Freya asked, but she simply shook her head. Freya watched her for a moment, waiting for her to at least look around the room. But she didn't. She just averted her gaze, then looked at her phone. "Care to guess?"

She looked up, shrugged, and nodded at the guy with no neck. "Him?"

"Is that your guess?"

Nodding, Chapman returned her attention to the phone, and Freya moved on.

"Cruz. Come on, you've always got an opinion."

It was as if he'd been waiting for her to ask. He leaned in surreptitiously.

"I reckon it's one of them," he said, with a sideways nod towards the two women.

"Which one?" Freya asked, and he turned to study them.

"The one with the white blouse. She's got copper written all over her."

"Is that right?" Freya asked.

"I'd stake my salary on it."

"That's a bold call, Gabby," Nillson said.

"I'm a bold guy," he said, even though the entire team knew that courage was not one of his attributes.

"Ben?" Freya said.

He took a cursory glance around the room, then his gaze loitered on the winning punter.

"Fella in the corner. The one reading the paper," he said.

"No. It's the bloke with no neck," Gold said, then backtracked. "But don't tell him I said that. It wasn't meant to be offensive."

"I agree," Nillson said. "Look at him. Straight back, fingers linked, steely gaze. He could be sitting at an interview room table scaring the hell out of a suspect."

"Interesting," Freya said, as Ben passed her a glass of wine. She took a sip, licked her lips, and then stared around the team.

"Well?" Cruz said. "Who is it?"

"Who's what?"

"The new team member?" he said.

"I think we should wait for Gillespie."

"Oh, come on–"

"It's only fair," Freya said. "We wouldn't want him to feel left out."

"He's going to be ages reading through my report."

"How would you feel if we left you out?"

"Ah, I suppose," he moaned. "Give us a clue, then. Male or female?"

"I'm not saying," Freya said.

"Has one of us guessed right?" he asked.

"Cruz. Be patient."

He took a sip of his beer, then looked around the pub again, sparking a renewed effort from the rest of the team. It was only Chapman who remained calm. She stared at the door, lost in thought.

Ben paid the bill, then raised his glass in the centre of the group.

"To Nillson," he said. "Congratulations, mate."

The team all toasted Nillson, who smiled her way through the attention with grace.

"Was it hard?" Cruz asked.

"I guess so. I was never any good in exams."

"But you got through it," Freya said. "And from what I hear, you did well."

"Cheers, boss," Nillson replied.

"Can anyone sit it?" Cruz asked.

"You have to demonstrate your competence at you current rank," Freya explained.

"Oh, right," he replied, defeated at the first hurdle.

Behind him, Gillespie pushed through the door and crept up behind Cruz with his index finger to his lips.

"Stick with Gillespie. He'll show you the ropes," Freya said.

Cruz shook his head. "I still can't believe I'm lumbered with that oaf."

"Oh, come on," Nillson said. "He's not that bad."

"Not that bad?" Cruz said, taking a mouthful of his drink. "He doesn't stop taking the piss out of me, he's the laziest man I've ever met, and if he doesn't have his morning coffee, he's like a bear with a sore head. Honestly, some mornings I'd rather be stuck with a rabid dog than Gillespie. It would probably smell better, too. And as for his bloody accent, I mean, I can't understand a word he says sometimes. It's like he's constantly drunk, or something. 'Aye this' and 'aye that,' and 'get doon there, laddie, or I'll sit ma big fat backside on ya.' I mean, surely he has to do the police fitness test every now and then. He's like a bad-tempered, flatulent, Glaswegian rhinoceros with a mop of greasy hair on his head."

He took another sip of his drink, and then his eyes widened as he took in each of their stares.

"He's behind me, isn't he?"

"Smell like a rabid dog, do I?" Gillespie said, winking at Freya to indicate he wasn't offended.

"Oh, crap."

"A bad-tempered, flatulent, Glaswegian rhinoceros, aye?"

"It's a figure of speech," Cruz said, without turning. He squeezed his eyes closed, expecting the worst.

Gillespie leaned in to whisper in his ear, but spoke loud enough for the team to hear.

"Rhinoceroses are rare. Hunted to near extinction. Did you know that?"

Cruz nodded.

"And we're also irritable. Very irritable," Gillespie said. "Do you know what rhinoceros do when we get insulted by filthy, wee, backstabbing, whining, and degenerate detective constables who have half a pint of lager and start shooting their mouths off?"

"Stomp them?" Cruz whined.

"No. No, we only stomp clean people. We don't like to get mucky feet. Especially when the detective constable in question has regular accidents in the trouser department. No, we prefer to make them suffer in other ways. Us rhinoceros are intelligent, see? We've hide as thick as your head and skulls like a rocks."

"What do you do then?" Cruz asked, still unable to turn and face Gillespie.

"Oh, we wait. We wait until our prey are least expecting it. We wait until they're on their knees and then we strike. You see, the thing about us bad-tempered, flatulent, rhinoceros is, and I'm talking specifically about the even rarer Glaswegian variety, is that we have no empathy. So, when our prey is begging for mercy, DC Cruz, when they are screaming for us to stop, begging for mercy, all it does is make us hurt them even more," Gillespie explained, as Ben handed him a pint of ale. "So, I'll leave you with that wee thought. And one day, when you're least expecting it, I'll remind you just how bad-tempered and irritable we can be."

"How long does it take?" Cruz asked.

"Oh, that all depends on the snivelling, wee, pants-pissing detective in question. Sometimes, it can take hours. Sometimes days. Weeks even. But you'll know. When the time is right, you'll know."

"That gives you something to look forward to, Gabby," Nillson said. She beamed at the team, delighting in Cruz's angst, then looked up to Gillespie. "The boss challenged us to guess who our new team member is."

"Guess the new DC?" Gillespie said, his face lighting up in delight at the game. "They're in here, are they?"

"Cruz thinks it's one of the girls over there."

He looked across at the two women, who, during the course of the last five minutes, had moved even closer together.

"Who them? No," he said, then scanned the rest of the room. "Do we have a wager running?"

"Not yet," Nillson said.

"Twenty quid says it's the girl in the corner."

With little care for discretion, the team all followed his gaze to the corner.

"I'm saying it's Mr No Neck over there," Nillson said.

"Yeah, me too," said Gold.

"My money is on the guy with the paper," Ben added. "Chapman?"

"Eh?" she said, looking up from her phone.

"Who do you think it is?"

She shrugged again. "I don't gamble."

"But if you had to?" Cruz said.

"If I had to what?"

"If you had to guess, who would it be?"

"I don't know."

"Alright," Gillespie said, and he slapped a twenty-pound note down on the bar. "Wee lass in the corner."

Ben followed suit but without the drama. He tossed a twenty-pound note onto Gillespie's.

"The fella with the paper."

"Alright," Nillson said, pulling two tens from her pocket. She placed them down on the bar with the rest of the cash. "No neck."

"No neck," Gold repeated, as she fished inside her purse for some cash. She produced three five-pound notes, four pound coins, and two fifties. "Sorry, it's all I've got."

"Money's money," Gillespie said, stacking it all into a neat pile. "It all counts. Anyone else? Cruz?"

"Ah, I erm..."

"Ah, come on, Gabby. Who did you say it was? One of the ladies?"

"I'm a bit short," Cruz said.

"A bit short?" Gillespie said. "They had to rewrite the force's minimum height restriction when you joined. They were worried the country would be policed by a bunch of school kids."

"Ah, leave off, Jim."

"I think the responsibility falls on you, Gillespie," Freya said, nodding at Cruz.

"Eh?"

"When I said you were joined at the hip, I meant it. You're

supposed to mentor him, look after him. And if that means you have to put your hand in your pocket every now and then, so be it."

"That wasn't in the sergeant's exam when I took it, boss," Gillespie said. "Did you see it, Anna?"

"I think it was question number nine, Jim. Right after the one about custody procedure."

"It's an unwritten rule, Gillespie," Freya said, cutting through the laughter. Then she held his gaze, adding weight to her point.

Ben turned away to answer a call, and the disruption was enough to break Gillespie's resolve.

"Alright, alright," he said, reaching into his pocket. He pulled another twenty out and slapped it down. "But if he wins, I get it."

"You get half," Freya said. "Think of it as a two horse bet."

Shaking his head, Gillespie stacked the cash again, arranging it in size order with the six coins on top.

"Right then. Let's do this," he said, and eyeballed Freya. "Who's our winning horse, boss?"

"No time," Ben said, stepping back into the group. "Who's had a drink? Cruz, you're out. Same for you, Gillespie. Sorry fellas."

"I've had a sip," Nillson said, seeing the urgency in Ben's expression.

"I haven't touched mine yet," Gold said.

"Freya?" he asked.

"I'm good to go," she replied, putting her untouched wine down on the bar.

"Good. That was the front desk. Someone just found a body over at Tupholme Abbey."

"Did they leave any details?" Freya asked, and Ben shook his head.

"Anonymous caller," he replied. "And before you ask, there was no trace."

Nillson zipped her jacket, indicating she was ready to leave. Gold, Chapman, Freya, and Ben made their way to the door, leaving Cruz and Gillespie behind.

"Ah, come on," Gillespie said, holding up the cash. "What about the bet?"

Freya turned at the door Ben was holding open. She glanced around the pub, giving no indication of who the new team member was.

Gillespie follow her gaze, hoping to gain some kind of insight, but found nothing.

"Well?" he said.

"Enjoy your winnings," she said, winking at him.

"Eh? I was right?" he said, glancing over at the young lady in the corner near the man with the newspaper. "Her?"

"Jenny?" Freya called out, and the girl looked over to them. Freya waved her over, and then watched Gillespie's reaction when she stood, collected her things, and walked confidently across the pub. He was smitten. It had been instant, and something that, if pressed, Freya would have admitted she had been a little concerned with.

"Holy mother of God," Gillespie mumbled under his breath.

DC Jenny Anderson had the long, flowing hair, the swaying hips, and the confident stride. Gillespie did little to hide his approval, staring at her as a child might, without shame of curiosity.

To everyone's surprise, Freya hugged the newcomer then, with her arm around her, turned to face the team. "Everybody, this is Jenny Anderson. Jenny, you'll learn names as we go. It's so lovely to see you again."

"Again?" Gillespie said. "You mean, you already know each other?"

"Oh, yes. We had the pleasure of working together in the Met," Freya explained.

"Ah, well, if Gab and I are staying here, we can give Jenny a warm welcome," Gillespie suggested.

"Are you leaving?" Jenny asked.

"We've had a call. You can stay here and get to know Gillespie and Cruz, or you can come with us and get stuck in."

"I'll come with you," she said, checking her watch.

Freya presented Nillson with a wave of her arm. "Good. You'll ride with Anna. I think you two will get along just fine."

Nillson gave her one of her warmest smiles and nodded a greeting as Ben led the team to the door.

"Isn't there a night shift?" Jenny asked, as she stepped out into the early evening.

Freya looked back inside to see Gillespie and Cruz staring after them in disbelief.

"This isn't London. This is the sticks. We work when we need to until such a time arises that the force recognises the need for more resources," Freya said with a smile. "Welcome to Lincolnshire."

CHAPTER THREE

The evenings were lighter for longer with every passing day, and the mood of the team seemed to lift in parallel.

Freya drove. There had been a time when Ben did all the driving, when Freya had been new to Lincolnshire and her little rental car proved inadequate for the job. But now she was settled in and had developed a mental map of the area, she had bought a new car and elected to do the driving. It was more than a control thing. It was comfort. Ben's old Ford had served them well, but Freya's Range Rover offered her all the comfort and luxury she looked for. She could have been sitting in her father's Chesterfield armchair, her feet being warmed by the fire.

"She seems nice," Ben said, leaving the comment hanging in the air, ready for Freya to tear apart.

"Gillespie seems to think so," Freya said. "She's prettier than I remember. I just hope the big oaf doesn't scare her off."

"Ah, he'll be okay."

"Here?" Freya said, surprised when Ben pointed to a small layby on the bend in the road. She slowed and pulled into the spot, recognising the little, white van that was parked there as belonging to the scene of crime team, or, as they were referred to here, crime scene investigators.

Nillson pulled in behind them, and a uniformed officer emerged from a gated track, approaching both cars wearing an inquisitive expression.

Freya took a breath.

"Ready for this?" she asked.

"I was ready for a pint," Ben replied, as he pushed open the passenger door. "Look how that turned out."

"Look at it this way. At least we won't have to listen to Gillespie and Cruz squabbling all evening," she said, and Ben leaned on the car bonnet waiting for her to finish. "The dead are far less irritating. Don't you think?"

He nodded back at Nillson's car, where Nillson and Anderson were climbing out. From their expressions, it was hard to read how their journey had been. Nillson wasn't known for her social skills and, if in the wrong company, was prone to offending people.

"Anything I should know?" he asked.

"About Anderson? No. She's a good detective who was looking for a break."

"A new start?"

"Something like that," Freya said, and the way she gazed at the younger female, Ben thought he saw something. Respect maybe? Or was it hope?

"Are you planning on bringing the rest of London to Lincolnshire, Freya? Have you pinned a leaflet to the bulletin board down there? Looking for a new start? Come to sunny Lincolnshire."

"She called me," Freya replied. "Who am I to turn down a fellow officer?"

"And you trust her?"

In Freya's opinion, the question was ridiculous. Why would she introduce somebody she didn't trust to the team? But she kept that thought to herself, and replied with a smile.

"With my life," she replied, then clapped her hands and raised her voice. "Right, Nillson, Anderson, let's go."

The walk from the road to the abbey took a minute or two. When Ben had explained to her the body had been found at Tupholme Abbey, Freya had expected to find a huge, old building, maybe even gothic in appearance. But, to her surprise, the abbey was nothing more than a pile of ruins with a few stone walls that had succumbed to gravity and decay. Empty window frames gave the old building charm, and invoked Freya's imagination. One day, a long time ago, the building had been grand. Not huge like Bolton Abbey, but grand, nonetheless.

A light blue, modern-looking Land Rover was parked near to the little gate that led from the track to the ruins. The keys were in the ignition still.

A white-suited crime scene investigator crouched in the distance beside a pile of tumbled stone, and even from two hundred yards away, the fleshy shape of a man was clear.

He had been laid out naked on the stone, spread eagle for all the world to see. It was as if he had fallen from a thousand feet and landed as a child might draw death with a crayon.

"That's no accident," Freya muttered to Ben as they drew near.

"No," he replied, scanning the scene with his keen eye. His gaze settled on a picnic blanket that had been laid out in the long grass a few metres away. "You can see the grass has been flattened where he's been dragged across."

"Nillson, Anderson. Guide uniform in. Have them lock this place down. We're going to need at least a dozen bodies here to carry out a detailed search."

"And get Chapman to run a check on the car," Ben added.

"And make sure the FME is on the way. I want to get the body out of here before dark if we can."

"We're on it," Nillson said confidently, and she led Anderson away.

"Good evening," the woman in the white suit said, standing up from where she was crouched beside the body. She peeled off her disposable gloves and pulled her hood back to reveal a mass of neat, blonde hair tied back in a ponytail.

"You beat us to it again, Michaela," Freya said. "It's almost like you have inside knowledge."

"Either that or I just don't have a life," she replied. "Do you want a run through?"

"Go for it. What are we up against?"

"Single stab wound to the back. No clothes. No ID," Michaela said.

"Looks like he was dragged from the blanket over there, rolled over, then laid out."

"Seems the obvious answer," Ben said, eyeing the blanket. "That was our assessment."

"Ah, but things are not always as they seem," Michaela said, then waited to be prompted for more detail. "You're right about the process. But not about the timeline," she continued. "You see, he was stabbed in the back, which implies that he was either lying on his front, or he was upright."

"Unless he was lying on somebody else's front," Ben said.

"Of course, DS Savage. How did I know you would highlight the seedier of the possibilities?"

"It's just an observation. I mean, there's a blanket, a bottle of wine or something. Plus, there are two glasses."

"So, if he was lying on top of somebody, as you suggested, how would the party he was lying on top of stab him in the back?"

Ben stared at her then at Freya, who rolled her eyes.

"You said things were not as they seem, Doctor Fell," Freya said. "We can get to the specifics later."

"Okay," Michaela replied, doing nothing to hide her smug grin. "If he was stabbed in the back then moved immediately here, there would be more blood. The trail in the grass would be soaked. The rock he's lying on would be covered. But it's not."

"He stopped bleeding by then," Freya said, and the doctor nodded.

"He was stabbed in his back on the blanket, possibly lying on somebody, or maybe just lying down. People do that, you know? Lie down without the need for it to be sexual. He was moved later. At least an hour. Maybe longer."

"Thank you, Doctor," Freya said. "So, we have a car, a body, and a picnic. There were definitely two people having a picnic, as identified by the presence of two glasses. Who was the other person?"

"Whoever it was didn't touch their glass," Michaela said. "The second glass is clean and he has traces of alcohol in his system."

"You tested for alcohol already?" Ben said.

"No. I smelled his breath. Old-fashioned, I know. But it works."

"When will you be finished?" Freya asked.

"An hour."

"Good. The FME is on his way. I want this on the pathologist bench ready for the morning. Anything else?"

"Only the trampled grass. I've asked my colleague, Pat, to see if there are any prints, but it's been too dry."

"That just leaves a detailed search," Ben said.

"How long before you get any DNA results back from the blanket and the glasses?" Freya asked. "I'm assuming you're not going to rely totally on old-fashioned methods?"

"Two days," Michaela said, as if she had been waiting for the question. She pulled on a fresh pair of gloves. "Now, if you'll excuse me, I need to see if he has any other injuries."

"One last thing, Michaela," Freya said, and Michaela turned with a single raised eyebrow. Freya nodded to the man's exposed genitals. "Are you able…"

"No, and no," Michaela said, finishing the sentence for her. "No, I can't test for signs of sexual intercourse here. That'll have to wait until he's on the bench. But no, I don't believe he did."

"What makes you so sure?" Ben asked.

"Old-fashioned methods," Michaela said with a knowing smile, and she sniffed at the air before pulling her hood into place. She gave him a wink, then added, "Tried and tested for more than a hundred years."

CHAPTER FOUR

"I'm surprised you didn't want to go back to the pub," Ben said, as they entered the farm track on which Freya's little cottage and Ben's house were located.

"What, and play catch up with Gillespie and Cruz?" she replied, as she brought the car to a stop at the junction. The track to the right would lead to Freya's house, while the track on the left led to Ben's house, which sat in a neat, little U-shape beside his father's house and his brothers' house.

Had it still been light, they could have viewed the land around them as far as the eye could see, all of which belonged to Ben's father. The Savage family had farmed the land for generations, and as a result, Ben knew every square inch of every field.

There had been a time, not so long ago, when Ben had thought that he might have to return to the family business. And that time would come. Maybe soon? Maybe not? But it would come.

"Although, that being said, a glass of wine sounds nice," Freya added.

"I've got a bottle at my house," Ben suggested. "I could do with a nightcap."

"Does the bottle have a picture of a little sailing ship on it, and a screw cap?"

"Probably," he said sheepishly.

Immediately, Freya turned right and sped along the track towards her home.

"It's the start of a new investigation," she said, when they pulled up outside the cottage she rented from Ben's father and killed the engine. "Let's do things properly, eh?"

"Fine by me," Ben replied climbing from the car. "I'll save my little sailing boat bottle for some other special occasion."

She heard the smile in his voice without having to turn to see it, then pushed open her front door.

"Don't tell me you've gone native, at last," Ben said, and Freya stopped on the threshold to look back at him. "Don't you lock your front door anymore?"

She laughed once, then entered, hanging her coat up on one of the three hooks on the hallway wall. When Freya had first moved to Lincolnshire, she had driven up in the family motorhome and found a spot on a local beach to call home. But the distance to the station in North Kesteven was too far, and the taxis in those first few days had been unreliable. It was only when they had closed their first case, and she had decided to stay, that Ben had offered her the cottage on behalf of his father. During those days, Freya had kept her coat on all night to fend off the bitter cold.

Spring had come and was merging with summer the way seasons do, and she enjoyed the freedom of walking into her home and changing into comfortable clothes.

"Wine or beer?" she asked.

"You've got beer?" he said. "Not just for me, surely?"

"No. I like a nice beer on a hot day. But you're welcome to have one."

"What are you having?"

"Wine. It's not hot yet. I bought the beers for when summer arrives."

"I'll have wine then," Ben said. "Besides, I'm guessing we have an early start tomorrow, so I'll just have the one and leave you to it."

"Wine it is," Freya said, pulling three glasses from the cupboard then grabbing the bottle from the fridge.

"Are you expecting anybody?" Ben asked, as he followed her through to the living room. But Freya didn't reply. She placed the bottle on the dining table beside her pile of papers, ignoring the figure in the armchair, and waited for Ben's reaction.

"Anderson?" he said. "What are you–"

He stopped mid-sentence and looked at Freya for an answer.

"She's staying with me until she can find digs of her own. I've given her three days. After that, she's on her own."

"Staying in the boss's house?" he said. "Wow, you two must be close."

Anderson smiled back at him from the armchair.

"Not really."

It was a curt answer, but not abrupt or dismissive. To the point. He could see why Freya liked her. She wasn't one to waste words.

"Let's just say that Jenny and I became allies in a male-dominated station," Freya said, as she handed them both a glass of wine.

"And now look at you. Women outnumber the men."

"Do they?" Freya said, pretending not to have noticed. "Interesting observation."

"When did you arrive?" Ben asked.

Anderson took a sip of her wine and settled back in the chair as if she had done the same thing for months.

"Yesterday. I drove up. I wanted to get a feel for the place," she replied. "Freya told me all about it, and the team. But you know what it's like. You have to see it for yourself, sometimes."

"I guess you do," Ben said. "How long has this been planned?"

"A month," Freya said. "And before you ask why I hadn't told you about it, I kept it a secret from everyone. Only DCI Granger and I knew."

"What about Harper?" Ben said, referring to the chief superintendent who had been off sick for months now.

"He'll find out when he comes back to work. He has bigger things on his plate."

"Right. So, Jenny, tell me about yourself. All I know so far is that you're a DC, you're good, and Freya trusts you."

"What do you want to know?" she asked, as Ben took a seat at the dining table.

The layout embarrassed Freya a little. She had planned on getting more furniture to make the place a little warmer and welcoming, but time had ticked by and she still hadn't done anything about it.

"What do you enjoy doing?" Ben asked. "In your spare time, I mean?"

"Boring," Freya said, and looked across at Jenny. "You'll have to excuse Ben. He has the social skills of a carrot. What he really means to ask you is, are you single? Gay? Rich? Or running away from anything?"

"I see," Jenny said, taking another sip of wine and eyeing Ben with more insight into his character. "Yes. No. No. Yes."

"You're running away from something?" he asked.

"Aren't we all?" she said cryptically. "How about you?"

"Yes. No. No. No."

"You're not running away from anything?" she asked. "A rare breed."

"Ben is rare," Freya explained. "Not only is he socially challenged, he's also part of the furniture here. This is his dad's farm. The Savages have been here for more than a century."

"Farming stock, eh?" Jenny said approvingly.

"Oh, and be careful. He also has a habit of flashing his bits to anything in a skirt," Freya said, then glanced down and saw Jenny was wearing a smart trouser suit. "Or trousers, for that matter."

"Freya?" Ben said, and she raised her glass to him.

"Other than that, Jenny, you'll find he's a solid detective, as reliable as they come, and a good friend."

"Wow, Freya," Ben said, shaking his head. "I'm amazed you don't host more social gatherings."

"People don't want to know the mundane, boring stuff," she replied. "They want the dirt. Speaking of which. I think we may have a little problem."

"What type of problem?" Jenny asked.

"Chapman. She's not herself. I want you both to keep your ears to the ground. If you hear anything, I want to know," Freya said, then looked across to Jenny. "We look after our own here. It's not dog eat dog like it is in London."

CHAPTER FIVE

For Ben, the ride into work was not the most comfortable. Anderson had taken the front passenger seat, leaving him the choice of either pulling rank and giving the wrong impression, or folding his six-foot-something body into the rear seat. It was her first full day at work, so he opted to leave her where she was. And it was only when he had pulled the door closed that the smell hit him. It was a sensory overload. He was used to the soft scent of Freya's perfume filling his senses, but coupled with Anderson's, it was like CS gas.

"So, this is what life is like when you're part of the minority gender, is it?" he asked.

"What's that?" Freya said.

"Emasculated, desensitised, and tortured," he joked. "I'll talk. Just tell me what you need to know."

"What are you going on about?" Freya said, glancing at him in the rear-view mirror.

"Nothing," he replied. "I'm sure my eyes will recover eventually. Just don't ask me to read anything for the next few hours."

The two women exchanged confused glances as Freya turned out of the farm track and onto the main road toward the station.

"What's the plan anyway?" he asked.

"We're meeting at the station for a briefing. Then we'll split up and see what's what," Freya replied. "I've got a plan in mind."

"Do you often get called in at the weekends in London?" Ben asked, directing his question at Anderson.

"We do shifts," she replied, turning in her seat to look at him while she spoke. She had nice eyes – serious, but kind, Ben thought. "Weekends and weekdays all kind of blend into one. You're either working, or you're not. If your day off happens to coincide with your friends and family, then great, you get to do something. But more often than not, your shifts never work in your favour. I found myself spending more time trying to swap shifts with colleagues than I did writing up statements."

"Oh, really?"

"Well, it's not quite that bad, but if you have a family event, like a dinner or something, you can guarantee you'll be on shift."

"Sounds rough," Ben said.

"Could be worse."

"Such as?"

"Having to work instead of finding a place to live," she joked.

"Two days and counting," Freya reminded her.

"What's the rush?" Ben asked.

"I'm bringing in a new team member. I don't want the others to think Jenny is getting preferential treatment. That's all. We have a good team right now, and with Jenny it'll be even stronger. But the team is a delicate ecosystem. People talk. We can't afford for that to happen."

"It's okay," Anderson said, turning in her seat again. "I get it. The last thing I want is to be the subject of gossip. I'm hoping to slot right in and stay below the radar. For a while, at least."

"If you want my advice, stick with Nillson."

"The Scottish guy seems like an interesting character," she said, and Ben heard Freya's intake of breath.

"Interesting is one way of putting it," Ben told her. "I can think of a few other terms."

"Such as?"

"Irritating, immature…" Ben began.

"Let's not cast a shadow just yet," Freya said, then glanced across at Anderson. "He saved a young boy's life last month. Dived into the river and pulled him out. Not to mention the time he managed to get a boy who rarely uttered a single word to not only talk, but even put him on a path to joining the force."

"The Scottish guy did that?"

"He might seem like he's all mouth and no trousers, Jenny. But deep down, that man has a heart as big as his appetite. And he has a very big appetite."

"What about Cruz?" Jenny said. "The little guy?"

"He's okay. He has a lot to learn, but I think one day he'll make a good detective. What he lacks in maturity he makes up for in being eager to please, and let me tell you something. What that man doesn't know about historical crimes, solved and unsolved, isn't worth knowing. He'll be good one day."

"Right. I wondered what it was he brought to the table."

"Everyone brings something, Jenny. Chapman is one of the best researchers I've ever met. She has no desire to step outside the station, but she doesn't need to. Gold is nicer than your favourite aunty. She's just been on an FLO course, and is our dedicated Family Liaison Officer. Seriously, she's all heart."

"And Nillson?" Anderson asked, saving her partner for last.

Freya eased the big Range Rover into the station car park and came to a stop in her spot. She killed the engine and looked across at Anderson.

"Ben?" she said.

"I think it's best you work that out for yourself," he replied. "But, if you want my opinion, in ten years' time, she'll be running a team of her own, and if I'm right, Freya teaming you with her puts you in an ideal position to be her number one when that happens."

"Like I said in the incident room," Freya added, "every DI needs a reliable DS behind them."

CHAPTER SIX

There was very little in the way of noise coming from the incident room, as Freya and Ben led Anderson up the fire escape stairs and into the first-floor corridor. The silence roused Freya's suspicions, and she stopped at the double doors and peered through the little windows.

Inside, Chapman and Gold were huddled around Chapman's laptop, Gillespie and Cruz were looking at the local map on the wall, and Nillson waited patiently, her notebook in front of her.

"Wow. I was expecting to find them throwing balls of paper across the room," Anderson said.

The corners of Freya's mouth teased into a grin at the more than accurate suggestion.

"I'd love to say they're better behaved than that," she said.

Leaning over the pair of them, Ben peered through the window.

"Why do I feel like a schoolteacher peering into the detention hall?" he said, clearly not expecting a response.

"Are you ready for this, Anderson?" Freya asked.

"Let's do it."

Freya pushed open the doors and the hinges squealed like nails being dragged across a blackboard. The team all looked up at the three of them, and Freya laughed at the grimace on Anderson's face.

"You'll get used to the doors. It becomes quite comforting after a while," Freya said, then clapped her hands three times and made her way to the whiteboard. "You all remember Anderson from last night, I hope?"

She studied Gillespie and Cruz for signs of a hangover, but found their eyes to be clear and them both sitting up straight, attentive. As if they were model students.

"Gillespie, how's the head this morning?"

"Right as rain, boss."

"And did you spend all your winnings?"

"No. We headed home after you guys left. We figured we'd be in today. Didn't want to let the team down, did we, Cruz?"

"That's right, Jim," Cruz replied. "I was in bed by ten o'clock."

"Aye, me too. Bright-eyed and bushy-tailed, boss. Ready and waiting."

"Why don't I believe you?" she asked, studying them again, this time for an indication of a white lie. There was none. "Alright. Well, I'll give you the benefit of the doubt. Anderson, take the desk beside Nillson."

In her usual casual manner, Nillson slid a spare chair back for Anderson, using her foot. Then she nodded at the space behind them indicating that's where she should put her bag and jacket.

"I appreciate it's the weekend. So, thank you all for coming in."

"Aye, boss. It's our pleasure," Gillespie said, and there was something about his tone that roused Freya's suspicions even further.

"Indeed," she said, then glanced around the room at the rest of the team.

Gold was sitting with her pen in her hand, ready to be given something to do. Chapman, who, if Freya wasn't mistaken, was wearing yesterday's clothes, waited with her fingers poised over her keyboard. Dark rings encircled her eyes, which she had attempted to mask with makeup. However, as she rarely wore makeup, all the effort did was draw attention to herself.

"We don't need to wait for pathology on this one. It's clear from the crime scene that our victim was murdered. So, let's get straight into it. Our victim, a middle-aged male, was found naked, laid out across a pile of old stones from the ruins of Tupholme Abbey. SOCO suggested he has a single stab wound to the back. We'll confirm that later when we pay Doctor Bell a visit. But what we do know is that the body was moved from a picnic blanket, where he was killed, to the stones. A distance of around ten to twelve metres."

"So, our suspect is a male then?" Gold said.

"Not necessarily," Nillson said, clearly offended.

"I just mean whoever moved him would have to be quite strong."

"I could do it," Nillson said, and she glanced across at Anderson. "You?"

"I'd struggle," Anderson said. "But we have to remember, adrenalin would have been flowing. People are capable of all sorts with adrenalin pumping through them."

"Good insight," Freya said. "We can't rule anybody out. We do know he was killed lying face down, then left for long enough that the blood congealed. Then he was moved. We estimate at least an hour between the murder and him being moved. That's all we have so far. Chapman, what did you find on the car?"

"Light blue Land Rover, ma'am. Belongs to one Theodore Wood. Forty-eight years old. Married with a daughter. He lives less than a mile away from the crime scene, in Bardney."

"Okay, good. So, he's either our victim or he's a suspect. Do we have a photo of him?"

"We do, but it's just his driving licence. We put him against the photos from the crime scene. Hard to say if it's him or not. The victim was around the same age with similar colour hair."

"Have you checked social media?" Anderson asked.

"We have, yes. He doesn't have any accounts."

"Right. Ben and I will pay the family a visit to get a lie of the land. By the time we're finished, I imagine pathology will have carried out an initial assessment. Nillson, take Anderson and knock on a few doors. See if anybody saw something. Maybe one of the locals walked their dog and saw the car?"

"Hold on," Cruz said. "We normally do the door knocking."

"And you normally moan and whine about it," Freya said. "I'm relieving you of that particular duty. Don't tell me you actually want to go door to door?"

"Well, no. But–"

"But what, Cruz?"

"What do we do then?"

"Oh, I have a real treat for you two."

"This doesn't sound good, Gabby," Gillespie said.

"You'll lead the detailed search," Freya said.

"Eh?" Cruz said.

"Talk to Sergeant Priest downstairs. You'll need uniform, at least a dozen. I want every inch of that area searched for the weapon, or anything else you can find."

"Lead the search?" Gillespie said. "Us?"

"And I want you leading from the front. You'll be on your hands and knees all day, so get the appropriate PPE."

"Ah, for God's sake, Gabby. Why did you have to open your bloody mouth?"

"But we normally do the door knocking."

"You've been promoted," Freya said, then addressed the team as a whole. "I want all information fed back through Chapman. Chapman, collate the findings for me, please, and prepare a report for DCI Granger."

"Ma'am," she replied.

"Gold. Work with Chapman until you hear from me. When the victim has been identified, you'll go in as FLO. Any questions, anybody?"

"Any point?" Gillespie said.

"None at all," Freya said. "Get to it. We'll meet back here this afternoon."

CHAPTER SEVEN

The address Chapman had provided Freya and Ben was a modest house in a pleasant-looking street in Bardney, less than a mile from the scene of the crime. There was no car on the driveway, but an upstairs window was open, indicating that somebody was home.

"This could go one of two ways," Freya said.

"Like you said before. He's either our victim or our suspect," Ben said, peering past her at the house she had parked outside.

"I'm going with suspect," Freya said.

"What?"

"Don't look so surprised. It's the weekend. I'm just injecting a little bit of tension, that's all."

"A man died, Freya."

"I know. And I'm betting it's not him."

"No. Categorically, no. I'm not betting on this, and even if I did fancy my chances, I wouldn't bet with you again. Not after last time."

"Oh, come on. Nobody needs to know. It's just a friendly wager."

"Freya, no."

"Twenty quid."

"You took twenty off me last night."

"Correction, Gillespie took that off you. Had you been paying attention, you would have seen my eye twitch a little when he called it."

"For God's sake, Freya."

"Twenty quid says he's our suspect."

"No," Ben replied, as he climbed from the car and made his way around to the pavement, where she met him and checked her appearance in the window. "Shame. I was telling Anderson how you could be relied on for a good laugh."

"I'm game for a good laugh but–"

"And how you never back down. Tenacious, was the word I used. A real man's man."

"What if I don't think he's the victim?" Ben said. "I don't exactly have much of a choice, do I? You've called the obvious choice."

"No. The obvious choice would be for the body to belong to Mr Wood. It was his car, after all."

"Right. But we all know things are never that simple. Which means the opposite is in fact true."

"You're beginning to think like me," Freya said. "I must be having a positive effect. So, come on then. If Mr Wood isn't the killer, and he isn't the victim, why was his car there?"

"I'm sure there's some perfectly reasonable explanation," Ben replied.

"That's a thirty thousand pound car. Who leaves the keys in a thirty thousand pound car in a field?"

"Like I said, I'm sure there's some perfectly good explanation," Ben hissed, and he pushed open the little gate at the top of a narrow footpath.

"Okay, okay. A tenner," Freya said.

"Freya?" Ben hissed again, and he knocked on the front door.

She held up her hands in defeat. "Alright. I'll just have to make sure Anderson knows how much of a coward you really are."

The door opened before Ben could respond, and he turned to find a teenage girl standing there.

"Hello," he said, presenting his warrant card. "I'm Detective Sergeant Savage. This is Detective Inspector Bloom. We're looking for a Theodore Wood."

"That's my dad. What do you want him for?" she said.

The sight of Ben's warrant card didn't seem to surprise the girl. She folded her arms, and leaned against the door, then brushed a loose lock of blonde hair from her brow.

"Do you know when he'll be home?" Ben asked.

"No," she said, in that defiant manner teenagers seem to adopt with such ease.

"Does he have a phone number, perhaps?" Freya said, butting in. "It's important we talk to him."

"He hasn't got his phone," she said, and she reached behind the door to a console table, then presented a cracked iPhone. "He must have left it here."

"Do you know where he is, then?" Ben said.

"No. He don't tell me anything."

"Is your mum home?" Freya asked.

"No," the girl replied. "And before you ask. No, I don't know where she is, or when she'll be back."

"How old are you?" Ben asked.

"Old enough to be left alone, if that's what you're getting at."

"Sixteen then?" Freya said, and the girl studied the carpet. "Ah, I see. Fifteen?"

"I'm sixteen in a month or two," she said. "Besides, you can't tell me if I can be on my own or not. I know the rules."

"Look, sorry, what did you say your name is?" Freya said, seeing no way through to the girl.

"I didn't."

"Well, perhaps you could tell me?"

She stared at them both, but said nothing.

"Unless, of course, you've something to hide?" Freya said, and she sniffed at the air. "Is that cigarettes I can smell? Do your parents know you smoke?"

"Franky," she said. "Francesca."

"Francesca Wood?" Freya said to confirm, and the girl nodded.

"Are we able to leave a message for your father, please?" Ben asked, and he fished a contact card from his inside pocket. "Have him call me on that number, will you?"

Ben turned and left, and Freya recognised the frustrated look on his face.

"What's it about?" the girl called. "If I see him, I mean, what shall I tell him it's about?"

"We found his car," Freya said. "If he wants it back, then have him call that number. Otherwise, it'll be destroyed."

"One last thing," Ben called out from the top of the path, one hand resting on the gate. The girl looked out at him, her face a picture of nonchalance. "Was he home last night, or yesterday at all?"

The girl shook her head confidently. "No. He hasn't been home for days."

"Did he take his car?" Ben said.

"I guess so," she replied, and she held his stare defiantly.

"It's important we speak to him?" Freya said, hoping her serious expression conveyed enough of a message.

But Franky slammed the door closed, leaving Ben and Freya no better off than they were ten minutes before.

Back inside the car, Ben rested his head on the head rest.

"And that," he said, "is why I shall never have kids of my own."

"You get used to it," Freya said, remembering the arguments she used to have with her ex-husband's only child, Billy. "You learn how to use it to your advantage. It's all about strategy."

"Strategy? I'd have to install a padded cell or a punch bag or something. It's like they know we can't make them talk and they enjoy watching you suffer."

"A wise man learns more from his enemies than a fool from his friends," Freya said, and she smiled across at him.

"What's that supposed to mean? Kids are the enemies?"

"No. Of course they're not. But it's a battle of wits and cunning. You have to learn how to play them at their own game," Freya said. "And if that doesn't work, throw their games console in the bin and smash their iPads with a hammer."

"Wow, parent of the year."

"Kids don't come with a handbook, Ben. You have to make it up as you go along. One day, you're their best friend. The next, you're the thorn in their side. You can't take it personally. All you can do is ride it out and stay true to what you believe in."

"Like corporal punishment?"

"I'll pretend I didn't hear that."

"Still think he's our suspect?" Ben asked. "He hasn't been home for days."

"Could be. If he's the victim," Freya said, nodding in the direction of the abbey, "he wasn't lying up there for days. Where was he before that?"

"If he's the victim," Ben said, "then you can be the one to tell the family. If the mother is anything like the daughter, I don't want to know."

"Alright. If he's the victim, I'll deliver the news. If he's not, then you can do it."

"Why are you so set on having a bet with me?"

"I'm not. I'm just trying to liven things up."

"You're bored."

"I am not bored."

"What is it? Lincolnshire? Not enough bodies for you?"

"This is the seventh murder we've had to investigate in as many months," Freya said. "I'd say that was enough, don't you think?"

"So, what is it then?"

She sighed, and hit the button to start the engine.

"The way I see it, we've had two bets. Both of which you have lost, and might I add, the last one was in truly spectacular style."

"Do you have to remind me?"

"I just want you to win one for a change."

"You want me to win?"

"Yeah. That's all. I want you to experience the glory."

"You're a terrible liar," Ben said.

"I'll have you know, I'm one of the best liars. I've learned from thousands of bad liars how to become a good liar. Something I'm actually quite proud of."

"What are the stakes?"

"I told you. Ten pound."

"Not enough. Something bigger."

"Like what?"

"If I win, you cook for me every night for a week," Ben said.

"Every night?"

"And you do my laundry."

Freya was a little taken aback.

"And my housework, come to think of it," Ben added.

"And if *I* win?"

"The same in reverse. Fully-dressed, I might add. None of this naked chef malarky."

"No. No, I'm not having you doing my laundry, thank you very much," Freya said. "Here's the deal. If you win, I buy you dinner at a restaurant of your choice. If I win, I get to choose the restaurant. You pay."

"One dinner?"

"And associated expenses," Freya said. "A new dress. Maybe some shoes."

"Alright, alright. I get the picture," he said. "The good news is that I know the most expensive restaurant in Lincoln."

"Do we have a deal?" Freya said, holding out her hand for him to shake.

They shook, and she put the car into drive.

"Right then," she said. "Maybe I won't need to tell Anderson how much of a coward you really are."

CHAPTER EIGHT

The road cut through fields that seemed to stretch for miles. An endless patchwork of greens, yellows, and browns. The earth in one field, Jenny noted, was so rich and fertile that it appeared black. Not brown like the soil she remembered in her mother's garden, but black.

Nillson drove well, using the gears to navigate any bends in the lanes. Although, many of the roads they used were dead straight. Like veins that interconnected small villages, or hamlets. She had never known which was which.

"Quiet, isn't it?" Nillson said, rousing Jenny from her thoughts. She glanced across to find Nillson offering a sympathetic smile. "You get used to it."

"Have you always lived here? In Lincolnshire, I mean."

"Born and bred," Nillson replied. "You? Where did you grow up?"

"London. Well, Kent and then London. But south. Born and bred."

"Kent's nice," Nillson said, inferring that her opinion of London was lower.

"DI Bloom said this was the seventh murder investigation since she's been here."

Nillson rocked her head from side to side, as if she was counting.

"Sounds about right."

"Seems like a lot for a place where nothing seems to happen."

"Oh, things happen, alright," Nillson said. "The difference is we don't see them. Nobody sees them." She pointed at a small holding a few hundred yards down a track, surrounded by fields with the glorious sun lighting the gardens and outbuildings. "What do you think is happening in those outbuildings?"

Jenny shrugged. "How should I know?"

"Exactly. There are thousands of properties like that here. No neighbours to keep a beady eye on the comings and goings. No neighbours to hear the arguments, the fights," Nillson said. "The gunshots."

"Gunshots?"

"This is the countryside, Anderson. I imagine it's hard to even arrive home with somebody noticing. In London, you probably couldn't even take the bins out without a neighbour noticing. Am I right?"

Jenny nodded.

"How often do you get calls from suspicious neighbours? The bloke next door is acting strange. Cars keep pulling up then leaving after two minutes."

"I don't know the numbers, but I get your point."

"Seven murders in, what, eight months?" Nillson said. "They're just the ones we know about."

"What made you decide to join up?" Jenny asked.

"Life," Nillson replied without hesitation. "What else was I going to do? Sit behind a desk? Cut people's hair? No thanks. I get to make a difference."

"Do you honestly feel that way?" Jenny asked. "Like you make a difference?"

"I know I do. I know *we* do. Not every day. Sometimes the odds are against us. But most days."

"Did you always want to be in major crimes?"

"I didn't even know it existed. I did my time in uniform and took the opportunity when it came."

"Same," Jenny said, peering out at a house encircled by a tall, brick wall and even taller trees. "Do you ever miss being in uniform? You know? Being out there on the street? Do you miss that?"

"Sometimes," Nillson replied. "Usually when Gillespie or Cruz are being irritating."

"What about DI Bloom? How do you find her?"

"Honestly?" Nillson asked.

"Always."

"Before DI Bloom came to Lincolnshire, we were split into two teams. Did you see the big empty space at the back of the incident room?" Nillson asked, and Jenny nodded. She had wondered what that big, dark area was used for. "I used to sit up there. Gillespie and Cruz, too. We used to report into DI Standing until he transferred."

"What about DS Savage and the others?"

"They reported into DI Foster."

"I suppose he transferred too?"

"Nope. He died. Cancer. Last October. Ben was being groomed to take over. But along came DI Bloom. It was a huge loss for the team. Ben especially."

"So, Freya took his place as DI?" Jenny said.

"Maybe. Maybe not. Either way, they seem to get on pretty well."

"Are they..." Jenny began, hoping Nillson would know where she was leading, and she did.

"No. Not as far as I know, anyway. Just good friends," Nillson said. "Besides, isn't there a rule about that sort of thing? We can't date members of our own team."

"Yeah, well... I'm sure there are a few exceptions to the rule."

"Well, if they are an item, then they do a good job of hiding it," Nillson said. "What about you? What are you running away from?"

"Who said I was running away?"

"Your face. Your questions. The fact that you left London and came here."

"Intuitive, aren't you?"

"Isn't it our job to be intuitive?" Nillson said. "Man trouble?"

"You could say that."

She caught Nillson eyeing her hand, probably searching for signs of a wedding ring.

"But not the type of man trouble you think," Jenny admitted, and she held up her hand. "No ring, and there's never been one either."

Nillson was silent, waiting for Jenny to continue, but making it clear there was no obligation to if she didn't want to.

"I was outnumbered," Jenny said. "Four to one. I couldn't stand in the urinal beside my DI. I don't play golf. And I don't drink beer by the pint. The world may have come a long way towards equality, but there are still advantages to being male."

"Ah," Nillson said, slowing as they passed the little layby where they had parked yesterday. She checked the rear-view mirror to make sure there were no cars behind, then came to a stop and lowered her window just as Gillespie was climbing out the driver's side of a maroon saloon car. Cruz emerged from the passenger seat and slammed the door, his face a picture of irritation. "Got your kneepads?" Nillson called out.

"Aye," the big Glaswegian replied, jabbing his thumb over his shoulder. "I was going to kneel on that idiot."

They all gazed past him to find Cruz fighting with the tail of his jacket, which was caught in the car door.

"See what I mean?" Gillespie said, nodding a casual greeting to Jenny.

"Jim. Help me out, mate," Cruz shouted. "Can you unlock the car?"

But Gillespie ignored the small man's plights, and leaned on Nillson's car door.

"Hope she's been saying nice things about us?" he said.

"All good," Jenny replied. "I've been hearing good things all round."

"What, even about dummy over there?" Gillespie said, and he stared at Nillson in disbelief. "At least give the wee lass a head start, Anna."

"I think I can make my own mind up," Jenny added.

"So, you two are knocking on doors, are you? Shame. Cruz here is an expert at it," Gillespie said, and again, they all looked to find Cruz working his jacket tail up and down, his tongue sticking from between his lips in full concentration. Gillespie flicked his head up the road. "There's a wee house up there. I'd start there if I were you. Other than that, the next house is all the way in Bardney. I don't think you're going to get much in the way of leads. But hey, someone has to do it."

"We'll be okay," Nillson said. "You just focus on searching every blade of grass in a square mile. I think DI Bloom has picked the perfect men for the job."

"Aye, well. We'll see who comes up with the leads, eh? That's what counts, Anna. Leads. And if it means Dopey and I have to crawl around on our hands and knees all day, then so be it."

Just as he said that, Cruz's jacket pulled free and he staggered back, nearly tripping over with the sudden freedom.

Nillson smiled across at Jenny. "See what we're up against?" she said, and then put the car in gear, checked the mirror again, and prepared to pull away. But before she did, she called out the window to Gillespie, "Do you still have that hundred quid?"

"Last night's winnings, you mean?" he said, suddenly interested in what Nillson had to say. "Aye, I do."

"Winner takes all. Whoever gets the best lead gets the money."

"Ah, come on. If you win, you get the money. But I've already got the money. What do I win?"

Nillson looked across at Jenny with a 'trust me' expression.

"A kiss," Nillson said.

"A kiss? From you?"

"And Anderson."

"A kiss from you both?"

"What are you doing?" Jenny hissed, but Nillson silenced her with a raised hand.

"So, I get a kiss from you both, but you get a hundred quid?" he said.

"That's the deal."

For a moment, Jenny thought the big Scotsman was going to turn her down. But he smiled hungrily.

"Aye, you've got yourself a deal," he said, and he wiped his mouth with the back of his hand.

"We'll see you back at the station," Nillson said.

"Lipstick. I want to see lipstick," he called out as Nillson pulled the car away.

"You have got to be joking," Jenny said, when they had left the two men far behind. "I'm not kissing him."

"You won't have to," Nillson said, as she brought the car to a stop in the driveway of the only house within a kilometre of the crime scene. She unclipped her seat belt and opened the door. Then, before she climbed out, she turned and offered Jenny one last morsel of confidence. "No man has ever beaten me, and I don't intend on breaking that rule now."

Jenny followed Nillson up the driveway and stood behind her while they waited for the door to be opened.

She wanted to say something. She wanted to contest her confidence. The idea of kissing Gillespie wasn't entirely disgusting. He was a big, strong man. There was a kindness in his eyes, and he was clean enough. But it wasn't the way Jenny had planned on starting her new life in Lincolnshire.

The door was pulled open, and a woman was standing there holding a dressing gown pulled around her to cover her modesty, but nothing to hide the veil of scorn on her face. A pretty wedding ring adorned the third finger of her left hand.

Her expression softened when she saw Nillson's warrant card, and her mouth hung open as Nillson explained why they were there.

"I'm afraid there's been a serious incident at the abbey ruins," Nillson explained. "We were wondering if you were around yesterday, and if so, did you happen to see anything suspicious?"

"An incident?" she whispered, the scorn replaced by what Jenny could only describe as fear.

"I'm afraid so, Mrs..."

"Carson," she said. "Leigh Carson."

"Thank you, Mrs Carson," Nillson said. "Were you home yesterday afternoon?"

"He's dead, isn't he?" she said, and she looked as though she was about to faint.

"I'm sorry?" Nillson said, giving Jenny a concerned sideways glance.

"My husband," she said. "He didn't come home yesterday."

CHAPTER NINE

"Alright, listen up," Gillespie called out to the dozen uniformed officers before him, and Cruz, who waited beside him like a bitter but faithful hound. Gillespie adopted his best motivational speech voice, and stepped up onto a small pile of fallen stone. "Your mission, should you choose to accept it, is to crawl across this wee patch of barren grass here in search of something. We'll be two metres apart, which means we can cover a thirty-metre strip of land. When we're done, we'll turn around and come back along the next thirty metres. And so on, and so on, until we're done. It's a thankless task, but someone has to do it. There will be blood. There will be thorns, and ticks, and sheep crap too. But we'll never give in. We'll never let them beat us. They can take our desk jobs. They can take our cushy little door to door numbers. And they can take our weekends from us forcing us to crawl across the bloodstained ground. But they'll never take our freedom," he cried, much to the amusement of a few of the uniforms, who sniggered in response.

He leaned down to whisper in Cruz's ear, who shook his head in absolute disgust.

"I've always wanted to do that."

"And you call me an idiot?" Cruz said.

"In all seriousness, lads. There's a lot riding on this. Be thorough. If you find something, raise your hand. There's a pint in it for you," he said, and winked at Griffiths, a uniform he had worked with on a few investigations. "Alright, two metres apart. Let's get this done."

"Ah, bloody hell," Cruz cried out, before he'd even got down on his hands and knees. He bent his knee and raised his boot to inspect the sole. "Bloody sheep crap."

"Just get on with it," Gillespie said, as he dropped down to his knees and looked along the line. "Take it slow, boys and girls. Let's go."

They worked their way across the large expanse of grass that the Scenes of Crimes team had declared ready for them. Every now and then, Gillespie looked along the ranks and called out for certain members to slow down, reminding them they were a team, and they needed to be thorough.

Twice though, Gillespie had to reach back and give Cruz a gentle tap on his head, accompanied by a wide-eyed glare to convey the need for him not to let the side down.

"I'm doing my best," Cruz muttered under his breath when Gillespie whacked him a third time. Then he gave a yelp and rolled onto his side, clutching his knee.

"Ah for God's sake, Gabby. Will you stop messing about?"

"My leg," he said, rubbing at his leg and pulling a face like a child having a splinter removed from his finger. "I knelt on something."

He ran his fingers through the grass, searching for the offending article. Then he stopped and looked at Gillespie like he had just discovered penicillin.

Dragging something from the tangled lengths of wild grass, Cruz held it up before him.

"Look," he said.

"It's a brick, Gabby," Gillespie said, shaking his head at the buffoon DI Bloom had suggested to be joined to his hip. *His* hip. James Gillespie. Cruz, of all the idiots in all the world, he thought to himself.

"It's got blood on it," Cruz said, holding the brick up for him to see.

"The victim was stabbed, Gabby. Besides, it was under all that grass. There's no way it had anything to do with what happened yesterday."

"I'm bagging it," Cruz said. "Look at it. That's blood."

It was half a brick with edges that had rounded with time. The type of brick that could be found at the abbey less than a hundred metres away. But the corner of it was stained in what Gillespie assumed to be a thread of iron. He shook his head at Cruz in utter contempt.

"Just get a bloody move on," Gillespie said. "You're slowing us down."

"Gillespie," a voice called out from the line of uniforms.

"What is it now? Don't tell me, you got a splinter?"

"No, mate," the man replied. It was Griffiths, and Gillespie baulked at his own reaction. He held up something black in his gloved hands. It was material. Lacy material.

"Is that..." Gillespie said.

"They're not my size," Griffiths replied. "They were lying right here on the grass."

"On the grass? Not under it?"

"On it," Griffiths said, as he dropped them into an evidence bag. "That's a beer you owe me."

"And me," a voice called out from further up the line. "I think you better come and see this."

CHAPTER TEN

The pathology department of Lincoln County Hospital was at the end of a long, bare corridor, with windows on one side looking out over a small, grassy knoll, overgrown, unkempt, and locked in by the irregular building on all sides.

It was perhaps the quietest corridor in the hospital, Freya thought, as they made their way towards the double doors.

"I dread this," Freya said quietly.

"And by that I assume you're not talking about seeing the dead body."

"No. Dead bodies are fine. I've seen hundreds of them. In fact, given the choice, I'd rather spend my time with a dead body. At least they don't make me feel like a naughty schoolgirl."

"Ditto," Ben said, as he pushed the button on the intercom and held his finger to his lips. They had made the mistake of being overheard on the intercom before and it hadn't been the ideal way to begin the meeting with the Welsh pathologist.

"You feel like a naughty schoolgirl?" Freya asked, and Ben laughed out loud. Although, the laughter was likely more to mask his unease. "I'm not putting up with it today. I'm not going to let her get the better of me. I'll give her a taste of her own medicine."

"Oh, this should be interesting then," Ben replied.

The door opened to reveal Doctor Pippa Bell, dressed in a clean, white smock with a multi-coloured pen in her breast pocket, and on her feet, a pair of red Crocs. As was custom with the fiery Welsh pathologist, her hair was dyed a bright, outlandish colour. This time it was an electric blue.

"Now then," she said, appraising them both curiously.

Their smiles faded and they waited to gauge the doctor's mood.

"Saturday," she said.

"Yes, we're not too pleased about it ourselves," Freya said.

"Saturday," the doctor repeated, somehow managing to prolong the delivery of that single word.

"Shall we get on?" Freya said. "Before it becomes Sunday?"

"I had plans, you know?"

"No, Pip. No, we didn't know. In fact, Ben and I were just saying how we had absolutely nothing better to be doing ourselves. We were rather pleased that somebody's life was torn apart, as it gives us something to do."

The doctor was taken aback at Freya's flippancy, and she cocked her head, as if the retort had impressed her.

"You know where the PPE is. I'll be inside," she said, holding the door for them both, then pushing it closed when they had entered. "I can give you ten minutes. That's all, I'm afraid."

"Any insight would be helpful, Pip," Ben said, as he tossed Freya a gown.

"Yes, well. Don't expect much. I haven't finished the preliminary examination yet. But I have some ideas. Now then. I'll see you inside."

She slipped through the door, and Freya felt the blast of cool air on her face as the door sucked closed behind her. She waited a few seconds for the doctor to be out of earshot.

"So far so good," she said. "I think I've cracked it."

"You've cracked it, have you?" Ben said with a smile. "You honestly think you've worked out how to deal with her?"

"You saw her. She didn't know what to do when I gave her as good as I got."

"Right," Ben said, as he fastened his gown. "Like I said. This should be interesting."

He held the door for her and followed her into the exam room, where a row of stainless steel benches awaited them. Doctor Bell was standing beside one of them, the only one with a mound covered by a blue sheet.

"Male, late forties," the doctor began. "Non-smoker. Given the condition of his hands, I'd say he was a non-manual worker. Office job probably. However, he worked out. He was fit."

She pulled back the sheet to reveal the man lying face down on the bench. A rolled-up towel supported his head as if he was there for a massage.

"Single stab wound to the back, penetrating his heart. Death would have been instantaneous."

"Any idea of the weapon?" Ben asked, only to receive a glare in reply.

"If you want to give me a moment, Ben, I'll tell you all I know."

"Okay. I was just—"

"I know what you were doing. Hurrying me along to get to the information you need."

"We're just keen to get to the bottom of this one, Pip," Freya said.

"And I'm keen to get home. Let me tell you. Tickets for Spiderman, I have. Three p.m."

"Spiderman?" Ben said, sounding surprised.

"Yes. It's the new one. Been looking forward to it, I have."

"Another new one?"

"Look, are we here to ascertain how our poor victim lost his life, or are we here to critique my choice in films?"

She spoke the final word as if it had two syllables, then stared at Ben with utter contempt.

"Go ahead," he said.

"Right. Thank you. The blade was at least eight inches long, maybe a little longer," the doctor explained. "An inch wide at the hilt, narrowing to a fine point."

"One inch wide?" Freya said. "That's narrow for a blade that long."

"Will you let me finish?" the doctor said. "Crikey, it's like presenting to a pair of excited puppies."

"Go ahead," Freya told her.

"Good. Now then. And this is key," she said, using her multi-coloured pen to indicate the stab wound by waving a circle in the air above it. "The knife went in here, but penetrated the heart."

"So?" Freya said. "We knew that, didn't we?"

"The heart, Freya."

"Yes, I understand."

"The heart isn't here," the doctor said, again using her pen to highlight the area, then waved a circle a few inches away. "The heart is over here. You'll have to wait for me to open him up and have a good look, but one thing I'm certain of is that the knife had some flex in the blade."

"A fillet knife," Freya said, and the doctor pointed her pen at her.

"Ah. Yes. Exactly. A fillet knife. The blade entered with some force, deflected off the rib cage, and found his heart. It was either lucky, or very unlucky. Either way. That's what we've got."

"Excellent work, Doctor," Freya said. "Do we have a time of death?"

"I ran some initial calculations. Some time between midday and four p.m. yesterday."

"He was found on his back," Freya said. "What do you make of that?"

"Ah. You're referring to the lack of blood," the doctor said. "You've been talking to Michaela."

"I wondered if you agreed with her analysis, yes."

"I do. See, I haven't even cleaned him up yet. What you see here is how he was found. Now, listen carefully," she said, and she pulled Ben towards her, turning him to face Freya. "Now, the wound to the heart would have stopped blood flow almost immediately. Almost being the key word. Had he been upright, some blood, not much mind, would have run down his back."

"That's what Michaela thought," Ben said.

"Well, she's right. But what she didn't tell you, I'm guessing, is that the knife, our fillet knife, was left in the wound."

"Sticking out of him, you mean?" Ben said, and the doctor nodded.

"Here's what I think happened. He was lying on his front when he was attacked. The killer left him there for a while."

"How long?"

"Long enough for coagulation to begin. An hour," the doctor said. "Then they removed the knife and rolled him onto his back."

"Yeah, they dragged him across the ground," Ben said. "Laid him out on some rocks and stripped him."

"Is there any sign of sexual intercourse?" Freya asked.

The doctor pulled back the sheet a little further to reveal the man's genitals.

"I'll take some swabs," she said, inspecting the face down man on the bench with a curious eye. "But he looks clean. I'll send you through the results along with my other findings, and, of course, we'll run his DNA through the database."

"Much appreciated, Pip," Ben said, as the doctor covered the man with the sheet. "How's your mum doing? Is the treatment working?"

"Oh, she's doing alright," the doctor said. "Still alive, at least."

"Well, that's good, isn't it?" Freya said.

"The cancer is eating her alive. Truth be told, it's only her bloody mindedness keeping her going. Anybody else would have given up a long time ago."

"Well, she has a lot to lose," Freya said. "A loving daughter, for example."

"Thanks. Although, I doubt she sees it quite so positively. That being said, she's looking forward to today."

"Today?" asked Ben.

"I told you. Spiderman," she said. "Come on, Ben. Keep up."

"You're taking your mother to see Spiderman?"

"Yeah. Loves the cinema, she does. Although, sometimes I wonder if she just likes the pick and mix and the milkshakes. But it keeps her happy, you know?"

"And who doesn't like a good pick and mix?" Freya said.

"Well, the doctor said I should keep her away from sugars. Said it could affect her moods quite badly. Because of the medication, you know? And he's right. Give her one chocolate mouse and she's up and down like a bloody yo-yo, she is."

"Right," Ben said, with a nervous glance at Freya. Agreeing for the sake of being agreeable could land him in a difficult position. "So, you just let her have what she wants?"

"Let her?" the doctor replied, and she laughed once, with a visible jolt of her neck. "Wild horses couldn't stop her. I might as well just buy her what she wants and suffer the consequences. I'm damned if I do and I'm damned if I don't."

"Right," Freya said, and this time both her and Ben exchanged nervous glances. "You could just tell her the cinema has been cancelled?"

The doctor stared at them both in turn, then settled on Freya, as if she'd just found the formula to calculate the meaning of life.

"Lie to her, you mean?" she said.

"Well... Not lie, as such. It's for her own good," Freya explained.

"Lie? To my own mother?" the doctor said. "What kind of monster are you? She's a dying woman."

"I was just–"

But before Freya could finish her defence, Pip was checking her watch.

"Right, you two. You've wasted enough of my time."

"So, you're going to the cinema then, are you?" Ben asked. "With your mother."

"Yes. But before then, I have to examine this poor man's heart, take some blood, and get his samples over to the lab," she explained. "With any luck, I'll have time to grab a McDonalds on the way home."

"A McDonalds?" Ben said, then checked himself. But it was too late. Pip had heard the tone and was ready with her own defence.

"Of course," she said, patting her backside. "You don't get a rock star body like this living on pick and mixes, now, do you?"

CHAPTER ELEVEN

"A rock star body?" Freya said, as she slammed the driver's door. "A bloody rock star body?"

"What happened to not letting her get to you?" Ben said.

"Oh, come on. You heard her. If she's got a rock star body, then I'm bloody Gillian Anderson. And as for picking up a McDonalds on the way home as if it's part of some diet plan. The woman's a lunatic, Ben. And what's with taking her dying mother to see Spiderman? I feel like that entire last five minutes of conversation was an out-of-body experience. How can any one person be that mad, Ben? How? I mean, it's bad enough she has blue hair. Blue hair, Ben? Not green, like it was a few weeks ago. Or orange. Blue. Like a porn star. That's what she looks like. A Welsh bloody porn star. Honestly, Ben. I feel like if you shook her head, her eyes would rattle about like one those poxy, furry things kids have. And the Crocs. I mean, I've turned a blind eye to them up until now. But not anymore. Oh no. What with all those tattoos on her feet, she looks like somebody's four-year-old was let loose with a marker and a pair of scissors. How can a woman like that be a forensic bloody pathologist?"

"Freya?"

"And as for you. You didn't exactly stand up for yourself, did you?

No. You just let her walk all over you. You just let her cast her magic wand and elevate herself up on this imaginary pedestal. I'm telling you, if everyone took a stand against people like her, the world would not only be a better place, it'd be safer. She needs locking up in a padded cell."

"Freya?"

"And did you hear her?" Freya said, then adopted the pathologist's accent. "*Saturday*? I had plans, you know? Well, welcome to the real world, Doctor. We all had plans. We'd all rather be doing something other than being patronised by a bloody lunatic with a multi-coloured biro, crappy tattoos, and a porn star haircut."

"Freya?" Ben said, raising his voice. It was only then that Freya realised she had been ranting, and she took a breath, letting her head fall back onto the head rest.

"I'm sorry," she said. "I let her get to me, didn't I?"

"Freya?" Ben said, and she turned her head lethargically to find him offering a look of solace. "I'm sorry to be the one to tell you this."

"What? You disagree?"

He nodded past her at the window.

"What?" she said. She refused to turn and look, but she did lower her voice. "Don't tell me she's there."

He gave a tight-lipped smile, almost apologetic in nature.

"Oh God," she mumbled. "Can you kill me? You know how to do it and get away with it. Just dig a hole somewhere on your dad's farm. A bullet in the head. Just make it quick. Honestly."

"No can do, I'm afraid," Ben replied.

"Oh, come on. I've seen you break laws when you have to."

"It's not a legal thing, Freya. It's a moral thing. It's against my principles."

"Is she still there?" Freya said, hearing the lifeless despondence in her own voice.

"Take a look," Ben said, and slowly, Freya rolled her head around to stare out of the window.

But all she saw was the hospital car park, with all the usual comings and goings of people. She turned back to Ben.

"She's not there," she said.

"Gotcha," he replied, and winked at her.

"You're going to hell for that."

"It stopped you ranting, didn't it?" Ben said. "If I hadn't of interrupted you, you'd still be going now."

"Yes, well. There's no shortage of material. What with her ridiculous hair, awful tattoos, and dying bloody mother."

"Freya?"

"Sorry. I know that was low. But that's what she does to me. Me? I pride myself on being courteous and polite. I'm a good person, aren't I? I deserve better, don't I? I don't deserve to be treated like this, do I? She does this to me, Ben. She makes me a horrible person. How can somebody do that?"

"Freya?"

"What?"

"Calm."

"I know," she replied, just as her phone began to ring over the car's Bluetooth system. She looked at the name on the screen. "Oh God, Ben. I can't do it. I don't think I can face him."

Ben leaned over and hit the button to take the call.

"DI Bloom's phone," he said.

"Ben. I've got some news. Is the boss about?"

"She's just stepped away for a minute, mate. What did you find?"

"Probably just as well. You know how uptight she can be sometimes. She can be a right old battle axe."

Freya's head snapped upright, reminding Ben of one of those wooden children's toys that snap into action at the pull of a string. She glared at him, mouthing her fury in silence.

"Go on, Jim. We're short on time. What did you find?"

"Well, first of all, we found some underwear."

"Underwear?"

"Aye, Ben. Saucy little number too. Black with little frilly bits on. Whoever was wearing them was out to please, if you know what I mean?"

"Where are they now?"

"Bagged and tagged, and on the way to the lab, along with our other find."

"Another find? Wow, you have been busy."

"Well, you know how it is, Ben. People work for people. It's not what you tell them to do, it's how you ask them."

"Jim, can I be honest? We've just had a hard meeting with Doctor Bell. I don't have the energy."

"Doctor Bell? Oh God. Sorry to hear that. How *is* the Welsh dragon?"

"Fiery," Ben said. "Come on. Put me out of my misery."

"Well, if I'm right, the underwear should give us the name of whoever was with our victim, right?"

"Right."

"What if I told you we found the murder weapon?" Gillespie said. "A nine-inch-long fillet knife. Covered in blood, lying in the long grass about fifty yards from the crime scene."

"You're kidding?"

"Nope. Couldn't believe it myself, if I'm honest," he said, then inhaled deeply, and Freya pictured him checking his fingernails, casually basking in his temporary glory. "I guess this has to go down as the biggest result of the day, eh? Should get me in the boss's good books, don't you think?"

"I think you'll have to work harder than that to get in *my* good books, Gillespie," Freya said. "You know what us uptight, old battle axes can be like, don't you?"

"Erm. Aye, boss," he replied. "I was just–"

"Save it. I'll see you back at the station," Freya said, and she hit the button to end the call. "Just when my ego needed a little massaging, I have to deal with that."

"All in a day's work," Ben said, just as his phone started ringing. He glanced down at the screen, hit the green button, and routed the call to loudspeaker. "Nillson. How's it going?"

"Bullseye," Nillson replied, her voice filled with confidence and conveying more than a little masculinity. "First door we knocked on."

"You said that like they gave you a winning lottery ticket."

"Better than that. We may have an ID on the body," she said. "A John Carson. Didn't come home last night, according to his wife."

"He might have worked late. He could be drunk in a ditch somewhere."

"Well, if it isn't him, he's a dead ringer," Anderson called out. "Pun intended."

Feeling Ben's stare, Freya continued to gaze through the windscreen, lost in the innocent to and fro of life.

"This is a pretty decent breakthrough," Nillson said, and there was something about her tone that reminded Freya of Gillespie. "I mean, it's not often we get an ID on the first door we knock on."

"Yeah, it's decent," Ben said. "I'll give you that much."

"Shall we send Gold round?" Nillson asked. "As family liaison? The wife was in a right state when we left."

"No. Not yet," Freya said, taking control of the situation. "Meet us back at the station."

CHAPTER TWELVE

Both Nillson's and Gillespie's cars were in the car park when they returned. Freya eased the big Range Rover between them and killed the engine.

"What are you thinking?" Ben asked.

"I'm still mulling over which restaurant we should eat at," she replied.

"Save your energy. I'll be picking the place," he said. "I still can't believe you managed to talk me into betting with you again. Not once has it ever turned out well for me."

"You know what they say about doing the same thing over and over and expecting different results, don't you?"

"It's a sign of lunacy," Ben said, easing himself from the car. He leaned on the bonnet while she gathered her bag and jacket. "What's your plan for the team?"

"Well, originally, I was going to send as many of them home as I could. We don't all need to be working at the weekend."

"But?"

"But I suspect tension in the ranks. I want to get to the bottom of it," she said. "They seem competitive, almost."

"Oh, right. And you're going to stamp out competitiveness, are you? Says the woman who just made a bet on who the killer is. If anyone got wind of that, you'd be front page news."

"We, Ben. We'd be front page news," she said. "If we can get a positive ID on the body, then we'll have made good progress. I'd like to be in a position to show DCI Granger how far we've come when he walks through the door on Monday morning."

She left him there, expecting him to follow like an obedient puppy. Annoyingly, he found himself trailing after her, and even ran the last few steps to hold the door.

They climbed the stairs to the first floor, then quietly pushed through into the corridor, where they were met with what Ben could only describe as the sounds of a classroom when the teacher takes a toilet break.

"They can take our desk jobs," Cruz said, mimicking Gillespie's Glaswegian accent, but unable to add the depth of his subject's voice with his own childlike tones. "And they can take our cushy little door to door numbers. And they can take our weekends from us forcing us to crawl across the bloodstained ground. But they'll never take our freedom!"

The effort produced a half-hearted applause from one or two individuals, and a little laughter, and by the time Freya and Ben reached the incident room doors and peered through the glass, they found Gillespie shoving Cruz back to his desk.

"I got results, though, eh? Didn't I?"

"Well, uniform did," Cruz said.

"Aye, on my watch. Under my supervision. It's motivational speaking like that that brings folk together. Creates unity. A pair of wee panties and the murder weapon. Eh? Not bad for a morning crawling round in the mud," he said with pride. "What about you, Nillson? Can you match that?"

"I'll take your panties and murder weapon," she replied. "And I'll raise you."

"You'll raise me what?"

"You'll have to wait and see," Nillson replied, and she winked at Anderson. Clearly the two girls were getting on just fine, and the little charade that was playing out, although considered unprofessional in most stations, was only a bit of fun.

"Want me to break this up?" Ben whispered.

"No. It's good for them. It's only banter. I'd rather they did this than didn't speak to each other."

"Fair enough," he replied.

"Ah, come on. You can't do that? I told you what I found."

"What uniform found," Cruz added.

"Aye well. I told you what we found. As a collective," Gillespie said. "Now you tell me what you found. It can't be better than the murder weapon."

"I'm not so sure about that," Anderson said, and Ben was surprised to see her joining in so early in her time there. It was a good sign. "In fact, with what we found, I think we might have even turned a corner in the investigation."

"Come on," Freya said, and she shoved open the incident room door, the squealing hinges cutting through the scene like a fire alarm. She strode over to the whiteboard, leaving Ben to his thoughts. "Take your seats, please."

Immediately, she began writing on the board, starting with a name in the centre of the space.

"John Carson," she said, while a wide-eyed Gillespie was still making his way to his desk. "Chapman, find out what you can on this man. Talk to Nillson for details. All we know is that he matches the description of our victim and didn't come home last night."

"Ma'am," Chapman replied, by way of confirmation.

Ben caught Gillespie mouthing something at Nillson, who tried to ignore him by listening to the briefing.

Freya wrote another name above the first.

"Theodore Wood," she said. "Hasn't been seen for days. Owns the car that was found near the murder scene. Where is he?"

"Probably done a runner," Cruz said.

"You could be right. In which case, we need to expand our reach. Talk to our neighbours in Yorkshire, Nottinghamshire, and East Anglia. Spread the word."

"What me, boss?" Cruz said, and she turned to stare at him.

"Yes, you. Is there a problem?"

"Well, no. But you just don't normally give me stuff like that."

"Well, it's a Saturday. Maybe I'm feeling generous. Use your head. Think outside the box. I want this man found."

"I'm on it," he replied, clearly excited at the prospect of doing something that didn't involve mundane police work.

"Nillson. I want you to talk to Doctor Bell. Arrange a viewing for Mrs Carson. We need a positive ID before we can move on this."

"Today, boss?"

"Yes. As soon as Mrs Carson feels up to it."

"Gotcha," she replied.

"Oh, and Nillson," Freya said, and the newly appointed DS looked up with raised eyebrows, "if you happen to do the viewing today, you might want to stop and pick a few things up for our crazy pathologist."

"Pick a few things up? I'm not following."

"A pick and mix," Freya said.

"A what?"

"You know? A little cup with little sweets inside. She's particularly fond of the chocolate mice, I hear."

"A pick and mix?"

"And a McDonalds," Freya added.

Ben smiled as Anderson looked on incredulously.

"Anything in particular from McDonalds, boss?" Nillson asked.

Freya gave it some thought, then grinned to herself.

"A happy meal," she said, and winked at Ben. "God knows she'll need it."

"Will do," Anna said.

"Everybody else, go home," Freya said. "We can't do anything until we get the results back from the lab, or until we get a positive ID."

"We could look into Theodore Wood, ma'am," Chapman suggested.

"No. Home. All of you. Anderson, you need to find yourself somewhere to live. Cruz, you need to clean that jacket, it's filthy."

"I got it caught in the car door."

"Clean it," Freya said. "Gillespie, keep pushing the lab for results, and Gold, stay on your toes. If we get a positive ID, I'll need you to go and babysit the wife. Is everyone clear?"

"Aye, boss," Gillespie roared. "I'll never turn down an early finish."

"It's more to save overtime than out of my kind heart, Gillespie," she said. "Now go. All of you. Enjoy your freedom."

CHAPTER THIRTEEN

The team were in high spirits in the car park. Cruz ambled along in his own little world, inspecting the grubby mark on his jacket. Gillespie strode behind him talking to Nillson, while Gold took the opportunity to get to know Anderson a little more.

As usual, Ben was deep in thought. And as usual, like a gentleman, he waited for Freya beside her car.

"Actually," Freya said, "second thoughts. I think I'm going to pop back upstairs."

"I'll wait for you," Ben said, shoving himself off the car.

"No. No, it's fine," Freya said. "I'll be a while."

"I can take you," Gold offered. "I don't mind. I'm taking Anderson anyway. She doesn't know the roads yet, so I said I'd take her to see a few places."

"If you're sure," Ben said, although the comment was rather subtly aimed at Freya and not Jackie Gold.

Freya nodded at him once.

"Go on. Enjoy your day off," she said, as Gillespie pulled out of his space to block Cruz from getting out first.

He wound down the window, and in that thick Glaswegian accent that Freya was growing to adore, he leaned out of the car, his big arm draping down the dirty door, and said, "Bye, losers."

Cruz honked on his horn, and Gillespie just laughed as he pulled out of the car park and disappeared. Driving, Freya thought right then, was an indication of somebody's personality. There was Gillespie, with his jerky steering and hard braking, followed by Cruz, who steered his mother's little hatchback from the spot as an elderly lady might. Not that there was anything wrong with taking care. It was just that the sight of a five-and-a-half-foot, twenty-something-year-old man holding the wheel at ten-to-two and revving the engine far too hard was a bit of a spectacle.

Jackie Gold drove competently, but cautiously. The last thing she would want to do is hurt somebody, or at the very least, offend them by driving too close. She reversed out of the spot, so that from his position in the passenger seat, Ben eyed Freya with curiosity. She knew that look. He was on to her. He knew she was up to something, and she'd have to make sure he didn't guess what it was.

Only when Jackie Gold's car had pulled out of the car park and disappeared up the high street did Freya re-enter the building. She took her time, keeping her footsteps quiet in the echoey stairwell. The first floor corridor was still. She liked it when it was quiet. Time to think. Space to breathe. And, best of all, no distractions.

Slowly, she peered through the incident room door, not daring to open them for fear of making a noise. But she found nothing inside but empty chairs and dark computer screens. That was when she caught the faint smell of something floral. She sniffed at the air, following her nose further along the corridor. Although the perfume was not to Freya's taste, she appreciated the quality. It certainly wasn't cheap, and it was strong enough to lead her to the female washroom, where she listened at the door.

Nothing. Not a peep could be heard. After a few moments of listening for the finest of sounds, she pushed the door open a crack, catching sight of a pair of jeans and a sweater hanging on the mirror above the basins. Then an inch further, she saw a female hand gripping the basin, as if the owner was leaning into the mirror, examining her face.

Carefully, Freya pushed the door open fully, and Chapman found her in the mirror's reflection.

"Ma'am," she said, her voice a little shaky. "I thought you'd all gone home."

"Ah, you know how it is. What am I going to do, Chapman? Sit at home and think about work is what. I might as well do it here. At least I have the resources to hand."

"Right," Chapman replied, turning away to pack away her makeup into a little, leather case.

"What about you? Thought you'd have left with the others."

"I'm meeting a friend. It's easier to get ready here than go all the way home and back again."

"I see. Off anywhere nice?"

"No. We'll go and see a film or something. Some dinner maybe. You know?"

"Ah, good for you, Chapman. It's good to see you getting out. You're normally so private."

"Well, with Gillespie and Cruz shouting their heads off, it's not always easy to get an audience, is it?"

"True. Well then. I'll stop invading your privacy. Have a lovely time," Freya said. "And Chapman?"

"Ma'am?"

"You'd tell me if there was something wrong, wouldn't you?"

Chapman's eyes widened a little, then settled, as she continued to pack away her things.

"Of course," she said.

"Good. You know what? I've changed my mind. I think I'll work from home. Enjoy yourself, Chapman. You work hard. It's healthy to cut loose once in a while."

"I'll try my best, ma'am," she replied, offering a weak smile.

Slipping from the bathroom, Freya stood against the wall for a few moments. Then, when she heard the sound of Chapman changing into her jeans, she made her way back to the stairwell, and down into the car park. She hadn't noticed it before, but Chapman's little car was parked in the corner out of the way. That was typical of Chapman. She wouldn't want to inconvenience somebody by taking a spot close to the doors. In a few short moments, Freya was in her car and pulling out of the car park. She revved the engine, feeling the comforting throb of the V8, then pulled out onto the quiet high street, making sure that anybody in the station heard her leaving.

But less than a hundred yards later, she slowed, indicated, then pulled into the pub car park.

There was no need to rush. Casually, she locked the car and walked back along the high street towards the station, this time using the main entrance, and then the main stairs to the first floor. The smell of floral perfume was strong again, but coming from the other end of the corridor. Freya traced it all the way back to the incident room.

She wasn't snooping. That's what she told herself. She was caring for her team. It was her duty as a leader. Although she couldn't shake the feeling that she was overstepping a boundary.

That was, until she peered through the window in the incident room door and saw exactly what she thought she would see.

CHAPTER FOURTEEN

It was two o'clock when Freya turned off the main road onto the old, bumpy farm track. She slowed while she found Ben's number in her phone, then hit the green button and set her phone down.

He answered after three rings, and through the car's speakers, she thought there was a slight echo to his voice.

"You're in your kitchen," she told him.

"What, are you spying on me now?"

"No. Just playing at being detective."

"What am I wearing?"

"Ben, for anybody else, that would be a fun game. But for you, my friend, it's pointless."

"Why?" he said dryly.

"Because I've only ever seen you wearing two outfits. Three, if you include the tracksuit bottoms you sleep in. You're either in your work clothes still, or you're wearing those tired, old jeans with a check shirt."

A pause followed, and she imagined Ben smiling to himself.

"What if I'm not wearing any of those?" he said.

"Oh, please tell me you're actually dressed."

"Alright, alright," he said with a laugh. "Jeans and shirt. Are you saying I need a new wardrobe?"

"You need new everything, Ben. Some variety. Some colour. Something that defines you."

"Did you call to insult my wardrobe, or was there something important you had to say?" he said. She had noticed he often moved the conversation on when it got too difficult for him or perhaps threatened to expose a weakness.

"I was wondering what you were doing?"

"Well, you know me. Predictable. Boring," he said. "I was thinking about mowing the lawn."

"Mowing the lawn? Wow. You must be bored."

"Not really. It's what you do, isn't it?" Ben said. "It's the weekend. You do chores. The sun is shining. There's barely a cloud in the sky. It's perfect grass cutting weather."

"I think our opinions differ on how best to enjoy the sunshine."

"I know. That's why there are, as yet, undiscovered tribes living in your back garden, Freya."

"Are you volunteering?" she asked, and felt herself biting down on her bottom lip in anticipation of his response. There was no way he would say no.

"You want me to come and cut your grass?"

"Oh, thank you, Ben. That would be lovely. Shall we say ten minutes?"

"Eh?"

"Thanks, Ben. I'll get the kettle on," she said, and hit the red button to end the call, smiling to herself at how easy he was to work.

Less than five minutes later, she was home. The kettle was boiling, and she had changed into a little summer dress, when she heard a familiar knock on the door. Three raps in quick succession. Ben's trademark knock.

"Ah, it's the community gardener," she said, when she opened the door to him.

"Don't push your luck," he told her, stepping past her into the hallway. He moved through to the back door, pulled back the bolts, and stared into the rear garden.

"Tea?" Freya said, hoping to soften the blow.

"Freya, your grass is nearly a foot tall."

"Is it?" she called back. "Oh. Is that a problem?"

He looked back her way, trying to read if she was joking or not.

"Have you even been out here?"

"Well, if I'm honest, I moved in last October and didn't even know I had a back garden until at least December time."

"What do you mean, you didn't know you had a garden?"

"Well, I just thought it was like some kind of wildlife thing. You know? For the farm. Plus, it was dark in the mornings and dark in the evenings. I didn't step outside there until last month," she explained. "Was that a yes, by the way?"

"A yes?"

"Tea," she said. "Did you want a tea?"

"I think I'm going to need something stronger."

"Me too," Freya said. "But if we get a positive ID—"

"Yeah, yeah. We'll need to go back to work."

"Wouldn't look very good if we waited until Monday, would it?"

He nodded, but his expression had lost that carefree smile. "Tea it is, then," he said, then stepped outside.

By the time Freya had made two cups of tea and taken them outside, Ben had fetched his mower from his car and was standing on the lawn. His feet and most of his lower legs were hidden by the grass.

She set the cups down on top of a low wall, then sat beside them, feeling more than a little guilty. The job would not be a quick blast around with the mower as she thought it might be. It was going to take some serious grunt to get through the thick thatch.

"What can I do to help?" she asked.

"Buy an apartment," he replied. "That way you won't have a lawn for me to mow."

"I'll be okay once it's done. I'll be able to keep it short."

"Do you have a mower?"

"Well, no, but I can borrow yours, I suppose."

He laughed and shook his head, then bent to grab hold of the pull cord. "This once," he said. "I'll get it under control. You keep it short."

"Of course," she said, sipping her tea. "I'll keep on top of it."

He stared at her, as if he could see the cracks in her promise. Then, with a final shake of his head, he pulled the cord and the mower fired into life. It was louder than Freya thought it would be. But then, out there in the middle of the Lincolnshire countryside, everything seemed loud. Even closing her front door.

"Ben?" she shouted, and he looked her way, irritated.

"What?"

"Can you do those stripes?"

"What?"

"Stripes. Can you make it stripy?"

He killed the engine, then, keeping a firm grip on his patience, he exhaled deeply.

"What?" he said, in the new silence.

"Can you do those stripes? You know? Like you see on the telly."

"Stripes?" he said, his expression a look of utter bewilderment.

"Yes. Up and down," she said, gesturing at the grass. "Like a tennis court."

"Like a tennis court?" he repeated. "Freya, small children could get lost in here. I'm sorry to be the one to break the news, but you're not going to be playing croquet on here for a while, or whatever it is middle-class people do on their lawns. You'll be lucky if the grass is even alive when I'm done."

He bent to start the engine again.

"So, no stripes, then?"

"No, Freya. No stripes."

"That's a shame," she said, just as she heard the sound of a car drawing up at the front of the house.

"That must be Gold and Anderson," she said. "I wonder if they found anywhere."

"I can't wait to find out," Ben said under his breath, and he gave the cord a tug, starting the engine for the second time.

The two women emerged through the back door, clearly amazed to find Ben mowing Freya's grass.

"Is that part of his job description?" Anderson asked, raising her voice over the sound of the mower.

"No. No, he just does it out of the kindness of his heart," Freya replied. "I told him he shouldn't bother. It's not like I'm going to keep on top of it. But you'll get to know what he's like. When he gets a bee in his bonnet, nothing will stop the man."

"Tenacious, is he?" she said, admiring Ben from afar. "I like a man who doesn't take no for an answer."

"Well, you might want to find some other tenacious man," Freya said, with a little wink at Gold. "He might be tenacious. But if you're looking for romance, he hasn't a clue. Am I right, Gold?"

"I fancied him for years," Gold said with a laugh. "He's the main reason I joined the force."

"Wasn't he interested?"

"I don't know," Gold replied with a shrug.

The three women all turned to watch Ben putting all his weight behind the mower to carve a path through the centre of the lawn.

"He's not very good with signals," Freya called out to the women, feeling her phone vibrate in her pocket. She retrieved the phone, then called out to Ben. "Ben?"

He didn't hear. He just kept on shoving the mower as hard as he could, and had already broken a sweat.

Anderson made a circle with her middle finger and thumb, then put them in her mouth to whistle.

Ben looked up instantly, peering at them from the far end of the garden with a confused look on his face. Freya held up the phone and dragged her finger across her neck for him to kill the engine.

"Nillson, talk to me," she said, when the engine had spluttered to a stop. She put the call on loudspeaker for everyone to hear.

"I've got some good news and some bad news, boss," Nillson said.

"Give me the bad news."

"Doctor Bell wasn't too happy about having to stay behind for Mrs Carson to ID the body," Nillson said. "And she really wasn't happy about being given a happy meal."

"Sorry, Nillson," Freya said. "I probably shouldn't have done that."

"No, no. It's fine by me. She just started ranting. I have no idea what she was saying. The only words I recognised involved her pen being shoved somewhere quite delicate."

"You can't blame her," Ben said. "She was supposed to go see Spiderman with her mum."

"Spiderman?" Gold said. "What is she? Twelve years old?"

"Tell me the good news, Nillson," Freya said, before they ventured down the same tangent they had earlier.

"Well, we can start our investigation," Nillson said. "Mrs Carson was right. It's her husband. John Carson."

CHAPTER FIFTEEN

"Right," Freya said, pocketing her phone. "Who wants some overtime?"

The three of them all stared at each other, then back at Freya.

"I'll take that as a yes," she said. "Gold. Family Liaison. Get yourself over to Mrs Carson's house. Introduce yourself. Keep me updated on anything you learn, and let me know when you think she's calmed down enough to answer some questions."

"Will do, ma'am," she said. She stood there for a moment, unsure of herself, then glanced at each of them and turned to leave.

"Jackie," Ben said, before she disappeared into the house. She turned and waited to hear what he had to say. "Good luck, kiddo."

The sentiment raised a smile, and she looked away shyly, before leaving and closing the door behind her.

"And then there were three," Freya said.

"What about Gillespie, Cruz, and Nillson?"

"I'm feeling guilty about sending Nillson to see Pip. Let's let her rest for a while. As for the boys, we'll call them if we need them. Jenny, how did the house hunting go?"

"Dire," she replied.

"Nothing at all?"

"Dark, dingy, old houses in the middle of nowhere. Not really my cup of tea, if I'm honest."

"Clock's ticking," Freya said.

"I know. I know. I'll find somewhere."

"Are you going to join us, or will you go and see a few more places?" Ben asked. "Letting agents will be closed tomorrow."

"Closed?"

"It's Sunday tomorrow. This isn't London."

Just as Gold had done, Jenny glanced at them both in turn, then nodded.

"Then I guess I should go."

"We'll keep you informed," Freya said, hoping to reassure her. "Ben? Shall we?"

"What about the lawn?"

"It's been okay for the past nine months," she said. "You can finish it tomorrow if you like?"

Inside the house, Ben was at the window watching Anderson's car as she headed back out into the world of house hunting.

"Do you think two days is a bit short? Especially given that one of those days is a Sunday."

"Have you ever had somebody stay for a night or two, and then that night or two becomes three or four? Or five or six?"

"Right," Ben said, nodding his understanding.

"I don't want to put myself in a position where I have to ask her to leave. But then I don't want to see her out on the street. Worst case scenario, she'll find an Airbnb. It's the expensive option, but I'm sure she'll work it out."

"So, it's just me and you, then? If I didn't know better, I'd say you engineered it that way."

"Just you and me," she replied, extending her arm to invite him to sit. "And I don't engineer. You of all people should know that."

"Of course. I forgot. Everything you need falls at your feet, doesn't it?" Ben said, taking one of the dining room seats.

"John Carson," Freya announced, changing the subject. "Single stab wound to the back with a fillet knife. Married to one Charlotte Carson."

She drew out the facts on a blank piece of paper just as she would have had they been in the office using the whiteboard. John Carson's name was in the centre of the paper, with a line connecting him to his wife. She made two bullet points to one side, where she noted the single stab wound and fillet knife details.

"What else do we have?"

"Theodore Wood," Ben said. Then added, "Blue Land Rover. Missing."

"Missing indeed," Freya said.

"Which reminds me," Ben said, rubbing his stomach. "I'm working up quite an appetite."

"It's not him," she said, and she peered at him across the table. "You do own a suit, don't you?"

"Of course."

"That's good."

"Why would I need a suit?" he asked.

"Well, if you've learned one thing about me over the past nine months, Ben, it should be that I've grown accustomed to the finer things in life. That includes where I like to dine."

"Dine?"

"Dine," she said. "Fine dining. The best there is. Are you still sure it's him?"

"I wasn't sure in the first place. It was you who convinced me to do the stupid bet with you."

"So that's settled then," she said.

"Whoa, hold on. What's settled?"

"My choice of restaurant. I know where we're going."

"*If* you win."

"Which I will."

"Alright then. Prove it if you're so sure of yourself. You're the one that started all this competitive nonsense. I think Theo is involved somehow. You think he's another victim."

"For that, we'll need to find him," she said.

"And how do you propose on doing that?" he asked. "We could get Chapman to talk to her man at the network provider. Have him locate Wood's phone."

"No. No, let's leave Chapman out of this. At least for today. Let's you and I do a little digging to see what we can find."

"Wow, you mean like old-fashioned police work?" he said. "Like Michaela's old-fashioned methods?"

"Yes. Yes, something like that," she replied. "What was John Carson doing at the abbey? Who was he with? And why would somebody want to kill him?"

"Well, judging by the underwear Gillespie found, I'd say it was more a case of *who* was John Carson doing at the abbey?"

"If the underwear is actually linked, which we don't know yet, it clearly wasn't his wife," Freya said. "You heard what Nillson said about her reaction."

"In which case, maybe he was having an affair? Maybe he was having an affair with the owner of the underwear?"

"Which leads us to two people. Mrs Carson, and the husband, or partner, of the owner of the underwear," Freya said. "We need those lab results."

"We won't get them until tomorrow at best. And even that's pushing it."

"Okay. The knife. Have we got photos?"

"Yeah, Gillespie said he emailed them through to the team," Ben said, fishing his phone from his pocket. He scrolled through his emails, then clicked open an image, holding it up for Freya to see. The image showed a pair of delicate hands, presumably Cruz's, holding a clear evidence bag with the knife inside. The handle was of redwood with three brass rivets. The blade was, as Pip had suggested, nine-inches long, and not an inch of those nine were free of blood.

"Okay. So, we pay Theodore Wood a visit again."

"He's missing. That's the point, Freya. We need to find him."

"No. No, we need to eliminate him from the investigation, Ben. We don't need to find him to do that."

"And how do you propose we do that?"

She smiled and snatched her handbag from where it hung on the chair. "Good old-fashioned police work, Ben. Just like I told you. Come on. Chop chop."

CHAPTER SIXTEEN

"Ah, if it isn't Lincolnshire's newest DS," Gillespie said into the phone as he wedged it between his shoulder and chin. With his hands freed, he cracked open a can of Guinness and began the slow, torturous, yet sensual pour of what he like to call black gold. "I thought the boss sent you to see our wee Welsh dragon?"

"Been there. Done that," Nillson said flatly. "What are you doing?"

"Already? I'm just in my garden, about to get stuck into a well-earned pint."

"Well-earned?" Nillson scoffed. "You haven't earned anything yet."

"Ah, come now, Anna. You know my find was better than your find."

"No way. I found the bloody victim's wife. You don't get much better than that. I just saved the team days of work trying to ID him."

"*I* found the murder weapon," Gillespie said. "And *I* found a pair of drawers."

"We don't know if they're linked yet."

"Oh, you know they're linked, alright. And I know they're linked. That's all that matters."

Nillson was silent, and Gillespie took the opportunity to savour the first sip of his drink. He smacked his lips and exhaled with the pleasure.

"Draw?"

"A draw? You mean I get to keep my money?"

"Our money, you mean."

"No. My money. I won it."

"You won it the first time. Then you gambled it, and we drew. That makes half of it mine."

"You're not having half of my money, Anna."

"Well, then I guess the bet is still on," she said.

"I guess it is," Gillespie said. He raised his glass to take another sip, but then stopped himself. "Wait. You said you'd done the ID already?"

"Yep."

"Well? Was it him? The Carson bloke?"

"Well, if I was to tell you that, I'd be giving away my lead, wouldn't I?"

"What lead?"

"Where do you think I am?"

"No way," he said.

"Yep."

"No. You're at the abbey?"

"Whoever makes the biggest contribution to the case wins the money. Deal?"

"You're there?"

"Deal?"

"I'm in my bloody garden in a pair of shorts and flip flops."

"You're not going to win that way," Nillson said. "You'd better get a move on, Jim. Who knows where this trail might take me?"

"Trail? What trail?" he said, leaving his pint on the garden table and running back through the house.

"Sorry, you're breaking up. It's a bad line."

"Don't you do this to me, Anna. It's cheating. That's what this is. Withholding information. That's an offence."

He put the phone on loudspeaker and set it down on the tallboy, then tore open his wardrobe to find something a little more suitable to wear.

"No, it's not. I reported it to my superior," Nillson said. "As per the protocol."

He found himself mimicking her last statement silently at the phone.

"Don't be a child, Jim."

"I'm not the one playing games, Anna."

"You just pulled a face at the phone, didn't you?"

He paused, then leaned over the phone to make sure no cameras had been enabled somehow.

"No," he said.

"You're too easy to read, Jim. Oh, hang on. What's this I've just found?"

"What? What?"

"Oh my God, Jim. You're not going to believe this."

"What? Tell me."

She paused for what felt like an eternity, and he stopped in anticipation, balancing on one leg with one foot in his trousers.

"Anna, bloody talk to me."

"See you soon, Jim," she teased, and ended the call.

He pulled his trousers on, buttoning them as fast as he could, before dialling Cruz who answered after a few rings in his usual, non-urgent, sleepy voice.

"Hey, Jim. You know it's a Saturday, right?"

"Aye. What are you doing?"

"I was about to watch a movie."

"A movie?" Gillespie said. "Lame."

"Lame? This is the latest Spiderman movie."

"The latest one is still out in the cinema. You must have the one that came out last year."

"Nope. I got it from one of the uniforms. He knows this bloke who knows another bloke."

"Oh, you mean it's dodgy? That's piracy, Gabby. Serious offence, that."

"No. No, everyone does it," Cruz said, his voice rising in pitch. "It's not really a serious crime, is it?"

"I wonder what the chief constable would have to say if he found out one of his officers, no, several of his officers, were engaged in illegal activity? I think he'd be severely disappointed. And imagine how that particular uniform would feel when he found out it was you who gave the game away?"

"You wouldn't."

"Top brass might even make an example of you. You could end up behind bars," Gillespie said. "Imagine that? Your wee little girlfriend would have to come and visit you in Lincoln nick. Shocking waste of talent if you ask me. Fit, young lad like you trapped with all those big, angry criminals. Do you know what they do to coppers on the inside, Gab?"

Cruz sighed audibly.

"What do you want?" he said.

"I want you, Gabby. Dressed and outside your house in ten minutes," Gillespie said, as he fastened his shirt and admired himself in the mirror. "Nobody has one over on James T Gillespie."

CHAPTER SEVENTEEN

"Here we go again," Ben muttered as Freya pulled her car up onto the kerb outside the Woods' house. "I hope he's home this time. I'm not sure I have the patience to deal with that bratty little kid again."

"Spoken like a true man, Ben," Freya replied. They climbed from the car and she waited for him to join her on the footpath. "We need something here. Anything. Just be nice to her. Let her insults wash over you, and let me do the talking."

"Sounds like one of those pep talks you give when we we're about to see Doctor Bell," Ben said. "And look how well they always turn out."

He leaned past her to ring the doorbell, then stepped back, leaving Freya at the front of their little party.

"Coward," she muttered as the door opened to reveal a middle-aged woman wearing a long, floral skirt and flowing, white blouse. In place of gold or silver, she wore multiple sets of beads both around her neck and wrist. Loose curls gave her long, blonde hair life and volume, and on first appraisal, Freya deemed her a voluptuous woman.

"Hello," she said. "Can I help you?"

"Mrs Wood?" Freya asked, and she nodded.

"Yes. Yes, that's me."

There was a hint of concern in the way her eyes narrowed at the sight of them, and a stiffness to her posture that belied her casual hippy-like appearance.

"I'm Detective Inspector Bloom. This is Detective Sergeant Savage. We were wondering if we might have a word?"

"Regarding?" she asked. It wasn't a denial. Nor was it aggressive in any way. But it was clear they would have to explain themselves a little better if they were to gain entry.

"We're investigating an incident not too far from here. We hope you can help us with our enquiries."

"The abbey?" she said, nodding. Then, when she saw Freya's expression alter, she added, "I saw the police cars yesterday. I wondered what was going on up there."

"May we?" Freya asked, and Mrs Wood relented, opening the door wide for them to come in.

"Go through to the lounge," she said. "I'll make some tea, shall I?"

She spoke softly, as if she had all the time in the world. Hers was a voice that suited her natural appearance. The living room was long and thin with a central, brick fireplace. A small wood burning stove took pride of place in the room, where the TV, although large, had been placed in the far corner. Not as an afterthought. It was clearly less of a priority to the family than the fireplace.

There were photos, of course. The types Freya had expected to find and had seen in their thousands. The holiday shots, wedding shots, family portraits, and even some of a black Labrador. Freya sniffed. There was no scent of dog, which there normally was when the family had one. And she would have expected to find black hairs on the floor or the sofa. But there were none.

"I'll see if she needs a hand," she told Ben, then slipped from the room and ventured along the hallway to the kitchen. "You have a lovely home, Mrs Wood."

"Thank you," she replied, then the stiffness eased. "It's Charlotte. Charlotte Wood."

"Have you been here long?"

"We moved in when I was pregnant with our daughter, Francesca,"

Charlotte explained, then pointed at the fridge, where several more photographs were held in place with little magnets in the shape of cubes. "That's her, there."

Making a point of studying the photograph, Freya opted not to mention they had been there earlier. Not yet, anyway. She was more interested in what Charlotte was doing, and as such, she sidled over to the kitchen island to watch her make tea.

She prepared three cups while the kettle boiled, and dropped a tea bag in each.

"Do either of you have sugar?"

"No, thank you," Freya told her, watching for the moment she opened the drawer to retrieve a tea spoon.

The kitchen was immaculate. The surfaces were clean and bright, and the floor gleamed. But when Charlotte finally opened the cutlery drawer, Freya was surprised to find an eclectic array of utensils, knives, and forks. She had expected to find them neat and orderly, and, at the very least, matching. But in those few seconds of opportunity, Freya saw nothing with a handle that resembled the knife Gillespie had found.

The tea was made, and Freya helped Charlotte carry the three cups through to the living room.

"Please do sit," Charlotte said, when they found Ben standing by the window. She set the drinks down on a coffee table, then waved her arm at one of the two sofas that faced each other beside the fireplace. "Now then. How can I help?"

Freya sat on the sofa, waited for Ben to join her, then watched as Charlotte lowered herself gracefully into the sofa opposite. She laid her hands on her lap and waited for Freya to begin.

"I'll cut to the chase, Charlotte. Do you know a John Carson?" Freya asked.

"John? Yes, of course I do. Why? What's happened?"

Freya and Ben exchanged glances, and Ben's expression told her he was equally as intrigued by her reaction.

"I'm afraid he's dead, Charlotte. How exactly did you know him?"

"Dead? John? How? When? I mean... Oh, God. Poor Leigh."

"Leigh?"

"Leigh Carson. His wife," Charlotte explained, then her eyes widened. "Oh God. Does she know? Is she okay?"

"She's being taken care of," Ben said. "We have a Family Liaison Officer with her."

"How exactly do you know the Carsons?" Freya asked, and Charlotte took a few deep breaths to compose herself.

"They're, erm, family friends. We're close. I should call her."

"Let's just wait a while," Freya advised. "We have a few questions we need to ask."

But Charlotte had changed tack. She now looked at them accusingly.

"Why are you here? Why have you come to see me?"

"We came earlier," Freya said. "We spoke to your daughter. Francesca. She told us your husband has been away for a few days. Where is he? Do you know?"

She shook her head.

"No. No, I haven't seen him."

"Are you worried about him?"

"Of course, I am. I'm always worried about him. But he does this. He goes away when things get too much. Leaves me to manage everything. The house, the business, Franky. What do you want with him, anyway? He hasn't done anything, surely. He's not capable. He needs looking after."

"You have a business?"

"It's small," she said. "Pays the bills. Just."

"Where does he go, Charlotte?"

"Oh, I don't know. He just takes some time for himself," she said, watching them with bloodshot eyes. "He's unstable."

"Unstable?"

"He's under a lot of pressure. It's how he handles things."

"Do you think he might harm himself?"

"No. No, of course not. Why? What's he got to do with this?"

"I'm sorry to be the one to tell you, Charlotte," Freya said. "But your husband's car was found at the crime scene."

"His car? I don't understand. You're scaring me—"

"Charlotte, we need to talk to your husband," Freya said. "He's a suspect in a murder investigation."

"I... I don't know where he is. I told you. I'm not lying. I haven't seen him."

"Okay, okay," Freya said. Clearly the free-flowing nature of the woman's appearance did not extend to her emotions. "Can you tell us when you last saw John Carson?"

"Last saw him?" she said, as if the question had some hidden meaning. "I don't know. Last weekend, I suppose. Yes. Last weekend. We all went round there for dinner."

"To the Carsons' house?" Freya asked.

"Yes. We took Franky. Francesca. They've got a boy around the same age."

"And you haven't seen or spoken to him since?"

"No. Of course. We don't live in each other's pockets. We're all just good friends," she said. "When you say he's a suspect... Do you mean, he could go to prison?"

"Well, only if he's found guilty," Ben said. "I think it's worth mentioning that, at this stage, all we're trying to do is eliminate close friends and family."

"I've heard that. Seventy percent of domestic murders are done by family."

"That's a strange fact to remember," Freya said.

"It's Franky. She listens to podcasts. True Crime. Want's to be a lawyer, although to get there she'll have to actually go to a class," she mumbled. "Oh, listen. I've got to go and see Leigh. She must be distraught."

"No. Not yet at least," Ben said, and he flashed Freya a message from Gold on his phone. "We'll be heading over there after this."

"One last thing, Charlotte. And I'm sorry to have to ask. But can you tell me where you were yesterday?"

"Where I was?"

"So we can eliminate you from our enquiries. I know it's a horrible question. But I'm afraid we have to ask."

"No. No, it's okay. I was here. I was here in the morning," she said. "Then I was out in the afternoon."

"Out where?" Freya asked.

"I went for a walk along the river. The sun was out, so..."

"Okay. That's fine," Freya said. "And can somebody verify that?"

"Verify it?"

"I'm sorry," Freya said.

"My daughter. Franky. She was here. Do you need to speak to her?"

"No," Freya said, taking a sip of her tea. "No, we'll get to her eventually. What I'd really like to do, Charlotte, is find your husband. If you can't tell us where he might be, perhaps you would be good enough to provide some DNA samples?"

"Samples? I don't understand."

"His toothbrush should suffice," Freya said. "That is, of course, unless he took it with him. Some people have a travel toothbrush."

"No. He left it. It's upstairs," she told Ben. "The one with the red stripe."

"We'll also need samples from yourself and Francesca," Freya added. "If you have no objection, that is?"

Charlotte hesitated for a moment, swallowed, but then nodded. "If you think it will help."

Ben left the room and the stairs creaked beneath his weight. They heard his walking about on the next floor, but while he was out of the way, Charlotte leaned in closer to Freya.

"Can I ask you something?" she said, with a nervous glance at the stairs.

"Of course. How can I help?"

"You don't really think it was my husband, do you?" she asked.

Freya took a deep intake of breath while she considered how she might respond.

"I hope not," she told her. "I really do hope not. For all our sakes."

CHAPTER EIGHTEEN

"I still don't get it," Cruz said, as they drew near to the crime scene. "So what if Anna's over here. Let her get on with it. If she finds something, then great. It saves us having to do it."

"You don't get it, do you?" Gillespie told him. "Where's your pride, Gabby? Eh? Where's your sense of accomplishment?"

"Eh?"

"It's our crime scene. We were told to oversee a detailed search."

"No. You were told to oversee a detailed search. I was just following your instructions."

"And what if Nillson finds something?"

"So what if she does?"

"It's going to make you look like you can't even crawl around on your hands and knees properly, isn't it?"

"Eh?"

"Well, I wouldn't take the blame, would I? No. The boss'll shout at me, and I'll just pass it onto you."

"Oy, that's not fair."

"It rolls downhill, Cruz. Remember that. It always rolls downhill."

"So, what are we going to do now that we couldn't have done earlier? We bloody scoured the entire field."

"We'll scour it again if we have to."

"What? Just us? We had a dozen uniforms before."

"Christ on a bike, Gabby. Will you just try and be positive for one minute in your sorry life? We've got an opportunity to really make a difference here. We could find something that helps us find the killer faster. And you know what that means?"

"We get to go home quicker?"

"The family get closure faster, Gabby. Plus, I'll be in the boss's good books, of course."

"We, you mean?"

"Aye, well. You know what I mean," Gillespie said, as he pulled off the road into the little layby near the abbey. He parked behind Nillson's car, nudging his old car as close as he could so she couldn't get out before him.

"What are you doing? Why are you parking so close?"

"Oh, for God's sake, Gabby. It's question after question. Relentless bloody questions. For once in your life, can't you just trust me?"

"Trust you?" Cruz said. "How the bloody hell can I trust you? All you do is laugh at me, ridicule me in front of the others, and make me look like an idiot."

"You do that yourself," Gillespie muttered. "I just feed the machine."

"See? That's exactly what I mean. You never take me seriously. Even when I found that rock."

"It was years old."

"It had blood on it."

"Don't be daft, Gabby. That was just iron or something."

"It was blood. I'm telling you it was blood."

"It was iron. That's where it bloody comes from. Rocks. They mine it."

"Here?" Cruz said, and gazed out of the window for effect. "Oh, that's funny. I can't see any iron mines here. You know why, don't you, Jim? Because there have never been any bloody iron mines here. Never will be. So, how the hell is there iron in a rock here?"

"There was iron all over the UK," Gillespie said. "You'd be surprised where they dug it up from."

"Yeah, and I'd go along with that if we found loads of the stuff, or if we found an old mine or something. But we haven't. It was a rock from the abbey ruins, and it had blood on it. None of the other rocks in the abbey have iron in them. Explain that."

"Well..." Gillespie began, seeing a valid point. "It's an anomaly."

"A what?"

"An anomaly, Gabby. You know? A freak of nature, or something."

"You're just saying that because it wasn't you who found it," Cruz said, as he climbed from the car.

Gillespie followed suit and locked the car. He was just about to head up the track toward the old abbey ruins when a voice called out from ahead.

"You two took your time."

"Anna?" Gillespie said, noting the wee rucksack she was carrying. "What's in the wee bag, there?"

"Ah, nothing," she said. "Just something I found. Thought it might be of interest."

"Aye, right. What was it?"

She winked as she sauntered between them both.

"Have a nice afternoon, boys," she said.

"Yeah, you too, Anna," Cruz called out. Then, when Gillespie stared at him in disbelief, he shrugged. "What?"

Gillespie just shook his head at the young DC.

"What?" Cruz said.

"That, Gabby, was the bloody enemy. You don't wish the bloody enemy a good afternoon, do you?"

"It's Nillson," he replied.

"Aye. The enemy," Gillespie hissed. "How in all that's holy in this world did I end up being chained to a moron like you?"

"I don't get it," Cruz said.

There was at least one saving grace. One final surprise in store for Nillson, which she would be finding right about now.

"Gillespie?" she called out. Her voice seemed to wash across the landscape like a gunshot, then echo to nothing.

He smiled to himself.

"You've gone and bloody made her mad, Jim," Cruz said, taking a step back to put Gillespie between him and Nillson. "She's a bloody lunatic. You're on your own with this one, pal."

"Gillespie," she called again, this time stepping into view in the open gate. She pointed at the cars. "Why have you done that?"

"Done what?" he said innocently.

"Move the car, Jim."

"Sorry, did you hear something, Gabby?" Gillespie said.

"Jim. I mean it. Move your car."

From thirty metres away, he was safe. Besides, he could outrun Cruz, and when it came to dealing with predators, as long as you can outrun your friend, you'll always survive.

"What was it you said, Anna?" he asked, offering his broadest smug grin. "Have a nice afternoon, or something?"

"Jim?" she growled.

He turned on his heels and began to walk towards the abbey.

"Jim? This isn't funny."

"Aye. You're right there," he called back. "But then again, nor is taking our finds for your own benefit. That's just not sporting."

"Your finds?"

"Aye. Our finds. Cruz and me. This is our site. You had your own tasks to do."

"Well maybe you should think about doing them properly in future? Then I wouldn't have to come along and pick up all the pieces you left behind."

"Pieces?" he said. "As in plural?"

"Yes. Plural. As in, more than one of," Nillson said. "Now move your bloody car."

"Not until you tell me what you found."

"For God's sake, Jim. What are you? Five?"

"Tell me what you found, and I'll move the car. It's not too difficult a concept to grasp, is it?" He turned to Cruz for some support, who held his hands up defensively.

"Don't get me involved."

"Right. Simple. You leave me no choice," she said, and disappeared from sight, heading back to the cars.

"Anna?" Gillespie called out. "What are you doing?"

But there was no reply. Not for a few seconds at least. And then he heard it. The sound of glass shattering, followed by the sound of his handbrake being released. A few moments later, the handbrake was wrenched back into place. He turned in disbelief to stare at Cruz.

"Has she...?" he said.

"I think so," he replied.

"No way."

"I warned you. She's a nutter, Jim."

A few moments later, Nillson's car fired up and reversed into view. She lowered the window and leaned out.

"You smashed my window?" he called out.

"You blocked me in," she replied. "I've got key evidence here. You were obstructing the line of duty."

"Obstructing my backside," he roared. "You owe me a new window."

"Like I was saying," she said, smiling at them both as she put the car into first gear. She winked again. It was a winning wink to accompany her smug grin. "Have a nice day, boys."

CHAPTER NINETEEN

The Carson house was a pretty, little farm house just a few hundred metres from where they had parked to walk to the abbey that morning. The old building, along with its converted stables and barns, were enclosed by a palisade fence and connected by wonderfully kept lawns and gravel pathways. The bare brick walls were alive with climbing roses and spouted colourful hanging baskets.

"They've got a few quid," Ben said, as Freya nosed the Range Rover into the property and came to a stop near Gold's little hatchback.

"You don't know that," Freya said, playing devil's advocate. "They might have had a few quid at one point, but a place like this can soon see to that. Imagine the heating bills, council tax, repairs. Not to mention just keeping the place looking like this. It must be a full-time job."

"But they could have money," Ben said. "Or they could be in debt up to their eyeballs."

"Something for Chapman to look into should we need a lead," Freya agreed. "Come on. Let's go and get the lie of the land."

"What do we think?" Ben said across the bonnet of the big SUV. "Two minute walk to the abbey from here?"

"No reason to drive, that's for sure," Freya agreed. "It's not like it was raining yesterday."

"Which raises one pertinent question. Who was he with and how did they get there? This is the only house around here. Unless she came from Bardney, which is possible."

"That's something I've been considering," Freya said. "Not the distance thing. People will do almost anything. But who did he meet?"

"I guess we'll find out when the lab results come back," Ben said. "The underwear Gillespie found might be the key to all of this."

"Let's keep an open mind, shall we?" Freya replied, and they moved towards the house.

The door opened before they had knocked, and they were greeted by Jackie Gold's smiling face.

"How's it going, Jackie?" Ben asked.

"Ah, you know? As well as can be, really," she said, looking back into the house and up the stairs. "Leigh is just having a shower. She's had a rough day, bless her."

"Has she said much?" asked Freya.

"Yes, and no, really. I think she's still in shock. She doesn't understand why it happened. I think she's more worried about the future than who could have done it. John was the bread winner. As far as I can gather, he handled all the finances. Poor woman hasn't a clue what to do," Gold said, then jabbed a thumb over her shoulder. "Did you want to come inside? I'm sure she won't mind."

With a wave of his hand, Ben invited Freya to enter first, then closed the door behind them. The house was old, but had been decorated to a high standard. Expensive frames surrounded abstract water colours, depicting scenes from the local countryside. And as they moved from the wide hallway through to the open-plan living space, the elegant yet minimal design continued. The soft furnishings were of a pastel, spearmint green. The walls were whiter than white, and the exposed wooden floors gave depth and contrast to what was a calm and peaceful interior.

"Nice, eh?" Gold said, and she gestured for them to take one of the three two-seater couches that formed a neat U-shape around an inglenook fireplace with a solid, oak mantle.

Above the mantle, again, framed in oak with gold beading, was a family portrait. Despite the image clearly being a professionally-taken photograph, it lacked the usual stiffness of people being asked to smile or convinced to relax. It was almost as if the photo they had elected to take pride of place on the wall was a candid image taken between poses. Each of them were laughing. The son gazed up at his father with adoration, while the man and wife exchanged loving and knowing glances.

The family wore what Freya would have called smart-casual clothing, but which Ben would have just called smart.

They were lying on their fronts on a faux-sheepskin rug before a plain, white background. John Carson was wearing a plain, white shirt that was open at the neck and a pair of smart, blue jeans. Leigh, a stunning looking woman with a mass of blonde hair, wore a white summer dress with lacy frills at the sleeve and the collar. The boy in the middle, who Freya presumed to be their teenage son, wore similar clothes to his father. Each of them were barefoot, adding to the natural feel the photographer was clearly shooting for.

Ordinarily, a framed photograph on a wall would not have captured Freya's attention with such ease. But the natural lighting, textures and tones, and the sense of family the image portrayed reminded her of a time long past. In fact, in her mind she could replace each of the faces in the photograph with that of her ex-husband, his son, and herself. The image spoke volumes.

"Beautiful, isn't it?" Gold said quietly, and Freya nodded without looking at her.

"This is a family who had everything," she said. "Somebody has torn them apart."

"How intuitive of you," a voice said, unfamiliar to Freya's ears.

Leigh Carson was standing in the wide doorway wearing a pair of light blue jeans and an over-sized knitted sweater despite the warm weather, which Freya deemed to be for comfort. Something to wrap herself in. To warm her where her husband's arms could no longer do so.

"I'm Detective Inspector Freya Bloom," Freya said, then gestured at Ben. "This is Detective Sergeant Savage. DC Gold suggested you may be able to answer a few questions to help with our enquiries."

She nodded, although her lower lip seemed to reach and swallow its counterpart. She was a sorry-looking thing, appearing lost and forlorn.

"Why don't we sit?" Freya suggested, taking the couch that Gold had offered a few moments before. She waited for Leigh to be seated, then glanced across at Gold. "Shall we have some tea?"

"I'll see to it," Gold said, and she disappeared through an archway at the end of the long room.

"I know this is a difficult time, Leigh. Do you mind if I call you Leigh?" Freya said, looking to establish where the boundaries were. The woman was in need of help, but putting her on her back foot at the beginning of the conversation could be detrimental to gaining any kind of useful information.

"Of course," she replied, her voice a sullen murmur. "It's fine."

"I was wondering if you tell me what type of man John was? How would you describe him?"

She shrugged and rocked her head from side to side while considering her response.

"Loving," she began, then bit down on her lip. "Warm, generous, and thoughtful. Everything a woman could want in a man. I'm sure that's some kind of cliché, isn't it? The perfect man."

"If only," Freya said. "What did he do for work?"

"Property. He inherited his parents' house when they died. Decided to do it up, you know? Then rented it out. That was fifteen years ago now. He used the money he made to buy another, then another. And so on," she finished.

"He must have quite the portfolio?"

"He does. Did. I do now, I suppose. Although, I haven't a bloody clue what I'm supposed to do with it."

"There are services that can help you. DC Gold will put you in touch with them. That's part of her role. But right now, I need to have a very difficult conversation with you."

Leigh glanced up at her, tearing her eyes from the empty coffee table for the first time. Her mouth hung open in anticipation, and the dark rings of grief had already begun to encircle her eyes.

"Do you know any reason why anyone would have wanted to do this, Leigh?" Freya asked, and Leigh shook her head in reply. "Tenants? Business dealings? Family or friends?"

"No. No, everybody loved him."

"Did he often go for a walk to the abbey?"

"I suppose. Not as often as we used to. But if we go for a walk, it's usually over there. It's nice. Quiet, you know?"

"What changed? You said you used to walk more often."

"We used to have a dog. Dogs need walking."

"I'm sorry," Freya said. "Did it die?"

"No. No, he went missing," she replied, and the new topic seemed easier despite the subject. "There was a spate of thefts a year or two ago. In Bardney, Bucknell, and Branston. Some men in a van, apparently. We tried to get him back. Put his photographs on social media. But nothing ever came of it."

"That's terrible," Ben said. "Did you report it?"

Leigh responded with a weak, tight-lipped smile that suggested her faith in the police had been marred as a result.

"We didn't get him back," she said. "So, we stopped going over there. There didn't seem to be much point, after that. Too hard, I suppose."

"We understand you're friends with Theo and Charlotte Wood? Close friends," Freya said, and again Leigh nodded but was clearly a little surprised to hear their names mentioned.

"How do you know that?"

She stared at Freya, searching for some kind of detail that might help her understand.

"Theo's car was found near to where John was found."

"So?"

"So, we traced the car's owner, and we've been to see them. We needed to know why it was left there."

"And?" Leigh asked. "Why was it?"

"We still don't know. Theo has been missing for a couple of days."

"Missing?"

"According to Charlotte, this isn't the first time."

"No. No, it isn't," Leigh said, as if she was piecing the information together as she spoke. "He suffers with his mental health. He's done it before. Just a few days. Enough for him to get some perspective, I guess. And enough for Charlotte to go out of her mind with worry."

"Charlotte mentioned they were up here last weekend. Was that the last time you saw them?"

"Yes," she said. "Yes, they came for dinner. John did a barbecue. He always loved a barbecue."

"Of course," Freya said. "It's a nice way to welcome the good weather."

"We have a pool out the back. Only a little one. Franky, that's their daughter, she gets on with Scott. They were splashing about while we talked."

"Scott? Your son?" Freya asked.

"Yes, sorry. They're roughly the same age. The water was still too cold for me, but the kids were in and out. To be honest, Scott has had a crush on Franky for years. He'd sit in ice water if she were there," she said. Then her expression dropped. It was like a few of the pieces she had been putting together in her mind had clicked into place.

"Is there something wrong?" Freya asked.

She seemed doubtful at first. As if what she wanted to say probably wasn't relevant. But the way her brow furrowed was a clear sign that whatever it was had caught her attention.

"Leigh?" Freya said, as Gold entered the room with a tray of cups.

Holding her hand up to Gold, preventing her from interrupting the moment, Freya leaned forward, and lowered her head to meet Leigh's vacant stare.

"If there's something I need to know, Leigh…" she said softly.

"They left early. Earlier than usual anyway," Leigh explained. "Hurried, you know? I'd been in the house with Charlotte. Just tidying away the dinner things. But when we came out, Franky was dried and dressed, and Theo was waiting for Charlotte. John was nowhere to be seen. Don't get me wrong, it wasn't a big deal or anything. I just thought it was odd. We normally finish at least two bottles of wine when they come over."

"Do you think something happened while you were in the house?" Ben asked.

"Yes," she replied. "Maybe. I'd completely forgotten about it until now. But now I think about it, I think they may have been arguing about something, or at least disagreed on something. John is very bullheaded. It wouldn't be the first time John and Theo have crossed swords."

"Leigh, I'm not sure how much you know about the procedures we have to undertake…"

"Not much," she admitted, bracing herself for a difficult conversation.

"When something like this happens, there are ways of doing things. Effective methods. For example, we couldn't even begin our investigation until you had provided a positive ID. That's just the procedure."

"Right," she said slowly.

"Once we have a positive ID, we then need to eliminate friends and family from our investigation."

"Okay. I don't see where this is going."

"It allows us to channel our focus into lines of enquiry," Gold added, her tone somehow softer, and the effect somehow more powerful.

"You want to know where I was, don't you?" Leigh said. "You want to know where I was yesterday. I'll tell you where I was. I was here. I was here all bloody day, just like I've been for twenty sodding years. That's where I was. And can anyone corroborate that? No. No, they can't, because I don't see anybody. I can tell you what happened in Steph's Lunchbox. I can tell you where yesterday's Escape to the Country was based. I can even tell you who won yesterday's Pointless. But can anybody vouch for me? No, they can't."

"That's fine. I'm sure we can work with that," Freya said, sensing a breakdown coming.

"Is that enough to eliminate me from your investigation?" Leigh asked, and all the sullen murmurings of grief had given way to the cauldron of anger, confusion, and fear. "Is it?"

Freya stared at her, forcing herself to remain impassive. To wipe the emotions from her reaction and remain flat and stable.

"Honestly? No. No, it's not enough. But like I said, we can work with it. Long enough for you to come to terms with your loss anyway."

"Thank you," Leigh replied. What Freya had said had clearly cooled the boiling pot of emotions, and that quiet, lost, little girl Freya had first seen standing in the doorway returned. "I'd appreciate that."

"DC Gold will stay here as long as you need her to," Freya explained. "If you have any problems, or if you think of something that might help, you call me. Okay?"

She nodded, and stared at the floor with more than a little embarrassment caused by her earlier tone.

CHAPTER TWENTY

BLUE AND WHITE POLICE CORDON TAPE FLUTTERED IN THE BREEZE, and the sun which had beat down on the rank of uniforms during the search now cast two lonely shadows that stretched across the flattened grass. To Gillespie, the shadows resembled a father and son, a thought that both horrified him and warmed his sense of pride in that he had been deemed qualified to mentor the wee lad.

"So, what are we doing, then?" Cruz asked. "Do you want to scour the grass again?"

"Not really. You?"

"No. I didn't even want to do it the first time," Cruz replied.

"We've missed something. We've missed something that Nillson found. What was it?"

"Could be anything," Cruz said, scanning the scene as if it might offer a clue, which, of course, it didn't.

Gillespie stared at him.

"What?" Cruz said defensively. He began touching his nose and his lips. "Have I got something on my face?"

"No, Gabby. No, you haven't."

"What are you looking at me like that for then?"

"Tell you what. Why don't you go and bag your wee rock? Tag it, and then come find me, eh?"

"What are you going to do?" Cruz asked, peering all the way down the field to where he estimated the rock was.

"Police work," Gillespie said, studying the old stones that John Carson had been laid across. "Good old-fashioned police work."

Cruz wandered down the field like he was barefoot walking the Mediterranean surf, feeling the sand between his toes.

"What an idiot," Gillespie said to himself. "What an absolute, twenty-four-carat idiot."

Ignoring Cruz, Gillespie strode over to where the blanket had been found with the two wine glasses and the hamper. The evidence would all be back at the station by now, but the area was marked by the flattened grass. He stood in the exact spot and gauged the distance to the stones where John Carson's body had been found.

"Fifteen feet?" he said aloud, studying the pile of stones and bricks. He estimated the mound to be around two-feet high, and each of the stones to be between five to ten kilos, give or take. Looking at the ruins, it wasn't clear exactly which part of the building the stones had come from. There was so little left of the building that, for all he knew, there could have been a chimney right where he was standing, and all the bricks and stone could have been lying right where they had landed. Or maybe they'd just been piled up since whenever it was somebody pulled the building down.

He crouched beside the pile. In the crevices where the sunlight rarely shone, a thin layer of moss indicated the pile had been there a while. A few rocks had been dislodged during the act of dragging John Carson onto the mound, but it was clearly an old pile of stones.

The question was, why did the killer drag him up there? Was the pile significant?

"Hey, Jim," Cruz shouted from way on down the field. He was standing waist deep in grass waving something in the air. "I found it."

Gillespie gave him a weak thumbs up.

"Good for you, Gabby," he muttered to himself. "You just discovered iron. We've only known about it for three thousand years, you moron." Then he called out, "Nice one, Gab," not wanting to put the lad down any more than was absolutely necessary.

Staring down at Cruz, Gillespie gauged the distance to be two hundred metres to where he found the rock. The underwear and weapon were found not far from there. Maybe it was significant? He looked further, thinking that the killer might have left the crime scene in that direction. But if that was the case, where were they heading?

"I got it," Gab said, when he got back to the ruins, slightly out of breath from the acute uphill. "Anna must have found something else."

"Aye," Gillespie said, still lost in thought. He pointed to the end of the field, where a line of tall trees formed the border between the heritage site and the farmland beyond. "What's down there?"

"Down where?"

"Down there, beyond those trees?"

"Fields, I suppose."

"You suppose?"

"Well, yeah. I haven't actually been further than the trees. There's a fence and trees in the way."

"Right. Well, then how about you go and take a wee looky loo, eh?"

"A what? A looky loo? What the bloody hell is a looky loo?"

"Aye, Gabby. A looky loo. Take a wee peep into the next field. Tell me what you see."

"I've just been halfway down there."

"Well, now you get to see the whole field, don't you?"

"This is a joke, right? You're just sending me on wild errands to keep me busy. DI Standing used to do this. That's why I spent half my first year in plain clothes standing in a queue to get coffee."

"Think about it. The killer drags the body from the blanket over there to the rocks over here."

"Right, so?"

"So, then they ran. They dumped the underwear and the weapon over there. Down the hill."

"And you think they carried on running?"

"Aye, I do. I think they panicked and ditched them."

"So how did my rock get there?"

"Ah, for crying out loud, Gabby. Your rock was buried under about a metre of grass. The killer didn't just toss it over there. It's been there the whole time. I'm sorry, mate."

Cruz stared down at the evidence bag, then back up at Gillespie, his face a picture of disappointment.

"So, what are you going to do while I'm down there?" Cruz said. "Don't tell me. Police work?"

"Alright, alright. You can help me," Gillespie said, and Cruz's face lit up. There were times when Gillespie genuinely thought the bloke was a twelve-year-old wearing his dad's clothes.

"Do what?" he said.

Gillespie looked at the spot where the glasses had been, and then at the rocks. He strode over to the patch of flattened grass where the glasses had been found.

"Right, come here," he said.

"Eh?"

Gillespie motioned with his index finger.

"Come here, Gab."

Cruz took the few steps with obvious trepidation.

"What?" he said, slowly, clearly expecting a trap.

"Lie down," Gillespie said.

"What? Lie down?"

"Yeah. Lie on the ground. Just there."

"Oh, for Christ's sake, Jim. This is a joke to you, isn't it?" Cruz said, his voice rising to what Gillespie had named fever pitch. "First of all, you want me to run down there. Then you want me to lie on the ground. This isn't police work, this is–"

"Gabby?" Gillespie said, raising his voice to quieten the outburst.

Cruz stilled.

"Lie on the ground and you'll see what I have in mind."

A few huffs and puffs followed, but eventually Cruz lay on the ground, his fingers interlocked on his stomach.

"Right, then. Hold tight," Gillespie said, and he reached down, grabbed Cruz under his arms, and began dragging him across the grass.

"Stop. Wait. Jim, what the bloody hell are you doing?" Cruz called out, and he rolled out of Jim's grip, dusting himself down. "Have you gone bloody mental?"

"Think about it, Gab. The killer dragged the body from there to here. I want to know how easy it is."

"Well, it's hardly a scientific experiment, is it? You're about twenty-five stone, and I'm less than half that. John Carson was a big man. A fit man. All that muscle. He must have been a heavy bloke. All you dragging me across the grass proves is that you're a Neanderthal. If you want to do it properly, the heaviest bloke needs to be lying down."

"Aye, right," Gillespie said, and he strode over to where Gab had originally been lying down, and dropped to the ground. "Come and get me then, wee man."

"You can't expect me to drag you?"

"Aye. That's exactly what I expect."

"But you're heavy."

"Aye, and so was John Carson. Come on, big boy. Give me all you've got."

Less than a minute later, Cruz was huffing and puffing. He had his hands under Gillespie's armpits, and was straining so hard he'd turned a deep purple colour.

He fell back onto the grass.

"I can't do it. You're too—"

"Careful what you say next, Gabby," Gillespie warned.

"Heavy. You're too heavy."

"Right. That's my point," Gillespie said.

"Eh?"

"Take your jacket off."

"No way."

"Take your jacket off, Gabby. I'm not going to do anything."

Slowly, Cruz slipped his jacket off and begrudgingly held it out for Gillespie, who then laid it on the grass in the same spot as before, then lay down on top of it.

"Now, grab the jacket and see if you can drag me."

"Eh?"

"Grab the jacket. It's not rocket science."

Muttering under his breath, Cruz stood, reached down, and grabbed hold of his jacket by the collar.

"Now then," Gillespie said. "Pull me across the grass."

"You're mental."

"Just pull. We haven't got all bloody day."

Cruz pulled, and to Gillespie's surprise, he felt the top half of his body rising up. Then he felt his backside slide across the grass a few inches. Not much, but it was further than before.

"That's it, Gabby. Keep it going."

"You're killing me."

"You're doing it. You're really doing it."

"I am. I'm pulling you," Cruz said.

It took more than a dozen short breaks, but eventually, Gillespie felt the hard stab of stone in his back.

"I did it," Cruz said, breathless. He leaned forward onto his knees and spat, as if he'd just broken the world record for dragging a man across grass. "I bloody did it."

"Well done, mate. Now see if you can get me on the rocks."

"Eh?"

"The rocks, Gabby. Come on, while the blood's pumping."

"Oh, for God's sake," Cruz said. Then he bent down, grabbed hold of Gillespie's arms, and heaved his top half onto the pile of stones.

"Easy, mate. It's not exactly a Silent Night mattress, you know?"

But clearly Gillespie had managed to get to him. Cruz was now in the zone, manoeuvring himself around Gillespie, heaving him this way and that. He swung one leg over him, and bent to grab hold of Gillespie's belt.

"Ah, get your backside out of my face," Gillespie said. "Ah, Christ."

But there was no stopping him now. With one final heave, the little DC had all of Gillespie's six-foot-one-inch of mass on the pile of old stones.

"There," he said, staggering backwards. "I told you."

"Aye, you told me, alright. David just conquered Goliath."

"Mohammed just moved the mountain, more like," Cruz said, and they exchanged a laugh.

"We've done it. You know what this means, don't you?"

"It means that whoever moved the body didn't have to be very strong," Cruz said. "And what with adrenalin pumping through their veins, anyone could have done it. Within reason."

"No, Gabby. You're wrong, mate."

"Eh?"

"I mean, aye. You're right to a point. But you're missing *the* point."

"What point?"

"We know the killer moved the body on the blanket, right? Because the blanket was over here not over there where the glasses were found."

"Right?"

"And we know that a bigger, more masculine man could have moved the body without the blanket."

"How?"

"Because I dragged you with one bloody hand, Gabby. That's how."

"Okay, I see your point," Cruz said. "So, if we know the killer used the blanket, then we can assume the killer wasn't a big, strong man."

"Aye. There you are," Gillespie said. "And that, my friend, is a key piece of information. But better than that. It's got to be better than whatever it was Nillson found."

He took a few steps away from the rocks, leaving the jacket on the pile, and stared down the hill at the tree line.

"We're going to crack this one, Gabby. You and me, son. You wait and see."

"Hold on," Cruz said, his voice sounding excited. Gillespie rolled his eyes and slowly turned to look at him. Cruz bent down, staring at the grass by his feet. "I've found something."

"What is it?"

"Keys, Jim. I've found some bloody keys."

"Keys?"

"Yeah. What if they belong to the killer? They could have fingerprints on. Give me a bag."

Gillespie stepped over to him and stared down at what he was getting excited about. Then he shook his head in utter dismay.

"They're my keys, Gabby."

"Eh?"

"Give them here."

Cruz was defeated again. He picked the keys up and dropped them into Gillespie's hand.

"Killer's keys, my backside," Gillespie said, and Cruz hung his head. "But good try, mate. Seriously. Nicely spotted. If you hadn't found them, we'd be stuck out here."

"Stuck out here? With you?"

"Aye. Imagine it? They'd find us in the morning huddled together for warmth."

"Oh, shut up," Cruz said, but Gillespie saw the smile beginning to take form. "Go on then."

"Go on then, what?"

Gillespie pointed to the tree line.

"The next field, remember?"

"Eh?" Cruz said. "But I thought—"

"You wanted to do some real police work, and I obliged. Now it's time to satisfy my whims."

"I'm not ready to satisfy anything, if I'm honest, Jim."

"Gab?"

"Yeah?"

"Tree line. The quicker you go, the quicker we can go home."

"So, you want me to walk all the way down there? To take a bloody looky loo into the next field, to see where the killer might have run to?"

"Aye," Gillespie said. "That's about the size of it. Except, of course, for one minor detail."

"Which is?"

"I don't want you to walk down there. I want you to run, laddie."

Clearly past the point of arguing, Cruz snatched his jacket from the rock pile.

"Ah, bloody hell," he said. "Look at the state of this."

"Aye. That's the price you pay for doing real police work, son. That's the price you pay."

"It's bloody ruined. Look," he said, and held the jacket up to show Gillespie the green stains that ran the length of the jacket, as well as the grubby grease mark from where he'd trapped it in the door. "My favourite bloody jacket."

"Are you still here?" Gillespie asked, and Cruz walked off in a huff.

"I'm not running," he called back.

"Fine by me. It'll all go in my performance report," Gillespie replied, and Cruz began a weak jog.

"Killer's keys," Gillespie said. He tossed his keys in the air, caught them, and slipped them into his trouser pocket.

Suddenly, he felt them slide from his pocket, down the inside of trousers, and then pop out onto the grass at his feet.

"Ah, damn it," he said to himself, feeling for the hole in his pocket.

A terrible thought struck him. In a panic, he slapped his hands against every pocket he had. His left trouser pocket, both rear pockets, then his breast pocket.

And that was when he realised something about DS Nillson. Something that he just knew would keep him awake for days and nights ahead, as he planned his revenge.

CHAPTER TWENTY-ONE

It was late afternoon by the time Freya and Ben got back to her cottage. Anderson's Ford SUV wasn't there, so Freya parked and killed the engine.

"So, what do we think?" she said.

"I think we need to wait until we get the fingerprint results from the car and the knife, and the DNA results from the underwear and the blanket. That's what I think."

"Not about the investigation. About Anderson," Freya replied. "Do we think she's found somewhere?"

"I hope so," he said. "Her current landlord is a right old witch."

"Hey, no need for that."

"She's been in the county for, what? Two days? She's jumped straight into an investigation, when by rights she doesn't have to start until Monday morning, and you're coaxing her out the door with the head of your broom. It's a bit harsh, Freya."

He softened the blow of his choice of words with that impartial smile of his. There was no judgement from him. There never was. And she was glad he felt comfortable enough to voice an opinion, or to provide an alternative perspective.

"Do you honestly think I'd kick her out if she hadn't found anywhere?"

"I don't know, Freya," he said. "But I'd like to see how good she is before she ups and leaves. At least that way we'll know if we lost somebody good or not."

"She's good. I told you she's good."

"Well, then I think we should cut her some slack," Ben replied. "Play nicely, Freya."

"This *is* me playing nicely," she said, peering through the windscreen at the cottage. "What a weekend, eh? Part of me hopes we don't get the lab results until Monday. At least then they all get a day off, instead of just Gillespie and Cruz."

"And Chapman," Ben added.

"True, yes," she said. "But Gold seemed happy enough. I think she'll do well as our FLO. Much better than bringing in a uniform, or somebody from another team."

"What are you doing for dinner?" Ben asked, which was his usual precursor for inviting himself over to eat.

"I haven't given it much thought. I quite fancy a quiet night in."

"Fair enough."

"You?"

"Ah, you know me. I'll knock something up."

"Beans on toast then?"

"Probably. But you know it'll be the best beans on toast going."

"Do you microwave the beans?"

"Of course. It saves dirtying a pot."

"And do you use the grill or a toaster for the toast?"

"A toaster. It's quicker."

"Well then, I'm afraid I cannot agree that will be the best beans on toast going," she said.

"It's beans on toast, Freya. It was a joke. There is no best beans on toast. It's just a cheat meal for when you're feeling lazy."

"Au contraire, Ben. If you're going to do something, do it properly."

"You think you can do better?"

"I know I can do better," she said, opening her car door. "Come on. I'll show you."

They met at the front of the car and ambled up the garden path, where Freya hoped he would notice how overgrown the front garden was getting.

"Is this some kind of precursor to the restaurant you've chosen, just in case you win our friendly little bet?"

"No, Ben. If that's what you're thinking, then I'm afraid you're really in for a shock."

She let them into the house and was immediately struck by the smell of lemons. Peering into the kitchen, she found the surfaces gleaming and every single item had been put away.

Following the smell of furniture polish, she walked the few steps to the living room door and peered inside. It was immaculate. The wooden floor had never looked so clean. The rug looked brand new, and even the blanket that had proved to be vital for Freya's first Lincolnshire winter had been folded and laid across the armchair neatly.

On the dining table, Freya's files had been straightened, but not organised, and as a centre-piece was a vase of gorgeous lilies.

"Is this the right house?" Ben said.

"I'm not sure," Freya replied. Then she noticed an envelope on the table leaning against the vase. She opened it, tossing the envelope onto the table. The front of the card showed a wide landscape with wild heather in the foreground and endless patchwork fields in the distance. She opened the card with trepidation.

Dear Freya,

I'd like to thank you for this opportunity, and for being kind enough to let me stay. You'll be pleased to know that I have found somewhere. So, I guess from this point on, our relationship will be more professional than personal. It's probably best for us both, and the team, as I know you'd hate to show favouritism, or for our history to get in the way.

I'm not sure what I'd have done had you not given me this chance. The world is much brighter for me now. Behind me is a darkness that I know will fade over time.

Forever in your debt,
Jenny.

P.S. I gave the place a quick once over as I imagine you've had a busy day. See you Monday, boss.

J.

Ben read the card over her shoulder and gave her arm a gentle, consoling squeeze.

"That's got to sting a little," he said. "I'm sure it reads harsher than she actually meant. You know how things in writing can be perceived differently."

"No," she said, closing the card and placing it on the table. "No, it's fine. I'm glad. It was a lovely thought."

She inhaled, long and deep, expecting him to say something to try and cheer her up. But he didn't. He said nothing, which, in her experience, meant he could see through the mask she was hiding behind.

"How about that dinner, then?" she said.

"You're going to cook in that kitchen?" Ben asked, sounding surprised. "I wouldn't even go in there in case I spoiled it."

"Well, then why don't you go out to the garden?" she replied. "Dinner will be ready by the time you've finished cutting the grass."

CHAPTER TWENTY-TWO

Satiated and stuffed, Ben dropped his knife and fork onto the plate and sat back in the chair, his hand massaging the swelling of his stomach.

"So?" Freya said, a good two hours after they had reached Freya's house. She set her knife and fork down on her plate, side by side, then wiped the corners of her mouth with a napkin. "What's the verdict?"

"I told you. There's not much we can do until we get the lab results back," Ben said, but as hard as he tried, he couldn't restrain the smile that threatened to give his game away.

Freya just stared at him, pulling her best unimpressed expression.

"Alright, alright," he said. "It was good. I don't know what you did to the beans, but it was good."

"And?" she said.

"Okay. The cheese was a nice touch, too."

"The best?" she teased.

"The best beans on toast I've ever had?" he said. "I don't know, Freya. I mean, that's a pretty bold statement."

She sipped at her water, then set it down, all the while maintaining a neutral yet knowing expression.

"Okay, okay. It was the best beans on toast I've had this year. How's that?"

"It'll have to do," she replied, then her demeanour softened. "Thanks again for doing the lawn. That would have taken me days."

"Listen, I don't like to eat and run, but..."

"No. It's fine. It's been a long day. Plus, I could do with a night to myself. You know what it's like when you've had somebody staying."

"No," he replied. "Not really. But I get it. You'll probably want to slip into something comfortable and unattractive, and put your feet up while you can."

"Something like that," she said.

An uncomfortable silence followed, which was broken by Freya abruptly standing, and her chair scraping across the floor. She gathered the plates in a hurry and carried them through to the kitchen.

By the time Ben had followed her, carrying the glasses, she was already running the water to wash up.

"Everything alright?" he asked.

"Of course," she replied, without looking up.

"I can stay if you want. I mean, I–"

"No. No, you go. It's fine. I just want to get this done, so I can, erm..."

"Slip into something comfortable?"

"Yes. Yes, that," she said.

"Shall I dry?"

"Seriously, Ben. You've done enough today. I've got a few things I want to sort out."

"Will you call me if the lab results come through?"

"Sure."

"We could even head out to Tupholme tomorrow? You know? Have a look around. We might spot something the search team didn't."

"Why don't you take a day off, Ben? Tomorrow's Sunday. Relax," she said, then gave a little laugh. "You didn't get around to cutting your grass, remember?"

"It'll still be there next weekend," Ben said. "I want to. Go to Tupholme, I mean."

"Okay," she said.

"I'll call you in the morning, yeah?"

"Okay. Night, Ben."

"Thanks again for dinner," he said, then left her to her thoughts. It wasn't the first time he'd seen her fall into one of her quiet, contemplative moods. But it had been months since the last time.

He'd already loaded the lawnmower into the car, and in a few moments, he was tearing up the farm track, kicking up a cloud of dust in his wake. The view in his mirror reminded him of when he and his brothers had been teenagers and they would tear across the same tracks on motorbikes, vying for first position to lose the others in the cloud.

Those days had long passed, and he rolled into the family's private driveway as the mature thirty-something-year-old he now was.

The front of the house was cool when he entered, but the rear had been warmed by the low sun, and his overgrown lawn seemed to perform a Mexican wave as the breeze rolled off the fens. He searched his pantry for something to drink. A cool beer in his comfy armchair would be the perfect way to finish the day.

Sadly, all he found was an old bottle of wine, from back in the days before he'd met Freya. Before she had converted him from cheap wine, steered him away from the expensive selection, and taught him how to find a good quality bottle in the mid-range section. He smiled as he picked up the cheap bottle. The label bore a picture of a little sailing boat, which was the reason he had chosen it. He'd been so happy with the price that he'd bought three bottles, the first of which Freya had used to paint a picture of him.

It seemed like years ago, despite the nine months that had passed.

He put the bottle on the counter. He wouldn't drink it. Not now he knew better. But he couldn't seem to bring himself to pour it away. There was something of him on that bottle. Something of a time before Freya. He'd always prided himself on living a simple life. He didn't own a TV. His furniture comprised of just two armchairs and a smattering of things his father might have thrown out.

"You haven't changed that much," he said aloud. "You're just older and wiser. That's all."

Even the fridge was bare. A carton of butter, some milk, and some random vegetables that were at best questionable.

He opted for a glass of water, then kicked his shoes off under the stairs and made his way through to the living room. During the winter, he would sit there for hours with the log burner warming the soles of his feet. But in the summer, he savoured the cool side of the house.

Once in his armchair, he peeled off his socks and fished his phone out of his pocket. He automatically navigated to Freya's number, and his thumb hovered over the green button.

Something had been wrong. Perhaps something had been on her mind? In which case, a good friend would try to help. Or at least make sure she was okay.

In the midst of deliberation, his thumb poised to either overstep their friendship or be the rock she needed, a knock on the door interrupted him.

He sidestepped into the hallway, studying the vague form behind the opaque glass in the front door. It wasn't either of his brothers, and it certainly wasn't his dad. The figure was far too short and slender.

He looked down at his phone and gave a little smile to himself, pocketing it. She needed him after all.

Adopting his warmest sympathetic expression, he opened the door and looked down at the guest.

"Evening, Ben."

"What are you doing here?" he said. "I thought you—"

"I lied," she said. "I didn't want to put Freya in a position. She's been good to me."

"I don't understand," he said, checking the windows in both his father's and his brothers' houses.

"I'm a bit stuck," Anderson said. "I need somewhere to stay."

CHAPTER TWENTY-THREE

The station car park was half empty. Whilst CID benefited from enough resources to apply a shift rotation, Major Investigations was not seen as anywhere near busy enough to warrant the budget allocation. That was fine by Freya. She had worked shifts during her career in London, and although investigations typically benefited from the continual drive, personal space was often a challenge. Desk sharing rarely ended well, and her processes didn't always align with those of the night shift.

But there was one car in the car park that belonged to a member of her team.

She climbed the fire escape steps to the first floor and crept into the corridor, then froze as she heard the incident room squeal open and then close with a loud bang. A figure ambled along the corridor away from her, then disappeared into the washrooms.

Freya slipped into the incident room, opening the doors as little as she could to prevent alerting anybody to her presence.

The room was long and narrow, and had originally housed the two Major Investigations teams. But now there was only one team, the lights at the far end of the room were rarely turned on. In fact, only one bank of lights were on – the row above Nillson's desk, Gold and Chapman's.

Freya moved to the dark end of the room, pulled out a seat, and waited. She didn't have to exercise much patience. Within a few minutes, the doors swung open with that arrogant squeal, and then slammed closed. A dark shape moved into the lit area and Chapman announced herself with a heavy sigh.

Feeling more than a little guilty of intruding, Freya forced herself to be silent for a while longer. At least until she had some kind of idea of what was going on. Again, her patience was rewarded.

"Hello?" Chapman said to somebody on her phone. "No. I'm out. I don't know."

One-sided conversations were Freya's speciality. A trick she had learned during the six months her husband had been cheating on her. The other person's voice played out in her mind. It was male, she thought, asking if Chapman was home, and when she would be back.

"This has to stop," Chapman said, then paused for a few moments. She sniffed loudly, then muttered, "Please."

Whatever the man said next was way beyond Freya's guessing skills. Chapman gasped, then ended the call, tossing the phone across the desk, where it slid all the way to Nillson's desk and came to a stop.

Chapman held her head in her hands and sobbed as a child might.

Slowly, Freya stood and made her way out of the darkness into the light, until she stood just a few feet from Chapman. Only then did Freya see the full reason for Chapman's obvious anguish.

"Denise," she said softly, and Chapman startled a little. Freya held her hands up to calm and reassure her. "It's okay. It's me."

Chapman's hands instinctively came up to hide the blue-grey bruise that surrounded her right eye.

"I'm sorry," she said, and began packing away her belongings. "I needed somewhere to go."

"Denise, stop," Freya said, her tone harder than Chapman was expecting. Then she softened. "It's fine. I'm not angry. But you need to tell me what's going on, okay?"

"I can't."

"You can't, or you won't?"

Chapman said nothing. Instead, she buried her face and sobbed.

"Right. Come on. You can't stay here."

"What?" Chapman said, wiping her eyes with a tissue she had tucked in her sleeve. She looked at Freya, her face panic-stricken.

"Get your things together. This isn't a hotel."

Chapman glanced behind her, where a small duffle bag sat beside the rolled-up sleeping bag Freya had seen through the windows only a few hours before.

"Okay, ma'am," she said quietly. She collected the things she had on her desk – her iPad, phone charger, and a small compact which she'd used to try and conceal her black eye. She looked up at Freya, her big eyes moist and red from the tears. "I've let you down. I'll go. I'm sorry. I didn't think anybody would find out."

"Just pack your bags, Chapman," Freya said, offering her very little in the way of comfort. "When you've done that, we'll put them in my car."

"Sorry?" Chapman said, not following.

"You can stay at mine."

"But–"

"I won't hear anything else about it. Pack your bags," Freya told her. "Come on. I've got a nice bottle of wine we can share."

"Stay at yours?"

"Have you eaten?"

Chapman shook her head.

"Right. I've got just the thing."

Chapman seemed unsure of the offer, like it might be a trap or something. Seeing this, Freya leaned on the desk and met her eye to eye.

"You don't have to tell me anything," she said. "But I've been around long enough to make my own mistakes. There's somebody I should have helped more than I did. I can't change that now. But I can help you. If you'll let me, that is."

It was the closest Freya had ever been to Chapman, who was usually quiet and reserved. She really was a pretty woman. Plain, but pretty in a natural sense.

"Will you let me?" Freya asked.

And Chapman, with her swollen and frightened eyes, nodded.

CHAPTER TWENTY-FOUR

Anderson was already up and dressed when Ben entered his kitchen in the morning. He followed the scent of coffee and found her clutching a mug in both hands, staring out at his garden. She smiled weakly when she saw him, but met his gaze when he thought she would turn away.

"You have good taste in coffee," she said, as his phone vibrated in his pocket. He pulled it out to find a message from Freya displayed on the screen.

Lab results back. I have a few things to do. Meet me at the station. F.

"Sorry," he said, realizing he'd ignored what Anderson had said.

"I said you have good taste in coffee."

"Ah. You can thank Freya for that. I used to be an instant man, until she taught me the error of my ways."

She laughed a little, but was reserved in letting it go freely.

"That sounds about right," she said. "She certainly enjoys the finer things in life."

"Have you known her long?" Ben asked, as he poured himself a cup, then offered the pot for a top-up. She waved her hand dismissively, then settled into the corner where the worktops met.

"No. It's funny, eh? I came all this way on a whim, really."

"A whim?"

"I admired her," Anderson said. "For a short time, at least."

"I'm sorry, it's none of my business," Ben said, then sought to move the topic on. "How long do you need?"

"You can ask, if you want," she said, then stared at him, waiting.

"You said you admired her," he said at last.

"I did. She was a strong, independent, successful female detective inspector. I'm a young, ambitious, female detective constable. And around us were men. From the bottom to the top. All men."

"You make it sound like Victorian times."

"Oh, don't get me wrong. There were women too. But you never heard them. We lived in the shadow of a select few men. Freya was brave enough to step out of that shadow. I respected her for that."

"Did you tag along with her?" Ben asked. "I mean, did you work an investigation with her?"

"The truth?" Anderson said. "I was assigned to her for one day. It was a huge investigation. She was at breaking point, although she never showed it."

"Just one day?"

"How well do you know her?" Anderson said, clearly not wanting to divulge Freya's history to just anybody.

"Better than I know myself, I think sometimes. I know her better than most, anyway. We've grown to be good friends."

"So, you know about her last investigation in London?"

"James Marley," Ben said. "The serial killer."

Anderson nodded.

"It was a challenging case for all of us. Freya more than most," she said.

Sure that she knew more than she was letting on, Ben halted the conversation, imagining that Freya would not appreciate a defining period of her life being discussed behind her back.

"A few days," she said at last, and Ben stared at her quizzically. "You asked how long I needed."

"A few days?"

"I just need more time to find somewhere."

"I'll have to tell Freya. I feel bad enough as it is."

"I see," she said, then gestured at the garden. "You know, it's funny. I saw you working your backside off in Freya's garden yesterday. Yet yours looks like it needs a bit of TLC. Why would you do that?"

"She's a friend. I like to help friends."

"Does that include *any* friends, or just special friends?" she asked, and Ben felt his eyes widening in shock. "Sorry. That was below the belt."

"There's nothing between us."

"Of course."

"There isn't."

"Right. You said. That's okay."

"Good."

"I mean, you're scared to tell her I'm staying, but you respect her enough to tell her. You cut her lawn even though yours needs doing."

"You're reading too much into that."

"Coffee's good," she said, repeating her earlier comment, insinuating that Freya had more than made her mark on him. "But there is one thing I don't understand."

"Go on," he said.

"The bottle of wine with the little sailing boat on the label, I'm pretty sure Freya would have had you throw that away. Which means she hasn't got her claws into you fully. Not yet anyway."

"What are you doing, Anderson?"

"Testing the water," she said, without hesitation. "What would you do if I threw myself at you?"

"What?"

"What would you do?"

"I don't know," Ben said, alarmed at this new direction. "I haven't really given it a thought."

"Sometimes, that's the best way," she said.

"Don't. Don't do this," Ben said.

"You'd push me away then?"

"Eh?"

"You'd push me away," she said, and she shoved herself off the kitchen counter, closing the distance between them. She was far shorter than Freya, and younger too, yet equally as confident. "You'd say no, would you?"

"Don't," he said, and she stopped before him, placed her hands against his stomach, and smiled up at him.

"Because you don't want to?" she asked. "Or because you don't want to upset Freya?"

Ben said nothing.

"I thought so. You really are a good friend, aren't you?"

"I try to be."

"Just to be clear," she said. "I wouldn't throw myself at you. I respect her too much. I just wanted to test the water. Now I understand."

"What is it you understand?" he asked, as she moved towards the hallway. She stopped and turned to face him.

"Why she loves it here so much. I just hope I make a friend as good as you, one day," she said.

"That was a test?" he called after her. "You were testing my loyalty to Freya?"

"I'm staying in your house. I need to know I'm safe," she said. "I just need a day or two."

He shook his head in disbelief. How close he had been to leaning down and kissing her. How close he had been to destroying everything he had with Freya.

"Anderson," he said, as he opened the front door. Again, she stopped and stared at him, eyebrows raised in anticipation. "There's a spare key under the plant pot in the garden. I'd appreciate if you kept our arrangement between us."

"My lips are sealed," she said, then winked and closed the door behind her.

CHAPTER TWENTY-FIVE

"This feels weird," Chapman said from the passenger's seat of Freya's car.

"It shouldn't," Freya replied. "How long have we known each other now? Nearly nine months?"

"I know. But you're my line manager. It doesn't feel right."

"You're vulnerable, Chapman. I've been vulnerable too. We all have."

"Yeah, right," Chapman said.

"It's true. It's these episodes in our lives that make us stronger. I'm grateful for the times I was down on my knees. It taught me who my friends are. Taught me who to trust, and who not to trust."

"I can't see a way out of this, ma'am."

"Firstly, it's Sunday," Freya said. "We may be heading into the office, but until we get there, it's Freya, okay?"

"That's even weirder."

"Yeah, well, be grateful it wasn't Gillespie who found you sleeping in the station."

"I think he'd have been okay about it. In fact, I think anyone on the team would have done the same."

"Yes, I agree. However, you would have woken up in Gillespie's house this morning. And I can only imagine what that must be like."

Chapman laughed. It was the first time since Freya had taken her back to her house that she'd heard Chapman laugh out loud. In fact, this was the most she had spoken. They had got home, had a cup of tea, and after making her feel welcome with a fresh bath towel and an extra blanket, Freya had left her to her own devices in her spare room, expecting her to come downstairs at some point for a chat. But she hadn't.

"Do you mind me asking what made you feel vulnerable?" Chapman asked. "Sorry, is that too forward?"

"No, it's fine. I'll spare you the graphic detail, but needless to say, if it wasn't for DC Anderson, I probably wouldn't be here today."

"Anderson?"

Freya nodded. "Surprised?"

"Well, yes. She seems so polite. So innocent."

"Oh, she is. Polite. As for innocent, I don't really know her well enough. But she's good. I trust her implicitly."

"Is that why she's here?" Chapman asked.

"No," Freya said, and gave her a sideways glance as she steered the car into the station. "But, like you, she's had man trouble. She needed a new start. And who am I to turn down a fellow female in distress?"

Chapman nodded, as if she had guessed that was the reason why Anderson was in Lincolnshire.

"I don't have man trouble," she said eventually, as Freya brought the car to a stop. She stared at Freya, waiting for her to press for more information. But Freya knew not to press.

"You don't have to tell me. I told you that."

"Someone's stalking me," she said, and then seemed to shrink as she spoke the words, as a defenceless animal might curl into a ball.

"Stalking you?" Freya said. "Are you sure? Of course you're sure. Denise, you should have come to me."

"I can't. He... He threatened me."

"Threatened you? How?"

Chapman covered her face with her hands, gingerly feeling the bruise she had done her best to cover with concealer.

"Denise?"

"I killed his dog," she said, although her voice was muffled by her hands.

"You did what?"

"I hit the dog. I was on my way home from work one night. It was dark and it just ran out."

"Oh God, Denise..."

"I stopped. Honest. I got out to see if... You know?"

"If you had actually killed it?"

Chapman nodded.

"It was pitch black. I was in the lanes," she said. "Then he came out of nowhere."

"The owner?"

"Yeah. Started screaming and swearing at me. I tried to help him. I said I'd take them to the vets. That I'd pay," she said, and the tears started to flow, and the next sentence was lost to her emotions.

"Did he hurt you?"

Slowly, she nodded.

"Talk to me, Denise. What did he do?"

"He shoved me. I fell over. But he came at me. He wouldn't stop. I managed to get into my car, but he took a photo of my number plate."

"You're sure about that?"

"Yeah. He sent it to me. Said he had proof, and that he would make me pay."

"Denise, you're a police officer. You have his phone number."

"It was a burner phone. I tried," she said, and glanced across at her apologetically.

"Denise, are you single? Is there anyone who can look after you?"

She shook her head.

"Has he come to your house?"

Chapman nodded.

"Oh God, Denise," Freya said. "Right. Leave this with me–"

"No, ma'am. Please. He said he would know if I reported him."

"He would know? How?"

"I don't know. But he found my address. He knows everything about me."

"That's why you were sleeping at the station. Because you're afraid to go home?"

"I'm so sorry, ma'am. It's all my fault."

"It's not your fault. But listen to me. You have to listen to me, okay?" Freya said, repeating herself until Chapman looked her in the eye. "We're going to find him, and we're going to stop him. I have a few things to do with Ben this morning. After that, we'll swing by your house, and you're staying at mine until all this is over."

"But–"

"And I won't hear another word of it. Is that clear?"

She nodded again.

"When did he do that to your eye?" Freya asked.

"The other night. He caught me at my front door."

"He did what?"

"He pushed me up against the wall. Pressed my face into the bricks."

"Did he touch you?" Freya asked softly. "Did he try anything?"

She nodded again, slowly, as if the memory numbed her senses. "He tried, but…"

"It's okay. You don't need to say the words."

"He's been in my house, too."

"Dirty bloody scumbag," Freya spat. "We'll find him. Whoever he is, we'll find him. I promise you that."

"Can we keep this to ourselves?" Chapman asked, with a sudden panic in her voice. "I don't want everyone to know."

"I'll need to enlist Ben's help," she said. "But nobody else, okay?"

"Okay," she said, after a while.

"We'll find him," Freya said. "And you can be the one to cuff him and read him his rights. How does that sound?"

"Honestly?" Chapman said, and the glimmer of a grateful smile shone through her tears, like the sun emerging from a cloud only to slip behind another. "Terrifying."

CHAPTER TWENTY-SIX

In the incident room, while Freya hung her bag on the back of her chair, she eyed Chapman, who slipped behind her desk. It was her safe place. That much was clear just by the way the sag in her shoulders seemed to give way to a straight back, and her fingers that had trembled in the car now rested on the home keys of her keyboard while she prepared for her computer to start.

"You're not on your own anymore," Freya said. "I'm right with you. Okay?"

"Thank you, ma'am," she replied.

Out on the corridor, the fire escape door closed. On any other day, the noise would have been lost to the commotion. But on a Sunday, with just Chapman and Freya in the incident room, the noise was loud and clear.

"Who's that?" Chapman asked. "Is anyone else coming in?"

"Only Ben," Freya replied. "I'll handle him."

The incident room door burst open a few seconds later and Gillespie entered, dumping his jacket on his desk. He snatched up his dirty mug from the previous day and turned immediately to head to the little kitchenette to make a coffee. He stopped at the doors, as if what he had seen had only just registered. Then he turned slowly, like he was unsure of what he might find.

"Morning, Gillespie," Freya said, sounding as cheerful as she could.

"Aye. Morning," he said, nodding to each of them in turn. "You know it's Sunday, right?"

"I could ask you the same question." Freya said.

"We have a lead. Or at least an idea. A theory, as such. I wanted to do a wee bit of research before we brought the team in."

"Sounds intriguing."

"Aye. It's a game changer, boss," he said. "How about you?"

"The lab results are back. For the blanket, glasses, and the car, at least. I want to make a plan for tomorrow."

"Equally as intriguing," he said. "Do you want coffee?"

"Sure."

"Chapman?"

"Yes, please," she said.

"It'll have to be that instant muck. Local shops are all closed on a Sunday. I've never understood that. You know? It's like the people that run the coffee shop don't realise that there are other people working at the weekends. Bloody selfish if you ask me–"

"Instant muck sounds delicious," Freya said, right before his rant gained momentum and became unstoppable.

"Instant muck it is then," he said dejectedly.

He stopped at the doors to eye them with acute suspicion, as if he had realised he hadn't asked why they were in on a weekend. But clearly he thought better of it and slipped through the doors, and they banged closed behind him.

"Don't worry," Freya said. "If he questions why you're in, just tell him I asked for some help."

Freya barely had time to clean the whiteboard when the incident room doors squealed open again.

"It's about time," Freya said, hanging the cloth on the corner of the board and collecting a marker. She turned to find Nillson staring at them both with a look of utter confusion on her face.

"Boss?" she said.

"Nillson. What an unexpected surprise," Freya said. "Pleasant, of course."

"Of course," Nillson said. She stood still, like she had been caught red-handed.

"What brings you here?" Freya said. "You realise it's a Sunday?"

"I just wanted to catch up on a few things. I might be onto something. I'm not sure yet."

"A lead?"

"Maybe," she said, keeping her cards close to her chest. "Give me ten minutes, and if it goes anywhere, I'll share it."

"Right," Freya said, just as Gillespie backed through the double doors carrying three mugs of coffee.

"Right then. Three steaming hot mugs of non-branded, bitter, weak coffee," he said, easing himself through the doors. He turned to deliver the coffee and froze. "Nillson."

"Gillespie."

"Do you two want to tell me what's going on here?" Freya said.

But neither of them spoke.

"I'm waiting," Freya said.

"I've got a theory," Gillespie said with a sideways glance at Nillson.

She followed with, "A theory? Is that all? I've got a lead."

"What's the lead?" Freya said, sensing an underlying friction between the two.

"Him first," Nillson said, retaining her usual calm and collected demeanour.

Freya nodded her agreement. "Gillespie?"

"Aye, well. I haven't had time to put it together yet."

"Just spit it out. You two are up to something, and I want to know what it is."

"We found something, boss," he said, then strode over to the whiteboard and began drawing a crude representation of Tupholme Abbey and its surroundings, marking the individual spots where John Carson's body, the knife, the underwear, the blanket, and the glasses were all found.

"What's all this?" Freya asked. "Or are we playing Pictionary, now? In which case, I give in. Just tell me the answer."

"This," Gillespie said, tapping the cross on the board that represented the abbey. "This is the abbey. This is where John Carson was found." He tapped the rest of the little marks he had made. "The blanket, the glasses, the knife, and the underwear."

"Great, you just drew what I already knew and dirtied the board I've just cleaned."

"Ah, but wait," he said, moving the marker back to where the glasses were found. "This is where John Carson was killed. I think we can all agree on that. The grass was flattened. Everything points to him being killed in this exact spot."

"So?" Nillson said, doing very little to add any niceties to her tone.

"So, he was killed here, then dragged to the rocks *here* using the blanket."

"We don't know the blanket was used for that," Freya said.

"Ah, but we do," he said. "Cruz and I carried out some experiments."

"You mean you dragged poor Cruz across the grass?"

"Ah, no. See, I did at first, aye. I dragged him with one hand. It was nothing. But when I asked him to drag me, he couldn't."

"You must weigh more than twice what he does, Gillespie. Where are you going with this?"

"But when I lay on his jacket," Gillespie said, snapping the lid back onto the marker, "he could do it."

"That doesn't mean anything," Nillson said.

"Yes, it does," Freya added. "It means the blanket was used, because whoever moved John Carson wasn't strong enough to move him without it."

"Aye, boss."

"It also means the rocks are significant. Laying him naked on the rocks meant something," Freya said. "So, what's your theory?"

"Eh?"

"Your theory. All you've done so far is confirm what I thought. I mean, good work on the whole jacket thing. But surely there's more."

"Yeah, come on," Nillson said. "You were acting like you had the whole thing worked out."

"Alright, alright," Gillespie said. "If you really want to tap into my genius, get yourselves ready."

"This better be good," Freya warned.

"Aye, it is. You see, if John Carson was killed here, and then dragged here..." he said, using the board to illustrate what he was saying. He glanced around the room to make sure everyone was following the end of the marker. They were. "And the underwear was found here, and the knife found here..."

"Then the killer ran down the hill to get away."

"Aye, boss," he said proudly.

"What's in the next field?"

"A derelict farm," Chapman said, speaking up for the first time. "I've got the satellite image open. Looks like a bunch of old buildings, overgrown trees, and some burned-out cars."

Freya looked curiously at Gillespie, who winked.

"I was wondering if you'd mind getting us some kind of warrant, boss?"

"If it's derelict, why don't you just go in and have a look around?" Nillson said.

"Two reasons," he replied, with more confidence than before. "Firstly, any evidence we might find would be inadmissible in court."

Freya nodded.

"And the second reason?"

"If we show up and get turned away, whoever owns it will have ample opportunity to clean the place up."

"You want the element of surprise?" Freya asked.

"Aye, boss. And I want a dozen good men to tear the place apart."

She nodded. "Okay. Good work. Better than I was expecting anyway," she said. "Nillson? What did you find? What's this lead? You've got a hard act to follow."

For the first time, Nillson appeared concerned. She eyed Gillespie, who was still basking in his glory with his feet up on Cruz's empty chair.

"Ninety-five bloody quid, no doubt," he mumbled.

"Sorry, Gillespie. Did you say something?" Freya asked, but he shook his head, and turned his attention to Nillson. "Nillson?" Freya said, rousing her from the dirty look she was giving him.

She fished in her bag for a moment, then produced a clear evidence bag with what looked to be a man's shoe inside, which she tossed onto her desk. The leather had long since lost its sheen and mould had started to form across the laces.

"It's a brogue," Freya said. "An old brogue, at that."

"It's a size eleven. I also found this," Nillson added, fishing once more in her bag. She tossed another clear plastic bag onto the desk, which landed with a metallic rattle. "A dog collar."

"A dog collar?" Gillespie said, with mock enthusiasm. "The religious type?"

"Very funny. No. The type dogs wear."

"Wow, Nillson. You really have stretched your abilities there," Gillespie said.

But Nillson, who Freya knew to have grown up with four older brothers, took the comments in her stride and waited for Freya to examine the bag.

"There's a tag," Freya said, holding it up to the light, and Nillson raised an eyebrow as if to say, *I told you so*. Freya read the faint inscription in the little, metal tag. "It's a phone number. Chapman, are you ready for this?"

Chapman's fingers fell into position, her head cocked and ready for the information, which she typed as Freya read out the number.

"Is that all?" Freya asked Nillson.

"For the time being, boss. Yes."

"Are you sure about that, Anna?" Gillespie asked. "You didn't happen to find anything else?"

"No. If I had found anything worthwhile, I would have bagged and tagged it, wouldn't I?"

"Not necessarily."

"Is there something I need to know?" Freya asked, glaring at them both.

"No," Nillson said without hesitation. "Gillespie is just being his usual immature self."

"Good. Thank you. Both of you. There's just one thing I'm concerned about more than anything."

"Aye?" Gillespie said, still basking in his glory. "What's that, boss?"

"You both worked yesterday, when I told you to go home," she said. "Why? I can't pay you overtime without a written instruction."

"Ah, come on, boss. You don't need to pay us. We were just pushing forward with the investigation."

"Is that right?"

"Aye," he said.

"Nillson?"

"Yes. We were just doing our jobs, boss."

"Right," she said, as Ben strode into the incident room, then stopped in obvious surprise at finding half the team there. "I hope that's the truth. For both your sakes."

CHAPTER TWENTY-SEVEN

"Am I interrupting something?" Ben asked, stepping awkwardly into the room. Nobody looked at him. They all seemed to be focused on Freya. At least, Gillespie and Nillson were. Chapman's gaze flitted from one to the other, then returned to her screen. "Does somebody want to tell me what's going on here?"

"Nothing's happening, Ben," Freya said. "Gillespie and Nillson were convincing me that they both worked yesterday afternoon out of the kindness of their hearts, and their duties to society."

"Dedicated detectives, eh?" Ben said, taking his seat at his desk. "So, what did we find?"

"The short version," Freya began. "Gillespie and Cruz worked out that the killer is most likely either a female or a weak male. He or she needed to use the blanket to pull John Carson from the picnic spot to the rocks. What does that tell you?"

"The rocks are significant," Ben replied. "Has anybody searched them?"

"Aye. They haven't moved for years. There's a layer of moss that hasn't been disturbed," Gillespie added.

"Can I continue?" Freya said. Then, when the team fell silent, she continued, using Gillespie's board to illustrate his theory. "The killer dragged John Carson from here to here. Then ran down the hill, discarded the knife and underwear here and here, and ended up in this derelict farm. From there, we don't know."

"That's pretty good," Ben said. "But I have two questions."

"Hold your thoughts," Freya said. "There's more. Nillson discovered an old shoe and a dog collar. Both of which look like they've been lost for years."

"A shoe and a dog collar?" Ben said, turning to Nillson, who rolled her eyes, and in turn stared at Chapman.

"Any luck tracing the phone number on the tag?" she asked.

"As it happens, yes," Chapman replied. "The number belongs to a John Carson."

"No way," Gillespie said, pulling his feet off Cruz's chair and sitting up straight. "The same John Carson?"

"The very man," Chapman said, reading the screen as if she was confirming it for her own sanity. "Yes. Definitely him."

"Leigh Carson said their dog went missing a couple of years ago. Could be the same one," Freya said. "It's something to bear in mind."

"Okay, I have four questions," Ben said. "First question. The shoe? How is that significant?"

"We don't know yet. But maybe the lab will find something," Freya said. "Next?"

"The underwear. Why did the killer throw the underwear away?"

"Maybe it belonged to the killer? Maybe she panicked?" Nillson said. "We've already established the possibility of the killer being a female. Maybe she killed John Carson? Panicked and ran, throwing the underwear and the knife away in the tall grass."

"Plausible," Freya said. "Next?"

"Okay," Ben said, not entirely convinced about the underwear theory. "Who owns the derelict farm?"

"Ah. I've got that one," Chapman said. "The freehold belongs to a man named Solomon Yates. No connection to the Woods, and no connection to the Carsons. Not that I can find anyway. No previous record. And more importantly, his driving licence is registered to the farm. It's not derelict. It's habitable."

"Good work, Chapman," Freya said, and she turned to Ben for the last time. "Next?"

"If the killer is either a female or a weak man, what was Theodore Wood's car doing there? He's not female, and judging by the photos in his lounge, he's not a small man, either."

"Ah, you want to see the lab results," Freya said, opening her file. "This is interesting. Theodore Wood's prints are all over the car."

"It's his car," Ben said. "Next."

"But the steering wheel was wiped clean," Freya added.

"Gold messaged me this morning," Ben said. "Theodore Wood still isn't home."

"Next. Charlotte Wood's fingerprints are all over the knife."

"Charlotte Wood? She would have had access to her husband's car. Do we think it's her?"

"Maybe, except for this key piece of information," Freya said. "The underwear."

"Charlotte Wood's?" Ben said.

"No," Gillespie said. "Don't tell me they belong to Carson's wife. What's her name?"

"Leigh," Chapman said.

"Both wrong," Freya said, clearly pleased with the look of confusion that spread around the room. "Francesca Wood. The daughter. We took DNA samples from them both. It's a match."

Nobody said a word while they digested the information.

Then Ben voiced his thoughts, "So, John Carson was at the abbey with Francesca Wood?"

"And Charlotte Wood caught them?" Nillson finished.

"Or Theodore Wood?" Gillespie said. "And that raises a whole new bunch of issues. Either way, we're about to accuse a dead man of sleeping with an underage girl. Consent or no consent, that's not a pretty picture."

"That's the problem," Freya agreed. She checked her watch and sat back on the desk. "Right. It's gone ten a.m. We need a plan."

"The obvious choice would be to raid the Woods' house," Gillespie said. "If Charlotte Wood did this, the clothes she wore might still be there."

"You're so cavalier, Gillespie," Nillson said. "We can't go in there gung ho. If John Carson was with the Woods' daughter, then we need to talk to her. Gently. Who knows how she's feeling?"

"You're both right," Freya said. "However, we don't want to show our hand. Not yet. If Charlotte really did this, us talking to her daughter will put her defences up. We've got her prints on the knife, but that doesn't mean she did it. The knife could be from her kitchen. Her husband is still in the frame. We'll only have one stab at this, if you pardon the pun."

"I say we see what the farm has to offer before we make any rash decisions," Ben suggested. "If we're going to get anything by CPS, we'll need a full account. Where did the killer go afterwards? Pathology confirmed the body was moved at least an hour after death. What happened in that time? Let's get the CPS on our side, and build a solid case before we make a move."

"Agreed," Freya said. "Gillespie, I'll get you your warrant. Nillson, I want you to go with him."

"Her?" Gillespie said.

"Do you have a problem with Nillson now?"

"Well. No, boss. But–"

"What's happening here?" Freya asked, switching her stare from one to the other. "You two have been acting oddly all morning."

"Nothing, boss," Gillespie replied, on both their behalf. "Nothing's happening."

She waited a few moments, clearly not believing him.

"Find me something. I want to know why the killer ran to that farm instead of running back to the road, which would be the obvious route to take. In the meantime, Chapman, can you look into phone records, please? See who called who, and if you can get any location data that might help us."

"Ma'am," she replied, her standard response.

"Right. Get to it," she said.

Both Gillespie and Nillson gathered their things in silence and made for the door. But before he followed Nillson into the corridor, Gillespie called out. "Boss?" he said, holding the door with one hand and his bag in the other.

She looked up, and Ben sat back in his seat to watch both sides of the conversation.

"I was just wondering. Are we okay to book this in? You know? A wee bit of overtime."

Freya smiled, but gave him a confused look.

"I thought you were keen on pushing the investigation along?" she said. "Or was that a lie?"

"Well, no," he said. "It's just…"

"Yes?" Freya said, making it clear she was all ears. "Are you no longer keen to push the investigation along? If you're not going to push the investigation along, then perhaps I should find somebody who will? Do I need to do that, Gillespie?"

"No, boss."

"Good. We'll discuss overtime when we've actually made some progress."

He let the door close and they heard him and Nillson bickering in the corridor all the way to the fire escape.

"What's going on with those two?" Ben asked, to which Freya bit her lower lip in thought, still staring at the doors.

"I'm not certain," she said. "But I don't like tension in the team."

"Tension? You think they've fallen out?"

"No. But I have an idea of what they're up to," she said, with that wry smile she wore when she was dreaming up a plan. "I just need to work out how to use it to my advantage."

CHAPTER TWENTY-EIGHT

"So, where are we going then?" Ben said, when he and Freya were in the car. "On this delightful Sunday morning?"

Freya eased along the country lanes, hoping more than anything to find somewhere that sold decent coffee.

"Ah, what else would you be doing?"

"Oh, I don't know. Cutting my grass, maybe? Doing some laundry. My life is action-packed, you know?"

"Right," Freya laughed. "Anyway, we're going to Bardney."

"I can see that, Freya. This is the road to Bardney. What I meant was what are we going to do when we get there? Are we going to see the Woods?"

"Do you want to go to the Woods?"

"Well, yeah. I'd be interested to see if Theodore Wood is home. He seems to be the missing link here."

"Oh, we'll be going to see the Woods, for sure. When we're done."

"When we're done doing what?"

"When we're done breaking into this house," Freya said, and she gestured at the house she was pulling the car to stop outside.

"When we're what?"

"Well, when I say *we,* what I really mean is *you.*"

"Breaking in?"

"Well, you don't have to actually break in. Just see if you can."

"You want me to test the security?"

"Yes. That's it. Just see how easy it would be."

"Are you thinking of buying this house?" he said. "Is that what this is about?"

"No, but I happen to know the owner. In fact, so do you."

"I know them?" he said, then gave it some thought. "Hold on. Chapman lives in Bardney. Is this…"

She nodded slowly.

"It's Chapman's house," she said. "There's something you need to know."

"Like what? She's got a guard dog?"

"No, but given the circumstances, that's not a bad idea," Freya said. "Somebody is stalking her."

"Chapman?"

"She hit a dog on the way home a few weeks ago. The owner went berserk. Started attacking her."

"Why hasn't she reported it? She's a police officer."

"She's frightened, Ben. You won't understand that. We're not all fearless. We're not all able to meet these things head-on."

"She could have come to me."

"He's threatened her. He calls her. And before you suggest it, the number is unregistered."

"Can we trace it?"

"Probably, but by the time we've done that, he'll have moved on. And more to the point, he'll know she's reported it."

"What's he asking for?" Ben said. "Money?"

"He isn't asking for anything. But he'll take whatever he can get. Lucky for Chapman, she fought back. But he's been in her house. He been through her things, and he knows everything about her."

"So, you want me to see how easy it is to get in so we can make her house secure?"

"Yes. And while you do that, I'm going to take a look around," she said. "Put your gloves on. I don't want to pollute any evidence he's left behind."

"Wow, you've done this before."

With her hand on the door handle, Freya looked across to him. "You know what? I have never broken into anywhere. This will be a first for me. I'm quite excited."

"You're a cheap date, then," Ben replied, as he climbed from the car. "I'll bear that in mind."

"Oh no. When it comes to dates, Ben, I am most certainly not cheap. You'll find out soon enough. Let's split up. Shout if you find something."

She left him to his own devices and opened the little gate to the property. It was the first time Freya had actually stopped and looked at the house in the daylight, having only dropped Chapman off at home once. But she was suitably impressed. Had somebody asked Freya to draw the house she imagined Chapman living in, she wouldn't have been too far off. It was a detached cottage, with roses in various states of bloom in the front garden. The windows were leaded and framed with ivy, and surrounding the building, neatly weeded and pruned flower beds were bursting with colour. It was one of those gardens that made Freya wish she knew the names of the flowers, and one of those houses that stirred a romantic view of village life in Freya's mind.

But it was the flower beds that Freya was interested in. It took a while, but after peeling back the plants along one side of the house and halfway along the rear, she found what she was looking for. A man's footprint, which meant that the window above it would likely have fingerprints on, as long as the rain hadn't washed them away.

She was just about to examine the wooden frame for signs of a break-in when the adjacent window opened, and Ben leaned out.

"Find much?" he asked.

"You're in," Freya said, slightly alarmed. "You're not supposed to actually get inside."

"You said to see if I can break in."

"But after that, I said you just need to identify..." she started, then gave up. "Oh, forget it. How did you do it?"

"Side window," he said, examining the window he was leaning out of. "See, these windows have a dead bolt. The one on the side doesn't."

"Which side?"

He pointed to the side Freya had yet to look at. "Over there."

"He's been here," she replied. "I think he tried this window. In fact, I think he probably tried them all until he found the one without the bolt. He's left a footprint."

Ben leaned out of the window to have a look. "You're not considering trying to trace the brand of shoe, are you?"

"Unless you have a better idea," she replied.

"How about some fibre from his jacket or something?"

"Sorry?"

He nodded at the side window he'd climbed through.

"He caught his jacket. Tweed."

Freya stared down at the print in the mud.

"Fibres would be easier," she said, and he nodded, as if the answer was staring them in the face. "Anything else?"

"As it happens, yes," he said. "But you can't tell Chapman. She'll go nuts."

"This is not the time for games, Ben. If you found something, then–"

"Sheep manure," he said, cutting her off.

"Sheep what?"

"Dung. Poop. Crap," he said. "Whatever you want to call it, it's all over the carpet beneath the window."

"So, he stood in some sheep dung before he came here?" Freya said. "There are bloody sheep everywhere. How does that help?"

"It doesn't. But it confirms which window he came in."

"So, he left footprints in the mud, fibres on the window frame, and sheep…"

"Manure," Ben finished for her.

"Right. That. He left sheep manure on the carpet. He's hardly the world's best criminal, is he?"

"What gets me is why he's going after Chapman," Ben said. "What did she say to him?"

"It's hard to say exactly. She was quite upset."

"Did she show her warrant card?"

"I don't know. Why?"

"Just a hunch," he said. "I'm going to lock this place up. Make it safe for her. Leave this with me, Freya. I'll take care of it."

She smiled up at him.

"You're a good friend, Ben," she said. "You never fail to amaze me."

"Stop it. I'll blush."

"I mean, it," she replied. "I can always count on you to never to let me down, can't I? You're loyal. That's a good trait to have."

He averted his eyes, choosing to look around inside the house.

"She's a woman on her own, Freya. I'm not going to let some lunatic get to her, am I?"

"She's staying with me at the moment. Until we can sort this out."

"Well," Ben said, "I hope for her sake you've given her longer than two days."

Freya leaned in through the window to look around Chapman's house, feeling Ben's wandering eyes only inches from hers.

"Get hold of Chapman. We're going to need a search warrant," she said. "I'll meet you out front in a minute."

CHAPTER TWENTY-NINE

"Right," Gillespie said, as he climbed from his car. Nillson had refused to share a ride, and had pulled in behind him in the layby near the abbey. He strode towards her before she had even switched the engine off. "You stole my money."

Nillson, being the cool, level-headed one of the two, said nothing and showed no signs of annoyance. She climbed from her car, ignoring him, which somehow made it worse.

"Well?" he said. "Are you going to answer me, or not?"

She said nothing. She just glanced at the sky, as if judging the weather, and then reached into the back of her car for her leather jacket. It was the short type, like a motorcycle jacket, and she fastened it up to her chest before locking the car and heading up the track towards the abbey.

"You won't get away with this," he called after her. "You don't know who you're messing with. Nobody steals from me, Anna. Nobody. You hear that? Aye? You hear me? Anna? Anna?"

She was already fifty yards ahead by the time he finished yelling, and after a moment's deliberation on whether or not he should get his jacket from his car, he ran after her. There was no point locking it anyway, after Nillson had smashed his window. He caught her up when they were close to the little gate that led from the track to the ruins, and grabbed her by the shoulder.

But that proved to be a fatal move. Within less than a second, she had reached up, grabbed his wrist, and twisted his arm behind his back, shoving him forward onto his knees.

"You don't touch me," she hissed into his ear. "You don't come anywhere near me."

"You stole my money—"

"I did no such thing. I'm not going to steal your money, you bloody idiot. Up until about an hour ago, we were friends. Why would I steal money from a friend?"

"I dropped it. Over there near the ruins. I had a hole in my pocket," he said, as she shoved his arm further up behind his back.

"If I had found it, I'd have been the first to tell you. I mean, sure, I might have made you work for it, but I wouldn't have bloody stolen it."

"You're serious?" he said.

"Of course I'm bloody serious," she replied, and she shoved him forward, stepping away before he could retaliate. "Are you saying you dropped it over there?"

"Aye. Then, when Cruz and I saw you, we figured you'd found it," he said. "You smashed my window."

"You blocked me in."

"That's going to cost me, Anna."

"Yeah, well..." she replied. "Maybe it was a bit over the top."

"Maybe?"

"I'm apologising, aren't I?"

"Ah, right. Is that what you call it?" he said, then eased off. "So, you didn't take the money?"

"No, Jim. I told you. I might be a lot of things, but I'm no thief, thank you very much."

"So, who did? This place was locked down all night and all morning."

"I have no idea," she replied. "Are we going to see this farm, or not?"

"Are you going to play nice?"

She held out a hand to help him up.

"That's some grip you've got there, Anna."

"I wasn't even trying," she replied, as they walked past the abbey and down the hill side by side.

"Aye, well. I wasn't quite ready for that. Lucky for you, mind. Had I had a wee bit of warning, you might have met your match."

"Is that right?" she said, as they came to the tree line and stared up at the overgrown farm ahead of them.

They were both silent for a few moments while they took in the sight. A few rusted, corrugated metal roofs jutted above the growth, and some bright blue oil drums lay on their sides by the side of the track.

"Not exactly Emmerdale Farm, is it?" Gillespie said.

"It's Emmerdale," Nillson said.

"That's what I said."

"No, it's just Emmerdale. Not Emmerdale Farm."

"Since when?"

"They changed the whole show. Modernised it years ago."

"Can't leave anything alone, can they? Always tinkering with stuff. Modernising, my backside–"

"Shut up," Nillson said, holding her hand up to silence him.

"So much for the nice Anna," Gillespie said. "That lasted all of, what? Two minutes?"

"I said, shut up," she hissed. "Listen?"

And then he heard it. Or at least he thought he did.

"What was that?" he said. "Was that a dog?"

"No. Not *a* dog," she replied, then turned to him. "Many dogs. Plural. We're going to need a K9 unit."

CHAPTER THIRTY

"Sergeant Priest. It's Ben Savage. We need a unit to collect a suspect, and one more to perform a house search. Do you have anyone free?" Ben said into the phone while Freya drove. Hearing just one side of the conversation, Freya could only imagine Priest's heavy Yorkshire accent grumbling away behind the custody desk. "It's an address in Bardney. Chapman is upstairs. She's dealing with the court now to get the warrant. She'll give you the details."

He paused for a few moments while Priest took his notes, then Freya heard Priest's familiar Northern grumble over the phone's tiny speaker. But it wasn't the short, curt thanks she had expected to hear. It was a long sentence, engaging, and judging by Ben's surprised expression, he hadn't been expecting it either.

"Thanks for letting me know, Priest," he said, and he ended the call. "Gillespie and Nillson have requested a dog unit at the farm."

"Are they going for a walk?" Freya asked.

"They also asked for handlers. Sounds like they've come up against a few challenges."

"Yes. Well, until my phone rings, I'll assume they can handle it."

"I still can't believe you didn't tell me about Chapman sooner," Ben said, when they were pulling up outside the Woods' house. He clicked off his seat belt and opened his door. But before he climbed down from the large SUV, he gave Freya a thoughtful look. "Did he try to hurt her? You know? Sexually?"

"I didn't ask," Freya lied, watching with curiosity as he mulled over the problem.

"Did she give any details about him? Hair colour, age, or height, even?"

"It was dark when she hit the dog, dark when he caught her outside her house, and dark when she found him standing at the end of the bed."

"I'll talk to her," Ben replied.

"Right now, I need you to focus on John Carson," Freya reminded him. "At least for the next hour or so. What are your thoughts?"

"My thoughts are that I'd like you to let me deal with Chapman's problem."

"And John Carson?" she asked. "What are your thoughts there?"

Ben sighed. "I think that if Theodore Wood still hasn't come home, then he's either dead or guilty. I don't care if people are telling us he disappears when he's down on his luck. It's just too convenient."

"But you hope guilty?"

"Of course," he replied. "We don't need another body."

"Is that your only motive?"

"I'd be lying if I told you I wasn't looking forward to seeing your face when I tell you where we're eating."

"Ditto," she said, as she slipped from the car and looked up at the house just as a curtain fell into place upstairs, as if somebody had been holding it back to watch them. "Somebody's home."

"You better get your credit card ready, then," Ben said, as he brushed past her and rapped three times on the front door. He stepped back to stand beside Freya, and waited for the door to open. "Do you think he's home?"

"Unlike you, Ben, I'm hoping he's not."

Ben took the statement to mean Freya hoped Theodore Wood was dead, and gave her a concerned look just as the door opened, and Freya forced a professional yet stern smile.

"Charlotte," she said. "Is now a good time to talk?"

For such a simple question, Charlotte seemed to take a little too long to answer, and she glanced over her shoulder furtively. She wore a baggy, floral top that hung from one shoulder, and a pair of loose-fitting jeans that seemed to be designed to wear with boots. Instead of boots, however, she had bare feet, and her toes clenched like fists while she considered her response.

"I suppose," she said, stepping back and opening the door wider.

Footsteps thundered across the floor above, and a shadow passed across the wall of the upstairs landing. But nobody stepped into view, and Freya chose not to question who it might be, certain of the answer.

"I'll make some tea," Charlotte said, when Ben and Freya were in the living room.

"Not on our behalf, I hope," Freya replied. "We won't be staying."

Charlotte seemed to loiter in the doorway, unsure if she should stay or go and make herself a cup. So, Freya made the decision for her.

"We have some news, Charlotte. But before we get into that, I wonder if there was something you wanted to say to me?"

"Something I want to say? Like what?"

"Like who killed John Carson," Ben said.

"I don't know. I told you, I don't know–"

"I'm giving you a chance," Freya said. "After this, it's going to be very hard for me to convince the CPS that you volunteered information."

"Information? But I don't have any information. I told you everything I know."

Freya glanced quickly at Ben to convey her regrets, then proceeded.

"We found the knife, Charlotte. We know you're involved somehow."

"Involved? Involved in what?" she gasped. "What knife?"

Over the course of Freya's career, she had learned to spot genuine panic from the type guilty parties portrayed. But of course, genuine panic did not necessarily mean the individual was innocent. More often than not, the panic was from the realisation that they had been caught.

"Oh, it's a fillet knife. The handle is wood, painted red. Probably matched a set years ago. But its counterparts have all been lost or broken. The blade is approximately nine inches long and covered in blood. John Carson's blood, to be exact. But do you want to know what else is special about this knife?"

Charlotte shook her head in denial and stepped back until she met the wall. "No," she whispered. "No. You're wrong."

"Wrong about the knife?" Freya said. "You see, I have two theories, as well as a few other lines of enquiry, that our colleagues are pursuing right now," Freya explained. "The first is that you killed John Carson."

"What?"

"You killed him, panicked, then ran," Ben said. "You ran into the derelict farm behind the abbey, didn't you?"

"No. No, I didn't—"

"What's there, Charlotte?" Freya said. "Why did you run to the farm?"

"I didn't. I don't know what you're talking about."

"Do you know who Solomon Yates is?" Freya asked, and Charlotte's face paled. She lingered too long before replying.

"No. I've never heard of him."

"I don't believe you."

"I don't. I've never met anyone by that name."

"I have a second theory," Freya said. "This one is a little harder to prove without your significant other though."

"Theo?"

"You see, if the knife came from your kitchen drawer, as I think it did, then even the weakest lawyer would be able to defend your fingerprints being on the weapon. But there are two things puzzling me. The first is that the handle has been wiped clean. There are no prints on the handle, yet the blade is covered in yours."

Charlotte did her best to appear unaffected by the news, but the fear was written all over her face.

"The second thing that's puzzling me is that your husband's car was found at the scene of the crime. Now why would he leave his car there?"

"I don't know," she said.

"One thing is for certain," Freya said. "Whether it was you or your husband that killed John Carson, I'm damn sure you were part of it."

"What makes you so sure?" she said, as Ben gave a little cough to announce the arrival of Priest's uniforms outside. Charlotte glanced at him once with a worried look on her face, then stared at Freya.

"We found a pair of women's underwear at the scene," Freya said. "Not far from the knife, in fact. It was almost as if whoever threw the knife also threw the underwear."

"Women's underwear?" Charlotte repeated, either not following at all, or doing a good job of pretending.

"Well, I say women's," Freya added, and she held Charlotte's stare and softened her tone, "more like a young girl's, really. A teenage girl's. Francesca's, to be precise."

"Francesca's?" she said, her eyes wide with horror. "You're sure?"

"You provided DNA samples. The chances of being wrong are no greater than one in a million."

"I don't understand," Charlotte said, as the uniformed officers rapped on the door.

"I'll get it," Ben said.

"John Carson and Francesca," Freya said. "I believe either you, or your husband, caught them. And until we find Theodore, I'm afraid you're the best we can get."

"No. No, you can't–"

"You found out about John Carson and Francesca, didn't you? You took the knife and went looking for them."

"No. No, you're wrong."

"You killed him, Charlotte. You killed him and took Francesca away. Hid her in the farm, I imagine. In one of the old, derelict buildings. But then you went back, didn't you? You came to your senses, and went back for him. To make a mockery of him. To show the world what he'd done. You laid him out naked on the rocks, didn't you?"

Charlotte shook her head, unable to speak. Her lower lip trembled, and she sank to the floor, her hands covering her face.

"I'm right, aren't I?" Freya said. "It was you and Theo."

A loud sob escaped Charlotte's mouth, and she wiped away the tears to stare up at Freya. Then she inhaled, long and deep, before nodding to confirm Freya was right on at least one account.

"I thought so," Freya said, then eyed Ben in the doorway with the uniforms lined up behind him. "Nick her. Then turn this place upside down."

CHAPTER THIRTY-ONE

The land had been given over to nature through idle hands. Tall grass concealed much of the waste, including an old washing machine and car tyre, and heavy brambles had almost consumed an old, rusted Ford Escort van.

"Would you look at that?" Gillespie said, peering into the bush. "I had one of those back in the day. Went everywhere in it, I did."

"It's going to take us weeks to search this place," Nillson said, ignoring his comment about the old car.

The two dog handlers, each wearing peaked caps, guided two snarling and growling German Shepherds around the corner on rigid nooses.

"Thanks, boys," Gillespie told them. "Wouldn't have fancied my chances with either of those two."

"No problem," the first handler replied. "They were chained up. Poor things are starving."

"My sentiment exactly," Gillespie said, as they watched the two handlers walk the dogs back to the vehicles. "It's the hunger that worries me."

The handler stopped and turned back to Gillespie, keeping the German Shepherd at a distance.

"Anything else?" he asked, to which Gillespie shook his head. "No. You're all done. What happens to them?"

"The pound. If they can be rehomed, then great. Otherwise, they'll be destroyed."

"Poor buggers."

"We see it all the time," the handler said, as he turned to re-join his colleague. "It's just a shame we can't do the same to the owners."

Gillespie and Nillson watched the two men struggling with the big dogs until they were a good one hundred metres away. Twice the dogs connected and snarled at each other, clawing at the other's face.

"Jesus. It was lucky you heard them," Gillespie said. "They would have torn us to shreds."

"Torn *you* to shreds," Nillson corrected him.

"Oh, I suppose you'd have calmed them down, would you? No, don't tell me. You would have got them in a headlock? Look at them. They're like bloody wolves."

"No," she said, flatly. "But I'd outrun you. And that's all that matters."

"Now then," a voice called out from behind them, gruff and irritated. "What's all this?"

They turned to find a mature man limping towards them from one of the old buildings. He wore an old, tweed jacket that was ripped at the collar, a sullied flat cap, and wellington boots that had seen their fair share of the weather. A mass of silver hair sprouted from beneath his cap, and Gillespie estimated at least four days' worth of fine, silvery growth on his face. But what was more noticeable than his dishevelled appearance was the shotgun that hung over his arm.

"Ah, you need to put the weapon down, sir," Gillespie said, stepping in front of Nillson and holding his hand up for the man to stay where he was. "There's no need to have that."

But the man's gaze found the two handlers over Gillespie's shoulder, and the two dogs they were controlling.

"My boys," he called out. "Where the bloody hell do you think you're going with my boys?"

His voice lacked the ups and downs of the English language. There seemed to be no intonation. Just a single syllable in which the words emerged as one low growl, as a drunk might ramble his thoughts before slumber takes him.

At the sound of the man's rumbling call, the two dogs' fight for freedom increased.

"Hey," he called out to the handlers. "You leave them alone. D'ya hear?"

"Sir, if you could just put the gun down," Gillespie said.

"Eh?" he replied, staring at Gillespie with utter amazement, revealing dark spaces where yellowed teeth used to be. "My land. D'ya hear? Trespassing. That's what you're doing."

"We have a warrant, sir," Gillespie said, taking a step closer with his arm outstretched to calm the man down. "I'm Detective Sergeant Gillespie. This is Detective Sergeant Nillson. We just want to ask a few questions. Maybe have a wee look around."

"You what, sonny? Look around? What for? Where you takin' my dogs?"

"Mr Yates? Is that right?"

He stared at Gillespie through big, bushy eyebrows, and without looking, he began loading the shotgun, sliding a cartridge into the breach.

"Mr Yates, there's no need for that," Gillespie said.

"Tell them to stop," he replied, gesturing at the two handlers in the distance.

Immediately, Nillson put her middle finger and her thumb into her mouth, and a loud, shrill whistle stopped the handlers in their tracks. She held up a hand for them to stay where they were.

"They've stopped," Gillespie said. "Just as you asked. Now put the gun down, Solomon. Nobody needs to get hurt."

"Get off my property," he replied. He hadn't shouldered the weapon yet, but the position of his hands would make it easy should he feel the need to. "Bring my dogs back and leave me alone. I ain't never hurt no-one. You've got no reason being here."

"We have a warrant, Solomon. Someone was murdered in the next field. We believe they came here. All we need to do is have a wee look around, and we'll be out of your way."

"Nobody came here."

"We'll be the judge of that," Gillespie said. "Just put the gun down. I'm guessing you have a licence for that thing?"

"Nobody came here, I said."

"What's in the buildings? You've no livestock, Solomon. You've no crops. What do you keep in there?"

"My things," he snapped. "Mine. D'ya hear that?"

"What do you need the dogs for?"

"They keep me safe."

"From what? Eh?" Gillespie said, making a show of looking about him. He took another step closer. "Nobody knows you're even here. Look at you. You're a bloody hermit, Solomon. A hermit, out here all alone. What do you live on, eh? I can't see any crops."

"That's far enough," Yates said, and he raised the weapon to his shoulder, aiming the shotgun at Gillespie. "Bring my boys back. You can't take them away from me. They're not for taking."

"Put the weapon down," Gillespie repeated, and he stepped to one side to get Nillson out of the line of fire. "Do you have a kettle, Solomon?"

"A what?" the man replied, his face contorting with incredulity.

"A kettle? Tea. I think you and I need a wee chat."

Slowly, Yates lowered the weapon, but kept his hands firmly in place ready to shoulder it again.

"Tea?"

"Aye. We're not here for you. A man was murdered, Solomon. We think the killer came here afterwards," Gillespie explained. "Now, you can either help us have a look around, and I can arrange for you to get your dogs back. Or you can make life difficult, and you'll never see them again."

"Never see them again?"

"Aye. All I have to do is give the word."

"You don't want me?"

"Not right now."

"Tea, you say?"

"One sugar."

"And then you'll leave?"

"And then we'll leave," Gillespie said, glancing once at the two handlers in the distance who were waiting for an instruction.

"Tea it is," he grumbled. "Now bring me my dogs back."

CHAPTER THIRTY-TWO

In Bardney, the liveried car pulled out onto the road, and through the rear window, Charlotte Wood stared out at Ben and Freya, her face a picture of misery and guilt.

"Well," Ben said, and Freya just knew he was going to make some sarcastic comment about her methods, "now all we need to do is prove it was her in case she denies it in the interview."

"For a man with such confidence and talent, Ben, you can be such a pessimist."

"I'm a realist," he replied. "What happened to us waiting? You know she's going to change her mind."

"Not if I have anything to do with it," Freya said.

She turned and marched back into the house to find the two uniforms that Priest had assigned to help them with the search. Happily, she recognised one of them as Griffiths, a man with a bright future, and who had helped Freya's team on several occasions.

"You two, take the downstairs. We'll take the bedrooms. We're looking for clothing and anything else that will help us put Charlotte Wood at the scene of the crime."

"Ma'am," Griffiths replied, and he led his colleague into the living room. Freya took a pair of blue latex gloves from Ben, which she snapped on. "Right then. Let's do this."

"Freya?" Ben said, and raised an index finger, bringing her attention to the footsteps they had heard on the landing. "Should we...?"

She shook her head. "All in good time," she replied, and he nodded his understanding.

She led the way, noting how the stairs creaked loudly when she put her weight on each one. The carpet was worn to the point of being threadbare in places, the scuffed, green underlay showing through in defiance.

"It's a big, old house," Ben remarked. "I tell you what. Throw a few quid at this place and I reckon it'll be up there with the Carsons' place."

"Do you think there was some rivalry there? Jealousy, perhaps?"

"Hard not to imagine it," Ben replied. "John Carson certainly did okay for himself. Maybe Theodore had plans for this place? Maybe things didn't work out the way he hoped them to?"

"The story of my life," Freya said, eyeing the doors to the five bedrooms. "How do you want to do this? Split up and meet in the middle, or shall we hit it together?"

Ben pulled a face. "I've always had a thing about being in people's bedrooms," he said. "On my own, you know?"

"Why?"

"It's just wrong, isn't it? It's the one part of the job I can't stand."

"More so than examining dead bodies on Doctor Bell's bench?"

"Well, not that bad."

"Okay. Let's start at the front in the master bedroom," Freya said, and she turned on her heels and burst into the bedroom, stopping only momentarily to appraise the room. "Wardrobe," she said, and she pulled open the doors, dropped to her knees and began searching for an item of clothing that Charlotte or Theo might have tucked away somewhere.

She found nothing. But Ben had upturned the laundry basket and was filtering through the dirty clothes, using the end of his pen to operate the garments.

"Not happy about going through people's bedrooms, but you're more than happy to have a rummage through their dirty underwear?"

"Behave," he muttered under his breath. "I've had an idea."

Freya watched him. He was forming two piles. The first comprised mainly of what Freya assumed to be Charlotte Wood's underwear, night wear, and a few other items. The second was made up of was she guessed to be Theodore Wood's boxer shorts, t-shirts, and jeans.

"What do you notice?" he said when he was done.

"That Charlotte wears more clothes than her husband."

"Not just wears more clothes. She had about five days' worth in here. He only has two."

"She might get changed throughout the day," Freya argued. "Or he might be one of those that wears clothes two days running."

"The difference is huge," Ben said.

"It won't stand up in court if that's where you're heading with this."

"I know that. I'm just trying to get some kind of hold on Theodore."

"Why?"

"Well, it strikes me that the guy is missing and nobody seems to be bothered by it. Least of all his wife. I know she's just admitted to killing John Carson, but you have to admit, it's a bit bloody odd that he's disappeared right when his mate has been killed."

"So, you do think it's him?" Freya said.

"I didn't say that. I just think it's odd that he's nowhere to be seen," Ben said. "Do you think she's protecting him?"

"What? As in taking the blame for the murder? I don't think that's part of the marriage contract. Not when I got married anyway. Until death do us part, yes. In sickness and in health, yes. Not when hubby sticks a bloody great knife in his best mate's back. No."

"You can be so flippant, sometimes, Freya."

"Well, what do you want us to do?" she said. "We have to be realistic. We can't halt the investigation until we find him. We've got a lead with Charlotte. We have to move on that. If her husband turns out to be part of all this when he does eventually turn up, then great. We'll nick him as well. But for the time being, we've got a murder weapon with fingerprints on, we've got the family car, we've got the underwear, and we've got an admission of guilt. That's means and motive, and let's face it, she hasn't put up much of a defence about the opportunity, has she?"

"I guess."

"You just want it to be him so you don't lose," she said.

"Oh behave. Like I care about that. It just doesn't sit right with me. He could be out there right now doing this all over again. If the knife has Charlotte's prints on but the handle was wiped clean, then it could easily have been him. It was his car we found, not Charlotte's. And let's face it, who stands a better chance of bringing a man as big as John Carson down, Charlotte or her husband? I'm just saying, that's all. We're missing a trick here. Something doesn't add up."

"How about this?" Freya said, and she shoved the bedside table to one side, reached down, and collected a handful of pills. "There must be fifty down here."

"What are they?"

"Sertraline, if I'm not mistaken," Freya replied, feeling Ben's quizzical stare. She rolled her eyes and explained. "Anti-depressants."

"On the floor?"

Then something caught Freya's eye on the bedside table. It was one of the pills just poking out from beneath the alarm clock.

"Looks to me like they were swept off in a hurry," Freya said, opening the top drawer. She found what she was looking for immediately, and held it up for Ben to see. "The box. Sertraline. One hundred milligrams. Strong dose."

"You seem to know an awful lot about anti-depressants," Ben said.

"I should do. I lived on them for six months. But nowhere near this strong. Mine were fifty milligrams. If the doctor prescribed these then he has a problem."

"Yeah. The problem is that he's obviously not been taking them," Ben said. "Looks like he's been saving them up to…"

He stopped mid-sentence, hearing somebody on the creaky stairs outside.

"In here, Griffiths," he called out.

But it wasn't Griffiths who appeared in the doorway. It was Francesca Wood.

"What are you doing in here?" she asked, her head cocked to one side. "Those are my dad's. What are you doing?"

"It's okay, Francesca. We're police. We're just–"

"Do you have a warrant?"

"As it happens, yes, we do," Freya said. "How does a fifteen-year-old know about search warrants?"

"Where's my mum?"

Ben inhaled and looked to Freya for support.

"She's been detained, Francesca," she said. "Would you like to see her?"

Francesca shrugged.

"Is there something you want to tell me?" Freya asked, and she glanced up at Ben, nodding sideways for him to make himself scarce.

"I'll be outside," he said, and edged around the bed, then slipped through the door.

Francesca watched him with curiosity, then turned her attention to Freya.

"Won't you sit?" Freya asked, and Francesca shook her head. She was dressed well, and she spoke with an air of authority that one day would serve her well. But at fifteen years old, Freya found the tone to simply be irritating and arrogant.

Francesca shook her head, declining the invitation to sit.

"You're friends with Scott Carson. Is that right?"

"Our parents are friends. I guess that makes us friends."

"Scott is having a hard time right now, Francesca. His father is dead. Did you know that?"

She neither nodded nor shook her head, choosing instead to intensify her stare.

"Is that why you've taken my mum?" she said. "Do you think she did it? Do you think she killed him?"

"Did she?"

A shrug was the only response Francesca gave.

"Do you know something?" Freya asked, eliciting nothing more than a trembling lower lip. "Did he hurt you, Francesca? Did John

Carson hurt you? It's okay. He can't hurt you anymore. But I have to know."

She stared at Freya, seemingly seeking empathy, then gave a slight nod of her head.

"Yes," she said. "But she was just protecting me. I should never have gone there on my own. She told me not to. It's all my fault."

CHAPTER THIRTY-THREE

BURIED AMONG THE OVERGROWN TREES, SURROUNDED BY A WILD landscape littered with appliances, car tyres, spent gas bottles, and the waste from a once functional farm, was an old farmhouse. Ivy had claimed the walls and most of the roof, and the damp had eaten away at the window and door frames.

"You live alone, do you?" Gillespie asked, as the old man held the front door open. He wore tatty, fingerless gloves from which grubby, pork sausage fingers protruded. And up close, his beard was wispy, like that of a man who hadn't shaved for weeks or months.

"That's how I like it," he replied. "I bother nobody. Nobody bothers me."

He took the only seat and dropped into it with the huff and puff of an old man whose body complained at every given opportunity. What sunlight managed to break through the overgrown trees outside was then further inhibited by the tiny window in the south-facing wall.

The room was sparse. Just a single wooden dining table, on top of which a smattering of used cutlery, crockery, crumbs, spills, and leftovers seemed to fill every inch. The floor comprised of what an estate agent might call exposed timber, but what Gillespie deemed to be absolute filth. No wonder the dogs chose to sleep outside.

"You must have some contact with somebody," Nillson said.

"Must I?"

"How do you survive?" she said. "Who does your shopping, pays your bills, does your laundry?"

Gillespie glanced back at her when she mentioned laundry with a roll of his eyes. He could probably answer that one.

"I get by," the old man said.

"With no contact with the outside world? I find that difficult to believe in this day and age," Nillson said, just as one of the handlers leaned into the room.

"The dogs are back on their chains, Sarge," he said.

"Righto," Gillespie replied.

"Those chains are against animal rights laws," added the handler. "And the conditions they're forced to live in probably break about five other laws."

"They're happy," the old man said. "What do you know about them? You don't know them. Not like I do."

"It's okay," Gillespie told the handler. "Bigger fish to fry and all that."

The handler appeared disappointed, but nodded that he respected Gillespie's decision.

"Will that be all?" he asked.

"No," Nillson said. "Do you have a K9 with you?"

"In the cars, Sarge. We've got three with us."

"Have them check the outbuildings, will you? They'll do it faster than we can."

"What is it you're looking for?" he asked.

"You'll find nothing," the old man interrupted. "Not on my land."

"At this stage, anything they can find," Nillson replied. "If Mr Yates here is right, then it won't take long."

"I'll get Buster. He's a good allrounder."

"Thank you," Gillespie said, watching the old man avert his gaze to some inanimate object on the cluttered table. "We'll be out in a bit."

"Why don't you tell me about this place, Mr Yates?" Gillespie said. "What is it you do here?"

"It's a farm, aint it?" he replied. "I farm, don't I?"

"Is it a farm? Looks more like a tipping ground."

"Ah, see, what do you know? Nothing. That's what. This here's a farm."

"And what do you grow?"

"Grow? Grow?" he said, the confidence in his voice waning.

"Aye. That's what farmers do, right? Grow stuff. Wheat or barley, or whatever."

The old man scoffed and waved him away with a gloved hand. "None of that. Vegetables. I grow vegetables, don't I? Man's got to live."

"So, you just grow vegetables to eat? You don't sell them?" Gillespie asked.

"Course not. I eat them."

"What about electricity and running water?"

"I've got water and power. When I need it," he said, then flicked his head to the rear of the house. "There's a generator out back. It does me."

"You're living off-grid," Nillson said. "Off the land."

"Is that what you call it? I call it surviving. Getting by."

"Mr Yates, when was the last time you had a visitor?"

The old man shrugged, and feigned interest in that inanimate object once more. "Not often."

"Who knows you're here?" Nillson asked.

"A few. Not many."

"Any names?"

"Nope," he said. "Not that I recall anyway. Memory is none too good these days."

"Should you really be handling a shotgun if your memory is going?" Gillespie asked. "You can find yourself having a nasty wee accident. Out here all alone. Don't fancy your chances much."

"I fancy them. Been here long enough to know what's what, and who's who. And as for visitors, you're the first for a while."

"How long is a while?" Nillson asked, and the old man sneered at her.

"From the last time to now. That's a while, or thereabouts."

"Mr Yates, you're not being very helpful."

"I suppose you want tea now, do you?" he replied, and Gillespie baulked at the idea of drinking from any of the man's old cups.

"Forget the tea," Gillespie said. "Let's cut to the chase. A man was killed at the abbey last Friday. The killer ran into your land. So, tell me, Mr Yates. Did you see them or not?"

"A killer?"

"Anybody?" Gillespie replied. "Anybody at all."

"A woman?" the old man said.

"What makes you say that?" Nillson asked, and Yates inhaled long and hard, like she was testing his patience.

"If you were looking for a man, you'd have said so. But you didn't. You just told me the killer came this way. So, you're looking for a woman. Tidy, too. If the opinion of an old man still counts."

"Tidy?" Nillson said.

"Pretty," the old man explained, and a string of saliva joined his lips, like an electric current arcing between opposing poles. He added a toothless smile for good measure, then admired Nillson as she switched from foot to foot in search of a comfortable posture.

"So, you did see somebody?"

"Might have," he replied. "Although, information don't come cheap. Not in these parts."

"How much?" Gillespie said, retrieving his wallet from his pocket. "A full description."

"Your money's no good to me, sonny," Yates replied, staring Gillespie up and down in wonder. Finally, he flicked his eyes at Nillson then back at Gillespie. "What am I going to do with money?"

Gillespie turned to Nillson. "Give us a wee moment, Anna, would you?" he told her. "Maybe go and see about the handlers. See what they might have found."

For a brief moment, Gillespie thought she might argue, stating something about being the same rank now. But the excuse to get out of the dirty, old house was far too appealing, and she left. Gillespie watched her through the window as she walked away on her phone.

"It's just you and me, Mr Yates," Gillespie said. "How about you start talking? Tell me what you know. You must have seen something."

"There's nowt to say."

"Well then, I suppose I could just have a wee look about. And I suppose I might find something I shouldn't."

"You won't find nowt."

"Oh, I'll find something. I always do when I need to."

Yates' expression altered. He understood exactly what Gillespie meant, and his brow furrowed so that, with his loose and aging skin, he resembled a bulldog.

"I see."

"Should I go out and have a wee look about? A looky loo, as they say."

Yates sighed and sat back in the old, wooden chair so that it creaked.

"Average height," he said.

"Average height?" Gillespie repeated. "Right. I see. And her hair?"

"Brown. Medium length."

"Thought it might be. Eyes?"

"Too far away to see."

"Clothes?" Gillespie pressed. "Was she wearing a jacket? Trousers? A skirt? Glasses?"

"A coat. A black one," he said.

"Average length, aye?"

"Yeah. That's it. Know her, do you?"

"I've just heard her description before from twenty other people, each with something to hide."

"Jeans," he said, revealing his bare gums. "Blue jeans."

"And where did our average lassie go to?" Gillespie asked. "Did she just pass through? Or maybe she stopped somewhere. In one of your outbuildings, maybe?"

His question was right on cue. Somewhere outside, the dogs began barking. Deep, wild, and threatening barks of the two German Shepherds.

"They'd have none of that," the old man said, gesturing at the window. "Kane and Abel, that is."

"The dogs?" Gillespie said, as Nillson reappeared between the trees, glancing back over her shoulder nervously.

"My boys," he said, letting his grin fade to something far more sinister. "Nobody gets past them. If they're on the chains, she'll be alright."

The dogs began barking again, and Gillespie smiled inwardly when he saw Nillson flinch at the sound. He'd found her weakness, at last. She called out to somebody out of view, then ran to the window and tapped on the glass, before wiping it with the sleeve of her leather jacket.

"Gillespie?" she said, squinting to see through the grime, and the sage skin on the old man's face paled.

"Aye?" he called back. "What is it?"

"The handlers. You need to see this," she said. "They've found something."

CHAPTER THIRTY-FOUR

"Is there anyone who can look after you?" Freya asked the young girl. There was no doubt in her mind that she could take care of herself. But she was a minor, and if anything should happen to her, it would be Freya who bore the brunt of the repercussions.

"No," she replied. "I'll be okay. I can wait here. In case my dad comes home."

"Do you think he will?"

She shrugged. "Don't know."

Freya softened, and sat on the edge of the Woods' bed.

"We need to get you checked out, Francesca. We have people that can take care of you. Nice people."

"Checked out?" Francesca said, taking a step back. "I don't need checking out."

"You said John hurt you."

"He did. You have to believe me—"

"And I do," Freya said. "But we have to be sure he hasn't... What I'm trying to say is..."

"You think I'm pregnant."

"Well... I don't think you're pregnant, Francesca—"

"It's Franky. Nobody calls me by my real name."

"Okay, Franky. But there are other things we have to check too. We have to make sure you're not hurt. Inside."

"I'm not hurt."

"Franky, you're fifteen."

"I'll be sixteen soon."

"The implications, Franky. Do you know what an STD is?"

She nodded, but wasn't following.

"If John hurt you, as you say he did–"

"He did. I'm not lying–"

"If he did," Freya said, raising her voice to be heard above the girl, but not too loud that she might frighten her off, "then he could have passed something to you. We can treat it, if he has. And if you're pregnant, we can help you deal with that too."

"Deal with it?"

Freya sighed.

"We can help you. Whatever you decide. Listen, I'm not the right person to have this conversation with. But I can find the right person. A doctor. Somebody nice."

"You just want me to come with you."

"No, Franky. I don't mean you any harm."

But it was too late. Franky turned on her heels and sprinted back across the hallway, and all Freya heard was a door slamming.

She had been fortunate enough in her previous marriage to have only had her husband's young boy to deal with, and he was far too young for hormones to have come into play when Freya had left. She hadn't dealt with the tantrums, the mood swings, and the slamming of doors. But there was a conversation to be had, and better it be her than Ben, who had all the tact of a shrew.

She found Ben wide-eyed on the landing, and he flicked his head at the one closed door, saying nothing.

Freya tapped gently on the door with a fingernail. It was loud enough for Franky to know she was there, yet soft enough for her to realise she meant no harm. There was no answer of course, so Freya tried the door handle.

"Franky, it's me. I'm coming in, okay?" Freya said, and with a final *wish me luck* look at Ben, she pushed the door open. She had expected to find Franky clutching a pillow in the corner of her bed, or lying down with her face to the wall so Freya wouldn't see her tears. But instead, she found Franky stuffing clothes into a holdall.

It was a scene Freya recognised. She remembered doing the exact same thing the day she made the decisions to leave her husband. Greg, of course, had tried to stop her, and that had only infuriated Freya. So, she adopted a different approach.

"Where will you go?" she asked.

"Anywhere. Far away from here."

"Do you have family somewhere?"

"No," Franky replied, fast, as if the word had been waiting on the tip of her tongue. "I'll be fine. I've looked after myself for this long."

"I thought your mum took care of you?" Freya said, and the child scoffed.

"She can barely look after herself. In fact, that's all she can do. Take care of herself. As long as she's okay."

"But, Franky... You just told me she tried to protect you. Why would you say that if she tried to protect you?"

The girl stopped for a moment, gave Freya one of those bitter looks that only children seem able to get away with, then continued stuffing a thick sweater into her bag.

"Don't forget your toothbrush," Freya said, and earned herself a glare as a reply. "I'm just saying. It's the one thing most people forget when they leave home."

"Oh, yeah? How many times have you left home?"

"Only the once," Freya said. "That was enough for me."

"And did you forget your toothbrush?"

"I forgot lots of things," Freya said softly, remembering that day with the clarity she wished fonder memories bore. "And there were things I just couldn't fit into one suitcase. I had to make some difficult decisions."

She glanced across at the holdall, then back at Franky.

"Do you think you can fit everything that's important in there?"

The child seemed to consider it for a moment. Long enough for Freya to know that a lie would follow.

"I'll get by. I'm resilient. That's what my dad says."

"Resilient? That's a good quality to have. Especially if you plan on sleeping in a park, or in a doorway. Resilience will help. It won't keep you safe, of course. But it'll help you block out the pain and the suffering."

Franky saw through Freya's scare tactic, and she pulled open the drawer in her bedside table, rummaged around at the back somewhere, and then drew out a roll of bank notes, which she stuffed into her jeans pocket.

"Like I said, I'll be fine," she said, then zipped up the bag, shouldered it, and gave her bedroom one final scan to make sure she hadn't forgotten anything.

"That's a lot of money for a fifteen-year-old to have," Freya said. "May I see that?"

"It's mine. I saved it."

"I'm sure you did. But may I see it? I'd be happier if I knew you at least had enough to get by."

"It's. My. Money," Franky said, and made to leave the room, but Ben stepped into the doorway, and she turned to glare at Freya, as if Freya might ask Ben to move.

Freya held out her hand, and eventually, Franky sighed, reached into her pocket, and handed the roll of notes over.

Pulling the elastic band from the roll, Freya flicked through the notes. There were four twenties, one ten, and a five.

"Ninety-five pound?"

"So what? I saved it."

"You found it, more like," Freya said, craning her neck to look her in the eye. "You've been to the abbey, haven't you? Either yesterday or today."

"No."

"Why did you go there, Franky?"

"I didn't."

"This money belongs to somebody I know. Somebody who was at the abbey. Somebody who'll be very upset about losing it."

"What?" Franky said, pulling that face that teenagers do so well. "I don't know what you're talking about."

"Franky, do you realise how serious this is? Your mother has been arrested for murder. Your father is missing. And you've been to the crime scene. You're not helping them."

"Them?"

"Yes, Franky. Them. They're both suspects in a murder investigation. Your mother has already admitted to killing John, and there's no doubt in my mind your father's involved somehow," Freya said, then softened again when she heard how hard her tone had become. "This places you there. This means all three of you might be involved."

"I'm not involved," she said, panicking.

"So why did you go to the abbey?" Freya said, coaxing more out of the stubborn girl. "What else did you take?"

"Nothing. I didn't take anything."

Freya held the money up and raised an eyebrow to contest that statement.

"So, you did go there?"

Franky gave a long sigh, and Freya sensed tears were not far away.

"I found it near the stones," she said.

"The stones?"

"The stones where John was... You know? But I didn't take anything else. I just wanted to see," she said, her voice trailing off. "That's all. I just wanted to see."

Freya nodded sympathetically.

"What are we going to do with you, Franky? I can't let a fifteen-year-old girl wander the streets while her mother is in custody and her father is missing. I have to know you're safe."

"I'll be fine."

"I need you to come with us."

"Not to the police station," she said, shaking her head and backing away from them both. "I don't want to go to a home."

"Just until we've spoken to your mother, or we find your dad. Somebody has to look after you. The doctor has to look at you, Franky. What you said about John is a serious allegation."

Her world was falling apart around her. She let her head fall back and squeezed her eyes closed. Probably wishing the nightmare would just end, Freya thought. But then she resigned to going with Freya and Ben.

"Okay," she said. "But when my dad gets back—"

"When your dad gets back, we'll talk to him. And if he wasn't involved, then the both of you will be free to go."

"And my mum?" Franky said, and behind her, Ben pulled his phone from his pocket and showed Freya the screen. It was an incoming call from Chapman's desk phone. He walked out of view to take the call. Freya returned her attention to Franky.

"I'm sorry, sweetheart," she said. "I can't make any promises there. You need to come with us."

"Freya," Ben said, stepping back into view as he pocketed his phone. "We need to go."

CHAPTER THIRTY-FIVE

A FEMALE UNIFORMED OFFICER WAS WAITING IN THE INCIDENT ROOM when Ben and Freya returned to the station with Franky in tow. She had a caring face, and when Chapman introduced her as PCSO McAlister, Franky looked to Freya, her eyes wide, silently pleading not to be palmed off to a stranger.

Sensing how awkward the conversation could get, Ben caught Nillson's attention, and then Gillespie's, and ushered them to the far end of the room, where DI Standing and his team used to work, which had become storage space for chairs, whiteboards, and even an old overhead projector on a trolley. Freya held a hand up for Chapman to stay where she was. Another female might help, should Franky offer any resistance, and Chapman had a calm way about her.

It was times like this that Freya wished Gold was around. She may be playing a crucial role as FLO, but it was these situations where her empathy really proved useful.

"It's okay, Franky," McAlister said softly. "I'm going to take you to see your mum."

"My mum?"

"Yes. She's downstairs. When we've seen her, we've arranged for you to see a doctor. Just to give you a look over. Make sure you're not hurt. How does that sound?"

"I don't want to see a doctor."

"I'm afraid you have to," Freya said. "There's nothing to worry about. There's no shame in it. In fact, it takes a huge amount of courage to go through what you've been through. I think you'll find the doctor will be impressed at how brave you've been."

The teenager glanced around the room, finding Chapman's warm smile.

"I've seen the doctor," Chapman said, and all eyes fell on her. Even the low rumble of voices from the far end of the room stopped, as Ben, Gillespie, and Nillson listened in. Chapman swallowed hard, refusing to meet Freya's stare. Instead, she focused her full attention on Franky, as if nobody else existed. "She's a good listener. She understands. I had to tell her that somebody hurt me, just like somebody hurt you. And you know what? I feel better for it. For talking about it. For not being afraid."

"Somebody hurt you?"

"They did," Chapman replied, and there was a notable break in her voice. "But you have to remember that it wasn't your fault. You're not to blame. It was him. The man who hurt you."

"But what's the point? He's dead. It's not like he can go to prison."

"No. No, you're right," Chapman said. "But there may be other girls out there. Girls just like you and me. They may be hurting. We have to find them and help them. Do you understand? You could really help somebody else by seeing the doctor."

"Will you come with me?" McAlister asked, and she held out her hand for Franky to take. A few seconds passed, as Franky processed all the information. Then, slowly, she reached out and took McAlister's hand. Freya handed Franky's holdall to the PSCO and stepped to one side before holding the door for them.

"You'll be fine," Freya told her, but could think of nothing to say that would add any weight to what Chapman had divulged.

The incident room doors slammed closed behind them and Freya caught Chapman's attention. They said nothing, although Freya hoped they would when the time was right, and when they didn't have Ben, Gillespie, and Nillson listening in.

"You can come back now," Freya called out to them as she strode across the office to sit on the edge of her desk.

The three were silent. Each of them took their places, choosing not to look in Chapman's direction. Freya waited a few moments, until she had the attention of the room.

"We have Charlotte Wood in custody," she began. "In case you hadn't worked that out from our conversation with her daughter."

"I thought you said we should wait until we had a case, boss?" Gillespie said. "Now we've just got twenty-four hours to prove it was her."

"She confessed," Freya replied. "All we have to do is record that confession and then make damn sure the evidence is watertight. Her trial might be six months away. Anything can happen in that time, and it wouldn't be the first time a suspect changed their plea to not guilty. In which case, the defence lawyer will look for any cracks we have in our armour."

"So, we need evidence?" Gillespie said. "Aside from the fingerprints on the knife."

"The handle was wiped clean. Her prints were found on the blade."

"The Land Rover?"

"That's her husband's car. And he's missing. That alone is enough for a jury to question her guilt."

"What about the wee girl's underwear, boss?"

"What about it?"

"Well, they were found next to the knife."

"That doesn't mean Charlotte Wood threw them there. It could just as easily have been Theodore Wood."

"Then why has she confessed?"

"To cover for him, maybe?" Freya asked. Then she spotted a wry grin creeping onto Gillespie's face, like a time-lapse video of a flower in bloom in a David Attenborough documentary. "You called Ben. What was so urgent, Gillespie?"

"Ah, you know? Just a few wee bits and pieces we discovered while we were at the old farm."

"Spit it out, Gillespie. It's a Sunday. I don't intend on being here all day."

"John Carson's clothes, boss," Nillson said, and Gillespie glared at her for ruining his big moment. "They were burned, but identifiable. A nice shirt, slacks, and a pair of expensive brogues. We dropped them at the lab, and called CSI to go over the place."

"Where, exactly?"

"In one of the old outbuildings. We sent a dog unit out to have a sniff about. Found them in about ten minutes. It would have taken us days to search the place. It's a tip."

"So, we don't know they're John Carson's clothes?"

"Not yet. Unless there's some other naked guy running around Lincolnshire with a bloody great hole in his back," Nillson added.

"Blood stains?" Freya said, and Nillson nodded.

"And..." Gillespie began, clearly hoping to ride Nillson's wave.

But she beat him to it.

"He said he saw a woman," Nillson spurted, and Gillespie glared at her once more, his mouth hanging open in disgust. But she ignored him, and focused on Freya. "I think Charlotte ran to the farm with Carson's clothes and hid them there."

"Is he prepared to give a formal statement?"

"Probably not, boss," Gillespie said, taking the narrative away from Nillson. "He's not the friendliest of chaps. Lives like a hermit, by the looks of things. He came at us with a bloody shotgun. Not exactly what I'd call a savoury character."

"He came at you with a shotgun?"

"Aye, an old Remington. Probably worth a few quid, too. And before you ask, it's licensed. I checked," Gillespie said. "Crazy old goat went berserk when the handlers took his dogs away."

"Dogs? As in plural?"

"Aye. Two of them. German Shepherds. Big ones too. The old boy keeps them on chains so nobody can get onto his property."

"Right," Freya said, and she glanced Ben's way to find him shaking his head in disbelief. "Ben, what are your thoughts?"

"My thoughts are," he began, with a loud intake of breath, "that Lincolnshire's toughest female detective, a.k.a DS Nillson, and our very own two-hundred-pound Glaswegian gorilla couldn't get past two guard dogs and a crazy old man with a shotgun."

"Aye," Gillespie said. "You didn't see them."

"But a woman of average build, average length hair, and a long, black jacket did."

"Well," Gillespie said, and he looked to Nillson for support, "we weren't exactly sneaking."

"But he let her walk onto his property, get into one of his outbuildings, and then proceed to burn the clothes of the man she had just killed?"

"Aye," Gillespie said, and it was clear he agreed with the point Ben was making. "Maybe we were a wee bit hasty with our conclusion."

"Maybe," Ben said. "Or maybe we need to look a little bit closer at old man Yates?"

"Go back a bit," Freya said to Gillespie. "To what you said a moment ago."

"About the woman, boss? Or about the clothes?"

"Neither. The bit about you two being too hasty in your conclusion," she said, and gazed at Gillespie and Nillson in turn.

"Well, aye. I mean, we were just pleased we found the clothes, boss. It makes sense. It means we can trace Charlotte Wood's footsteps. You know? Complete her story. Evidence, right? You said we need to fill the gaps."

"It's funny," Freya said, when it all clicked together in her mind. "You haven't once yet mentioned the dog collar Nillson found."

"Aye, well. It's a dog collar, boss–"

"And you, Nillson. You seemed very keen to be the one to report what the pair of you found."

"It's good news, boss. I wanted to share it."

"You know, I could be mistaken, but I'd swear the pair of you are in some sort of competition?" Freya said.

"Competition?" Gillespie repeated. "With her?"

"The more I think about it, the more it makes sense. You've had a bet," Freya said. "Don't tell me, whoever brings the most valuable piece of evidence to the investigation wins? Or something along those lines. Am I right?"

"Ah, come on, boss," Gillespie said. "You don't think we'd..."

He stopped when Freya produced the roll of bank notes from her pocket and held it up for the room to see.

"You were saying, Gillespie?" she said. "Do you want to know what I think? I think that yesterday morning, when you, Gillespie, took Cruz to the abbey, and you, Nillson, took Anderson to go door knocking, you met up, and through some kind of heated debate about the allocation of tasks, you ended up having a bet. Am I right?"

"Well..." Gillespie began, and he was about to deliver some kind of fabricated truth when Freya, who was tiring of the charade, stopped him.

"Gillespie, I've worked with you long enough to know that should ninety-five pound land itself in your grubby, little mitts, you'd have spent the lot in the pub in under two days. Unless, of course, you had some way of doubling your money," Freya said, turning to Nillson. "And given the way you pair have been behaving, it's pretty clear that there's some kind of competition going on. Friendly, of course. Any other bystander might have deduced some kind of grievance between you. But, again, I know you both too well. If there had been some kind of grievance, Gillespie would be sporting an injury of some kind."

"Eh? Hang on," Gillespie said, but Freya ignored him.

"Therefore, there must be a competition with financial gains. Am I right?"

"Yes, boss," Nillson said, laying her cards on the table. It was typical of Nillson. She wasn't afraid of anything.

"How right am I?"

"Scarily right," Nillson replied.

"And when you presented your findings earlier, Gillespie asked if you had found anything other than the dog collar. He was referring to the money he'd lost."

"Yes, boss."

"The dog collar means nothing. You just had to have something in your bag to make him think you had found something important."

"Jesus Christ," Gillespie said in amazement. "You're like the love child of Sherlock Holmes and Mystic Meg."

"I'll take that as a compliment," Freya said. "Do you know what DCI Granger would say if he found out?"

There was a pause, during which time Gillespie and Nillson exchanged guilty looks.

"I doubt he'd be too happy, boss," Nillson said, her chin up, ready to take the flack.

"Quite right. He'd be extremely disappointed. Lucky for you, I have a rather more liberal view of gambling," she said, staring directly at Ben. "Whether for money, favours, or experiences. I won't say anything about this matter."

"Sorry, boss," Gillespie said, holding his hand out. "If you just hand me my cash back we'll forget all about it, eh? It won't happen again."

Freya stared at the money in her hand.

"I've got a better idea," she said.

"Eh?"

"The bet stays on," Freya said, an idea coming to mind. "But I'm expanding it."

"Expanding it?" Gillespie said, with his usual irritating way of repeating what Freya had said.

"That's right," Freya continued, the plan now fully formed in her mind. "To the whole team. Whoever makes the largest, most significant contribution to the investigation wins."

"No," Gillespie whispered in disbelief.

"Oh yes," Freya replied, pleased to see the beginnings of a grin replacing Chapman's forlorn expression. "And to make it fair, all submitted evidence, as of now, doesn't count. I'm drawing a line in the sand, as it were. So, if either of you want this, I suggest you buck your ideas up, and either find me something to get the CPS behind us with Charlotte Wood, or even better. Find me Theodore Wood. Dead or alive."

CHAPTER THIRTY-SIX

Custody Sergeant Priest had assigned interview room two to Freya and Ben. Then the heavyset Yorkshireman with the baritone voice and barrel chest followed up with, "Mrs Wood will see you now," and then winked, grinned, and fished his pen from his breast pocket before getting back to his work.

"Thank you, Michael," Freya said. "Has her legal representative arrived?"

"Duty Solicitor arrived ten minutes ago," he said. "Which makes a nice change."

"I don't know what we'd do without you," Freya replied, then pushed through the double doors into the ground floor corridor. "Do you want me to lead?"

"Well, you arrested her," Ben replied, overtaking Freya in time to open the door for her. "And after all, I am forever in your shadow."

He shoved open the door and stepped back.

"Mrs Wood. How nice to see you again," Freya said. "We'll keep this as brief as we can. Ben, can you do the honours with the recording, please?"

While Ben prepared the tape and set the recording up, Freya flicked through her file, much to the annoyance of the duty solicitor.

He was a slight man with feminine hands, a long, pointed chin, and sunken eyes encircled by dark rings.

"Will you be submitting further evidence?" he said, his monotone, almost robotic voice matching that of his appearance – weak and without substance. He held up a similar file to that of Freya's, only thinner. "Or is this all you have?"

Glancing across at Ben just as he pressed the record button, Freya waited for the long beep to finish before she began. She announced the date and time, then introduced herself and Ben, leaving a space for the solicitor to follow suit.

"Harold Gough. Legal representative," he said, then, with a slight movement of his head, he advised his client to do the same.

"Charlotte Wood," she said quietly.

"Mrs Wood," Freya began, "I'll begin by reminding you of the charges against you. Then perhaps we can go over the events that took place three days ago. You are under arrest on suspicion of murder. You do not have to say anything, but it may harm your defence if you do not mention when questioned something which you later rely on in court. Anything you do say may be given in evidence. Do you understand, Charlotte?"

She nodded, as they always do.

"For the recording, please."

"I understand," she said, her voice cracked from emotions and exhaustion.

"You have verbally accepted responsibility of the crimes that took place at Tupholme Abbey, namely the murder of John Carson. I wonder if, for the benefit of the ladies and gentlemen of your jury, should this lead to a trial, if you could supply an account of those events?"

"You want to know what happened?" Charlotte said. "You want to know why I did it?"

"That's correct."

"But I've admitted to it. I told you I did it."

It was then that Harold Gough leaned in and whispered in her ear. No doubt reminding her that she had the right to withhold any information at this point.

"No," she said, pulling away from him, as if he'd just offended her. "I'm telling them what happened."

The response clearly displeased him, and he took to his notes before raising a hand.

"Before we get into the details. I asked previously if you would be submitting further evidence. I am yet to receive a response."

"We have made a partial submission," Freya said.

"So, there will be further evidence."

"As and when we're obliged to submit it, yes."

"It's just that, right now, there doesn't seem to be any conclusive evidence that my client is guilty of this crime."

"Other than her admission."

"You know as well as I do that the evidence you've submitted to me is refutable," he said, and he referred to his file. "A knife with my client's fingerprints on the blade, not the handle. Some underwear with DNA that suggests it belongs to my client's daughter. And a motor vehicle that belongs to my client's husband."

"We also have a report stating that the deceased raped Mrs Wood's daughter, Mr Gough," Freya said. "I think you'll find that gives us the means, the motive, and the opportunity."

"But it's inconclusive. My client's husband could quite easily have carried out the murder."

"Could he?" Freya said. "Perhaps you know where he is then? You see, Mr Gough, had you read the report we've provided you, you will have seen that Theodore Wood hasn't been seen for nearly a week now. He went missing a few days before the murder took place."

"That doesn't mean it wasn't him."

"No, it doesn't," Freya said. "But it also raises quite a pertinent point, and I thank you for bringing this to my attention. You see, your client, Mrs Wood, has admitted responsibility for the murder of John Carson. So, when I learned that her husband, one Theodore Wood, has also been reported missing, I wondered if she was not, and this is purely my thought process, you understand, responsible for his disappearance, too."

"How dare you," Charlotte said, and she stood, shoving her chair back so it scraped across the concrete floor. "My husband is missing—"

"Mrs Wood, please sit," Ben said, raising a hand for the officer at the door to stand down. "Nobody is accusing you."

"She has a funny way of showing it."

"I merely said," Freya began, "that it was purely my thought process. It was by no means an accusation. However, now that you have made it clear where you stand on the matter, we could perhaps move forward?"

"I haven't seen my husband for days."

"Okay, that's fine. Can you sit, please?" Freya said.

The solicitor beckoned for her to do so, and she dragged her chair back to its place, eyeing Freya with complete disdain.

"Shall we start again?" Freya said. "By which I mean, perhaps you could give us an account of the events that took place three days ago."

"Am I being accused of killing my husband?"

"No, Charlotte. Nobody is accusing you of anything other than the charges against you. We just need to know how the events took place."

"But I already told you I did it. I told you I killed John Carson."

"Mr Gough, perhaps you could explain to your client why we need her to provide a detailed account?" Freya said to the solicitor.

He cleared his throat, fiddled with his pen for a moment while he selected his words, then closed his file.

"Mrs Wood, you are being asked to provide an account of the day's events so that your admission to the crime may be recorded and used against you, should you, at a later date, opt for a plea of not guilty," he said. "Right now, all Detective Inspector Bloom and DS Savage have is a verbal statement from you, which if I am honest, is inadmissible in a court of law."

"What does that mean?" she said.

"It means that right now, Mrs Wood, it's your word against theirs. You could deny you said anything and they would have nothing. Except, of course, a knife with questionable fingerprints, some of your daughter's underwear, and your husband's car. None of which would convince a jury of your guilt. There are simply too many other possibilities. Your husband, for example."

"Thank you, Mr Gough," Freya said. "Do you understand, Mrs Wood?"

There was a pause while she considered her options.

"I understand."

"Good. You mentioned before that you believed the deceased, John Carson, had forced himself on your daughter. Is that right?"

"He did," Charlotte said softly, despite Gough's attempt to advise her otherwise.

"How was it you came to believe this?" Freya asked. "And I apologise for the sensitive nature of the question, but if we are to get to the bottom of this, then I'm afraid we will need to have some very difficult conversations."

With Harold Gough having proved himself to be an adequate legal representative, Freya would need to play by the book. She would need to demonstrate that she had Mrs Wood's best interests in mind, while still pushing the investigation forward.

"I understand," she said again. "It's okay."

"So how did you learn of the relationship?" Freya asked.

"Relationship? There was no relationship. He raped her," Charlotte said. Then her face altered. She was remembering the event. "I caught him. I caught him doing..."

She paused, unable to complete her sentence. But the three others in the room all knew how the sentence ended.

"How did you react?" Freya said.

"Isn't it obvious?" she said. "I killed him."

"How?" Ben asked. "How exactly did you kill John Carson?"

"With a knife. In his back."

"Did you stab him once or twice?" Freya asked. "Or perhaps more?"

"Once," Charlotte said after a while, and she cast her eyes down to her fumbling hands. "Just once."

Freya felt Ben's stare, and she glanced his way, and if she read his expression correctly, he was thinking the same thing as her.

"And how was it you came to have a knife with you, Charlotte?" Freya said, and Ben nodded his agreement. "It seems odd that you should carry a knife with you."

Laying her hands flat on the table, Charlotte looked up and met Freya's stare.

"Because I knew he would do it, and I knew where."

"How?"

Charlotte inhaled long and hard, as if preparing to divulge information she would rather forget.

"It was last weekend," she began. "We were at the Carsons' place. You know? Like a get-together. The two families."

"Did you do that sort of thing often?" Ben asked, and she nodded.

"At least twice a month. We'd go to theirs, or they would come to ours. Leigh will never speak to me again, will she?"

"I think Leigh not speaking to you is the least of your worries, Charlotte," Freya said. "What happened this time to make you believe John's intention?"

"It was something Theo said," Charlotte explained. "They argued about it. John and him. He said he caught John upstairs with Franky. Nothing happened. Not then, at least. Apparently Franky had gone inside to use the loo, and John had followed."

"And that made Theo suspicious, did it?" Freya asked.

"Yes. He followed John. Found him in the bathroom with her. She was cornered," Charlotte said with a look of disgust on her face. "But when Theo interjected, Franky ran for it. Ran all the way home. The men argued. Leigh and I tried to calm things down, but I knew things would never be the same again. It was too weird."

"So, you left the party?"

"It wasn't a party. But yes. We left. We went home and found Franky in her room. I asked her what he did, and what he said, but she just clammed up. She refused to talk about it. She still hasn't told me what happened."

"And your husband? Did he say anything else?"

"He didn't have a chance. A few days after that, he went on one of his little jaunts."

Freya cocked her head at the use of the word *jaunt*. It seemed an odd expression to use.

"You honestly don't know where he is, do you?" Freya said softly, still playing to the rule book and keeping Charlotte's best intentions in mind.

Charlotte shook her head.

"The week passed. Theo was gone. Franky still hadn't said a word to me. It was like she blamed me or something. You know how kids can be?"

Freya nodded.

"They don't come with a handbook, do they?" she said, and Charlotte laughed a little, but it was a weak effort.

"I paid them a visit. The Carsons, that is. Last Friday. I was going out of my mind. I know it was the wrong thing to do. But I had to know what happened. I had to..." She sought the right words to use. "I had to get inside Franky's head. I had to know. She's my daughter. Do you understand that?"

"I understand," Freya said. "You were treading a fine line. You didn't want to accuse your friend's husband of something, but you still needed to know what happened."

"Exactly. Franky was nowhere to be seen. She said she was going for a walk. But she'd been gone for hours. And Theo... Well, he would have been bloody hopeless even if he was there."

"What happened when you arrived at the Carsons' house, Charlotte?"

"I took Theo's car. It was blocking mine in, so I just grabbed the keys. I wasn't even thinking. It was like something had taken me over. Another me. An angry and scared me," she said softly. "Leigh answered the door," Charlotte said, fumbling with her hands again and lowering her gaze. "I asked to speak to John. I could barely look her in the eye."

"But John wasn't there, was he?"

Charlotte shook her head, a sad expression transforming her emotionless eyes into a picture of pain and suffering.

"Leigh said he'd gone out looking for Franky. But his car was there." She looked up once more. "That meant he'd walked. You've seen where they live. It's remote. There's only one place to walk to."

"The abbey?" Freya said, and Charlotte's lips tightened in confirmation.

"It's where Franky sometimes goes when she's sad. Everybody knows that."

"How did John know she would be there?" Freya asked.

"Simple. I texted Leigh when Franky hadn't come home. I usually call her, but I couldn't bear to hear her voice. Not then. She must have told John. They knew I was worried. She said he'd gone out looking for her. But I knew. I can't explain how, but once I knew what was happening... Once I knew where John was, I knew she would be there. And I knew she would be in trouble."

"So, you drove straight there?" Ben asked.

"No. No, I went home first. I didn't really know what to do. I didn't know if I should call the police, or if I should try and find Theo, or…"

She dropped her face into her hands, and the tears rolled through her fingers. She'd done well so far to keep them at bay. But in Freya's experience, once the tears started, they wouldn't stop.

"I suggest we call a break," Gough said. "My client is clearly upset–"

"I have just one more question," Freya said, cutting him off. "And then we'll stop for a while. Is that okay, Mrs Wood? We have somebody here who wants to see you."

"Franky?" Charlotte said, her voice almost a breath. "She's here?"

"You can have some time with her after this. But I do have one more question. Are you okay with that?"

Charlotte nodded, and Ben handed her a box of tissues that were always to hand in the interview rooms.

"What did you do with John Carson's clothes?" Freya said. "You killed him. You moved him to the pile of stones. And you stripped him. What did you do with his clothes?"

The question seemed to catch her off guard. She averted her gaze while she thought of a response that would match her performance so far.

"I burned them," she said. "I took them home, and I burned them in the garden. There's nothing left of them."

CHAPTER THIRTY-SEVEN

IT WAS MCALISTER WHO BROUGHT FRANKY TO THE INTERVIEW room. Hard as it seemed, the interview room was far more conducive to a meaningful meeting between the two than a cell with just a plastic-covered, blue mattress to sit on.

She stood in the doorway in front of McAlister, seeming smaller than Freya remembered. But there was no grateful expression at seeing her mother. No look of thankfulness, as Freya had imagined there might be. Instead, Franky was cold. Almost scared to enter the room. Charlotte sprang up from her seat to hold her daughter, but Franky flinched away. It was only when Charlotte held her by the shoulders, and looked into her eyes, that Franky softened.

"It's me," Charlotte said. "I'm still me, baby."

"I think we'll leave you to it," Freya said to Charlotte. "But we can only give you five minutes, I'm afraid."

"Five minutes?" Charlotte replied, appearing outraged at the short time with her daughter.

"It's important that we get Franky to the hospital. Somebody needs to look at her, Charlotte. You understand why, don't you?"

"I do," Charlotte said eventually, turning to face Franky. "It's for the best, sweetheart."

But then something must have clicked in her mind. Some delayed motherly instinct.

"I should be with her."

"We can take care of her—"

"I'm her mother."

"And you're under arrest for the murder of John Carson," Freya stated. "There's only one place you'll be going from here, Charlotte. As for Franky, PCSO McAlister will be with her the whole time, and the doctors are all female. We have strict procedures in place. I can, at the very least, assure you of that."

If there was any fight left in Charlotte, it sank beneath the surface. She took a breath, smiled at her daughter, and squeezed her shoulder, then agreed.

"You'll be okay," she said. "You'll be fine. Just tell them the truth. Okay?"

"Your five minutes starts now," Freya said, and she edged past them to get out of the door, where Gough was waiting. Ben followed, and was closing the door behind him when Charlotte called out once more.

"Does she have to stay?" she said, pointing at McAlister. "This might be the last time I get to speak to her alone."

"She stays," Freya said. "Like I said, we have strict procedures for this type of thing."

She gave Ben the nod to close the door, and then turned to Gough, expecting a grilling from the man who, now she had seen him standing, appeared to have no spine in either the physical or descriptive sense. His back hunched under the weight of his head, and his feeble hands gripped his case before him, as a child might carry heavy textbooks to school.

"Do you have everything you need?" Freya asked, without meeting his stare. She was far more interested in Ben, who had stepped away to take a call.

"Not really," Gough replied. "You have your confession. But I still don't believe it's enough for the CPS to go ahead. She can change her plea at any time. Right up to the moment she steps up to the dock. Do you really think CPS would risk that? Because I don't. Imagine the costs of keeping her on remand. Imagine the costs of the case. But most of all, imagine the force's embarrassment. All that hype about a confession and she changes her plea. The press would have a field day. But most of all, the real killer could be loose." He sucked in a breath, sharp and designed to strike a chord in Freya's reactions. "I imagine they'd bring in someone else to run the investigation. You'd be shamed. Imagine that."

Freya smiled the best she could, watching Ben, whose animated behaviour gave her reason to believe one of the team had discovered something tangible. Something concrete, as Granger would probably say in her next meeting with him.

"You imagine a lot, Mr Gough," she said, "for a duty solicitor. What are you hoping for? Are you hoping this goes to trial, and your client submits a not guilty plea? Are you hoping for the jury to find the evidence refutable? Is that it? Maybe then you can get a job in a practice. Maybe then people will take you seriously. I mean, you'd have to invest in a few decent suits, of course. But you know that. You're hoping that, off the back of this little gem that has rolled into your lap, your career will take off. You'd be the solicitor who stopped an innocent woman from spending the next fifteen years in prison. The solicitor who stopped a young girl from being thrown into the cold hands of a care home owner, who will have no doubt received extra benefits for their trouble." Finally, Freya turned to examine the scrawny waste of skin and bone. "Imagine that."

"You must have more evidence to submit," he said, the strength gone from his voice, leaving the same nasal tone as before, but with a slight stammer, almost imperceptible. Like he had suffered with a speech impediment as a child, but had worked hard to overcome it.

"When my team finds the nail in the coffin, Mr Gough, I can assure you, I'll make sure you're there to watch me hammer it home," Freya said. "Now, if you'll excuse me. It's been a long day."

"You can't leave," he said. "You have my client in custody."

"Oh, I think I can," she replied, as she made her way along the corridor to Ben, who was just finishing his call. "I've got a confession, remember. We'll be charging her in the morning, when she's had time to think about where her husband is."

Ben pushed open the door to the fire escape stairwell and held it open for Freya. He gave Gough a final nod and one of his casual smiles, then followed.

"What did he have to say?" he asked, when they were climbing the stairs.

"Oh, he was just telling me he's a little short in the trouser department and wants to prove to everybody he's got more to offer."

"And has he?" Ben asked, when they reached the first floor. He held the door again, and ushered her through with a sweep of his arm.

"Judging by his weak hands and poor posture, and how easy it was to put him back in his box, I very much doubt he'll ever find somebody who wants to find out."

"I wasn't referring to the contents of his trousers, Freya," Ben said.

"Neither was I," she replied, pushing open the incident room door. "Who was on the phone?"

"Gold," he said, and Chapman looked up from her desk when they entered. "She has some news from Leigh Carson. She's finally got her to open up."

"And?"

"It seems Charlotte Wood's story about the two men having an argument last week was accurate."

The news stopped Freya in her tracks. She caught Chapman's attention and gestured for her to get her coat.

"What did she say the argument was about?" Freya asked.

"She didn't know. It was between the two men."

"Interesting," Freya said. "Yet another hole in the confession. Charlotte said that her and Leigh tried to calm the men down after the argument. It's not looking promising."

"Do you want me to do anything?"

"No. It can wait until the morning. I just need to figure out a way to get DCI Granger on our side. If I can do that, there's a chance he can talk CPS around," she said. "Let's go home."

"I'm not going home," Ben said.

"You're what?"

"I'm not going home. At least, not to my own house," he said, and he held out his hand to Chapman. "I need your house keys."

"What are you going to do?" Chapman said, a little frightened, but still she searched for her keys in her handbag. She found them and tossed them to him. "It's the one with the yellow tag."

Ben caught the keys and slipped them inside his pocket.

"Ben?" Freya said. "Chapman asked you a question."

"What am I going to do?" he repeated, offering Chapman a reassuring smile. "Some good old-fashioned police work. That's what I'm going to do."

CHAPTER THIRTY-EIGHT

The wine of choice for the evening was a chianti, Freya's favourite. She surrendered the only armchair to Chapman and sat on the floor on a cushion leaning against the wall.

They had watched Ben leave then driven home in an awkward silence. Both had changed into more comfortable clothing, which for Chapman was a matching loungewear set, and for Freya, her dressing gown with a pair of tracksuit bottoms that belonged to Ben. She had borrowed them once when she had stayed at his, and had to roll the waistband over several times. They looked terrible on her, but they were the most comfortable tracksuit bottoms she had worn in a long time.

"To good old-fashioned police work," Freya said, raising a toast to Ben in his absence.

"To good old-fashioned police work," Chapman replied quietly. She raised her glass and leaned forward to clink glasses.

"Ah," Freya said. "We don't clink glasses."

"We don't?"

"It's poor etiquette," Freya explained. So, they simply raised them instead, then each took a sip.

Freya let her head fall back against the wall, and she closed her eyes, savouring the wine. It was a bottle she had been saving for a special occasion, but deemed it suitable, if anything, to lift Chapman's mood.

"I hope he's okay," Chapman said, voicing her thoughts more than she was starting a conversation. "What's wrong with clinking glasses, anyway?"

"Well, according to folklore, it was a practice used to ward off evil spirits. It was deemed a working-class belief, which the snobs and toffs ridiculed. Society then adopted the practice of simply raising one's glass during a toast. It was another way to separate themselves from the working class. Silly really."

"Ward off evil spirits?" Chapman said. "They didn't believe in all that, surely?"

"Perhaps we should chink?" Freya suggested, seeking to raise a little hope in Chapman. She held out her glass and they chinked with a laugh. "Goodbye, evil spirits."

"Goodbye, evil spirits," Chapman repeated, and she drank.

But the elation was temporary. She closed her eyes, gently at first, as if she was trying to urge dark thoughts from her mind. But then she squeezed them tight, a sign that that particular battle was becoming harder to win.

"Denise," Freya said softly. She reached out and touched her hand, and Chapman instinctively slid from the chair onto the floor, then fell into Freya's arms. "It's okay. You're safe now."

Freya heard herself say those three words. *You're safe now*. They were the same three words somebody had told her less than a year ago. That same somebody who was now fighting her own mental battle.

"I lied," Chapman whispered. "I'm sorry. I should have said–"

"You don't need to apologise for anything," Freya said, strengthening the hug. "Do you want to talk about it?"

"No," Chapman said. "But I should. That's what they tell you, isn't it? That you should talk about your problems. A problem shared is a problem halved."

"That's what they tell you, yes. But I tend to think whoever coined that particular phrase had very few problems of any significance. You don't have to talk about it. Not if you feel you can't. When I had my own problems, I found that focusing on the future helped more than discussing the past."

"Sounds like good advice. Except, I can't see a future. I can't see myself without this burden. He raped me, Freya. I told you I fought him off, but the truth is, I couldn't. I wanted you to think I was stronger than I am. That I could take care of myself. And I think I could have pulled it off. I think I could have just gone on without anybody knowing. But when I saw little Franky, I felt I could help. That somehow by using my own experiences, I could help her. And I could heal a little in the process. Does that make sense?"

"You helped that little girl, Denise. There's no question of that. And if you felt good about it, even if it was just for a few moments, then yes. That makes total sense."

"I woke up and he was there at the end of my bed," Chapman said. "In case you're wondering when it happened."

"I wasn't."

"First there was the incident. When I hit his dog. I told him I'd call the police. That I'd hand myself in. But when I got my phone out, he shoved me, and then he hit me. I mean, a full-on punch. I kicked out and managed to get away."

"Denise? Oh my god—"

"Then he came to my house and threatened me on my doorstep. That was a few days later. After that, he would park outside my house. I think he even walked around the garden, peeking in through the windows. Whatever he was doing, he wanted me to know he was there. He wanted to frighten me."

"You should have told me sooner."

"He said if I told anybody about what happened, he'd know, and he'd be back."

"But it was you who was in the wrong," Freya said, and she pulled her away to look her in the eye. "Sorry. But, I mean, you hit his dog. What was it you were supposed to tell anybody?"

"That he attacked me, I guess. I don't know. Maybe he's got a record of violence? Maybe he acted in anger and he's scared of being put away again. I don't know."

"He came back again, didn't he?" Freya said, and she pulled another cushion across the floor for Chapman to sit on. She leaned against the armchair, and Freya handed her wine to her. "Just relax, Denise."

"Like I said, he was there. A few days ago. I woke up and saw a shape in the room. I fumbled for my glasses, but I wish..." she said, stopping to catch her breath and to stifle her tears. "I wish I hadn't. He said he'd seen me with the police. It must have been when Jacobs dropped me home. I had to put my car in to have the bumper fixed, and I asked Sergeant Priest if anybody was free to run me home. He must have seen me getting out of the car."

"And that's when he did it, was it? That night?"

She nodded, and wiped away a tear from her cheek. She was doing well. For somebody who had been through what she had all alone, she was stronger than anybody gave her credit for.

"You've been to the doctor, right?" Freya asked. "You've had yourself checked?"

"He used protection. He was careful. He knew what he was doing."

"He planned it."

"I think so. He wore latex gloves, too."

"Was there any hair?"

"He was shaved," Chapman said, and gave Freya an awkward look, then quickly averted her eyes. "Everywhere."

It was something that Freya's girlfriends back in London would have said without flinching when discussing new boyfriends, and may even have made a comment on the effort he had made. But something told Freya that even if the act had been consensual, Chapman would have still felt awkward talking about it.

"Definitely planned," Freya said. "Premeditated. He watched you for a few days to see if you had a partner. A boyfriend or a husband. When he knew you were single, he made his move."

"And how about you?" Chapman said, taking Freya off guard a little.

"Me?"

"You said you'd been through something similar," she said. "You said you had your own problems, or something."

"Ah, you don't want to hear about that. This is about you."

"No. I do," Chapman said. "The distraction would be welcome."

Freya took a sip of her wine, but somehow her palette only tasted iron at the thought of the time Chapman was referring to.

"I can't tell you it all," she said. "It's a long and boring story. And besides, I've told it to more therapists than I care to remember."

"Is that what the therapist was for? Last year?"

"Oh, you heard about that."

"Jackie knew about it somehow. And when Jackie knows…"

"Everyone knows. Yeah, right," Freya said. "What did she tell you?"

"Surprisingly little. For Jackie, I mean. She just wanted me to know that you might not be yourself. I think she was looking out for you. She never means anything malicious. She's not like that."

"Yes. I know. She's got a good heart."

"And a big mouth," Chapman said, smiling just a little.

Freya took another sip of wine, then leaned back against the wall, twirling the glass in her fingers.

"It was a serial killer investigation. A big one. Probably the biggest of my career."

"James Marley?" Chapman said.

"Yes. How did you know?"

Chapman looked embarrassed, and suddenly defensive.

"I wasn't looking into you. Not behind your back, I mean. It's just, he was caught last year, right? Thankfully there aren't serial killer stories every week. Not in the UK, anyway."

"You heard about the case?"

"Yeah, of course. I didn't know you were part of the team," Chapman said. "Jackie never told me that part."

"Well, I guess that saves me having to rattle on about it for too long," Freya said. "The long and short is that I was kidnapped. He locked me in a room, hooded me, and left me there."

"He didn't…" Chapman said. "You know… Touch you?"

"I wasn't sure at first. It took me months to remember. And it was Ben who actually helped me. During the Jane Blythe murder investigation. Do you remember that?"

"I do, yes. That was before Christmas."

"Yes. Yes, it was. It seems like an age ago now."

"How did you get away?" Chapman asked. "From James Marley, I mean?"

"Ah. That's where things come full circle," she replied. "A good friend came to my rescue."

"A good friend?"

"I didn't know it then. But yes. A good friend. Somebody I'll always be grateful to," Freya said, and she swirled her wine, losing her focus to the pattern of cut glass and the tiny bubbles that formed. "I just need to learn how to show it more often."

CHAPTER THIRTY-NINE

An hour after Freya and Chapman's heart to heart, and more than half the wine bottle, Freya placed her empty glass on the wooden floor, topped it up, saving the remaining glass for Chapman, then leaned back against the wall. She stretched her legs out before her, flexing her toes. It was nice to have bare feet. Her first winter in Lincolnshire had been a cruel one. Slowly, as spring passed and the wild fens glimpsed the first rays of summer, the number of layers Freya had worn throughout the ever-lightened evenings had reduced. But to feel the cool night's air on her bare feet was a pleasure she had almost forgotten. Until now, that is.

She drank, she swallowed, and slowly, the woes the two women had shared waned, and the fog of John Carson's murder returned. But tonight did not belong to John Carson, just as it didn't belong to the force. Tonight belonged to Denise Chapman. The all-too-often unsung hero of the team's success. The quiet one, who despite shining light with her impeccable research from the shadows, now bore her own darkness. She was suffering.

Freya scrolled through her phone and, finding the familiar name in her recently dialled numbers, she hit the green button.

"Freya," he said, his voice quiet, and somehow Freya could hear the silence of his surroundings.

"How are you getting on?" she asked.

"I don't think anybody saw me arrive. I parked my car down the road," he said, and it sounded like he was settling down in the armchair Freya had seen through Chapman's window. "How's Chapman?"

"Taking a bath," Freya replied. "She's been through it, Ben. She's suffering. She really is. She told me things. Things I'll never repeat. Things nobody should have to repeat."

"I get the idea," Ben said softly. "It makes me ashamed to be a man. I hate it. I hate that some men see fit to treat women that way."

"You're a good man, Ben. I'm not going to judge you."

"Even still."

"What about you?" she asked. "What are you doing?"

"What do you think I'm doing?"

"I imagine you sitting in Chapman's armchair," Freya said, closing her eyes and letting the sounds and silences of the call inspire an image. "The lights are off. You're waiting for him to come. I imagine you're fixated on the front door. You're listening for the faintest of sounds. Like a guard dog. Keen and alert. Salivating."

"Salivating?"

"Well... I might have added that bit."

"You're surprisingly close. Except the salivating part, and the bit about being fixated on the front door. But I am in her armchair, and yes, the lights are out."

"What will you do if he doesn't come tonight?"

"Come back tomorrow. And the day after, if necessary."

"I always said you were tenacious," she said, and smiled as she sipped at her wine.

"You're drinking."

"It's a girls night in. We have wine," she said. "Do you want the good news?"

"Some good news might help me while away the time," he replied.

"Why not?"

"He's coming back for her. Whoever did this to her saw her getting out of a marked vehicle. He thinks she's gone to the police."

"He doesn't know she works for the police, then?"

"I assume not. If he does, he's either brave or stupid. But I don't think he does. I think he's found a source of enjoyment. He gets off on the power."

"You're psychoanalysing him."

"I know what he did. It was planned. He left no trace. Not even a hair."

"Don't tell me, she didn't go to the hospital?"

"If she had, they would have reported it to CID. She wouldn't have risked that. It was only when she saw little Franky that she felt she could somehow use the experience to do some good."

"Jesus, that takes some balls," Ben said.

"Metaphorical balls, I presume," Freya said. "So, how do you feel about our little wager? Are you still confident Theodore Wood has something to do with John Carson's murder?"

"You're changing the subject. Did I strike a chord?"

"No. Not at all. I just wanted to gloat. Did I tell you I found the restaurant where you'll be buying me dinner?"

"Do they have a happy hour?"

"*Non*," she replied. "*Nous ne sommes pas des paysans*."

"How much wine have you had?"

"Not nearly enough," Freya said. "So? John Carson. What are your thoughts? I haven't had a chance to bounce ideas off you."

"Well, you arrested the only other suspect, and we'll be charging her in the morning, so unless I find him, I don't really stand a chance, do I?"

"But still. Your thoughts still count."

"I think Charlotte Wood had something to do with the murder. But I don't think she acted alone," Ben said quietly. "She was wrong about the clothes. She's covering for her husband."

"Or she's afraid we'll find his body," Freya suggested. "I guess time will tell. Are you staying there all night?"

"Shh," he hissed.

"Ben?"

A few heavy clunks came over the phone, and Freya guessed Ben had put the phone down on a hard surface.

"Ben?" she whispered. "What is it?"

But he didn't reply. The silence now was deafening. And for the first time that evening, Freya wished she hadn't drunk so much.

"Ben, talk to me. Is it him? Is he there?"

A door creaked open somewhere on the end of the call, and Freya's heart was in her mouth. A footstep on her own stairs distracted her for a moment as Chapman stepped into view, bringing with her the warm fragrances of essential oils and shampoo.

Chapman came to stand in the doorway. For the briefest of moments, she appeared more relaxed than Freya had ever seen her. She was drying her hair while she stood there, and gave Freya a questioning look. But as hard as Freya tried to conceal anything from her expression, Chapman's intuition proved as great as her research skills.

"Is that Ben?" she said, gesturing at the phone in Freya's hand. Freya need not say a word. Chapman read all she needed to know in those few terrible moments. "Is he okay?"

The heavy clunks that had earlier indicated Ben placing the phone on a hard surface repeated. And a man's heavy breathing took precedence.

"Ben?" Freya said, and she fought every instinct to cry out to him. Keeping her voice calm and controlled, if anything, for Chapman's sake. "Ben, are you there?"

A silence followed, as long and terrible as the nightmares Chapman had no doubt endured and with only the sounds of a man's heavy breathing to accompany the darkness.

Then a man's voice. Confident. Breathless, but confident. "I'm here," he said, and the wet sounds of him swallowing hard came across the call. "I'm sorry, Freya. He got away."

"Oh, Ben. How? Was he in the house?"

"Walked straight through the front door. Bold as brass."

"And you saw him? You'd recognise him?" Freya said.

Chapman was watching her from the doorway, her face a picture of terror.

"The lights are off. He must have heard us talking."

"But you went after him—"

"He was too fast, Freya. I'm sorry. Tell Chapman, I'm sorry."

"I'll tell her. It'll be alright. At least he knows we're on to him. Or at least, that somebody is on to him," Freya said. "What are you going to do?"

"What can I do? Go home, I guess. Lock this place up the best I can and get out of here. He won't be back. Not tonight, at least."

"Well, then, I guess I'll see you in the morning," Freya said.

"Bright and breezy," Ben replied, his voice sullen and filled with disappointment. "Tell her, Freya. Tell her I'm sorry. I did my best."

"I will, Ben," Freya said. "I'm sure she knows. You're a good friend."

He laughed once, but it wasn't really a laugh.

"I mean it," Freya said. "Not many people would have risked everything like that. I'm glad you're on my side. Go get some sleep, okay?"

"I'll see you at the station in the morning," he replied, and then ended the call.

Freya let her head fall back against the wall, and she set her phone down to take another sip of her wine.

"He didn't get him, did he?" Chapman asked.

"He did his best," Freya said, and it warmed her to think that she could be so close to a man like Ben. Somebody so dependable and fiercely loyal. She looked up at Chapman and hoped in that single, solemn expression that she could convey enough faith and trust to help her through the night. "Just like I knew he would."

CHAPTER FORTY

Despite the beautiful spring sun, and the promise of a glorious morning the view from Freya's bedroom window had offered, a cold chill hung in the house. She was barefoot in her kitchen, wearing only her dressing gown, and stood with one foot placed atop the other for warmth, switching every thirty seconds or so to let one foot recover from the bite of the terracotta floor tiles.

The coffee machine seemed to be taking an age, but the smell of the beans was alluring enough for her to remain where she was, staring out across the fields. Although the roofs of the three houses Ben's family occupied could be seen, they were too far away for Freya to make out any detail. It was probably for the best. Had she been able to, she might have found herself standing, one foot atop the other, staring out of the window more often, coffee machine or not.

"Good morning," a voice said from behind her, and Freya turned to find Chapman in the kitchen doorway.

"Morning," Freya replied, then gestured at the coffee machine. "I think it knows it's Monday morning. I've never known it to take this long."

"That's okay," Chapman said.

For work, Chapman usually wore a knitted cardigan, a floral dress, below knee-length, of course, and flat shoes. It was as if she did everything possible to turn a man's eye the other way. There was nothing wrong with how she dressed, of course. In fact, Freya rather admired Chapman's ability to stick to her own personality, rather than adhere to fashion.

"How did you sleep?" Freya asked.

"I've always found that a strange question," Chapman replied. "How would I know? I was asleep. I don't remember having a nightmare, if that counts? And I certainly wasn't lying awake all night."

"That's good enough for me," Freya laughed, as the drips from the coffee machine halted, signifying it was ready. "How do you take it?"

"Black, please. No sugar."

"One black coffee coming up," Freya said, as she filled a cup and slid it across the worktop to her. She poured herself the same, then set the coffee pot down in the machine to keep it warm. "Are you ready for today?"

"I'm ready for the distraction," Chapman said. She cradled the cup in two hands and Freya followed her gaze to the window, and beyond. "Is that Ben's house?"

"One of them," Freya said. "Have you never been to Ben's house?"

"No. I've been here before. When you had that little party," Chapman said, and a hint of a smile crept onto Chapman's face – a welcome sight. She was referring to the time Ben had lost a bet to Freya and, as a result, had agreed to wait on her hand and foot wearing only a pinny. It wasn't one of Freya's proudest moments, but it was a good team building exercise. At least for the females in the team who had all admired his backside.

"What you can see is three houses in a U-shape. Ben's is on the left, his brothers' house is on the right, and his father's house is the one in the middle. The old farmhouse. The original."

"They're like a clan, then," Chapman said. "I couldn't imagine living that close to my family. Although, there are times when I wished I did."

"I think that's why he's so loyal. Did you know his family have owned this land for generations? I can't imagine staying in the same place for that long."

"Have you always moved about?"

"No. Not really. My father was a gentleman. Or at least, he considered himself one. Middle class. Born into money and all that."

"And your mum?" Chapman asked.

"She was the daughter of a traveller. A gypsy. Not the fortune-telling type. Nothing romantic like that. Just an ordinary gypsy who fell in love with a rich man," Freya said, as fleeting memories of her own childhood showed themselves, then faded. "How about you, Chapman? Where are your family?"

"I don't know," she said, and Freya forewent the view of Ben's house and studied her face. "Dead. Moved on. Forgotten."

"In that order?" Freya asked, and Chapman agreed.

"Dad died. Mum moved on. I don't know where. And my sister…" she said, pulling an uninterested expression. "Who cares?"

"I get it," Freya said. "Have you always lived in Lincolnshire?"

"Born and bred. I don't think I'll ever leave. Although, I haven't always been in Bardney. You could say I've lived in all four corners of the county."

"Well, I'm glad you're here. I'm glad you're on my team," Freya said, and she inhaled long and hard. "Shall we get ready? Big day today."

"Of course," Chapman said. "I imagine it *will* be a big day. In more ways than one."

It was nice to have another girl in the house, Freya thought. Someone to call out to when she was drying from her shower. To hear somebody else moving around somehow brought life to the old house.

"Seems weird," Chapman said from the spare room. "Charging somebody first thing on a Monday morning after working all weekend. I can't remember the last time we worked all weekend. I suppose it's common in the city."

"The days tend to roll into one in the city," Freya said. She was pulling on the jacket of her trouser suit and checking herself out in the full-length mirror. "I haven't really thought about it since I've been here. But I suppose you're right. I think we've just been fortunate so far. The thing is, the first few days following a murder are critical. We couldn't have sat around waiting until today to do anything. Imagine it. We wouldn't have a confession yet. No doubt Joe public would have decimated the crime scene. Everything would be harder, and our chances of success would be even smaller. That said, we still have a lot of work to do. We still have gaping holes in the story, and if I can't get DCI Granger on board, then there's no chance in hell we'll get CPS to give us the go-ahead."

"How are we going to fill those holes?" Chapman called out. "We need Theodore Wood. Without him, there are too many other possibilities. Even if CPS did give us the go-ahead to charge Charlotte, there's no way a jury would come to a unanimous conclusion."

"That's exactly my problem," Freya replied, as she sprayed her perfume into the air, walked through the cloud, then applied a little to her wrist for good measure. She stepped out of her bedroom onto the landing. "That's what makes me think this is all a very good plan. Without Theodore Wood, we can't charge him, and we charge his wife. It doesn't matter which one is guilty, does it? If we don't have him, then they both get off."

"What if he's dead?" Chapman asked. She stepped from the guest room, dressed exactly as Freya would have guessed she would be dressed. Although, her cardigan wasn't knitted and she was wearing a cute scarf, the type women wore in the fifties.

"And that's my second quandary. How do we find him?" Freya said, then smiled. "You look lovely today. Shall we?"

The longer Freya spent with Chapman, the more the woman seemed to come out of her shell. Even in the passenger seat of Freya's car, she seemed to no longer sink into the seats as if she wasn't there. She was upright, observant, and inquisitive.

"So, that's Ben's house over there, is it?" she asked, when they reached the junction on the farm track. Turning left would lead them to the main road and to the station. Heading straight across would lead them to the Savage clan.

Freya was about to turn left when she had an idea and sped across the junction towards the three houses.

"Are we going to his house?" Chapman asked.

"Yes, why not? Let's go and make him coffee or something. We have plenty of time."

They parked beside his old Ford, and a few moments later, they were at his front door. Freya gave her usual three raps and stepped back.

The door opened a few inches, and Ben peered out through the crack.

"Morning, Ben," Freya said. "We thought we'd come and say thank you for what you did last night."

"Last night?" he said. His hair was a mess, but that wasn't unusual, but there was no way of knowing if he was actually dressed or not.

"Do you want to let us in? We'll make you some breakfast."

"I'm good, thanks," he said, and he glanced over his shoulder. "I've had it."

It was the first time he hadn't opened the door to her. Something was wrong. Something was very wrong.

"Ben, are you okay?"

"Yeah, I'm just–"

"Ben?" another voice called out from inside the house. A female voice.

Ben's expression shifted immediately. He closed his eyes, the way he did when he knew he'd messed up.

"Ben, do you have a hair dryer?" the voice said. "Is somebody here?"

He let the door go, and Freya nudged it open to find Anderson at the top of the stairs with a towel wrapped around her.

Anderson froze, clutching the towel.

"I can explain," Ben said.

"Don't bother," Freya replied. "Just don't bother."

CHAPTER FORTY-ONE

The incident room doors squealed when Ben pushed them open. He held them for Anderson to enter, then let them swing closed with a bang. The whole audible episode was the only sound in the room, despite the entire team being in the office. Everyone had their heads down and were getting on with work. Gold was flicking through her notebook, typing up what she had written. Nillson was poring over satellite images of the crime scene. Chapman was typing away, as she normally was. Gillespie and Cruz were, as they normally were, doing their best to appear busy.

Freya was at the whiteboard with her back to the door, and Ben sensed the whole fractious mood was emanating from her, like she was some kind of power source capable of silencing entire groups of people with just a glare from her cold, grey eyes.

Anderson took her seat beside Nillson, who greeted her politely, and a low hum developed as the two began sharing details of their weekends. Nillson no doubt sharing what they had discovered in the investigation, and Anderson sharing her efforts at finding somewhere to live.

"Boss?" Gillespie said, either brave enough or stupid enough to poke the beast. "Seeing as it's Anderson's first real day at work, how about we celebrate with some decent coffee?"

"Be my guest," Freya replied without turning.

"What I meant was, how about the station gets us all a decent coffee?"

"Have we found Theodore Wood?" she replied, again without turning.

"Not that I know of."

"Have we eliminated every other possibility that John Carson's murderer could be anyone but Charlotte Wood?"

"No. Let's face it. It could have been anyone."

"Well then, I see no cause for a celebration," Freya said. She snapped the lid back onto her marker, and turned around. She looked good. Ben always liked her in that trouser suit. And on a similar vein, he always hated it when she refused to meet his stare. "Now that we're all here, we need a plan. Time is running out. DCI Granger will be wondering why we've had Charlotte Wood in custody for over a day and haven't charged her yet, not to mention why we haven't found her husband. And if I'm honest, I'm wondering the same."

"Hold on. I thought we weren't going to bring her in until we had something on her," Cruz said. "Did you all work this weekend?"

"She confessed," Freya said. "And yes, some of us worked."

"I would have worked. I could have done with the overtime."

"It was a freebie," Gillespie told him. "For the love of our jobs, apparently."

"Duty," Freya said. "And don't worry. You can book it in as overtime. I'm not as cold as some might think."

"So, Charlotte Wood killed John Carson?" Cruz said. "I thought they were friends."

"You'd be surprised what friends do. Even those who you think are loyal."

The last line was clearly aimed at Ben, and he felt himself redden at the words.

"Think yourself lucky, Gabby," Gillespie said. "You don't have any friends, so there's very little chance one of them will stab you in the back, in the metaphorical sense, and the physical sense. Now get down to the wee coffee shop and get a round in, eh?"

"Me? Why do I have to go?" Cruz said.

"Because you're the youngest and fittest."

"No, I'm not missing the briefing. I've already missed out this weekend."

"He's right," Freya said. "He needs to catch up. I suggest we send somebody else. I'll let you decide who."

Gillespie looked around the room.

"Don't even try it," Nillson warned him.

"I'm typing up my notes," Gold said.

"I don't want a coffee," Chapman said.

He couldn't ask Anderson. She wouldn't even know where the coffee shop was. And besides, it was her first day. What kind of welcome would that have been?

He turned in his seat and found Ben staring at him.

"Mine's a latte," Ben said. "No sugar."

"Ah, for crying out loud. Alright, alright. I know when I'm beat. Who's having what? The usual, aye?"

"Sounds good," Nillson said, and Gold mirrored her response.

"Actually, come to think of it, Jim," Chapman said, "I'll have a black coffee, please. No sugar."

"It's bloody great, this," he said to Ben. "A bloody decade in the force, and I'm still the bloody tea boy."

"You used to love going down there," Nillson said.

"That was until he found out the girl behind the counter was engaged," Cruz added. "I was there when he found out. Crushed, he was. Devasted, in fact."

"Aye, alright alright," Gillespie said, as a few of the others laughed.

"What was her name? Jenny, wasn't it?" Cruz said, and he adopted a Glaswegian accent, frowning with the effort. "Aye, I'm heading down to see my wee Jenny. I'd let her froth my latte any day of the week, if you know what I mean. Eh? Eh?"

The accent was terrible, but the team laughed. All except Freya, Anderson, and Ben.

"Very funny," Gillespie muttered, seeing he was beat on this particular occasion. He stopped at the double doors and turned back to the room. "You all may laugh. But it's me who's getting your coffee. You just think about that when you take your first wee sip, eh?"

He sauntered through the doors, clearly pleased he'd got the upper hand.

"He wouldn't, would he?" Gold said.

"Spit in our coffees?" Nillson said. "No. Not if he wants to see his next birthday."

"I wouldn't put it past him," Cruz added. "He can be a right–"

"I can be a right what?" Gillespie said, and he stepped back into the room.

"Right, enough chit-chat," Freya said, cutting them off before they began their childish bickering, and Gillespie left, the door closing behind him. "We've got Charlotte Wood in custody with a full confession. However, we still have gaping holes in the investigation. The knife could have been from anywhere. It may even be from the Carsons' house, in which case it's plausible that Charlotte's fingerprints are on the blade from when she helped wash up after dinner, perhaps?"

"I checked, ma'am," Gold said. "There's no match between any of the knives at the Carson house and the one in the photos Chapman sent to the team."

"That's good to know. Thank you, Gold," Freya said. "We have some of Francesca Wood's underwear. A fifteen-year-old girl. And we have a statement from the daughter accusing John Carson of rape. Needless to say, this is a route I am not prepared to go down until we have positive proof. Accusing a murder victim of rape is asking for trouble. His family would have every right to file a complaint. Nobody needs that."

"Bloody typical," Cruz said. "The first time we actually get someone to confess and we can't even charge them."

"It's a game," Freya told him. "She knows we can't charge her. The last piece of evidence we have is the car. Her husband's car, which she had access to. But without knowing his whereabouts, we don't stand a chance in hell of convincing either DCI Granger, the CPS, or a jury. So, today we find him."

"Ma'am," Chapman said. "Sorry to interrupt. I've had an email from the lab. They've got the DNA results from the blanket and the glasses."

"Go on," Freya said.

She had given the entire speech without once looking Ben's way.

"The blanket was clean. Freshly laundered, in fact. And there were two wine glasses. Both of which had John Carson's fingerprints on. Nobody else's."

"Why would somebody take a blanket, wine, and glasses if they were going to look for a missing kid?" Anderson said, her first contribution to the briefing. "Unless, of course, he was seducing her."

"True," Freya said, again without looking her way. "Seduction is a powerful manipulation technique. Although, where children are concerned, I'd rather think of it as grooming."

Anderson glanced in Ben's direction, and he nodded to confirm that Freya's statement had also been a dig at the two of them.

"There is one more thing, ma'am," Chapman said, and all eyes fell on her. She was doing well for a woman who had been plagued by a stalker. She no longer covered her bruised eye with makeup. Freya must have been having a positive effect on her. "PCSO McAlister is at the hospital. The doctor examined Franky. She found no sign of sexual interference."

Freya gave that comment some thought for a moment, although she did little to hide her confusion.

"Well, at least that's something," she said. "She's uninjured. Although I am sensing a *but* coming."

"She's also missing, ma'am," Chapman said. "McAlister says they left her alone to get dressed, and she did a runner."

CHAPTER FORTY-TWO

"Well, she can't have got far," Freya said. She glanced around the room to find her team wide-eyed and pausing for thought. "Does anybody have anything to say?"

"Check the car parks," Ben said. "CCTV."

"McAlister is already on it," Chapman said.

"Why would she run?" Cruz said.

"Do you know what the examination entails?" Nillson replied, shaking her head. "Do you realise what women have to go through?"

"Well... No, not really."

"Do you want to know?"

"I don't think we need to go there," Freya said, with a sideways glance at Chapman, who appeared to be busy dialling a number on her desk phone. "Needless to say, it's intrusive and unpleasant, and happens at a time when all the victim wants to do is curl up in a dark room. So, let's move on. Cruz, I want you and Gillespie to work with uniform. Find Francesca Wood. She has a mobile phone, and if you ask nicely, Chapman might just help you out with tech support."

"No worries, boss," Cruz said in Gillespie's absence. "We'll find her."

"Good. Nillson, you're with me today," Freya said, and she was just about to distribute more tasks to Ben and Anderson when DCI Granger entered the incident room. Freya stopped and looked up at him. "Guv?"

"A word, Bloom," he said. "My office."

"May I finish my briefing?"

"No. I'm sure DS Savage can pick up where you left off," he said. "You too, Anderson."

He left the room, letting the doors slam closed behind him.

"Anderson," Freya said, and for the first time, she actually looked her in the eye. "Get your things together."

"Get my things?" she replied. "Am I–"

"You're going to see DCI Granger."

"So why do I need my things?"

"Because when he's finished with us, you can go home," she said, collecting her file from her desk. "DS Savage. Perhaps you can shine a light on a new line of enquiry in my absence?"

She pushed through the double doors, not waiting for Anderson, and then entered Granger's office.

"Guv?" she said.

"I thought I asked you to bring Anderson," he replied without looking up from his paperwork.

"I'm here," Anderson said, slipping into the room, eyeing Freya with caution.

"Ah," Granger said, closing his file and removing his glasses. "Well then, let me begin by welcoming you to the team. I trust DI Bloom has made you feel welcome."

Anderson contemplated her words before speaking. As much as Freya felt betrayed, she admired the ability to hold one's tongue before speaking. It was a good trait to have.

"DI Bloom has done everything in her power, sir," Anderson said, with all the diplomatic honesty she could.

"Good. I expected nothing less. Now then, what have you got her working on, Freya?"

"DC Anderson will be working on the John Carson investigation, guv."

"Will be?" he said. "She's here now."

"There's the small matter of finding her feet, guv. A place to lay her hat, as it were."

"Oh. I would have thought one of the team would have put you up, Anderson. They're friendly enough."

"I'm trying to encourage independence. Besides, speaking from experience, it's best if Anderson finds a more permanent home before she gets too integral to an investigation."

"Ah. Wise words, Freya," he said. "You stick with Bloom, DC Anderson. You'll not go far wrong."

"Thanks for the vote of confidence, guv," Freya said, and Anderson smiled politely.

"Well, then, that's it really. Except, of course, to say that, should you feel the need, my door is always open. I daresay DI Bloom will have all the answers you might need. But it's nice to know you have an alternative. Keep your head down and your chin up, Anderson. You'll find Lincolnshire is rather a pleasant place to be."

"I like what I've seen so far," Anderson replied.

"Yes, well," Freya said, "it's probably best to stick to putting down some roots. Focusing on the job, as it were."

"Sound advice," Granger grumbled. "See what I mean, Anderson?"

"I do," she replied.

"Good. Well, that'll be all."

"One thing, sir," Anderson said, and he looked up in anticipation. "Will I get to meet Detective Superintendent Harper? I'm told he hasn't been in for a while."

"Ah," Granger replied, tucking his chin into his chest as he took a long breath to consider his response. He looked up in earnest. "I hope so. He's dealing with some personal issues. But he's a tough, old soul."

He opened his mouth as if he was going to add to his last statement, but thought better of it, and smiled softly instead.

"Remember what I said. My door is always open."

"Thank you, sir," she said, and Granger collected his pen and flipped open his file.

Anderson left the room, and Freya was about to follow when Granger's voice grumbled into life.

"Bloom?"

She stopped. He had a knack of waiting until she was nearly away before calling her back inside. Usually, it was to twist the knife a little further.

"I understand you have Charlotte Wood in custody with a confession."

"That's right, guv."

"Are you charging her?"

"I could, but–"

"But what?"

"But we don't have enough to go on. There are too many inconsistencies in her story. I could, of course, develop the narrative, but even if the CPS decide to get behind us, a jury will see through it."

"So, why is she in custody?"

"She confessed, guv. What was I supposed to do? Let her go?"

"Don't get smart, Bloom," he said. "You may recall I was singing your praises less than two minutes ago."

"Sorry, guv."

"What do you need?" he asked.

"I need her husband. He's been missing for a week now. He would have had access to the car, the murder weapon, and he would have had just as much motive for killing John Carson as his wife."

"Do you have any leads on him?"

"None. Nobody seems to know where he is."

"What does your gut tell you?"

"That he's dead, guv," she said, with no hesitation.

"And you believe Charlotte Wood killed him as well?"

"It would make sense. It would add complexities to her trial."

"You're worried she might change tact and enter a not guilty plea?"

"Worried isn't the word I would have used, guv," she replied.

"What word would you use?"

"Foresight. Through experience, guv. The suspect confesses with half a story. The police sit back and celebrate. Then, when the trial date arrives, they enter a not guilty plea. The prosecution look like fools and the suspect walks away."

"What are you doing to remedy the situation?" he asked, clearly unimpressed with the situation the team were in.

"We're looking for the husband now," she said. "And the daughter."

"The daughter?" he repeated, then referred to his file. "Francesca Wood. The one John Carson raped? I thought we had her? Who the bloody hell is looking after her if her mother's in here and her father's missing?"

"She bailed on us, guv. At the hospital."

"You lost her?"

"It appears so, guv. Yes," she replied.

"Well, I for one am surprised, Freya," he said, and he waited for Freya to prompt him further.

"What are you surprised about, guv?"

"Well, if you must know, I'm surprised you sat there and listened to me sing your praises to the newest member of your team without blushing. Are you that arrogant?"

"I'll sort it out, guv. It's a setback. That's all."

"I'll tell you what you'll do, Freya. It's not often I find myself stepping into one of your investigations, but I will if I have to," he said, lowering his voice. "Charge Charlotte Wood."

"Guv?"

"Or release her. Your call. Whatever you choose, just get on with it," he said. "I'll leave it to you and your wealth of experience to decide which is the best path to take."

"Guv," she heard herself mumble.

"Close the door on the way out," he said, as he pulled his glasses on, and returned to his reading.

In the corridor, Freya glanced into the incident room. She noticed that everyone was working, except for Ben. He wasn't there. She walked to the stairwell, listening for the door to the car park on the floor below to open and close, and then she slipped through the first floor door, where a large window looked out over the car park.

That was when she saw him. He was waiting by Anderson's car, leaning on it, the way he leaned on Freya's car. He said something to her, but Freya couldn't hear. She was expecting them to hug, or be close, but it was like he was making a show of keeping his distance. Then he handed her something. It was a piece of paper, which

Anderson opened, then she gazed up at him while he explained something. An address of a property, maybe? That was a good sign, at least.

She hated having any kind of ill-feeling towards him, and the pit of her stomach rolled at the idea that she might have messed things up with him, over what could have been an overreaction on her part and an oversight on Anderson's. There was something about her that was jarring Freya. Her mannerisms. The way she stood with her feet apart. Unladylike, Freya thought. Uncivilised, even.

Was he just helping a friend? After all, he was famously useless at understanding the female mind. Or was there something between them?

Either way, Anderson should have known better.

Down in the car park, Anderson climbed into her car and Ben shoved himself off, tapping on the bonnet three times, as he often did on Freya's car. He strode back toward the fire escape doors, and Freya slipped back into the corridor, and then into the incident room.

"Cruz, are you still here?" she said.

"I'm just waiting for Jim," he explained. "He's gone to get the coffees."

"Have you spoken to Sergeant Priest? You could make yourself useful and rally some troops while you wait."

"Right, boss. I'll get to it," he said, and left the room in a hurry.

"Gold, how about you?" Freya asked.

"I was going to see Leigh Carson, ma'am. You know? To see how she's holding up."

"Good. What's keeping you?"

"Well, nothing really," she said. "I was just catching up."

"Catch up in your own time, please."

'Ma'am," she replied, and began gathering her things, red-faced.

Freya stood at the whiteboard. There were far too many white spaces and much too little information. Behind her, the incident room doors squealed open slowly, then crashed closed.

She daren't turn. She couldn't face him. Not now. Not after Granger's clear message. She was losing this one.

"Who died?" Gillespie said, his voice loud and clear.

Freya turned to find him standing in front of the doors with a cardboard tray containing coffees for the entire team.

"John Carson died," Freya said. She grabbed her jacket and walked past him, collecting one of the coffees; she didn't care which. "Nillson, I'll see you by the car."

She pushed through the double doors, sipping at the coffee. It was sweet. A hazelnut latte, which, if she was right, was probably either Cruz's or Gillespie's. She burst into the stairwell and came face to face with Ben.

"Freya?" he said, just as surprised as she was.

She paused, and searched his eyes for a moment, before looking past him.

"Not now, Ben," she said, and she began descending the stairs.

"It's not what it looked like," he said.

"I said, not now, Ben."

"Do you remember what I told you when you first came to Lincolnshire? To this station?" he said, and she paused on the halfway landing and looked up at him. "The stairwell. It's rank free."

"I remember," she replied. "An informal place where anybody can speak their mind without fear of reprimand. Is that right?"

He nodded.

"So? Speak your mind."

"Open your eyes, Freya," he said. "She's hurting. Anderson. She's suffering, just like you were. You should talk to her. She can't be alone. She's frightened."

"And along comes Ben Savage. Healer of broken women from the south," she replied. "You should stick with her, Ben. She has your style."

"My style?" he said, as Freya descended the last few steps and opened the door to the car park. "What style?"

"Exactly," she replied. "My point, exactly."

CHAPTER FORTY-THREE

"What's this?" Cruz said, as he climbed into Gillespie's car. He held out his coffee with a look of utter disgust on his face. "This isn't mine."

"It's a flat white," Gillespie said.

"Where's my hazelnut latte?"

"The boss took it."

"Eh?"

"The boss took it. She's in her car over there if you want to go and ask her to swap."

Cruz stared through the windscreen then back at Gillespie.

"Not likely. She's in a right mood. What do you think happened?"

"Ah, I don't know. She seems off with Ben, too. That's when you know it's serious," Gillespie said, as he put the car into drive and eased out of the parking space, avoiding eye contact with the boss in her Range Rover.

"Something to do with Anderson, maybe?" Cruz suggested, when they were safely out of the boss's reach and on the main road heading towards Bardney. "She got sent home."

"Bloody hell. It's like being back at school," Gillespie said. "Where are we heading anyway?"

"Tupholme Abbey," Cruz replied.

"We're supposed to be looking for Francesca Wood, Gab."

"I know. So, I figured we'd have a look round the farm."

"I've looked around the farm—"

"I haven't."

"Why would she be at the farm? The last report we had was from PCSO McAlister stating that the kid had done a runner."

"Which one is McAlister?"

"Ah, you know her. She's the one with nice eyes and lips like a *Spitting Image* puppet. You know? Like she's allergic to something she had for lunch. If she got too close to a window, she'd stick to it like a cheap *I've been to Skegness* souvenir."

"Ah, her," Cruz said, clearly remembering who Gillespie was describing. "I spoke to Sergeant Priest. He's got a unit heading to the hospital to look for her."

"To look for McAlister?"

"No. To look for the kid. They're checking the CCTV and bus routes. Until they find her, we can't really do much. Unless, of course, you want to drive the streets looking for a fifteen-year-old girl with an attitude problem?"

"That wasn't at the top of my agenda, if I'm honest."

"Exactly," Cruz said. "So, I figured we'd go to the abbey and the farm. Have a quick looky loo, as you would say."

"I was there yesterday."

"I know. But I wasn't."

"Who have you been speaking to?" Gillespie asked.

"Eh? Nobody."

"Don't lie to me, Gab. I know when you're lying."

"I haven't. Honest."

"You know, don't you?"

"Know what?"

"You've been speaking to Chapman."

"What?" Cruz said, the pitch of his voice rising higher than ever.

"You have. She's the only one that knows."

"Knows what?"

"About the money," Gillespie said. "You want to go back to the farm to have a stab at winning the cash. My cash, I might add."

"Well... It would be nice," Cruz said.

"Ah, I knew it. You slippery wee–"

"You might have missed something."

"Right. And you think you stand a chance of finding it, do you? You think you can find what two dog units couldn't find?"

"Well, it would be nice to level the playing field."

"Level the playing field?" Gillespie said, and then an idea struck him. It was cruel, but it might just brighten up his day. "Alright. Alright, let's stop at the abbey so you can have a wee looky loo around the farm. After all, another pair eyes would be useful. You're right. I might have missed something."

"Good," Cruz said, although the way his eyes narrowed suggested he was far from convinced Gillespie's intent was all above board.

"Where's your jacket anyway?" Gillespie said, as they took the turning to Bardney.

"My mum has it. She's going to see if she can get those stains out. She wasn't happy about it, mind. She bought me that coat and it wasn't cheap. If it's bloody ruined, I'll be upset. I love that jacket."

"Right. Is she getting you a trilby for your birthday, so you can complete your private eye costume? Or have you asked for a cigar so you can look like Columbo? I'll poke you in the eye if you really want to look the part."

"You're funny, Jim. Too funny," Cruz said.

It was odd. Usually, he would have sulked, or moaned and whined, at least. Usually, he was easier to wind up. It was like Cruz was maturing, or growing immune to Gillespie's jokes.

"Gab, listen," Gillespie said. "Have you noticed you've been having funny dreams recently?"

"Eh?"

"You know. Sexy dreams."

"What're you talking about, Jim?"

"Is your voice getting deeper?"

"Have you gone mad?" Cruz said. "Has the job finally got to you?"

"What about hair under your arms? I mean, your body will be going through some changes."

"Oh. I see. Brilliant. Very droll."

"Jesus. What's happened to you? You had one day off, and it's like you're made of Teflon," Gillespie said, as he pulled into the little layby beside the abbey.

"If you must know, I'm trying to be taken more seriously."

"More seriously?" Gillespie repeated, feeling his mouth hang open in amazement that somebody could actually admit to that and not expect some kind of comeback. "Alright, alright. I'll respect that. It's good to see, if I'm honest. You should be taken more seriously."

"You think?"

"Aye. Of course," Gillespie said, and he nodded toward the abbey. "Shall we go have a wee looky loo? See if you can see something I haven't."

"Sure," Cruz said, straightening his collar.

"One thing, though," Gillespie said, trying his hardest not to smile as he said it. "Have you still got super sleuth powers without your Columbo jacket?"

Any confidence Cruz had gained over the last few minutes waned. They climbed from the car and Cruz stretched and yawned. He poked the plastic sheeting Gillespie had crudely taped over the window that Nillson had smashed.

"Haven't you got this fixed yet?" he asked.

Gillespie stared at him and the broken window.

"Does it look fixed, Cruz?"

He prodded the plastic to be sure, then looked up at Gillespie.

"No."

"I can see why you wanted to be a detective, Gabby. That was fine police work right there," Gillespie said, shaking his head. "Come on. Let's get this over with."

Gillespie walked fast. Mostly because he was fed up of being lumbered with somebody whose brain worked at an entirely different level to his own. It wasn't that Cruz was stupid. The boy had his moments of genius. He also had an uncanny ability to store information and recall tiny details from previous investigations they'd both worked on, or that Cruz had read about. He was basically a walking reference library. An annoying, walking reference library, Gillespie thought to himself.

He took long strides up the track and past the abbey ruins. He enjoyed hearing the sounds of Cruz struggling to keep up behind him with his much shorter legs. They reached the end of the field and passed through the open gate onto Yates' land. Had it been a well-maintained farm, they could have seen across the entire property. But the small plot had been handed over to nature, and clumps of brambles and weeds stood like islands among the sea of unkempt grass, which, just like the real oceans, had been polluted with human debris.

"Hold on, hold on," Cruz said, as he caught Gillespie up. "Can you slow down?"

"We've things to do, Cruz. No time to dilly dally."

"Dilly dally?"

"Aye, dilly dally. It's a phrase."

"Yeah, right. In Mary Poppins, maybe. Or in a Roald Dahl book."

"Shhh," Gillespie said, listening for movement. He sniffed at the air. "Do you smell that?"

Cruz made a show of trying to smell what Gillespie was talking about.

"Smoke?" he said.

"Aye. A fire. Tell you what. Why don't you go up that way?" Gillespie said, pointing at the vague pathway between the two eight-foot-high clumps of brambles he had used the previous day. "And I'll go this way."

"Split up?"

"Aye," Gillespie said, keeping his voice low. "We'll cover more ground. Go on. I'll see you at the other side of the property."

Reluctantly, Cruz stomped off with all the stealth of an embittered rhinoceros. He had his hands in his pockets, and could just as easily have been a young man out for a stroll in the country, lost in his thoughts.

Gillespie counted down from ten.

"Ten. Nine. Eight..."

That was when the two dogs began to bark, and the first scream echoed through the property.

"Seven. Six. Five. Four..."

The sound of a stampeding rhinoceros could be heard between the distinct snapping and snarling of the German Shepherds.

"Three. Two..."

"Run, Jim. Run," Cruz said, as he came hurtling around the corner. He passed Gillespie without looking back, his little legs tripping and stumbling through the tall grass.

"I forgot to mention, Gabby," Gillespie called out, his smile broader than it had been all day. "Look out for the dogs."

Cruz didn't stop. He ran from the property back towards the abbey and disappeared from sight.

The dogs silenced, until Gillespie rounded the corner. Having been there before, he knew the extent to which the chains would reach, and forged a path through the overgrown vegetation to circumvent the ever-watchful guard dogs. All the while, he followed the smell of the smoke until he could see the white plumes against the thick hedge that bordered the property. He rounded the last of the bramble islands and found the source. It was nothing more than an old incinerator, the type that looked like an old, metal waste bin with holes drilled into it.

But behind the old bin, lost in a haze of smoke and heat, the old man stood before an old shipping container; its doors were wide open, but the contents were lost to shadow.

"What are you doing, Yates?" Gillespie said.

The old man stiffened at the sound of Gillespie's voice. Then he replied, his voice cracked and dry, "Housekeeping." He dropped a pile of old newspapers into the fire and stepped back.

"What are you burning there?" Gillespie asked.

"Yesterday's news," he replied.

Gillespie stepped over, feeling the heat of the flames on his face as the newspaper took light. He kicked at the bin, toppling it onto the ground, and Yates jumped backwards, then began to stomp the flames before the grass took light.

But Gillespie wasn't interested in the grass. The whole place could go up in flames for all he cared. It was the contents of the container he was interested in, now glowing in the light of the fire.

There were at least four large dog cages, each with its door wide open. He kicked through the embers to find the smouldering remains of what looked like old clothes, but on closer inspection, he found them to be blankets, ripped and torn to burn faster.

"Dogs?" he said, and Solomon Yates stared at him defiantly. He scratched at his face with a grubby, old finger.

"They have to sleep somewhere."

"Four of them? What are the other cages for, Yates?"

"I used to have more," he replied.

"You used to have more?" Gillespie said, not hiding the disbelief in his tone. He kicked at the blankets, sending smoke and ash into the air. "Why don't I believe you?"

"Perhaps you have trust issues?" the old man said, eyeing the embers on the ground. Gillespie followed his gaze, and with the sole of his boot, he scattered the hot coals and logs Yates had used to build the fire.

Then he heard it. A faint metallic click. It was out of place in a fire of wood, paper, blankets, and coal. He spread the embers some more, searching for the sound.

And there they were. The charred remains of two leather dog collars, each with a little silver dog tag.

Gillespie looked up at Yates, who steeled himself, trying not to give anything away through his expression. Then Gillespie stepped over to the container.

"Like I said, I used to have more," Yates said.

"You stay there," he said, jabbing a finger at the old man. He peered inside, baulking at the stench of dog faeces. He could see that each of the cages had a padlock on the open doors. "What's the newspaper for?"

"To soak up the piss," Yates said. "Can't have my boys lying in their own mess, can I? That would be inhumane."

"Aye. Aye, it would. Do you know what else would be inhumane?"

The old man said nothing, and Gillespie stepped over to him as the breeze caught the thick smoke and engulfed them both.

"Stealing wee dogs from their owners."

"Ah come on–"

"Solomon Yates," Gillespie said, sure he was onto something. He looked the old man in the eye, and damn well knew he was lying. "I hope you don't have plans today. You're coming with us, sunshine."

CHAPTER FORTY-FOUR

The events of the morning weighed heavily on Ben. He sat in his car just two hundred yards from the station, alone and lost in thought. A vehicle passed him, rocking his car with the momentum, and he saw it was Freya, probably with Nillson in the passenger seat.

Ahead of him, parked in a side road, Anderson's SUV was parked. The car was so bland and common that nobody would look twice at it. It was the ideal car for somebody looking to disappear and start again somewhere else.

A few minutes later, there was movement in his rear-view mirror, and he saw Anderson running from the station. She opened the passenger door and climbed in, then breathed a sigh of relief.

"Anybody see you?"

"I don't think so," she replied.

"Did you speak to Sergeant Priest?" Ben asked.

"I did," she said, and nodded. Then she reached into her pocket for her notebook. "He was exactly as you said he would be. Very helpful. Very discreet."

"He's a good man is our Priest," Ben said. "Did you give him the number plate I gave you?"

"I did. He ran it through ANPR."

"And?"

"And," she began, "we have a name and an address. We also have a potential disciplinary if we get caught."

"Potential?"

"If we get caught."

"We'd better not get caught, then," Ben said. "Where am I heading?"

She opened her notebook to the last page, then flashed it at him.

"I know it," he said, indicating and pulling out into the road. "Are you sure you want to go through with this?"

"Of course," she replied. "She needs our help."

"And Freya?"

Anderson rocked her head from side to side.

"It's not the start to my new career I was looking for. But she'll get over it. In time, that is. I'm just sorry you've been dragged into this. You two are close, aren't you?"

"We are. Hopefully we still are, anyway," he said. "But, if I try to see it from her point of view, I can see why she's hurt."

"She thinks we slept together."

"She knows me better than that," Ben said. "The issue is never the issue, with Freya."

"What does that mean?"

"It means that whatever reason she gives for being upset at you, there's usually another far more obscure underlying reason. Something bigger. Yes, it may have looked like we had spent the night together, but the real issue will be something bigger. She's hurt. Betrayed, maybe."

"Well, then I hope what we're about to do is worthwhile," Anderson muttered.

"It'll be worthwhile, alright. Legal though? I'm not one hundred percent on that one," Ben said. "You don't have to do this. She'll calm down, you know?"

"I'm not doing it to get in her good books, Ben. I'm doing it because it's the right thing to do. I'm doing it because today is my first day in a new job and I've been sent to go and find a place to live, instead of making a difference. That's why we do this, isn't it? To make a difference."

"Most of us, yes," Ben said. "Not all of us. There are those that see this as nothing more than a day job. A means to an end."

"Like Gillespie, you mean?"

"Jim? No. He's like us. He's one of the good ones. In fact, everyone on the team is here to make a difference in their own way. Gillespie has a colourful background. The force gave him a way to channel his energy into doing good with his life. Chapman and Gold are both angels. I couldn't imagine either of them doing anything else. Nillson will go far. She just needs to tame her temper a little. But she'll do well."

"What about the little guy? The young one?"

"Cruz?" Ben said.

"Yeah, what's he all about? It's like he's fresh from school, but he's clearly in his twenties."

"Sometimes I think Cruz plays that role very well. I think deep down he's an intelligent guy who just needs a break. He's keen, a hard worker, and naturally inquisitive. He's just…"

"Just what?" she said.

"He's not street smart," Ben said. "I think that's the nicest way I can put it. But he'll get there. We all have our learning curves, don't we? Some are more pronounced than others."

She said nothing at first, seeming to appraise him until he looked her way, then turned his attention back to the road.

"You care for them, don't you?" she said, to which he shrugged.

"Of course, I do. We've been through some pretty tough times together."

"I feel like an outsider," she said. "I think that's my problem. Now that I hear you talk about the others like that, it makes me realise something."

"What's that?"

"I don't think I've ever belonged. Not really. Not like you just described."

"Well, for what it's worth, I think you'll fit right in here."

"You think?"

"I know," Ben said. "If the team didn't like you, you'd know by now."

"You mean, getting sent home on my first day isn't a sign?"

"That's a sign that Freya is under pressure. She's good, and I think you know she's good. You wouldn't have come all this way, otherwise," Ben said, as he turned into the street that was written on the scrap of paper she was holding. "Number thirty-two, right?"

"That's right," she said, looking for the house numbers. "It's on my side. Slow down."

Ben slowed the car to a crawl. The houses were modest but well-kept. Good, honest, working-class homes, his father would have said. Lawns were cut, windows were clean, and the cars on the driveways mostly shone in the early summer light.

"There," he said, spying number thirty-two. The house was semi-detached, one of a pair as opposed to the end of a long terrace. The walls were stippled and painted white. The windows were old, wooden frames painted black, and the roof sagged between two great chimneys. The two cottages were older than the rest of the street, set in larger plots than the neighbouring houses, which were far more modern and regimental in size and features. "I'll drive past. We can walk back."

He found a side road a hundred yards away, then turned in, coming to a stop behind a parked van before killing the engine.

"Did you see those old windows?" Anderson said.

"I did. They won't put up much of a fight."

"It's not the windows putting up a fight I'm concerned about," she said.

"I didn't see a car. I don't think anybody is home. With any luck, we can be in and out in under five minutes. Before any nosey neighbours come snooping about."

"Well, if you see anyone, call me," she said.

"What do you mean?"

"You're not going in."

"Eh? We said we'd do this together—"

"You're not going inside, Ben. I can't let you. It's my fault Freya's mad at you. If anyone is going to lose their job, it's far better to be me."

"No way–"

"I'm not letting you go in, Ben."

"I outrank you," he said. "Since when do you give me orders?"

"Not here, you don't," she said. "And it's not an order. It's a request. I couldn't live with myself if you lost your job because of this. Just let me go. I'll be in and out in a few minutes."

He stared at her, reading the sincerity in her face. She wasn't going to budge.

"Do you know what you're looking for?" he asked.

"Anything that links him to Chapman's house," she replied.

"Check for boots," Ben said. "Muddy boots. He was watching her through the window. I saw his prints in the flower bed."

"What a creep."

"What do you have in your pockets?" Ben said, and she removed her warrant card, slipping it into the glove box.

"Nothing," she replied.

"Good. Are you sure about this?"

"It's not the first time I've had to do something like this, Ben," she said, opening the car door. "Keep the engine running, and don't follow me."

She closed the door quietly, and, bold as brass, she made her way back towards number thirty-two.

"What am I doing?" Ben said, letting his head fall back onto the head rest.

He pulled his phone from his pocket. It was an involuntary move, and he hadn't even realised he'd done it until he was checking his messages. There was nothing from Freya. No missed calls, no text messages, and no emails. There wasn't even anything from Chapman, which was rare. She usually had some snippet of information to share with the team. Little nuggets of gold, he'd heard Freya call them.

He considered composing a text to see if she would respond. But she'd see through the attempt. She was far more versed in the games people play. Far more adept at pulling strings and pushing buttons. And she was pushing all his buttons, that was for sure. By simply ignoring him, she had sent him into a ruminating spiral. And it hurt, he thought. It hurt far more than he could have possibly imagined.

His finger hovered over Freya's name in the list of recently dialled numbers. But at the last minute, he scrolled down to the next name and pressed it to dial. He routed the call through the car's speakers and closed his eyes. He didn't really know what he would say. The call was a distraction more than anything.

"Ben?" Jackie said when she answered. "How are you getting on?"

"Ah, you know? One step at a time," he said. "Where are you?"

"I've just got to the Carson house. Leigh is in the shower and the boy is in the garden, sulking."

"How's she bearing up?"

"As well as can be," Jackie said. "It's all been a bit much for her, if I'm honest. I don't know how she's going to cope. You know how some people can just get on with stuff, like calling the bank, calling the lawyer, and all that?"

"Right?" Ben said, unsure where she was going.

"Well, Leigh doesn't seem to be one of those people. She doesn't even know where all the paperwork is kept."

"Her husband has been killed, Jackie. Give the poor woman a break."

"I know. I know. It's just... She seems so fragile. Every time I mention her affairs, she seems to curl into a ball and break into tears."

"Isn't it your job to help her through that?"

"No, it is not. I'm not a nurse maid. My job is to work with the victim's family as a conduit to the investigation."

The car door opened suddenly and Anderson climbed in. Ben held his finger to his lips to silence her.

"Ben? What was that?" Jackie asked.

"Oh, nothing. I got a ham roll from the coffee shop. I just threw it out the door."

"Lost your appetite?" she asked, as Anderson quietly produced something from her pocket. It was a photo, which she proudly turned to reveal in all its glory. "What's up with DI Bloom, anyway? She seemed really off with you this morning."

"Are you busy?" Ben said.

"Busy? Well, not right now. Leigh takes about an hour, and the boy—"

"I need a favour."

"A favour?" Jackie said, and Anderson smiled at the plan. "That doesn't sound good, Ben. When do you ever need a favour from me?"

"When I'm being outcast and I need something checked out."

"I don't know, Ben. I'm doing alright here. This FLO role is good for me."

"What if I said it was to help Chapman?"

"Chapman? How? What is it?"

"Do you have your laptop?"

"Of course. I have to take it–"

"Open it," Ben said. "I need a name checked out."

CHAPTER FORTY-FIVE

Freya and Nillson were entering Bardney when Freya's phone rang out over the car's speakers. She expected the caller to be Ben, but she felt a mix of both pleased and surprised when she saw Gillespie's name flash up on the little screen.

Nillson's expression remained impassive while she waited for Freya to hit the green button.

"Gillespie. I presume you have good news?" Freya said.

"Eh? Oh, aye, boss," he replied. "I think you need to see this."

"See what? Where are you?"

"We're at the derelict farm behind the abbey. I'm not really sure what to make of it, if I'm honest."

Freya glanced once at Nillson, who knew better than to comment while Freya was in one of her moods.

"Sit tight," Freya said. "We'll be there in two minutes."

She ended the call and said nothing to Nillson, who to her credit, also kept quiet. It wasn't until Freya had stopped the car behind Gillespie's in the little layby that Freya finally felt compelled to speak.

"I know I can be difficult," she said, and again, Nillson revealed no indication of what she was thinking. "I'm not mad at you. You should know that. I just go quiet when I have things on my mind."

"You don't need to explain, boss."

"I do," Freya said. "I should. A leader shouldn't let their emotions affect their team. But on this occasion, I'm rather distracted. Preoccupied, as it were."

A liveried police BMW was parked beside Gillespie's car, which intrigued Freya.

"Is there anything I can do?" Nillson asked.

"Turn back time?" Freya said, and she offered Nillson an apologetic smile then stared out of the windscreen at Gillespie's car. "What's wrong with Gillespie's window? It's broken. How long has he been driving around like that?"

Nillson shrugged and looked away. Then, moments later, she inhaled and turned back to Freya, as if she was about to confess to a major crime.

"If we're being honest, boss, it was me," she said, and gestured at Gillespie's broken window. "He blocked me in and refused to move."

"So you broke his window?"

"It was either that or physically attack him," Nillson said. "I figured that wasn't the correct way for a newly appointed DS to behave."

"And smashing a window is?"

"It's the lesser of the two."

Freya stared at the young woman, admiring her honesty and her courage. She really was fearless. Most of the team would have denied any knowledge and lied, especially when Freya was in such a mood. But Nillson had owned it. That took courage.

"Well, I'm glad you stood up for yourself," Freya said. She pushed open her door and made her way toward the track that led past the ruins and down to the farm, walking slowly to allow Nillson to catch up.

"What do you think he's found?" Nillson asked, when she was walking beside Freya.

"Oh, you know Gillespie better than I do. Whenever he finds anything, he enjoys making a song and dance about it. He likes to celebrate his little wins," Freya said. "But whatever it is, he's had to ask for some support. As far as I'm aware, the site is no longer locked down."

"A body, maybe?" Nillson asked.

"Are you heading towards making another bet, DS Nillson?" Freya asked. It was a light-hearted question, but given her mood so far that day and the light telling off she had dished out to Gillespie and Nillson only the previous day, it was understandable for Nillson to become defensive.

"No. Not at all. I was just—"

"It's okay, Nillson. My humour is a little off," Freya explained as they neared the ruins. But it was during the lull in conversation that Freya heard grunting. A man's grunting, to be more accurate. She exchanged confused expressions with Nillson, and when they came alongside the ruins, they saw a man on his hands and knees at the exact spot John Carson's body had been discovered. He was shifting the pile of rocks.

Quietly, they entered the field and, keeping to the well-trodden path that led from the track to the old building, they approached the man from behind.

"Can we help you?" Freya asked, when they were just ten feet away.

The man froze. Then he pushed himself to his feet and turned around.

"Boss?" he said, breathless from his exertion.

"Cruz?"

He was covered in mud. His hands were bleeding, and even his forehead had a layer of grime across it from where, presumably, he'd wiped away his sweat.

"What the bloody hell are you doing?" Freya said, and all Nillson could do was smile at the sight of him.

"Dogs, boss," he said, licking at his dry lips. He jabbed a grubby thumb toward the farm.

"Where's Gillespie?" Freya asked, and again, he jabbed his thumb in the direction of the farm.

"Two big German Shepherds," he said.

"I saw them yesterday," Nillson said. "They're on long chains, though. Right?"

"Chains?" he said, suddenly doubtful. "I didn't see any chains."

"Just tell me what happened, Cruz," Freya said.

"Jim and me, boss, we went down to the farm. He said he wanted to have a look at something. But there were dogs."

"And you ran?" Freya said, waiting for him to confirm. He did. He nodded slowly. "You left Gillespie behind with two savage dogs while you saved your own skin?"

"Yes, boss."

"And where is he now?"

Cruz shrugged.

"And what is it, exactly, you are doing?" Freya said, fighting the urge to reprimand him there and then. But she had a sense that Cruz wasn't entirely to blame where Gillespie was concerned.

"Thought I'd have a look at the rocks, boss. To see what's under them."

"I thought Gillespie said they were covered in moss? They hadn't been moved recently."

"Just thought I'd check boss."

"Because you were too scared to go back and check on DS Gillespie?"

"Yes, boss," he said, with more than a hint of sorrow in his tone.

"And have you found anything?" Freya asked.

Cruz nodded and swallowed, eyeing her with caution.

She peered into the hole he'd made in the pile of stones, but she was interrupted before she could question the find.

"What's all this then?" a voice called out, and they turned to find Gillespie walking towards them with two uniforms behind him escorting an old man wearing fingerless gloves, an old overcoat, and a thick layer of grime across his unwashed face.

"Solomon Yates?" Freya said.

"Aye. That's him," Gillespie said, holding the gate for the uniforms to escort the man through.

Freya waited for them to get close, then questioned the man's handcuffs with a single inquisitive expression directed at Gillespie.

"I found a secret little hidey hole," Gillespie explained.

"A little hidey hole?" Freya said with a shake of her head to convey that she would need more than that to understand why the man had been arrested.

"Aye, well. Not exactly secret. It's a shipping container buried under the brambles."

"And what was in this shipping container?" Freya asked.

"Cages, boss. It's a kennel."

"And is that illegal?"

"The kennel isn't. But the stolen dogs he keeps there are," Gillespie said, then nudged the old man into life. "Ain't that right, Solomon? You've been illegally trading stolen dogs, haven't you?"

"And what does that have to do with our investigation?" Freya asked, before the old man could open his mouth to speak.

"Nillson found a dog collar, boss," he said. "The Carsons lost their dog. Remember?"

"Oh, I remember alright," she said, then clicked her fingers for the old man to open his eyes. She pointed to what Cruz had uncovered in the stones. "Perhaps you can tell me how this got here then, Mr Yates?"

CHAPTER FORTY-SIX

Rounding the last bend from Bardney to the abbey, Ben and Anderson passed the Carson home, noting Gold's car in the driveway. Moments later, he slowed when he saw a liveried police car pulling out of the layby where the team had been parking to access the abbey.

"What were they doing here?" Anderson asked.

"I don't know," he replied, as he pulled into the empty space. "Maybe one of the team found something. Who knows?"

"Ever get the feeling we're being excluded?"

"I do. But it won't last," Ben said, as he climbed from the car, feeling the ground crunch under his feet. He looked down, then up at Anderson. "Broken glass."

"A bottle, maybe?" she said.

"No. This is a car window." He stared down the road where the liveried car had disappeared from sight. "It might explain the uniform presence, though. Car crime, maybe?"

"That's a little coincidental. Don't you think?"

"You're right," he said, after a short pause. Then he locked his car, checked the door to make sure it was locked, and led them both up the track.

"Are you sure it's here?" she asked.

"I'm positive," he said. "But again, it's all too coincidental."

It was as they were passing the ruins that Ben glanced across at what was the crime scene only a few days before.

"Hold on," he said, and he stopped abruptly, pointing at the ruins.

"What is it?"

"The stones. They've moved."

Anderson followed his gaze, then gasped.

"You're right. Bloody hell, Ben. Somebody has been here."

Ben pushed open the little gate and ran to where John Carson's body had been found. The pile of stones which had once stood nearly a metre high were now strewn across the area.

He stared down into the pile as Anderson came to his side.

"It's a skull," she said. "A dog's skull."

"Nillson found a dog collar," Ben said. "With the Carsons' details on it. And Leigh Carson told us they lost their dog a couple of years ago. What's the bet this is their dog?"

"Gillespie said the stones hadn't been moved for at least a couple of years. Something about the moss on them."

"A couple of years," Ben said. "Well, we've solved one mystery."

"But made another more complex," Anderson said, and she walked off back towards the gate. By the time Ben caught up with her, she was already verbalising an idea. She walked fast, forcing Ben to take long strides. "What if we can put the two crimes together? The missing dog and the John Carson murder?"

"Don't get carried away, Anderson. It's just a dog's skull right now. And besides, we're not exactly in the know. We need to share this information with Freya."

"No. No, we need to keep this to ourselves. It might be what we need to get you back into her good books. If we can prove that was the Carsons' dog—"

"Stop," he said, as they neared the bottom of the track and entered the old farm property. "We can't withhold evidence. We can't hold information back. It doesn't matter if Freya is upset with me or with you. This is a crime. We could have somehow discovered something that could make all the difference."

She was silent for a moment, but then nodded. "You're right. I'm just mad that I've got you into this. If it wasn't for me, you'd still be a part of the investigation."

"I am still part of the investigation. So are you, Anderson."

"Jenny. Please. Call me Jenny."

"Alright, well so are you, Jenny. Freya's upset. She's keeping us at arm's length. That's all. You're supposed to be out finding somewhere permanent to live, and I'm..." He paused and gave it some thought. "She didn't actually give me any instructions, but you can bet your life she expects me to report any findings. We need to tell her."

They stopped at the base of the property where two informal tracks diverted from the main track. The first led to the house which was guarded by the two dogs. The second led into the maze of overgrown brambles and bushes.

"Where's the photo you found in the house?" he said, and she fished a six-by-four print from her pocket and handed it to him. He held it up to see it side by side with their surroundings, then pointed at the second of the informal tracks. "This way."

He led them along a winding path, and they had to duck several times to avoid being slapped in the face by overhanging branches of oak and what looked like hazelnut trees.

"Somebody's been here recently," Anderson said. "Look how trodden the grass is."

"More than one person, I'd say," Ben agreed, as they rounded a corner and found a shipping container with its doors wide open.

The remains of a fire smouldered on the ground not five feet from the steel wall. Paper had been burned, judging by the charred remains, but what they had been was anybody's guess.

He peered inside the container and saw a row of cages, each with an empty water bowl and old newspapers on the floor. "And I think I know why too. This must be where the German Shepherds live."

Once more, he held the photo up to the landscape.

"There's no water. These bowls are bone dry," Anderson said, sniffing the stale air inside the container. "It stinks. This is no place to keep a dog. Guard dog or not. This is bloody animal cruelty. That's what this is."

Agreeing with her, Ben felt his phone vibrate in his pocket. He pulled it out, hoping that Freya had seen sense and was reaching out to apologise, or at least move forward.

But it wasn't Freya.

"Jackie," he said with a sigh.

"Oh, don't sound so pleased to see me," she said.

"Sorry. I am pleased. Of course I am."

"You thought I was DI Bloom? Hasn't she contacted you yet?"

"Hell hath no fury, Jackie, like a woman scorned."

"I *am* a woman, Ben. You know that right?"

"No offence meant. I'm just—"

"Sensitive?"

"Keen to move forward, Jackie. I want things back to how they were."

"Do you want to hear some news?" she asked, and he could hear her smile. Jackie's family had moved to Lincolnshire from Edinburgh when she was a child. Despite growing up in the fens and going to school with Ben, she had somehow retained a faint Scottish accent. It wasn't harsh like Gillespie's, who could make singing a lullaby sound like he was gearing up for a fight. Jackie's was gentle and kind. And when she smiled, her voice smiled with her.

"I could ask you the same thing," he replied.

"Me first," she said. "The name you gave me. You said it has something to do with Chapman. Is that right?"

"It is, but I can't go into detail."

"Well, I'm not sure what she's up to. But the name, Andrew Sykes, is a local guy. Mid-forties, single, lives in Potterhanworth Booths."

"Yeah, we've just been to his house. What did you find out about him?"

"Alright, alright," she said, teasing him. "He has a list of previous offences."

"Hold on," Ben said, and he gestured for Anderson to come closer, then set the phone to loudspeaker so she could hear what Jackie had to say. "Go on. What type of man am I dealing with here?"

"Well, breaking and entering for one. Three counts of it. Plus, there's some car theft, and a rape charge that was dropped."

"A rape charge?"

"The victim withdrew her statement," Jackie explained. "Probably harassed, but the investigating officer couldn't prove anything."

"What else?" Ben said.

"Isn't that enough?"

"You're hiding something. I can hear it in your voice."

She laughed. "Just saving the best until last," she replied, then revealed the final card up her sleeve. "One count of dognapping and one count of trading live animals without a licence."

"He's a dog thief?" Anderson blurted out, and Ben glared at her.

"Who's that?" Jackie asked.

"Nobody," Ben said.

"That's Anderson. What's she doing with you? She's supposed to be out looking for a place–"

"I didn't tell you so you can deny any knowledge of it, Jackie," Ben said. "We're looking into something personal."

"DI Bloom will go mental, Ben. What are you doing?"

"Freya won't be going mental, Jackie. Because Freya isn't going to find out, alright? At least not yet."

"Ah, Christ, Ben. Are you two–"

"No, we are not," Ben said.

"But that's what Freya thinks, isn't it? No wonder she's mad at you."

"Just leave Freya to me," Ben said. "We're working on something for Chapman."

"What is it?"

"I can't really say. I'm sworn to secrecy."

"Oh, right," Jackie said. "I was sworn to secrecy once. A sergeant I used to work with disobeyed a direct order, and a detective constable too. They asked me to keep their little secret. But you know? To keep a secret, you have to get something in return, I feel."

"Alright, alright," Ben said. "But you have to keep it quiet."

"You know me, Ben. They don't call me the keeper of secrets for nothing."

"I mean it, Jackie. This is personal. Serious stuff."

"My lips are sealed," she said, and he could hear the smile in her voice again.

"Chapman has a stalker."

"A what?"

"A stalker. Some bloke has been harassing her."

"Andrew Sykes?"

"Yep. He broke into her house while she was sleeping. I won't go into detail, but needless to say, she's scared out of her wits."

"Bloody hell, Ben. Why didn't you tell me?"

"Because it's personal."

"She's a police officer, for crying out loud. Why didn't she come to us?"

"Because he's threatened her. And what you just told me about the dropped rape charge supports that, don't you think?"

"Did he..."

"Yes, Jackie. He attacked her. So, you can see why we're trying to keep this under wraps."

"Oh my god. I should see if she's okay."

"No. You do not talk to her. If you do, she'll know it was me who told you," Ben said. "She's staying with Freya until we can get this sorted. I waited at her house last night and nearly had him. All I got was his number plate."

"You ran him through ANPR? Ben, that's an offence if it's not linked to a crime."

"I know. I know. I called in some help."

"Don't tell me. Sergeant Priest."

"He was the only one I could trust."

"For god's sake, Ben. The whole station is in on this. If she hasn't reported it, she doesn't even have a crime number."

"I know, Jackie. But she's one of us. We need to help her."

"And where are you now? What offence are you committing right now? Or shouldn't I ask?" Jackie said.

Ben felt Anderson's apologetic stare, and he waved it off.

"We're at the derelict farm beside the abbey."

"The abbey? What does that have to do with Andrew Sykes?"

"We found a photo in Sykes' house."

"In his house?" Jackie said. "How did you get a warrant?"

Ben said nothing. There was nothing really to say.

"Oh, Ben. You don't have a warrant, do you?"

"Not technically, no," he said. "But the photo showed Andrew Sykes at the derelict farm. We're standing in the exact spot the picture was taken."

"So what? I don't see how all of this is linked."

"Solomon Yates is in the photo, Jackie."

"Again, I don't see how any of this is anything but a massive coincidence."

"You asked where we're standing," he said, "and you told us Andrew Sykes has previous for stealing dogs and selling them on the black market, right?"

"Right?"

"Three feet from where I'm standing is an old shipping container."

"So?"

"It's full of cages, Jackie. This is where Andrew Sykes keeps the dogs before they're sold on."

"But how is Solomon Yates involved?"

"That's what we need to find out," he said, and he took a deep breath. "That's what I need to find out from Freya."

CHAPTER FORTY-SEVEN

"Sergeant Priest," Freya called out, as she emerged from the fire escape stairwell and caught the old Yorkshireman heading towards the custody desk. "Where am I?"

"Ah, Freya," he replied, his baritone voice grumbling in the empty corridor. An age ago, in some other life, Freya had called out to somebody in one of the London stations she had served at. Her voice had been lost to the din, and she'd had to fight her way through the hustle and bustle to catch up with her intended target. But in the remote Lincolnshire station, his voice seemed to penetrate the thick walls as an earthquake in Japan might cause a tremor in neighbouring China. "Solomon Yates?"

"That's him."

"Interview room two," he replied. "I've lined up a cleaning squad for when you're done."

"Is it that bad?"

"He looks and smells like he hasn't bathed for months. Is he homeless?"

"As near as damn it," Nillson added. "He doesn't have electricity or running water."

"That explains it," Priest said, and nodded a farewell, leaving them with a curt, "I've had Friday night specials covered in puke and God knows what else who smelled better than him."

"Thank you, Sergeant," Freya said, as he slipped into the custody room. She turned to Nillson. "Are you ready for this?"

"As I'll ever be," she replied, just as Freya's phone began to ring. Ben's name flashed up on the screen.

"Take this, will you?" Freya said, handing her the phone. "Tell him I'm busy, and meet me in the interview room."

"What if he has news?"

"If he has news, he can file his report as per the protocol," Freya said, and she shoved her way into the interview room only to be hit with the smell of urine, sweat, and an unwashed body. The air was thick, as if she could part it with the flat of her hand. "Mr Yates. I hope you're comfortable."

He growled something unintelligible whilst fishing something from between his yellow teeth. With one elbow on the table, he rested his head in his hand as a schoolboy might daydream about football while his science teacher explained the reproduction process of a flower.

Nillson entered the room shortly, and, assuming Ben's role, began setting up the recording while Freya arranged her notes.

"This gonna take long?" Yates said, his hand still supporting the weight of his head.

"That all depends on your answers, Mr Yates," Freya replied, as Nillson hit the button to start the recording. In Freya's experience, every recording started with a prolonged beep, designed to prevent any communication from starting early and potentially being missed. She stated the time, date, and then introduced herself and Nillson before gesturing for Yates to follow suit. "Would you care to introduce yourself for the recording?"

"Not really."

"Then I shall do it for you. Solomon Yates. Is that correct, Mr Yates?"

"What if I said no?" he said, and the folds in his cheeks deepened with a wry smile.

"Then I would continue with this interview, and should your case go to trial, a jury of your peers would gain an invaluable insight into your body language, attitude, and dare I say it, your cognitive abilities."

"Cognitive abilities?"

"Your desire to manipulate the interview, Mr Yates," Freya explained. "If you lie about your name, then you, by assumption, are clearly willing to fabricate other truths."

"Right," he said, his furrowed brow bringing his two caterpillar-like eyebrows together as if they were kissing.

"Shall we start again?" Freya asked. "Are you, or are you not, Solomon Yates?"

"I am," he said, after a short pause.

"Good. We're on a roll. I'd like to reread you your rights," Freya said. "Solomon Yates, you are under arrest on suspicion of theft and trading in live animals without a licence. You do not have to say anything. But it may harm your defence if you do not mention when questioned something which you later rely on in court. Anything you do say may be given in evidence. Do you understand?"

"I suppose so," he replied. "I don't have to say nowt?"

"No. In fact, you can remain silent for the remainder of this interview if you so wish."

"Well, I'll do that then," he said.

"Okay. One more thing, you realise you are entitled to free legal representation if you feel you need it?"

"Do I need it?"

"Are you guilty?"

He smiled and bared the yellow tombstones in his gums.

"We're all guilty of a thing or two, aren't we?"

"Of the crimes I have just announced, Mr Yates," Freya said. "Theft and trading animals without a licence."

He placed his free hand on his chest.

"I have stolen nowt, and as for the trading thing—"

"The illegal trading of animals," Nillson added.

"Right. That. Haven't done that, neither."

"So, the choice of having a legal representative is entirely up to you, Mr Yates," Freya told him, and she steepled her fingers beneath her chin while she waited for him to make a decision.

"How long will they be if I said yes?"

Freya shrugged and glanced at Nillson for an answer.

"An hour or two, maybe?" Nillson said. "At a guess. It's a Monday, so I doubt anybody will be sitting around waiting for a call."

"An hour or two?" Yates replied.

"I'm happy to postpone this interview," Freya said. "I'm sure we can find you a comfortable cell to have a lie down while you wait."

"How long do you think this will take?"

"This interview? Let me explain the process. In this interview, we'll just be gathering information before a second and potentially a third interview."

"Gathering information? Second and third interviews? What is this?"

"It's a procedure, Mr Yates."

"What do you need to know?"

"What were you burning when my colleague, Detective Sergeant Gillespie, arrived on your farm earlier today?"

"Nothing. Just keeping the place clean, is all."

"And the shipping container on your property. If we traced the serial number, we'd find a record of sale, would we?"

He shrugged. "Don't know. Been there years, it has."

"Years?"

"Decades. Bought it when we used to work the land. S'all gone now, course."

"The farm is no longer active?" Freya asked. "You no longer grow crops or keep livestock?"

"No point," he said. "Price of diesel is up. Supermarkets pay less and less each year. It'd cost me more to run the machinery than I'd get back. No. Sold most of my fields on. What I've got is enough for me."

"Enough for what?" Freya asked, and his eyes narrowed at her attempt to get him to give away a snippet of information.

"My allotment. S'all I've got now. A little patch to feed myself and some space for the dogs to run about."

"Ah, yes. Speaking of dogs. My colleague suggested you had several crates in the container."

"Aye, I do."

"Five, in total," Freya said.

"Aye. S'right."

"And you only have two dogs. Two German Shepherds."

"Yep."

"So why do you have five crates?"

"Used to have more, didn't I?"

"Ah. I see," Freya said. "You used to have five dogs, but now you only have two."

"S'right."

"And you have no running water."

"S'right again."

"Or electricity."

"Thieves. The lot of 'em."

"How do you live, Mr Yates?" Freya asked, genuinely interested to hear how the man coped during the winters.

"I've a borehole. Gives me all the water I need."

"A well?" Freya asked, and she looked to Nillson for an explanation.

"Kind of," Nillson said. "It's a closed well. They're quite common here."

"I see," Freya said. "And electricity?"

"Don't need it. And when I do, I've a genny."

"A genny?"

"A generator," Nillson explained. "It's like an engine that produces—"

"It's fine. I know what a generator is," she said, remembering the loud and monotonous drone of one particular camper's generator that Freya shared with her ex-husband around five years ago. They had lights and music and, in Freya's opinion, all the things a night beneath the stars could have done without. "What do you do for heat? In the winter, I mean?"

"Same as what we've done for hundreds of years," he replied.

"You have a fireplace?" Freya asked. "You must get frightfully cold."

"I suppose I must," he agreed. "But better to put on a few layers than give my money to those greedy buggers like everyone else. No. I don't need it. It's not illegal, you know?"

"I didn't say it was."

"Nobody even knows I'm there, mostly. Keep myself to myself. Just me and my dogs. S'all I need."

"Ah, yes. Your dogs. What did you do with the dogs that died?" Freya asked.

"Died?" he said, cocking his head.

"Yes. You told us you once had five dogs, hence the five crates, and now you only have two. Forgive my assumption, Mr Yates, but I can only imagine that three of them must have died."

"Buried them, didn't I?" he said, his eyes darting from Nillson back to Freya.

"I see," Freya said, making a show of believing him. "And the two dog tags my colleague discovered in your fire. How did they get there?"

"Like I said. I was clearing stuff out."

"Old dog collars. Must have been a tough decision to make. I know I'd find it hard to burn anything to do with our family dog."

"I'm not the sentimental type," he said, and he rubbed his chin, producing a sound akin to fingernails running across sandpaper. "What are you getting at exactly, lady?"

"If we could keep to my line questioning, Mr Yates," Freya said. "We're nearly done here. I'd just like to know if you can shed any light on the skeleton of the dog we discovered at Tupholme Abbey earlier. And for the benefit of the recording, the ruins of Tupholme Abbey are in the adjacent field to Mr Yates' property."

"Bones?" he growled. "What do I want with bones?"

"I was wondering if you could tell us how they got there, and why they were covered in stones?" Freya said.

Yates leaned in close, his foul breath warming Freya's face. But she didn't recoil. That would have given him some kind of mental advantage. Instead, she held her breath, waiting for him to speak.

"You reckon on me nicking dogs?" he said. "Nicking 'em and selling 'em on?"

"Stealing dogs and selling them on the black market. Yes, those are the charges against you, Mr Yates," Freya said. "I believe that's a source of income to you. One which I'm keen to prove."

He shook his head.

"Stealing dogs?"

"That's right."

"Selling 'em on?"

"That's it," Freya said.

"So, if I'm such a dastardly dognapper," he said, and for the first time, he held Freya's stare, "why would I kill one and bury it up there by the ruins?"

"Mr Yates, forgive me for saying, but I'm finding your demeanour to be somewhat aggressive. I'm sure you can see things from our perspective."

"Your perspective?" he said, as a throwaway comment.

"Yes. We have the body of a man found a few hundred yards from where you claim to live, and a shipping container full of dog crates on your property."

"Like I said. I had five dogs, and now I have two."

"And I presume you know nothing of the murdered man found at the ruins?"

"What murdered man?" he said, baring his stained teeth with a grin that did little else but entice Freya to find something on the disgusting, old man.

"Well, then perhaps you can tell me about the fire?" Freya said. "My colleague informs me that when he found you, you were burning something. What were you burning, Mr Yates? Other than old newspapers and dog collars?"

He shrugged, and he leaned his head on his hand again, as if the weight of it was too much for his neck to bear for too great a time.

"My life," he said.

"Your life?" Freya repeated.

"Bills, records, photographs," he said. "All the junk a man might collect over a lifetime."

"Photographs? Why would you burn photographs?"

He paused for a moment while he considered his response. The smugness faded from his expression, and he pushed his chin out to belie his true thoughts.

"Mr Yates?" Freya said, sensing his difficulty in answering. "Why would you burn your photographs?"

"I don't need them," he said eventually, and he met Freya's stare. "Not where I'm going."

Freya stared at him. His carefree approach to hygiene and life suddenly made sense.

"You're sick?" she asked, hearing her tone soften.

"S'right," he replied. "So, you can lock me up, and you can do what you will. But it'll be him upstairs who has the last word with me."

CHAPTER FORTY-EIGHT

Ben ended the call and dropped the phone into his pocket, very aware of Anderson's intrusive stare.

"What did she say?" Anderson asked.

"Oh, you know. This and that," Ben replied.

"She fobbed you off, didn't she?"

"Nope. She didn't even answer the call. Nillson did," Ben replied, and studied his surroundings for a distraction.

"Did she say anything?" Anderson asked.

"Nillson? No. Only that she was about to go into an interview with Freya."

"Charlotte Wood?"

"No, even better than that," Ben said. "Solomon Yates."

"The guy who owns this place?"

"Apparently. Dognapping," Ben said, and jabbed a thumb at the cages.

"Well, what else did she say?"

"Nothing," Ben said. "Nothing at all. You can't blame her really. She doesn't need to be on Freya's hit list."

"This is ridiculous," Anderson said. "Right, that's it. I'm going back to the station to have it out with her."

"Don't be ridiculous," Ben told her. "What are you going to do? Walk in there in front of the rest of the team and tell her that you and I didn't sleep together? It would be all over the station within minutes. And that includes DCI Granger. You could kiss your quiet, non-intrusive entry into the team goodbye. And if you expect Freya to roll over and forgive us, you really don't know her as well as you think you do."

Anderson sighed.

"You're right. Of course you are. But..."

"But what?"

"But I expected you to have a bit more of a fight in you. Look at you. Six foot what?"

Ben shrugged. "Six foot something."

"You don't know how tall you are?"

"It depends," he replied.

"On what?"

"What shoes I'm wearing. And as for having fight in me, if there's one thing I've learned working with Freya, it's knowing when to pick that fight, and how to win."

"And how do we win?" Anderson said. "Wait for her to calm down?"

"No," Ben said, and he stared at the roof of the old farmhouse three hundred yards away. "I have an idea. Follow me."

"Where are we going?" Anderson said, before Ben had even gotten into his stride. "The house? We're going to the house?"

"Nillson said Yates had been arrested for dognapping."

"So?"

"So why is a detective inspector who is currently up to her neck in a murder investigation interviewing an old man about a dognapping charge?"

Anderson was quiet, leaving Ben to navigate his way around a random copse of trees and brambles.

"You think he's linked to this, don't you?" she said, and Ben stopped in his tracks and turned to face her, a little too abruptly, as she clearly startled.

"John Carson was murdered up there," he said, pointing up the hill towards the abbey beyond the tree line. "Chapman has a stalker who we know to have a previous record for dognapping, and who is an acquaintance of Solomon Yates. The man who lives, what? Four hundred yards from the ruins where Carson was found?"

"It's not a coincidence, is it?"

"There's a link. I don't know what it is, but there's a link. And if Freya won't let us in, then we'll have to brute force our way in."

"With something she can't turn her head at."

"Exactly," he said, returning to his long strides.

"You don't have a warrant," she said, struggling to keep up with him, and she silenced when he glared at her.

"It hasn't stopped us so far today," he said, and he held a hand up for her to remain quiet, then stepped quietly around the next corner. He waved her over to him, gesturing for her to keep the noise down.

"What is it?" she said, peering around the bushes. She gasped when she saw what he was looking at. "Dogs."

"They guard the house," he whispered. "We need to get past them."

Anderson nodded.

"Alright," she said, slipping out of her jacket. She tossed it to the ground and took few deep breaths. "Are you ready?"

"You can't be serious?" Ben said. "They'll tear you apart."

She smiled weakly. "Only if they catch me," she said, then her face turned serious, and she ran.

Ben watched her for a few seconds in utter disbelief. She was light-footed, and the dogs merely cocked an ear when she first started out. But then as she grew closer, they paid the intrusion a little more attention. Their heads raised up. Ears like satellites tuned in to the source of the noise.

And in an instant, they were on their feet, teeth bared, eyes narrow, and hackles raised like a hundred thousand soldiers ready for war.

They were chained to posts on either side of a narrow pathway between two vast clumps of bushes and trees. Anderson, sprinting now for all she was worth, darted between them, narrowly avoiding their snapping teeth. She ran and ran until the dogs reached the limits of the chains, and the heavy links snapped the growling German Shepherds back.

Ben was so lost in the sight that he nearly missed his opportunity.

"Run," Anderson shouted, as one of the dogs turned and caught sight of him.

And the charade began again, only this time, the savage dog had Ben in his sights. He ran and didn't stop until he hand slapped against the wooden doorframe of the old farm house. The dogs were circling now. Defending their territory on either side. They strode up and down like two sentries passing on a castle wall. Keen eyes watched Ben's every move, as he slipped through the front door and took in the sight before him.

The kitchen was like something straight out of a Dickens novel, save for a few modern utensils made of plastic. The overgrown bushes outside blocked most of the light, and a layer of dust lay undisturbed on old, wooden cabinets and surfaces. Two candlesticks adorned with rolls of wax sat atop the old kitchen table as if the scene had been frozen in time, the flames snuffed with its molten liquid in a perpetual solid state.

Ben moved through the kitchen to a small sitting room. There were three armchairs and no TV. He found it mildly amusing that despite the lack of electricity, the filth, and the fact that Solomon Yates clearly lived a frugal life, he still had one more armchair than Ben, who also elected not to own a TV.

Of interest were the open drawers of an old bureau. It was the type with a roll top and little cubby holes where men of money in another age would have filed letters, expensive pens, and perhaps a pocket watch. But not Solomon Yates. He was neither a man of wealth nor the type to own an expensive pen. It was as if the old desk had been searched, and the burglar had found them empty and left them open. Ben checked the drawers that were closed and found them all to be empty. A few scraps of paper had fallen to the old, wooden floor, but they were nothing of interest. An old newspaper cutting featured an article on Lincolnshire farms, and another described the rising costs of agriculture and the falling prices of produce. They were articles from nearly a decade ago, and ones that Ben's father would have read then tossed into the fire.

He bent to check for any more beneath the desk when he heard a footstep behind him.

Daring not to move in case he made a noise, he slowly straightened and searched through the dirty window for Anderson.

But then he saw it. Movement. A shadow passed across the kitchen wall, and he stepped back, hoping that Anderson had somehow found a way past the dogs.

But it wasn't Anderson. The shadow was too small, the footsteps too heavy and clumsy.

Slowly and tentatively, a young girl stepped into the room.

"Franky?" Ben said, more from surprise than any other intention.

She took one look at him, gazing up with wide eyes.

Then she ran.

She ran with the familiarity of somebody who knew the layout of the house. She bolted past the kitchen table, flinging a chair backward into Ben's path. He climbed over it and stepped out into the daylight where he found her stopped dead in her tracks with a dog on either side of her. They circled her as wolves might pace the ground beneath a tree that offered refuge. And beyond them, Anderson stood just out of the dogs' reach.

"Stay still, Franky," Ben called. "Don't move a muscle."

She glanced down at the dogs, but seemed wholly undisturbed.

Then he saw it. The dogs' eyes. They were different somehow.

"What are you doing here, Franky?"

"I could say the same to you," she replied, her tone filled with the venom of hatred.

"Why did you run?" he asked. "We're trying to help you."

"You can't. You can't help me. Nobody can. Not now."

Ben studied her. It was a mask. The type of mask an adolescent girl wears to cover her weaknesses. She had been crying. Her eyes were puffy and her hair was unwashed. He stared across to Anderson, who shrugged, as if to indicate she had no idea how Franky had got past her.

"You were in here when I arrived, weren't you?" he said to the girl, and he took a step closer. "They know you. The dogs. You're familiar to them."

He stared at them. It was clear they were only really interested in Anderson and him.

"They trust you," Ben said. "You've been here before."

"So what?" she said, and her neck moved as she swallowed hard.

"Solomon Yates. Who is he to you?" Ben asked. But the girl said nothing. "Talk to me, Franky. You're not in any trouble."

"You're the copper. You work it out," she said, and then she darted from between the dogs, slipping past Anderson, who reached for her but was deterred by the snapping German Shepherds.

"Franky?" Ben called out, seeing that he was now trapped. But she disappeared into the maze of brambles, leaving the two of them dumbfounded, awestruck, and with yet another question to ponder.

"Shall I go after her?" Anderson called.

Ben shook his head, but said nothing. He was distracted by a niggle of a thought. A memory. Something he'd seen. He strode back into the house, marched into the kitchen, and there it was, lying on top of the kitchen table. The connection he'd been looking for.

CHAPTER FORTY-NINE

"Mind if I take a shower?" Chapman asked, as Freya closed her front door behind them. She leaned back onto the door and let her head bang against the wood.

"You don't have to ask, Chapman," she replied. "I told you. Treat the place like your own. I want you to be comfortable."

Chapman smiled a thanks, but seemed unconvinced.

"How about I cook you dinner tonight?" she said. "To say thanks."

"That'd be nice," Freya replied. "As long as it comes with a glass of wine."

"Of course. It's not about the dinner, ma'am."

"Freya, Chapman. Please call me Freya."

"Sorry. But it's not about the food, is it? The food is just a canvas for the wine, and I popped out at lunch today and bought us the perfect bottle."

"That sounds lovely," Freya said, and Chapman left her to her own devices. A moment's peace and quiet. A few minutes for her to organise her thoughts.

But it was not to be.

Her phone vibrated in her pocket, and she fished it out without even thinking. Any ideas of some quiet contemplation fell by the wayside when she saw the name the screen.

"Ben," she said, exhaling her despair.

"Wow. You really are mad at me."

"Is that you seeking some kind of gauge as to my mood or disposition, DS Savage?"

"I think I'd rather not venture down that little path," he replied.

"That's wise. Is this work related?"

"Yes. Well, yes and no, really."

"Let's keep it professional."

"I'd rather talk off the record."

"Then it can wait," Freya said. "I really am not in the mood to discuss–"

"I found Chapman's stalker," Ben said, cutting her off. She hated being cut off, and he bloody well knew it. But what he said was intriguing enough for her to offer him a little more carrot in the way of some well-practiced feminine silence. "I lied the other night when I told you I lost him. I got his number plate."

"You lied to me?" Freya said, and she moved into the lounge to avoid Chapman overhearing, then dropped into her armchair. "Do you realise what she's going through? I'm beginning to question if I know you at all, Ben."

"I wanted to surprise her. You too. Plus, you seemed so..."

"So, what?"

"So focused on the John Carson murder, Freya. You don't need the distraction. I figured I'd just deal with it so you didn't have to."

"I see," Freya said. It was typical of Ben to have some kind of reason that gave him the moral high ground. And if she was honest with herself, what he was saying was exactly something he would do.

"Andrew Sykes," Ben said. "Self-employed courier."

"He's a white van man?" Freya said.

"Something like that. He has previous for a whole list of petty offences, including dognapping."

"Dognapping?" Freya repeated. "Are you sure?"

"We checked him out."

"We?" Freya said, realizing that she had simply repeated what Ben was saying, adding little. But her mind was whirring, and tiny cogs were interlocking, however blurred their purpose might be. "Not Anderson, Ben. Tell me Anderson hasn't been working this with you."

"I asked Gold to run some checks for me."

"Why Gold?"

"Right now, she appears to be my only ally, Freya. You wouldn't even take my call earlier."

"And Anderson?" Freya said, dismissing his statement and seeking an answer to her own line of questioning.

"She helped. I couldn't stop her."

"I'm sure you tried very hard, too."

"Nothing happened, Freya. She needed somewhere to stay. That's all."

"So where is this Sykes character?" Freya asked, again driving her own agenda. If she was going to talk to him, she would keep the conversation on track.

"I don't know. We've done a little digging on him, and I can link him to Solomon Yates."

"And how did you make that connection?" Freya asked.

"I found a photo of him and Yates at the farm."

Freya digested the information in light of what Gillespie had found earlier. But the link to Solomon was overshadowed by Ben's methods.

"Where exactly did you find the photo, Ben?" she asked.

"Do you really want to know?"

"Please tell me you didn't go to his house."

"We made the link. That's all you need to know, Freya," Ben said. "We even went to the spot on the farm where the photo was taken, and do you know what we found?"

"Oh, I don't know. Dog cages, maybe?" Freya said. She always enjoyed knowing what somebody was excited to tell her. "Evidence of a small dognapping industry? Nillson and I have already interviewed him."

"Nillson?" he said, clearly disappointed that his spot beside Freya was being filled.

"There's nothing to link him to the murder. I've passed on the details to CID to follow up. I doubt very much if DCI Granger will appreciate his Major Investigations Team spending time on a dognapping offence, if indeed there is one. If they find something, then perhaps they can re-arrest him."

"Re-arrest him? You let him go?" Ben said. "He was burning evidence. We need him, and you let him go?"

"Of course. Why would I keep a dying old man in custody for an offence I have no business with? The last thing I want is for his last days to be spent sitting in a ten-by-ten cell. That's asking for trouble. Besides, we have Charlotte Wood's confession. And unless we find her husband, we're going to have to charge her or let her go. We can't hold her forever."

"Dying?" Ben said. "Did you say Solomon Yates is dying?"

"He wasn't burning evidence, Ben. He was burning his life. He was making preparations."

"Dying how, exactly?" Ben asked.

"Cancer. Chapman has confirmed it with the hospital."

Ben was silent for a moment while he composed his thoughts. But then he spoke, and he did so with practiced professionalism.

"We need to get him back," he said. "Dying or not. We need him back."

"And why do you say that?"

"He's Franky's grandfather," Ben said. "I found her there. At his house."

"So? That doesn't make him her grandfather."

"No? So then how did she get past the dogs?"

"How did you get past them?" Freya countered.

"Anderson," he said. "She made a bolt for it. Created a distraction."

"She did what?"

"She's a brave girl, that one," Ben said, clearly trying to sway Freya back into singing Anderson's praises.

"She's a fool," Freya said. "She wasn't supposed to be working. If they had got her—"

"Then she would have dealt with the consequences, and we would have all done what we could to help her," Ben said. "The fact of the matter is that Franky Wood walked through those two guard dogs as if they were pets. She knows them. She's familiar to them."

"And where is she now?" Freya asked.

"She did a runner."

"Again?" Freya said. "Why can't we pin this girl down? She's the bloody victim here."

"I've got a theory," Ben said, and he waited for her to show interest. This would be his cards laid out on the table.

"Go on," Freya said, trying not to sound overly interested.

"Andrew Sykes and Solomon Yates are involved in the illegal trading of stolen dogs. Sykes steals them. Yates hides them until they have a buyer."

"Right?" Freya said. "Are you looking to transfer to CID here, Ben? The last I knew, you were a sergeant in a Major Investigations Team."

"Hear me out," he said. "Chapman said she hit a man's dog. Sykes' dog. But it wasn't Sykes' dog."

"It was a stolen pet?" Freya said, seeing where he was leading her. "And he threatened her in case she heard about the missing dog and went to the police?"

"Exactly. I think Chapman was submissive. He took it too far."

"What?" Freya said, angered by Ben's lack of empathy. "She was bloody terrified—"

"I know. I know," he said. "And I'm not blaming her. God knows, none of this is her fault. He's a dog thief. I doubt he's used to losing dogs. But on this occasion, the dog got away. He was chasing after it when Chapman hit it. I think he panicked. He went after her."

"And you think he just got carried away?" Freya asked.

"I don't think he planned any of it. If he knew what he was doing, he wouldn't have left footprints in the mud outside her house, and he probably wouldn't have caught his jacket on the window."

"Okay," Freya said. "So, what next? How do we bring him in? I'm guessing if we find him and can match the prints to him, and the fabric from the window, then we've got him?"

"I think we need Yates to find him," Ben said. "And I think Yates is linked to the murder somehow."

"What? That's a big jump, Ben."

"I found something else," Ben said. "It didn't register at first. I had to go back and look."

"What? What did you find?"

"On his kitchen table. A bread knife."

"A bread knife? So?"

"With the exact same handle as the murder weapon, Freya," Ben said. "I think you might have just let our killer go, but if we find him, he'll lead us to Sykes."

"Well, that remains to be seen," Freya said.

A silence followed, and Ben's breathing was heavy over the line.

"So?" he said finally.

"So, what?"

"So, what do we do now? I could come over," he said. "We could make a plan. That's normally how we get through moments like this, isn't it?"

"Normally, yes," she said, and a pang of warmth formed in the pit of her stomach. Then it cooled, like a breath of that north-easterly wind that winter brings. "But not tonight. I don't think it's a good idea."

"Oh, Freya, come on–"

"I'll see you in the morning, Ben," she said, and found herself biting her lower lip. "We'll make a plan as a team. We'll do things my way. No more renegade tactics. We're a team, remember?"

"It hasn't felt like that today, if I'm honest," Ben said, and there was a sharpness to his tone that she hadn't encountered from him before. A bitterness that she somehow felt was justified, yet wouldn't succumb to.

"Goodbye, Ben."

She ended the call, then clutched the phone to her chest, letting her head fall back against the wall. She closed her eyes, fighting the urge to call him back. He could come over. After all, that's how they usually got through these moments.

"Freya?" a voice said from the doorway, and she opened her eyes to find Chapman dressed in full loungewear clutching a bottle of wine.

"Chapman," she said, although her throat allowed only a whisper.

"Are you okay?" Chapman asked, her expression one of growing concern. "You look pale."

"I'm fine," Freya said, and she clambered to her feet, smoothing her clothes. From somewhere inside one of those cupboards in her mind where she stored the disguises that had helped her through life, she found a smile, albeit weak and far from sincere. "Now then. We'll need two glasses for that wine, won't we?"

"Ma'am," Chapman replied, and she appeared grateful that Freya was okay. The sign of somebody who truly cared. She started for the kitchen, and Freya called out to stop her. It seemed like a good time to tell her.

"Chapman?" Freya said, and she emerged in the doorway again, eyebrows raised in anticipation.

"Ma'am?" she said, then corrected herself. "Sorry. Freya?"

"I've had some news," Freya told her. "He's found him. Ben, I mean. He's found the man who's been stalking you. I'll pass the details to CID to follow up."

CHAPTER FIFTY

"How did that go?" Anderson asked from the living room doorway. She was dressed in a pair of old gym shorts with a tight-fitting Leyton Orient Football Club shirt. She waited with her hands behind her back, accentuating the snug fit of the shirt. He hadn't known it was a Leyton Orient shirt and had to study the emblem on the front to find out. That was when she repeated the question, and he realised he was staring at her chest. "That was Freya, wasn't it? On the phone, I mean."

"Yeah," he said, feeling his face redden. An awkward silence followed.

"I wasn't..." he began. "The shirt. I was seeing which team it belonged to."

"Orient?" she said, and she pulled the fabric away from her to peer down at the two opposing dragons on the club's badge. "The whole family support them. Started with Grandad, I think. Who do you support?"

"I don't," he said, as she let go of the fabric and it snapped back to her body. "I don't follow football at all."

"I suppose you'd be an Imps fan, wouldn't you?" she said. She was barefoot and placed one atop the other as she leaned against the doorframe.

"A what?"

"Imps," she said. "That's what they're called, aren't they? Lincoln City. The Imps. You're a local lad. You should know that."

"We didn't really do football when I was a lad," he replied, tearing his eyes from her bare legs.

"What did you do, then?" she said. "If you didn't do football, what did you do? You must have done something."

"I got up to no good," he replied. "Rode my motorcycle, shot rabbits, helped my dad. You know. Farm life."

"So, you're not a football fan?" she said. "What about beer?"

"Depends what it is," he replied.

"Oh, so you're the silent outdoors type, yet you're a bit fussy about the beer you drink? What if I told you I've got two bottles of warm beer in my bag?"

"Warm?"

"My bag isn't chilled."

"Then, I'd say let's put them in the fridge for half an hour."

"What if I wanted a beer now?" she said. "Would you let me drink alone?"

"You don't seem to need any support from me, Anderson. I won't judge you."

"Jenny. Please call me Jenny," she said.

"Okay, Jenny, why don't you get those warm beers, and I'll drink with you?" he said. "But I'm warning you, they'll be nicer chilled."

"Well, it's a good job I chilled them then, isn't it?" she said, and produced two bottles of blonde IPA from behind her back.

He gave a little laugh as she sauntered into the room and fell into the other armchair beside him. Then, handing him a beer, she held hers up as a toast.

"To cold beer," she said, and they chinked bottles.

He took a sip. It was good ale, and it quenched a thirst he hadn't realised he'd had.

"You know, Freya would never allow you to chink glasses or bottles."

"Oh? Why's that?"

"She says it's poor etiquette. A symbol of the lower classes."

"Everybody chinks glasses."

"Everybody accept Freya," he said, and he took another sip, savouring the cold on his throat. "What was all that about warm beer?"

"I wanted to see if you'd drink with me," she said, smiling to herself. "But for the record, I don't do warm beer."

"That's good to hear."

"So?" she said, taking a mouthful so large the beer spilled from the side of her mouth. She wiped it away with the back of her hand and took another. "How did it go with Freya?"

"How do you know I was talking to her?"

"By your tone," she replied. "You speak differently when you're with her, or talking to her on the phone."

"I do not–"

"There's nothing to be ashamed about," she said. "It's good to know who wears the trousers in your relationship."

"We do not have a relationship, Anderson."

"Jenny."

"Jenny, then. We do not have a relationship."

"Okay, okay," she said, her smile growing. "But you are upset that she's mad at you. You'll admit that much?"

"I'm not upset. I just..." He paused, unable to complete the sentence. She was right. "We're good friends. Freya and me. We're close. So yes, I am upset that she's mad at me. Especially when it's one of her friends I'm helping out."

"Whose friends?"

"Freya's friends. You're her friend, aren't you?"

"I wouldn't say we were friends. Do friends give you two days to find somewhere to live then just kick you out?"

"You told her you found somewhere."

"Only because I didn't want to put her in an awkward position."

"Did you even look for somewhere?"

"I did. Yes."

"And they were all terrible, were they? All the places you saw? None of them suited you? Not even for a short period while you found somewhere more permanent?"

"As it happens, yes. Some of them were nice. One in particular. It was stunning. The villages here are truly remarkable."

"Don't change the subject, Jenny," he said. "Why didn't you take one of the places you saw?"

"Because..." she said, as if that single word explained everything. As if it was an entire sentence, or monologue that divulged her reasoning. She accompanied that single word with a casual shrug, and took another mouthful of her beer.

She was the exact opposite of Freya. The way she slouched in the armchair like a teenager, where even in those relaxed surroundings, Freya would have retained a far more elegant posture. The way she took mouthfuls of beer and held the bottle, where Freya would have either requested a glass or taken sips in more ladylike measures.

"I don't like being alone," she said finally. "I don't want to be on my own."

Ben listened, digested, and waited for her to add something. But nothing followed.

"Your ex?" Ben said. Any frustration or grievance his earlier tone had carried was dropped.

She nodded in reply, staring at the unlit log burner in the fireplace.

"Do you want to talk—"

"He beat me," she said, cutting him off as if she'd been asked the same question a thousand times. "He drank. I worked. He wanted sex. I didn't. He hit me, and I let him."

Her head remained still, but her eyes tracked to his as if to punctuate the finality of her statement.

"Is he—"

"Free?" she asked. "Yes. And before you say it, I know. I should have pressed charges. But you know what? I can't be bothered. I'd sooner be away from him. I'd sooner not have to deal with him at all than to go through the trials and tribulations. It's one of the downfalls, isn't it? Of being in the force? You get to see how it all works. You never think it could happen to you, but when it does, you know what the future holds. Interview upon interview. Being made to feel like it was my fault."

"It's not like that—"

"It is like that, Ben. And not just in London. That's how it is. That's why so many men get away with it. That's why Chapman hasn't said anything, isn't it?"

"I don't know about Chapman."

"It is. Trust me, it is," she said.

"And that's why you wanted to help her."

"What did she say?" Anderson asked, taking another mouthful of beer and ending the conversation about herself.

"Who? Freya?" Ben said, but she neither confirmed nor denied the question. "They picked up Yates."

"The old boy?" she said, suddenly coming to life. "The bloke that owns the farm?"

He nodded. "Gillespie found the cages before we did. They pulled him and let him go. Looks like Freya is going ahead with the charges against Charlotte Wood."

"No way. Why did they let him go? You told her about the knife, right?"

"Of course I did."

"And about him being Franky's grandfather?"

"Yes, yes. I told her all of it. Sounds to me like her mind is made up."

"But yours isn't," she said, as if she had known him for years rather than days. "You think he's part of all this, the same as I do."

He nodded.

"I just can't prove it."

"What about Sykes?" she asked. "What did she say about him?"

"That she'd hand the details over to CID to follow up."

"What? But what about Chapman? How is she going to feel about the whole station knowing what he did to her?"

"They won't. He'll serve time for the dognapping offences. No doubt forensics will find plenty of evidence in his van."

"Is that what Freya said?"

"No, it's what I extracted from the very short conversation with her, Jenny. Chapman won't press charges even if it was us that was processing him. Which it won't be. At least this way, he won't go after her when he gets out and she can go on with her life."

"That's terrible."

"Is it?" Ben said. "What do you suggest she does, run away?"

"That's low," Anderson said, and her anger faded as fast as it had come. "But you're right. I guess we deal with things our own way. I'm not really in a position to talk about pressing charges, am I?"

"All I want is for Chapman to be happy. With Sykes behind bars, she will be. Job done."

"As long as CID can get evidence on him," Jenny said, and she took the last mouthful of beer from her bottle, then placed it on the floor beside the chair.

"What's that supposed to mean?"

"Nothing," she said. "It's just that CID might not put as much effort into finding him, as, let's say, a friend of Chapman's."

"You're saying we should gather the evidence for them?"

"Well, it's one thing to hand a lead to CID. But it's an altogether different thing to hand them a lead with everything they need to charge the bloke. What if he gets off?"

"He can't get off. Chapman will be devastated," Ben said.

"Well, then I guess it's down to you and I to make sure they have everything they need to charge him, isn't it?"

"What do you suggest?" Ben said, not liking the direction this was heading.

But Anderson, unperturbed by the prospect of breaking a few more rules, leaned forward in her chair, crossing her legs beneath her, and once more, Ben was drawn to her smooth, toned flesh.

"Gold said he was a driver. A courier, or something, right?" Anderson said, and she clicked her fingers to rouse Ben from his stare.

"Eh?" he said, blushing again. "Yes. A self-employed courier. White van man, as Freya put it."

"Okay. Let's get a list of his regular customers. We need to take a look inside his van. Can we get Gold to help, again?"

Ben nodded. He hated the idea of going against Freya's wishes. But he knew it was for the greater good. It was funny, he thought, that he and Anderson had had a similar chat to the ones he and Freya normally had, and had come up with a plan from nothing. But he had a bad feeling about this one, and he couldn't be sure if it had anything to do with Anderson's body, or betraying Freya.

CHAPTER FIFTY-ONE

It was the morning, and even three strong coffees had not quenched the burning sensation in the pit of Freya's stomach. She felt like a teenager with a crush on a boy who continued to snub her. Yet it was her who was doing the snubbing, and there was no crush; at least, the crush was not the cause of the issue. Not directly anyway.

She sat at her desk staring at the whiteboard. Eight names stared back at her, all somehow interlinked. John Carson, and his wife and son. Then Charlotte Wood, Theo, and Franky. Solomon Yates and Andrew Sykes completed the set.

Eight names, one missing person, and one confession. She could close the case right now, if she wanted. All she would have to do was walk downstairs, ask Sergeant Priest to fetch Charlotte from her cell, and then formally charge her. Mrs Wood would be held on remand until her court date. Freya could then hand the paperwork to Granger, and it would be done and dusted.

Perhaps then she would have time to be a little more involved with Andrew Sykes. Perhaps then she could help Chapman get back on her feet.

But she knew deep down that even if Sykes confessed to assaulting Chapman, the young investigator would never want to press charges.

However, if Sykes was put behind bars for some other crime, such as dognapping, then he would have no reason to go after Chapman when his sentence was complete. It was the least Freya could do to see that, should the opportunity arise, he be sent down for as long as possible.

"It's just our luck, isn't it?" she said to nobody in particular. "John Carson knew Franky had run off, and where she was likely to be. It's the summertime, so he takes a blanket and a bottle of wine, then waits for her to arrive."

"You think he seduced Franky?" Nillson said, speaking for the first time that morning, other than the brief good morning she had offered on arrival.

"She doesn't have any bruises or cuts. Not that I saw anyway."

"In that case, is it still…" Chapman began, unable to say the word.

"Rape?" Freya finished for her. "She's a minor. It's sexual assault whatever way you spin it."

"Aye, he got what was coming to him, that's for sure," Gillespie added. "If it hadn't happened in the outside, it would have happened on the inside. Worse, probably."

"It's not our job to judge people, Gillespie," Freya said.

"That's what we do though, right?" he said.

"No. We process evidence. We determine if there is enough of it for CPS to pursue with a trial or a conviction. And if there isn't enough, we find it. And if we can't find it, then we leave it. We're looking for black and white here. Facts. Indisputable facts."

"But surely finding wine glasses with his DNA and prints on beside his dead body, and her underwear not far away, that's enough to go on? And that's even without Charlotte Wood's confession."

"There's something wrong," Freya said. "You're right, Gillespie. Although it pains me to say it. But there's something off. I can't put my finger on it."

"We've got the confession, boss," Gillespie said. "We've been down Solomon Yates' path and found nothing but an old, dying man who steals dogs."

"He doesn't steal dogs," Freya said. "He holds them. Andrew Sykes steals dogs."

She pointed to the board where she had added Sykes' name.

"But there's nothing to link him to the murder," Nillson added.

Freya checked her watch. It was nine-fifteen. Ben should have been in by now. And so should Anderson. Not a good start for her first full day in the office.

She inhaled long and hard, and collected her thoughts.

"Right. Listen up," she began. "We've got a confession from Charlotte Wood. In about fifteen minutes' time, when DCI Granger finishes his coffee, he's going to walk in here and ask me why we haven't charged Charlotte Wood yet. If I know him as well as I think I do, then he'll give me an ultimatum. He's already told me to either charge her or let her go. He'll be worried about backlash. I have to do something."

"I'm thinking the same, if I'm honest, boss," Gillespie said.

"And if it wasn't for one thing, one key piece of evidence, then I might agree with you, Gillespie," she told him, then turned to Cruz, who was doing a poor job of feigning interest in his laptop, pretending to work. She always knew when he was pretending to work, because he looked engaged, as opposed to when he was actually working, when he looked as if he might fall asleep at any given moment. "Cruz?"

"Eh?" he said, and clicked a few buttons on his laptop. "I was just—"

"Yes?" Freya said.

"I was just checking through the lab results. You know? To see if anything jumped out at me."

"And did anything jump out?" Freya asked.

He smacked his lips and shook his head once. "Nope," he said, with a sharp and disappointed intake of air, as if to say, *I did my best, boss, but not this time.*

She knew it was all hot air and he was likely browsing the internet for an upcoming film at the cinema.

"It was your find that is causing much deliberation, Cruz," Freya said.

"Me? What find?" he said. Clearly he hadn't been listening, as his tone and body language was defensive.

"Yes, you, Cruz. The dog. The bones under the stones."

"Right," he said, still unsure if this was a good or a bad thing.

"If you hadn't have found those bones, then perhaps I'd be inclined to walk downstairs and charge Charlotte Wood."

"But you're not going to?" he said.

"No, Cruz. I am not. It wasn't her."

"Eh?" Gillespie said.

"You what, boss?" Cruz added.

"It wasn't her."

The rest of the expressions on the faces of her team mimed what Gillespie and Cruz had both so eloquently expressed. Confusion.

"Last night, I spoke to DS Savage. It seems that Solomon Yates is Franky's grandfather. It's just a hunch, but Chapman, that's one for you. Prove it or disprove it, please. I'll need an answer by the time DCI Granger gives me an ultimatum."

"I thought he was just a mad, old man," Gillespie said.

"A dying, old man, yes," Freya said. "But not mad. Ben also found a knife in his house. A bread knife."

The team were expressionless while they waited for her to finish.

"With the same red handle as the murder weapon," she said.

"Eh?" Gillespie said.

"You what?" Cruz added.

"But we let him go," Gillespie said.

"And why did I let him go?" Freya snapped.

Gillespie was a little taken aback by Freya's tone. He shrugged.

"No link to the murder?" he said.

"Exactly. I had no link to the murder," she said. "Despite you being in his kitchen, Gillespie."

"Eh?"

"Were you, or were you not, in his kitchen with him?"

"Aye, well…"

"Were you, or were you not, standing beside his kitchen table?"

"It was a wee bit cluttered, for sure," he countered.

"Well, I suggest next time, you should look harder. DS Savage saw it."

"So, he's the killer?" Cruz said tentatively. "The old man?"

"That's what we need to find out," Freya said. "But first, we need to find him."

"Ma'am," Chapman said. "I've just had some more results back from the lab."

"More results? Are we expecting anything else?"

"I think so," Chapman said. "The case number matches the Carson investigation. Unless they've made a mistake."

"I would hope the lab wouldn't make administration errors, Chapman," Freya said. "What is it?"

Chapman made a show of rereading the information on her laptop, screwing up her face in confusion.

"It's a rock, ma'am."

"A rock?"

"That's what it says," she replied, and sat back, inviting Freya to come and see. She walked around the desks to stand beside Chapman and read the email.

"Blood stains on a rock found at Tupholme Abbey?" Freya said.

"Who submitted this as evidence?" Freya asked the team, glaring at them all in turn.

"Aye, well… I tried, boss, but I couldn't stop him," Gillespie said, pointing his finger at Cruz, who, as a schoolboy might, rolled his eyes at Gillespie's spineless lack of support then turned to face the consequences of his actions.

"Sorry, boss. I thought it might be something."

"Aye. And I told you it wasn't blood. Iron, laddie. It's iron."

"Well, Cruz, you might have just helped me make a connection."

"Eh?" Gillespie said.

"You what, boss?"

"The stains on the rock were not iron, as you claim, Gillespie. They are, in fact, blood."

"Ha," Cruz said, his chest swelling before Freya's eyes. "I knew it."

"But not human blood."

"Eh?" Cruz said, whilst Gillespie remained silently dumbstruck at his DC's good fortune.

"Dog blood. A Labrador," Freya stated.

"Dog blood?" Nillson said, and opened her mouth to voice the connection. But Freya's mind was working far too fast to wait for her team to fall into place.

"The blood is more than a year old, as, I would guess, are the bones that Cruz found."

"Somebody killed the dog with a rock?" Cruz asked, then repeated it again, this time less like a question and more as a statement, as if he'd put the pieces together. "Somebody killed the dog with the rock, then tossed it into the field."

"Not just any dog," Freya said, and turned to Nillson. "The Carsons' dog. Somebody stole the Carsons' dog and killed it up near the abbey. Who do we know that steals dogs?"

"Yates," Gillespie said.

"And Andrew Sykes," Chapman added, her eyes belying the hope in her tone.

"Right," Freya said. "There's the link. All we need to do is understand why they stole the dog and killed it."

"Ma'am," Chapman said, and Freya looked down at her screen where one of several national databases she used every single day was open, and a list of results was displayed. Chapman tapped away, her fingers a blur, and the results reduced to five lines of data. She tapped away again, and four of the results vanished, leaving one name on the screen.

"Solomon Yates?" Freya said, and Chapman nodded, sitting back to allow Freya a full view of the screen.

"This is the Births, Marriages, and Deaths records," Chapman explained, as the door to the incident room squealed open and then slammed shut. But nobody turned to see who had entered. They all knew who it was, and they waited with bated breath for Chapman to finish. "He's Theodore Wood's father."

CHAPTER FIFTY-TWO

"DI Bloom. My office, please," Granger said, reaching for the incident room door again.

"Wait," she said. "This is important."

"Excuse me?" Granger replied, clearly not impressed with being told to wait in front of Freya's entire team.

"Sorry, guv," she said. "We've just had a breakthrough."

"I don't care if you've just solved world peace, DI Bloom. My office. Now."

"Guv, I know what you're going to say," Freya said, staying beside Chapman. "You're going to tell me to charge Charlotte Wood or release her."

"Very intuitive," Granger grumbled. "Well? What'll it be?"

Freya waited a few seconds. She knew what she had to say, but in moments like this, delivery counted.

"Neither, guv."

"Excuse me?"

"Neither. I need more time."

"She's been in that cell for two days now, Bloom. Now, are you going to charge her or not?"

"Not right now. No," she replied.

"Then perhaps Sergeant Priest can have his cell back?"

"I can't do that either, guv," she said.

"Talk," Granger ordered. "Fast."

"Okay. Okay, here goes. A year ago, the Carsons lost their dog. Leigh Carson said there was a spate of dognapping in the area. They never saw it again. It was a black Labrador, guv."

"So? Are we investing a murder or the illegal trade of animals?"

"This weekend, Nillson discovered an old dog collar at the ruins. The tag on the collar suggests it belonged to the Carsons."

"Again, shall we call David Attenborough? This is more his field than yours, Bloom."

"Meanwhile, Cruz discovered a rock with old blood stains on it. DS Gillespie thought it was iron ore running through the rock, but Cruz followed his instincts."

"Aye, well..." Gillespie said. "I mean, it was faded–"

"Then yesterday, Cruz discovered a pile of bones beneath what we thought was a cairn at the abbey. It turns out they are the remains of the Carsons' dog."

"And the rock is the weapon used to kill it?" Granger asked.

"Yes, guv."

"Right. That's the murder of a Labrador solved. How about we solve the murder of a human being? Namely, John Carson."

"Guv, there's something you should know," Freya said, and she rested her hand on Chapman's shoulder, peering down at her for some kind of assurance. Chapman closed her eyes, then gave a slight nod. "A little while ago, DC Chapman was on her way home from work. As you know, she lives in Bardney."

"Wow, you're pulling every tangent out of the hat today, Bloom."

"She hit a dog, guv. It was dark. She stopped and who she thought was the owner starting laying into her. She just about escaped."

Granger digested the information, then stared at Chapman.

"Is this true, Denise?" he asked, and she nodded, but from her expression, she daren't even begin to try and speak.

"Why didn't you come to me? Or Freya? Or any of us?"

"The fact is, guv, that the owner of the dog then hounded her. He found out where she lives and broke in."

"I'm guessing he didn't actually own the dog?" Granger said.

"You'd be right," Freya said. "His name is Andrew Sykes. He has previous for dognapping, and we've subsequently linked him to Solomon Yates."

"The old guy that was here yesterday? What's he got to do with this?"

"He owns the land beside Tupholme Abbey, or so the paper trail led us to believe. We found dog cages on his property inside an old shipping container buried in the brush."

"So, he stores the dogs until Sykes can find a buyer?" Granger said. "He just owns the land."

"That's right, guv," Freya said, enjoying his focused attention. "He also owns a bread knife with the same handle as the murder weapon."

"And you think he could be the killer?" Granger said. "Where does Andrew Sykes come into this?"

"I don't know," Freya said with a sigh. "Aside from working with Yates, I can't see a link."

"But there's no way that old man could have done it. He barely has the strength to get dressed in the mornings."

"I don't think he even gets undressed," Gillespie added. "Smells like he's been wearing those clothes for months."

The team turned to Gillespie, even Granger. But nobody replied. They were following the story, and Gillespie's flippant rhetoric was unwelcome when everyone was so focused.

"We found John Carson's clothes on his land, guv," Freya said.

"But if he's Theodore Wood's father, then Charlotte Wood would have access to his property. She'd know it well."

"You're a grandfather, aren't you, guv?" she said, trying a new approach.

"I am, yes. But I don't see what that has to do with it."

"Two grandsons and a granddaughter. Am I right?"

He nodded, falling in to where she was leading him.

"What would you do if you found somebody..." She paused, not wishing to upset Chapman any more. "Assaulting your granddaughter?"

"What I would do has no bearing on this investigation, Bloom."

"I disagree," she said. "I think Charlotte Wood is covering for her dying father-in-law. I think he caught Carson assaulting her daughter, and he did what any grandfather would do."

"That doesn't explain why Theodore Wood's car was found at the scene," he said, finding a new way to unravel Freya's arrangement of the facts.

"Yes, it does. Charlotte had access to the car. He's been missing for days. She called the Carsons to see if Franky was there, then went out to look for her. But she was too late. That's why there was a delay in the body being moved," Freya said, the facts coming together even as she spoke. "That's why the clothes were found on his property. There are two possible scenarios. Either Solomon Yates caught John Carson in the act, and killed him. Which suggests that Charlotte arrived moments too late. He wouldn't care about the consequences. He's dying."

"Or?" Granger asked.

"Or she did it, as she suggests. The same theory, but a different perpetrator. In both scenarios, she stripped Carson to get rid of any evidence either her or her father-in-law may have left behind. She stripped him and took the clothes to the farm to burn, getting rid of the knife and Franky's underwear in the long grass."

"Why get rid of her daughter's underwear?" Cruz said. "She's the victim."

"Because the underwear links the family to the crime. Victim or not."

"So why drag him to the rocks?" Granger asked. "That's what the report said, wasn't it? Why drag him to the cairn?"

"Because the rocks are significant," Cruz said, speaking up for the first time in a while. It was one of those moments when he spoke before he'd fully thought about it, and now the entire team was staring at him, and he teetered on the verge of crumbling under the pressure.

"Go on," Freya said, reassuring him, hoping for the love of God that he would voice what Freya was thinking. "Why are they significant?"

"Because that's where Yates buried his dog," Cruz said.

"Okay. And why did Yates kill John Carson's family pet?" Granger said. Freya was sure he was thinking the same as her, and she was pleased to see him bring Cruz on a little more.

"Simple," Cruz said, shrugging. "Because it wasn't the first time he'd assaulted Franky."

The team were silent, and Cruz looked at each of them, clearly hoping somebody would say something. But they didn't, and he felt compelled to substantiate his theory with facts.

"The report, boss. From when you first spoke to Charlotte Wood. You were talking about the family problems, and why Theodore Wood goes missing for days at a time." He pulled open his file and searched through the text, mumbling to himself as he scanned the pages. "Here it is. She said the family prefer to deal with their problems their own way. It's a family trait."

Cruz looked up from the file and searched the team for some kind of response.

"So why would Charlotte Wood and her husband carry on talking to the Carsons?" Nillson asked. "I mean, if they knew what John Carson had done, then why would they go there? And why would they take Franky?"

"It's a family trait," Freya said. "They didn't know what John Carson had done. Only Franky's grandfather knew about it. I think the dog was just a warning."

"A warning?" Gillespie said. "You mean, like the Godfather cutting the head off the horse?"

"Something like that," she replied. "And if it happened again, there would be no more warnings."

"And it did happen again," Granger said, and he turned to Freya, jutting his chin out while he made his mind up. "What are you going to do with Charlotte Wood?" he asked.

"She's an accessory, guv," Freya said. "At the very least."

"You can't charge her for being an accessory to murder unless you have the actual individual responsible for the murder. Otherwise, your case is just conjecture. You have to prove the murder to prove the accessory."

"Well, then I suggest we let her go."

"Eh?" Gillespie said.

"We let her go," Freya repeated. "She's been here far too long already, as DCI Granger quite rightly pointed out."

"You're going to let an accessory to murder and a murder suspect walk free?" Granger said.

"Like you said, guv, we can't hold her for murder, and we can't hold her as an accessory without the actual murderer," she said. "Therefore, until we know if it was Solomon Yates or Charlotte Wood that killed John Carson, we can't hold her. Full stop."

"There is a third scenario we're overlooking," Granger said. He nodded his agreement, but his eyes searched Freya's for something else.

"Guv?" Freya said.

"You mentioned Theodore Wood. Where is he? According to Chapman's reports, he's been missing since a few days before the murder. Have we managed to find him?"

"Not yet," Chapman said. "I've had every hotel, Airbnb, and caravan park in a fifty-mile radius checked. Nobody by that name has checked in anywhere."

"What about his phone?" he asked.

"He didn't take it," Freya said. "No car. No phone."

"Taxi firms?" Granger asked.

"Checked," Chapman replied. "None of them received any calls."

"He's on foot, guv," Freya said. "Unless his wife dropped him somewhere before all this happened. But that would indicate a premeditated murder. It doesn't support the idea that John Carson was assaulting Franky and one of them caught him in the act."

"Your theory stacks up," Granger said with a sigh. "I agree that Solomon Yates and Andrew Sykes were involved in the Carsons' dog being taken. And I agree that killing the dog could easily have been a warning shot across John Carson's bows. But the second time? This time?" he said, shaking his head. "This could easily have been either of them. Charlotte Wood, Theodore Wood, or his father, Solomon Yates. And given Andrew Sykes' involvement in the dognapping episode, and from what you've told me about his run in with Chapman, I'd say he was a strong contender, too. He's clearly a nasty piece of work."

"That's why I want to let her go, guv," Freya said, perching on the edge of Chapman's desk. "If we let her go, my hope is that she'll lead us straight to him."

"Straight to who?" Granger asked. "Be clear now."

"To the killer," she replied. "Whichever one of them that might be."

Granger mulled the idea over for a few moments before nodding his agreement with obvious reluctance.

"You'll follow her?" he said.

"Gillespie and Cruz will be in one car. Nillson and I will be in another," she replied, and Cruz glanced across at Gillespie, visibly enthused at the idea of tailing Charlotte Wood.

"You'll need support," Granger added.

"I'll ask Sergeant Priest to mobilise a team," Chapman said.

"Wait until I've spoken to her," Freya said.

"Are you suggesting another interview, DI Bloom?" Granger said.

She straightened and stepped over to the window that overlooked the high street and the station car park. The space where Ben's car should be was empty, and that empty sensation returned to the pit of her stomach. Across the road from the station, parked outside the charity shop, which was yet to open, was a dark grey BMW. A single occupant sat at the wheel, and from Freya's elevated viewpoint, she could see the driver was looking at a phone.

"Just one last little chat," she replied. "I'd like to run our theory by her."

"And DC Gold? Where does she come into this?" Granger asked. Gold stopped typing at the mention of her name. After three days of sitting with the victim's wife, she had plenty of notes to type up and had been working away in silence while the team discussed the theory.

"I'm going to send her to Leigh Carson's home."

"You want me to go back there?" Gold said. "She'll be sick of the sight of me by now."

"I've got a feeling that Leigh Carson hasn't been entirely honest with us. If this isn't the first time her husband has assaulted Franky, or anyone else for that matter, then maybe she knows something. Be direct. You're going to have to ask some difficult questions. Gauge her responses, her body language, and her tone. We've got a theory. Maybe she can help us prove it."

"I'll try my best," Gold said.

"Do you want to take a uniform with you?" Granger asked. "For support?"

"No," Gold replied. "I'll be fine. She'll open up more if I'm on my own."

"Looks like your team has everything covered," Granger said, and he looked around at them, then back at Freya with a slightly concerned look on his face. "Except Savage and Anderson. Where are they?"

CHAPTER FIFTY-THREE

"Another interview?" Charlotte Wood grumbled as a uniform ushered her from the corridor into interview room two. She held her cuffed hands before her, as if to prove a point. "I've told you everything. I've even confessed to the crime. What else do you want from me?"

"Sit down, Charlotte," Freya said, and she gave Nillson the nod to begin the recording.

Charlotte Wood kicked the chair from opposite Freya and slumped into it. Her hands rested on her lap, and she stared at Freya as a teenager might eyeball a headteacher from across a desk. The recording began. The long beep ensued and finished, and Freya introduced the parties present, then looked up at the uniform by the door. "I'm expecting Mrs Wood's legal representative. I imagine he'll be arriving shortly. Please see him in."

"Ma'am," the uniform replied, and slipped out of the door.

"Now then, Charlotte. Before your legal representative arrives, I wondered if there was anything you'd like to say."

"You called Mr Gough?" she replied. "How did you know I would request anybody to represent me?"

"Because you're stalling for time, Charlotte. Just like you've been stalling for time ever since you arrived here."

"I don't follow," she said.

"How long have you been here, Charlotte?"

"Two days," she replied, without hesitation. "And a bit."

"And how long are we permitted to keep you before charging you?"

Charlotte shrugged, feigning ignorance. "I'm not a copper," she said.

"Oh, don't give me that. You blurted it out in your first interview. You told me that I had twenty-four hours to charge you, and I replied that the CPS would grant me thirty-six given the severity of the crime," Freya said, keeping her voice calm. "Now, perhaps I can ask the question again? How long are we permitted to keep you in custody?"

Charlotte resumed her bitter sneer, and mumbled her response, "Thirty-six hours."

"And how many times have you complained to the custody sergeant about how long you've been trapped in that cell? I imagine you must be growing tired of flimsy sandwiches, microwave pasta, and warm water."

"What's your point, Bloom?" Charlotte said.

But her acceptance of Freya's observations was all Freya was looking for. She was about to move on to her next point when there was a knock at the door, and the uniform who had left to fetch Harold Gough stepped inside, holding the door for the duty solicitor.

"Ah, Mr Gough. Take a seat, please," Freya said, nodding her thanks to the uniform, who waited by the door. "For the benefit of the recording, Mr Harold Gough, Mrs Wood's legal representation has arrived." She stared at the little man who drew out the remaining seat and placed his files on the table. "I presume you received the updated evidence submission?" Freya asked.

"I did. About fifteen minutes ago," he replied. "But I must say, I'm surprised to find my client already being interviewed."

"Oh, it shouldn't be a surprise, Mr Gough. A man like you with a hunger to advance his career would have been counting down the thirty-six hours until Mrs Wood here was either charged or freed. In fact, I'd go as far as to say that was you sitting in your car across the road from the station this morning. Dark grey BMW. Am I right?"

"It's a long way to come from the city, Inspector Bloom. I imagine you'd have remarked upon my tardiness had I been late."

"And what do you make of the evidence submission?" Freya asked.

"Well, I haven't had a chance to discuss the matter with my client."

"Not to worry. We can go through it all now," Freya said, cutting the weak, little man off and opening her file. She flicked through the papers to find the notes she prepared prior to the interview. "Shall we begin with the good stuff? The murder weapon. A fillet knife with a red handle. Quite distinguishable. It must have come from quite a nice set once upon a time. Sadly, it was found not far from John Carson's body with your fingerprints on the blade, Mrs Wood. The handle had been wiped clean, of course. Then we have your daughter's underwear, found a few feet from the knife. The knife is the means and the underwear provides the motive. All we need is an opportunity, which, of course, is provided for by your statement, during which you explain that you discovered your daughter, Franky, had run off. You then called the Carsons to see if they had seen her, and then went to search for her. You took your husband's car, seeing as he hadn't been seen for days. It was there you discovered John Carson's body."

"No," Charlotte replied. "I found him and Franky. He seduced her. He was..." She stopped, biting her lip as if she daren't even think the words let alone verbalise them.

Freya enjoyed her little outburst. It was exactly what she had expected from Charlotte.

"Then we found the victim's clothes, burned in a corner of a neighbouring plot of land," Freya said. "A plot of land owned by your father-in-law."

"What?" Charlotte said.

"Oh, yes. We made that connection. What was it you told me when we first met? You said the family deal with their problems themselves. It's a matter of pride. Is that right?"

"So?"

"Here's what I think happened. I think you found John Carson dead with his killer standing over him. I think you helped strip John

Carson and then burn his clothes, tossing the knife and the underwear on your way. Then you returned to the scene to move the body."

"And why would I move the body?" Charlotte asked, just as Gough made an attempt to convince her to say nothing. He inhaled and sat back a little. Clearly, he had realised Charlotte's mistake, even if she hadn't.

"That's what I was wondering," Freya said, unable to hide the smile that was spreading across her face. "Why did you move the body?"

Charlotte glanced at Gough, who leaned forward, and although Freya couldn't hear what he said, Charlotte's response told her all she needed to know.

"No comment," Charlotte said, albeit with very little confidence.

"Can you explain why you moved the body?" Freya asked.

"No comment."

"What was so significant about the stones on which John Carson's body was discovered?"

"No comment."

"Do you know who moved John Carson's body?"

"No comment."

"Do you know who killed John Carson?" Freya said.

"No comment."

"Are you concealing the identity of John Carson's murderer?"

"No comment."

"Charlotte Wood, despite your confession, I do not believe it was you who killed John Carson–"

"What? It was me. I told you it was me."

"Then why did you move the body an hour after he was killed?"

Charlotte's mouth hung open. But she said nothing.

Freya had no more points to prove. There were no more questions to be asked. She turned to Gough.

"I'm sorry, Mr Gough, but you'll be disappointed to learn that this will not be your opportunity to progress your career with a big win at a murder trial."

"I'm sorry?" he asked, but Freya had already turned her attention back to Charlotte.

"Charlotte Wood, I'm sure at this stage you'd be expecting to be escorted to the custody desk to be charged. But I can see no case here. We need irrefutable evidence that there was nobody else who could have possibly killed John Carson."

"But I confessed—"

"Despite your confession," Freya added, raising her hand to catch the attention of the uniform. "Escort her to the custody desk to collect her belongings, please."

"What? No," Charlotte said, as the uniform approached her and attempted to unlock her handcuffs. "No. Get off me. I did it. It was me."

"Mrs Wood, you're not helping your cause," Gough said.

"Oh, shut up, you pathetic, little man," she snapped at him, then turned back to Freya. "I told you it was me. I killed him. The knife is mine. I drove the car there. I killed him."

Freya announced the end of the interview and the time, then Nillson hit the button to end the recording.

"Mr Gough, it's good manners to offer your client a lift home, regardless of the outcome. But I'm sure you already knew that."

He clearly did, and as Charlotte Wood was ushered back through the door, he followed.

"I wasn't expecting that," Nillson said, when just the two of them remained.

"I was," Freya replied. "I needed to be sure it wasn't her. Thankfully, Gough is smarter than he looks. There was no way Charlotte Wood would have realised her mistake otherwise. I'm certain it wasn't her."

"But are you certain where she will lead us?" Nillson asked.

Freya closed her file and laid her hands on top.

"No. Not yet," she said, and then turned to face the young DS. "But I have a feeling this afternoon will be one filled with surprises. Now, get your stuff. I'll meet you in the car park. Bring Chapman, too, will you? I think she needs some fresh air."

"What about back-up?" Nillson asked. "Shall I ask her to call Sergeant Priest to organise a unit?"

"No," Freya said, mulling over the facts in her head. "No, we'll manage."

"Are we going after Charlotte Wood, boss?" Nillson asked. "If so, we'll need something a bit more subtle than your Range Rover. She'll spot that a mile off."

"Leave Gillespie and Cruz to go after Charlotte," Freya replied. "The plan has changed. We have our own target."

CHAPTER FIFTY-FOUR

The morning traffic had died down, and the country lanes that connected the Savage farm to Bardney were as good as empty. The only delay Ben and Anderson faced was when a tractor pulled out from a field gate ahead of them. Many people would have put their foot down to get ahead of the lumbering beast. But Ben, being of farming stock who had faced the same difficulties the tractor driver had been facing, let him out and slowed to a crawl behind.

"I guess this is rush hour in farmland," Anderson remarked.

"If we didn't have the farms, Jenny, we'd be a county of housing estates in a country full of hungry people."

"Sorry, did I touch a nerve there?"

"No. But I've sat behind the wheel of a tractor many a time. It's not an easy task, you know."

He spoke quietly while he unlocked his phone, and his concentration was on finding a number.

"Driving on the phone?" Anderson asked, and Ben glanced down at the speedometer.

"I'm doing five miles an hour," he replied.

"Oh. I didn't realise there was a speed limit associated with that particular crime."

He hit dial, rolled his eyes at her, and then dropped the phone between his legs as the call routed through the car's Bluetooth system.

"Ben?" a familiar voice said. She was driving and had to shout to be heard over the road noise.

"Jackie. How did you get on?"

"Oh God, Ben. She nearly caught me. I was pretending to type up my notes."

"But she didn't catch you?"

"No," she replied. "Thankfully. I managed to get into Andrew Sykes' company bank account. Don't even ask me how I did it. I swear I'll be repaying favours for the next month after this."

"You sound quite positive, though," Ben said. "You must have found something."

"I did. But I wish I hadn't. It turns out that Andrew Sykes' biggest customer is a little company out on the edge of Bardney. They lease a warehouse on Juniper Farm."

"Juniper Farm?" Ben said, making sure he'd heard correctly. "I know it. It's up past the bridge over the river."

"That's not the news, though," Jackie said. "Guess who owns the business?"

"I don't know," Ben said, as the tractor in front of them indicated to turn into the next field. Ben slowed even more to give the driver some space.

"Charlotte and Theodore Wood," Jackie said, her slight Edinburgh accent adding to her conspiratorial tone. "I looked them up on the government website. They buy stuff in from China and sell it all on Amazon. The turnover is low."

"The Woods? I don't get it."

"He's a self-employed courier–"

"I know, I know. You told me," Ben said, and he heard the sharpness in his tone, and he softened. "But..."

"But what, Ben?" Jackie said. "You asked me to have a look. All I'm doing is telling you what I found."

"Sorry, Jackie. I shouldn't have snapped. It's just that now he's linked to the Woods, it's even more confusing," Ben said, and he glanced across at Anderson, who nodded her agreement, wide-eyed.

"We had Sykes and Yates down as dognappers. That's one avenue. Then yesterday we linked Yates to the Woods as the girl's grandad. But that's as far as it went as far as Sykes was concerned. Now you're telling me he's in with the Woods."

"So?" Jackie said, and he imagined her shrugging off the comment. "It doesn't mean anything."

"It means he's very likely more involved than we think, Jackie. What did Freya have to say this morning?"

"Do you mean before or after Will Granger gave her hell for not knowing where two of her team were?" Jackie replied.

"Oh, God," Ben said. "I hoped he wouldn't miss us."

"Well, he did. And DI Bloom had no other option but to tell him she didn't know where you were."

"She could have lied."

"You're right. She could have. But she didn't."

"What did she have to say about the investigation? I spoke to her last night, and she said she was going to make a plan in the morning."

"She did make a plan," Jackie said, her tone still not as warm as it had been. "They've gone after Charlotte Wood."

"What do you mean they've gone after her? She's in… Oh, don't tell me she let her go?"

"Granger gave her no other option. She can't charge her for murder when there are so many alternatives. At best, Charlotte Wood is an accessory."

"And she can't be charged as an accessory if we can't prove who actually killed John Carson," Ben finished.

"Exactly."

"So, Freya let her go in the hope that she'll lead them to the killer? If she is an accessory, that is."

"That's the idea. Gillespie, Cruz, Nillson, and DI Bloom are all following her."

"Jesus. Is that what it's come to? What about you?"

"I've been sent back to Leigh Carson's house. They were toying with a theory that John Carson had assaulted Franky before. Sometime last year."

"Why?" Ben said. "He can't have. Why would the families still be friends?"

"They think it was Sykes and Yates who stole the Carsons' dog and buried it by the ruins. DI Bloom thinks Leigh Carson might know something. She wants me to press her."

"So, the theory is that Yates and Sykes took the dog as some kind of warning?" Ben said, remembering the first time they had met Charlotte. "That makes sense. She made a point about the family taking care of their own problems. She said it when we first saw her."

"Yeah, that's what DI Bloom said as well. It was in her report."

"So, let me get this straight," Ben said. "Yates caught John Carson the first time he assaulted Franky. A year ago. He killed the dog as a warning, which suggests Carson didn't actually harm her, but was close."

"Right," Anderson said, nodding, and speaking up for the first time during the call. "If he had actually been found doing anything more serious, Yates would have killed him there and then."

"That's what we thought," Jackie said.

"But he did do it again, and this time it was more serious, judging by the fact we found Franky's underwear. The question is, who caught him? Charlotte has confessed, but she could be covering for Yates, her father-in-law."

"Or Theodore," Jackie added. "They said he hasn't been seen for days, but that could all be a ploy to keep him hidden."

"But why hide only to let his wife take the blame?" Ben said. "That doesn't add up. But you're right. It could have been any one of them. Charlotte called the Carsons to ask if they'd seen Franky. Then she could have taken her husband's car to search for her. She knows the ruins are Franky's favourite place, so she goes there. The question is, did she arrive too late, and discover Yates or her husband with John Carson's body? Or did she arrive just in time, and do the killing herself? Either way, it explains why her prints were on the knife. She stripped him, then took his clothes to her father-in-law's farm to burn them. Then she went back and moved the body to the rocks. That explains the delay in Carson dying and his body being moved."

"Wow," Jackie said. "You're like the male version of DI Bloom. That's her exact theory."

"But one thing doesn't make sense," Ben said. "If Yates killed the dog as a warning, but didn't tell his son or daughter-in-law about Carson, then why would she go back and move the body to the rocks? She wouldn't know the significance. It had to be Yates who went back."

"No," Anderson said. "He's too weak. He's an old man. There's no way he could have moved John Carson's limp and lifeless body."

"So, then it had to be Sykes," Ben said. "He's young and strong. That's how he's involved."

"You just made a link that DI Bloom hasn't," Jackie said.

"Good," Ben said, as he turned into Juniper Farm. The surface was gravel and bumpy, so he slowed, dropping down into second gear. "Keep it to yourself, will you? If Freya and the team are on Charlotte Wood's tail, and she really is going to meet the killer, then Freya will be onto Sykes."

"What does it matter who brings him in?" Jackie said.

"It matters, Jackie," Ben said, seeing a van heading towards them. He pulled into a passing spot, which was nothing more than a piece of verge that had been worn down by passing vehicles. "I want Sykes before he's taken in custody. He's got a lot to answer for, that man."

"Oh, Ben. Don't do anything stupid. Chapman wouldn't want you to."

"I can take care of myself, Jackie," Ben said, as he raised a hand to acknowledge the passing van driver, who mirrored the move.

"You're a fool if you do," Jackie said. "This is your career."

But Ben's attention was elsewhere. He studied the van in the rear-view mirror.

"Jackie, what was the number plate I gave you and Chapman? Sykes' van?" he said, moving his foot to the brake pedal.

"How do I know? I wrote it down in my pad, but I'm driving," she said. "It ended in CKV. I'm sure of it. Why?"

Shoving the gear stick into reverse, Ben backed onto the track, searching for a place to turn around.

"I've got him," Ben said, glancing across at Anderson. "He's leaving Juniper Farm in his van."

"Ben, promise me," she said, her voice suddenly anxious. "Ben? Ben?"

"I've got to go," he said.

"Promise me."

"Thanks for all your help, Jackie," he said. "I mean it. It's good to know you've got my back."

She began to argue, but he ended the call and took a long breath, processing all the information Jackie had divulged.

Then, with a final look across at Anderson, he put his foot down hard.

CHAPTER FIFTY-FIVE

"There he is," Ben said, pointing at the roof of the white panel van, just visible above the hedgerow that separated Juniper Farm from the B-road that led from Bardney to Branston. "He's heading back towards Bardney."

"Shall I call it in?" Anderson asked, slipping her phone from her pocket. Her thumb poised over a name on the list of recently dialled numbers, and Ben glimpsed Freya's name at the top.

"No. No, we'll handle this ourselves."

"Ben, this could be serious. He could be dangerous."

"Correction. He is dangerous," Ben said, as he pulled from the farm track onto the main road.

"You heard what Jackie said. Even she told you not to do anything stupid."

"We can't call it in, Jenny," he said. "The only link we have to him is a photo we took during an illegal search of his property and some intelligence garnered through scrupulous means. Granger would have a fit if he knew we'd been in his house without a warrant. And as for Gold. I have no idea how she got the information on Sykes' bank, and I'd rather not drag her into this any more than she already is. And then there's the misuse of the ANPR system that I asked Priest to help me with."

"It shows how much people think of Chapman," Anderson said.

"It's just a shame we can't use any of it," Ben replied.

"So, we can't actually arrest him?"

"Not until we have something on him. Something formal," he added. "Something that a decent lawyer wouldn't pick up on and have slung out of court."

"So, what are you going to do?"

"We're going to follow him and wait for him to make a mistake. And if I'm right, he'll be making one in about thirty seconds' time."

Anderson looked ahead, wondering what Ben was talking about. And as predicted, Sykes slowed then pulled into a side track without indicating.

"Where's he going?" Anderson asked.

But Ben said nothing. Everything would become clear in a few minutes. Ben indicated, waited for an oncoming car to pass, then slowly, he entered the track, keeping a healthy five hundred yards behind Sykes' van. The track was bumpy, and the car rocked from side to side as he navigated pot holes and overgrown trees that reached across, trying to block the way. Branches scraped at paintwork as Ben passed, and at every slight bend, he slowed to ensure Sykes was still way in front.

But when they rounded the last corner, the white van was stopped up ahead. Around the van, overgrown brambles and bushes spilled from where they grew. And in the distance, the roof of the old, rundown farmhouse stuck out above the trees.

"It's the farm," Anderson said.

"The back entrance," Ben explained. "This track led to the ruins. But he's not going there."

They waited to see if Sykes was nearby, but after a few moments, Ben's impatience got the better of him. He switched off the engine and climbed out. Anderson followed suit, and he met her stare over the roof of his car.

"You don't have to come, Jenny," he said. "You've done enough. You've more than proved your worth to the team."

"I'm not doing this to prove my worth, Ben," she said, almost appalled that he could even think that. "I'm doing this for Chapman."

She walked ahead and Ben had to run a few steps to catch up. As they neared the van, each of them quietened their footsteps. Ben pulled the rear doors open, hoping to catch Sykes unawares. But the driver's seat was empty, and in the rear of the van was everything Ben needed.

"There's his mistake," Ben said.

"A dog cage?" Anderson replied, searching the empty space for anything else of interest.

Ben shook his head, and she stared at him curiously.

"The jacket," he said, and he gestured at the old tweed coat that had been tossed over the passenger seat. "There'll be a rip in the arm with a piece of material missing."

"The shipping container," Anderson said. "I'll bet he's there."

"No, he's in the house," Ben said, and he ran. They navigated the maze of pathways with familiarity and came to a stop close to where the dogs were chained up.

Stopping beside him, Anderson caught her breath, and spoke quietly.

"You want me to distract them again?" she asked.

She was a brave woman. A fool, according to Freya. But brave, nonetheless.

"No," he said. "Not this time."

He strode around the corner, making little effort to be stealthy. And just as he had thought, the dogs were gone. Two chains were lying on the ground, but everything around them was still.

"Where are they?" Anderson whispered.

"Yates has them. He's scarpered," Ben said, and he crept towards the house. The front door was open, as it had been on his previous visit. But where before the house had been silent, now the sound of drawers and cupboards opening and closing came from the living room.

With Anderson behind him, Ben took the few steps to the living room door. He must have blocked the light or made a noise somehow, because Sykes stopped his frantic search of the place and looked up at him. It was the man Ben had seen at Chapman's house. He was dark-haired with tanned skin. His face, though, bore the pockmarks of teenage acne, and every inch of his arms were covered in tattoos, illegible in the poor light.

"Andrew Sykes?" Ben said, and the man simply stood straight and turned to meet Ben head-on. "I don't know if I should arrest you for dognapping or rape."

"Neither," a voice said from behind them, and Ben turned to find Freya and Nillson in the kitchen doorway. A few seconds later, Freya's perfume caught them up and seemed to fill the dingy, old house with the essence of expensive oils and leather. She stepped closer, staring Ben in the eye, before moving past him and standing between him and Sykes. "Unless, of course, Mr Sykes has something he wants to tell us. In which case, we could add murder to that list."

"I've got nothing to say," Sykes grumbled. His deep voice seemed to be swallowed by the dust in the room, and by the way he adjusted his feet, he seemed to be preparing to fight his way out.

"Do you want to do this the hard way?" Freya asked him. "There's a dog cage in the back of your van, Mr Sykes. The same type as the others in the shipping container on this property. Given your previous record for illegally trading stolen dogs, I'd say we have a good case against you, and we haven't even started trying yet."

"Dognapping?" he scoffed. "Not my style."

"Okay, then. How about rape?"

"Eh?"

"And we'll throw in actual bodily harm, too. Just for good measure," she said.

"I don't know what you're talking about," he said, in that tone that Ben and every other police officer had heard a hundred times or more. The words were a denial, but the tone hinted at a challenge to prove it.

Freya gave Nillson the nod, who in turn leaned out of the kitchen door and muttered something to somebody.

That was when Chapman entered the building. She paused for a moment, as if she had doubts about what she was about to do. But, spurred on by encouragement from the team, she took a breath and walked the few steps to the living room doorway. Ben stepped back to give her space, nodding his support, which she received with the faint hint of a smile.

And then she stood before him. Freya, being very cautious, remained where she was. Between them. A guard. The senior officer in what was turning out to be a complex investigation involving many crimes.

But there was only one crime that mattered right then. And the right officer was there to bring it to a close.

"Andrew Sykes," Chapman said, her voice wavering with fear and hatred. She cleared her throat, refusing to break eye contact with the man. "I'm arresting you on suspicion of rape, ABH, and the illegal trading of dogs. You do not have to say anything. But it may harm your defence if you do not mention when questioned something which you later rely on in court. Anything you do say may be given in evidence."

CHAPTER FIFTY-SIX

"Do you understand? Mr Sykes?" Freya asked. But his mouth hung open in amazement, and his stare remained fixated on Chapman.

"You're a copper?"

"Afraid so," Chapman replied.

It took both Ben and Nillson to wrestle the man to the old, wooden floor, and they held him there for Chapman to snap the cuffs on. And when she had finished, she exhaled. She would never heal, of course. Even Ben knew that victims of sexual assault never truly healed. But the act of snapping those cuffs on and delivering the police action would ease the pain a little.

Nillson and Anderson dragged Sykes out of the house, along with Chapman, leaving Ben and Freya alone in the house. He nodded at the kitchen table, but said nothing.

"The knife," she said quietly. "Good spot."

"I don't know how we missed it the first time."

"There's a lot we missed on this one. I'm afraid none of us have been at peak performance, have we?"

"I didn't..." Ben began. "Anderson and me. We didn't–"

"I know," she said, cutting him off. "I suppose I always knew you wouldn't do that to me. I just let my heart rule my mouth sometimes."

"You're not the only one guilty of that, Freya."

"I know," she said. "I know this is hard. But I don't want to lose you. No. It's more than that. I saw what you did for Chapman, and it just reiterates what a good friend you are. The truth is, Ben, I don't want to share that with anyone."

"Even the person who saved your life?" Ben asked, with a little sideways nod towards the kitchen door.

"Anderson? She told you all about it, I suppose."

"You know she's scared, right?" Ben said, ignoring Freya's question. "You know she's scared of being alone? She thinks the world of you. That's why she left your place when you asked her to, despite not having anywhere to go."

"She didn't have to leave."

"She came to my house that night. You must have pointed it out as you passed it."

"I did," Freya said, then sighed. "If I could turn back time."

"I wouldn't have changed a single thing," Ben said as his phone began to ring. "There's more good to come out of this yet. You mark my words."

He answered the call, but didn't turn away from Freya.

"Ben, it's Jackie."

"Hi, Jackie. Everything okay?"

"No, Ben. No, it's not. I put some pressure on Leigh Carson. God, it was horrible. After all she's been through."

"What did she say?" Ben asked, and Freya cocked her head, tuning into the call from afar.

"John Carson didn't assault Franky, Ben," she said. "It was Charlotte."

"He attacked Charlotte?"

"No. It was consensual, Ben. They were having an affair."

"An affair?" Ben repeated, and Freya took a step back, as if she had lost her balance.

"It all began about a year ago. Leigh found out. They all knew about it. But it was over. They put it behind them. Just a drunken episode that shouldn't have happened."

"This changes everything," Ben said.

"What do you want me to do?"

"Stay there. Stay with Leigh. Where is she now?"

"I was hoping you wouldn't ask," Jackie said. "I had to tell her and the wee lad, Scott, about Charlotte confessing. I hope that's okay? I mean, it's common knowledge now, isn't it? And it's not like we're charging her."

"How did they take it?" Freya asked, and she eyed Ben cautiously.

"I'm not so sure. They disappeared upstairs a while ago. Leigh seemed quite upset. Maybe she's taking a bath. She does that a lot. What should I do? Shall I go and find her?"

"No. No, give her some space. Just call up to make sure she's okay," Freya said.

They heard Jackie walk across the room then clear her throat.

"Leigh," she said, in that gentle, motherly tone that made her a perfect FLO. "Leigh, it's me."

"Is she okay, Jackie?" Ben said.

"Hold on. I'll pop my head upstairs," she replied. Then, a moment later, "Leigh, it's me. Listen, I just need to make sure you're okay? Leigh? Leigh?"

A muffled voice could be heard over the line, but it wasn't the voice of a woman.

"Ben?" Jackie said, and her voice carried a hint of panic. "Ben, she's gone. Scott said she left a while ago. He said she's gone to the farm to see Franky's grandad."

"Well, she won't find him there," Freya said. "Whatever you do, don't leave. Stay there and call me when she gets back. Good work, Jackie."

Ben ended the call and stared at Freya, who was leaning on the back of an old, wooden chair, processing the information she'd overheard.

"All roads point to Theodore Wood," he said.

"Indeed," she replied. "That is exactly what I was thinking."

It was then that her phone began to ring.

"Looks like things are back to normal," Ben joked, as one of their phones seemed always to be ringing.

She looked up at him, phone in hand.

"I'm glad they are," she said, then answered the call. She routed it through the loudspeaker and held it out for Ben to hear. A slight pang of relief sprouted in his heart. Things really were back to normal.

"Boss?" a man's voice called out.

"Gillespie? What is it? Where are you?"

"We followed her to Metheringham, boss. To the train station. Gough dropped her off and drove away. She's on the platform on her own."

Ben knew the station well. And they both knew the station was a sore spot for Gillespie. Only a few months ago, a suspect had thrown himself in front of a train right before Gillespie's eyes.

"Where is she heading?" Ben asked. "Into Lincoln or out toward Peterborough?"

A few seconds of silence ensued, and then Gillespie's heavy breathing returned.

"I don't think she's going in any of those directions, Ben," he said. "I think she's looking for a one-way ticket, if you catch my meaning."

"Stop her," Freya said. "Keep her calm. Don't make a fuss. Offer her a lift or something. Anything, Gillespie."

"I'll do my best, boss," he said. "I'll let you know how I get on."

"Gillespie?" Freya said.

"Boss?" he replied, his tone far from chirpy.

"Are you okay? Do you think Cruz could handle it?"

"I'll be alright," he replied, and the speaker rasped as he exhaled. "I'll take her home. There's no train due for ten minutes anyway. For all we know, I might have drawn the wrong conclusion."

"It's better to be safe than sorry," Freya said. "She's scared. She needs to be with somebody, and we still don't know where Franky is."

"I could take her to the hospital?" Gillespie suggested. "If I'm right, then she needs help."

"If you're right, she needs to be admitted into an institution," Freya said. "But not yet. Take her home, Gillespie. With any luck, her daughter is there to take care of her."

"Will do, boss."

The call ended, and Freya puffed her cheeks out in a mixture of what Ben guessed to be disbelief and hope.

"So much for her leading you to the killer," Ben said, and the comment caused Freya's eyebrows to raise in curiosity. But she said nothing. "Why would she want to kill herself? It doesn't make sense."

"No. It's not right. You should have seen her, Ben. At the station. It was as if she wanted to go away. To prison, I mean. It's almost like she doesn't want to be on the outside."

"She doesn't feel safe on the outside?" Ben suggested, and Freya nodded. Then her eyes widened, just as a terrible thought hit Ben.

"When we searched the Woods' house," Freya said. "We found pills by Theodore's bed. Do you remember?"

"I do," Ben replied. "Are you thinking what I'm thinking?"

"I am, but I'm also kicking myself. What if he overdosed? Why didn't we think of it before?"

"Because we've all been caught up in our own worlds, Freya," he said.

"Where's Chapman? We need her to make some calls," Freya said, and marched from the room. She stopped in the doorway and turned to look at Ben. "Well? Aren't you coming?"

"Where to?" he replied.

"The hospital, of course. If Theodore Wood attempted suicide by overdose, then that's where he'll be. A least until he has recovered. Then he'll either be moved to an institution or home. It all depends on the assessments the doctors make."

"You want me to come with you?" Ben said, a little surprised at the sudden turn of attitude.

"You are my right-hand man, are you not?" Freya asked. "And besides, if we're right about this, and he is in hospital, while I'm talking to him, you can find out how he got there. He didn't bloody well walk, did he?"

CHAPTER FIFTY-SEVEN

Freya and Ben had been on the road for fifteen minutes, heading towards Lincoln County Hospital, when Freya's phone rang out over the car's speakers. Chapman's name displayed on the screen, and Ben leaned forward to answer the call, leaving Freya to focus on the road.

"Chapman," he said. "That was quick."

"This isn't the first time I've had to navigate the hospital's phone options, Ben," she said. "You get to know the shortcuts."

"Well?" Freya said, biting down on her lower lip.

Chapman sighed audibly. Somewhere close by, Anderson and Nillson could be heard, and Freya imagined them all escorting Sykes to the main road ready for the transporter to collect them.

"You were right, ma'am," she said. "Theodore Wood was admitted to A and E last Thursday. He was unconscious and needed his stomach pumped and a heavy dose of Naloxone. I told them you're on your way."

"What's that?" Ben said.

"The opposite of pain killers," Freya said. "Like an antidote, but not quite. You said he arrived last Thursday. So, unless he slipped out for a few hours, we can strike him off the list. Did they say if he arrived alone?"

"No, ma'am. Sorry, I didn't think to ask. I was just focused on making sure he was there and still alive."

"No need to apologise, Chapman. Anybody else would still be looking for the right number to call. We're just pulling into the hospital now."

"Right. I'll forward you the name of the ward," Chapman said. "Should I head back to the station?"

"Yes," Freya replied. "I want Sykes processed, and if you'd like to be the officer to do that, then be my guest."

"I would, ma'am. Thank you."

"You deserve it. Tell Nillson I want her with you, while Anderson mans the phones," Freya said, as she pulled into the entrance to A and E, parking off to one side to make room for ambulances. "We'll be in touch when we've spoken to Theodore Wood."

She ended the call and fished her warrant card from her pocket in preparation for the security guard who was no doubt just waiting to ask them to move the car.

They strode side by side through the automatic doors, and the guard, as predicted, rose to his feet, opening his mouth.

"We'll be thirty minutes," Freya said, holding her card up, all without breaking stride. "Keep an eye on my car, will you?"

The guard was left dumbstruck and hadn't uttered a single word.

"Did that make you feel good?" Ben asked.

"I'll take any uplift I can get right now," Freya said, glancing up at the sign on the wall. "This way."

She led Ben down a side corridor, with framed photos on the wall of the hospital in years gone by. There were images of doctors with patients and rows of beds. The images were mostly monochrome, taken in a time when things had a habit of seeming to be simpler, though Freya doubted they ever were.

They stopped at the entrance to the ward Chapman had sent through, and she waited for Ben to push the intercom button.

A female answered, and the speaker made her voice sound nasal.

"Hello, it's Detective Inspector Freya—"

The door buzzed open before Freya could finish, and they entered side by side. The ward was quiet, with just a few nurses moving from room to room. A woman was sitting behind the reception, and she gathered some paperwork while Freya and Ben approached.

"You're here to see Theodore Wood. Is that right?" she asked in a thick and alluring Southern Irish accent.

"That's correct," Freya replied. "We were wondering–"

"Follow me," the nurse said, cutting Freya off again. She walked ahead of them, speaking over her shoulder as she made her way along the corridor. "Mr Wood is stable but sensitive. I'm afraid only one of you will be able to speak to him."

She stopped at the door to a private room, addressing them both with solemn professionalism.

"I'll go in," Freya said. "Perhaps–"

"I imagine you'll have some questions for me then," the nurse replied, talking directly at Ben. It was as if she had very little time for chit chat, yet had foreseen any questions they had.

"I do," Ben said, and he nodded to Freya. "I'll be out here when you're done."

The nurse swiped her access card through the reader, then pushed the door open for Freya.

"Good luck," Ben muttered as she stepped inside, out of the nurse's sight.

"You too," she replied, glancing once at the abrupt nurse.

The door closed and an electromagnetic lock clicked into place.

"I was wondering when you'd be here," a voice said, and Freya turned to find a rather handsome, dark-haired man lying on the single bed. The mattress was raised, allowing him to sit upright, and he tossed a well-fingered paperback onto the side table, then took a deep breath. "I suppose you're going to analyse me, put me in a straight jacket, and cart me off to the Francis Willis Unit."

"The Francis Willis Unit?" Freya said

"The mental hospital," he replied. "That's where you're from, isn't it?"

"Mr Wood, I'm Detective Inspector Freya Bloom. I'm with the Lincolnshire Major Investigations Team."

"The police?"

"I'm not a doctor, Theodore," she said, using his first name to both put his mind at ease and convey that she knew about him. His reaction to her next statement would tell her all she needed to know. "I'm investigating the murder of John Carson."

His face dropped. He said nothing at first, merely stared at her in disbelief. Then a weak smile appeared, followed by a feeble laugh.

"You're kidding, right?"

"I'm afraid not. His body was discovered last Friday. I was wondering if you could tell me anything about it."

His face paled, and he shoved himself upright on the bed.

"How?" he asked, and then he stammered, stumbling over the many questions he must have had. It appeared to be the reaction of an innocent man. However, from that moment on, he couldn't look Freya in the eye for any longer than a fleeting glance. In Freya's experience, that was a sign of guilt, direct or indirect.

"He was stabbed in the back," Freya said. "At Tupholme Abbey."

"The ruins?" he gasped.

"Would you happen to know why anybody would want to murder Mr Carson, Theodore?"

"Theo," he said. "Please. And no. I wouldn't. I mean, he's successful. His business does well. But I wouldn't know if he'd made any enemies."

Freya glanced around the room. There were no bouquets of flowers, boxes of grapes, or well-wishing cards. Aside from the pile of clothes on the little armchair and the paperback, he could have arrived twenty minutes ago.

"How are you, Mr Wood?" she asked.

He laughed once. A single snort of breath that conveyed anything but humour.

"I'm here again, aren't I?"

"Again?"

He looked at her, then stared at the door.

"This isn't my first attempt," he mumbled.

"You suffer with depression, I'm guessing?"

"All my life. It's a curse. I guess I'm weak."

"No," Freya said. "No, in my experience, anyone that can speak openly about how they feel is braver than any man that bottles their problems up. Was it the tablets?"

"Painkillers," he said. "They say you just slip away. Like slipping into a warm bath."

"It's not as easy as that. From my limited experience, you have to wait for the bath to run, and once you've turned on the taps, there's no turning back."

He cocked his head, as if the statement had resonated somehow.

"That's more accurate than anything the doctors have ever said. Have you...?"

"No," she said. "You meet all sorts in my line of work. I'm glad to see you're looking well. Your family need you. Franky especially."

"Ah," he said, and his expression softened at the mention of her name. "She's a jewel, that girl."

"Do you want to tell me what happened?" Freya asked.

"Do I have to?"

"No, but you could help us find your friend's murderer if you do."

"What does my being in here have to do with John?"

"Why don't you tell me how they are linked? What made you attempt suicide?" she asked, choosing not to ponder on the words, but rather speak them out loud, directly. Without shame.

"I told you. I was depressed."

"What about?" Freya asked. "What is it that gets you down?"

"Is this a therapy session? I thought you said you weren't a doctor."

"I'm not. I'm sorry, I was hoping..." Freya began, and then she sighed, and perched on the side of his bed. "Theo, I'm sorry to be the one to tell you this. But your wife has confessed to the murder."

"Charlotte? That's impossible."

"She made a statement. Twice, in fact."

"So why are you here?"

"Because you know, as well as I do, that your wife didn't do it."

He let his head fall back onto the bed's steel frame.

"You know then, I suppose."

"I have a theory. I'd like to hear it from you, though. An unprompted version, if you like. I'd hate to sway your perspective."

"My perspective was swayed a long time ago," he replied. "They had an affair. A long time ago."

"How long?"

"A year. Maybe more. I don't know," he said. "But it was over. Or, at least, we thought it was over. A drunken mistake was what they said."

"But it wasn't a solitary event, was it?"

"No," he said, with a slight shake of his head. He closed his eyes, but Freya caught the shine of tears before he hid them.

"And that's why you're here?" Freya asked.

"What would you do if you found out the person you loved was seeing somebody else? Because they thought you were weak. Because you're so caught up in making your business work that you can barely function in a relationship."

"I'm not the best person to answer that," Freya said, and refrained from telling him that she had indeed been in that very position less than a year before. "How would you describe Charlotte's relationship with your father, Theo? Solomon Yates?"

He sighed again and opened his eyes, giving them a wipe with his sleeve.

"You found him then."

"He flies beneath the radar, but not that low."

"There is no relationship. He can't stand her."

"Because he knew about the affair?" Freya asked.

"That was the icing on the cake. But yes. Mainly because of that." He sat up again and crossed his legs, and for a moment, it was as if Freya was speaking to her ex-husband's son, Billy. Talking him through a problem he was having at school. "He caught them at it. That's how we all found out."

"You all?" Freya said.

"Leigh knows. But, like me, she soldiers on, hoping the problem will go away."

"What about Franky? We found her at your father's house. Are they close?"

"Two peas in a pod," he replied, with a proud smile.

"Theo, did your father warn John off, when he first found them?"

The whites of his eyes had reddened, and the tears rolled down freely, until the growth on his face broke their descent. He inhaled, long and deep, and pursed his lips and exhaled slowly.

"My father is of a different generation. He prides himself on the fact that our family takes care of our own problems. He doesn't like outsiders interfering."

"It doesn't sound like you share the sentiment."

"I'm afraid that particular family trait passed me by," he said, and presented the room with a sweep of his arm. "Look at me. Look at where I am. I don't have the strength. I don't have those same family values."

He stopped. Not because the emotions had become too much. But because he was afraid of saying too much. It was the flick of his eyes in Freya's direction that gave him away.

"Is there something you'd like to tell me, Theo?" Freya asked.

"Is she going to prison?" he said. "Charlotte. Is she in custody?"

"No," Freya replied. "We've sent her home."

"Home?" he said, and his eyes widened.

"Where else would we take her? She didn't kill John Carson, and until we can prove she was an accessory–"

"You have to go there. You have to stop it."

"Stop what?" Freya said, and the temperature in the room suddenly dropped a degree or two, as an icy chill ran the length of Freya's spine.

"I may not have inherited the family values, inspector," he whispered. "But my daughter certainly did."

CHAPTER FIFTY-EIGHT

They sped from the hospital car park on the wrong side of the road, to the tune of several angered drivers on their horns, who, to be fair to them, merely saw a shiny, black Range Rover with an impatient driver. They weren't to know that the occupants were police, and they weren't to know that somebody's life was at risk.

Using Freya's phone, Ben dialled Gillespie's number, and they waited for the ringing to come through the speakers. It took four rings for him to answer.

"Aye, boss," he said, when he answered the call. "She's safe and sound. Didn't say much, but we dropped her home."

"Where are you now?" Freya said.

"We're just on our way back to the station. Thought we'd help Chapman out. We heard Sykes was picked up."

"You left Charlotte alone?"

"Aye. I mean, I offered to go in and wait. But she was adamant she would be okay."

"I told you not to leave her alone."

"What was I supposed to do? Barge my way in, boss?"

"Was anybody else there?" Ben asked, and he pointed to Freya which way to turn off a roundabout.

"At the house? I think so," Gillespie replied. "Somebody opened the door for her, but I didn't see who it was. Like I said, she didn't say much. Well, she didn't say anything actually. Not until we pulled up outside the house. Then she seemed to cheer up a bit."

"She's a danger to herself," Freya said. "You just bloody well stopped her stepping in front of a train and now you leave her alone?"

"Aye, well. She promised me she'd be fine. Said something about the family takes care of its own problems, and not to take it personally."

"We're close to the house now. Do me a favour. I need an ambulance and uniform on the scene."

"I don't think she'll do anything, boss. Honestly. Not now."

"Just do as I ask, please."

"Aye," he said. "You're the boss."

She leaned forward and hit the button to end the call.

"Tell me what the nurse told you," Freya said.

Ben took a breath and gripped the door handle as Freya rounded a fairly tight bend far faster than she normally would have.

"He was dropped off at A and E last Thursday. He was conscious, but could barely stand or walk. He'd vomited down himself."

"And how did he get there?"

"A Land Rover. Which I'm guessing is the same one we have in the lab," Ben said. "She said she made enquiries to find his next of kin. Security told her that as soon as Theodore Wood was being wheeled away, the driver sped off. Clipped a kerb on the way out. He told her she was in a hurry to get away."

"Don't tell me. The driver was a middle-aged blonde."

"Nope. I don't even think Charlotte knew he was there. The driver was a young female with dark hair. Seventeen at the most," Ben said.

"Are you telling me a fifteen-year-old girl drove her father to the hospital?"

"A fifteen-year-old girl who spent her childhood on her grandfather's farm, driving around in old trucks and tractors," Ben said.

"She's fifteen, for crying out loud."

"I did the same," Ben said. "Younger, probably. By the time I took my driving test, I'd been driving on my dad's property for years."

Freya wrenched the steering wheel to the left and pulled up outside the Woods' house. She switched the engine off, processing the new information.

"Okay. I don't know what we're going to find in there. But be prepared," Freya said, looking up at the house.

"Do you want to wait for uniform?"

"I'd love to wait," Freya said, and she shoved open the car door. "Sadly, I don't think we have that luxury."

Freya had been so distracted by the investigation during her earlier visits that only now did she appreciate the potential in the property. Ben had, of course. He'd said it could be as nice as the Carsons' home if somebody could afford to pay for the work. The house was larger than average with large windows and a sprawling floorplan. The gardens appeared as if they might have been maintained at some point, but not in the last year or two. The windows needed replacing, or at the very least a lick of paint. The front door was in a similar state, flaking around the letterbox. It was only when Ben reached past Freya to knock on the door that they realised it was ajar, and it opened a fraction at his touch.

They exchanged nervous glances, then Ben pushed the door open further. Neither of them called out. They just listened at first. It was just as Ben said that he would check upstairs that a soft sound came from the kitchen. A sob, and then a hiss.

"Charlotte?" Freya called out in as soft a tone as she could summon given her dislike for the woman. "Charlotte, it's DI Bloom. I'm just checking you're okay. Are you home?"

A notable silence hung in the air like a bad smell, and although when she peered through to the kitchen Freya could see nobody, her senses tuned into something or someone.

She motioned for Ben to follow her and stepped quietly towards the kitchen door, where the eerie silence was explained in a horrifying picture of reality.

The kitchen was, as Freya had noted before, immaculate. Cold and unwelcoming. A single door led out to the rear garden, and a smattering of shoes and wellington boots were scattered on the floor beside it.

The kitchen table was old and stained with careless use, but large enough to seat eight comfortably. Ten at a squeeze, Freya thought.

Charlotte was seated at the end of the table. Her hands lay flat on the wood, and her eyes rolled up to meet Freya's, as she was not daring to move her head. A knife was held to her back. It was a long carving knife with a familiar red handle. One of a set.

CHAPTER FIFTY-NINE

"Franky, put the knife down," Freya said.

"This is our problem. We fix our own problems."

"Franky. She's your mother. Look at her. Look at what you're doing to your own mother."

"You don't know what she did."

"I have an idea," Freya said. "Why don't you put the knife down so we can talk about it?"

"There's nothing to talk about," Franky replied. For a teenager, her voice was deep, and there was a tenaciousness to her tone. Like anything Freya said would brush off like she was Teflon. Nothing was going to stop her. "You've been to see him, haven't you?"

"Your father? Yes," Freya said. "He's looking well. Considering."

Charlotte's brow furrowed, and she tried to turn to stare at her daughter, who simply pressed the tip of the knife harder to still her.

"Don't even think about it," Franky hissed.

"You didn't tell me you know where he is," Charlotte whined. "Where is he? I've been bloody worried sick."

"The only person you ever worried about, Mum, was yourself."

"That's not true. The things I've done for you."

"The things? What things? It was Dad who brought me up. It was Dad who was always there. Not you."

"I was running a business."

"You were out having fun, while Dad was left to pick up the pieces. I told the hospital you were dead. When I visited. I told them it was just us. Dad and me."

"What? The hospital?" Her hurt expression then morphed seamlessly into one of dread. "Are you telling me-"

She paused, seemingly unable to complete the sentence. Franky nodded; the disgust evident in her eyes.

"That's what you drive him to," Franky said. "That's what you do to him. He'd rather kill himself than be with you."

"Franky, I'm his wife. I'm your mother."

"No, you're not. It might be your name on my birth certificate, but you're nothing to me. You have no idea what you've done to him, have you?"

"Franky? Stop this, please."

"You can't even see how much you've hurt him. You and Carson."

"Franky, put the knife down," Ben said. "This can all be resolved."

"Yeah, it can. And it'll be me who resolves it," Franky said.

"Where is he?" Charlotte said, her eyes once more rolling towards Freya, keeping her head perfectly still. "Where's my husband?"

"Shall I tell you what *I* think happened?" Freya said, and she stepped forward to pull a kitchen chair out. She held a hand up to indicate she wasn't a threat to Franky, and then lowered herself into the seat. Then, taking her time, mostly to antagonise Franky into making a mistake, but partly to consider where she might begin, she crossed her legs. Once she was comfy, Freya cleared her throat. "I'll start from the beginning. I'd appreciate if you could let me finish before you voice your arguments. This is just my theory, after all."

"Just a theory?" Franky said. "Why don't you keep your nose out of our business? Go on. Get out. We don't need you. Any of you."

"It is just a theory, Franky," Freya said, ignoring her request for her to leave. She smiled at the young girl, who did indeed at that moment appear more akin to a seventeen-year-old than the fifteen years she actually was. "Charlotte, you'll have to excuse the content of what I'm about to say. I wouldn't usually speak of such things in front of a minor. But given the circumstances..."

"Just say it," Franky hissed. "And you talk to me. Not her."

"Okay. Have it your way," Freya said. "Your mother here has been having an affair with John Carson."

"Tell me something I don't know—"

"I asked you not to interrupt. Please. Show some decency. If you go ahead with this, you'll want me on your side. I can assure you that."

Franky sneered. She shifted her feet and wiped the sweat from her palm before placing the knife back into position.

"Go on," she said.

"The first time they were caught, because there *was* more than one occasion, it was you, Franky. Wasn't it? You caught them up at the ruins. But at that time you were, what? Thirteen? Fourteen? What could you do? You couldn't go to your father. The news would destroy him. He's sensitive. Unlike your grandfather. Am I right?"

Franky licked the underside of her two front teeth, seeming to delight in the memory.

"I can rely on Grandad. He's strong. He doesn't take crap from anyone."

"Yes, yes," Freya said dismissively with a wave of her hand. "The family takes care of its own problems. I've heard it all before. But the fact remains that he, and his counterpart, Andrew Sykes, decided to warn John Carson, at your request. It was you, Franky, who asked them to do it. It was you who masterminded the theft of their dog. It was you who ensured the Carsons were distracted while Sykes took the dog. But you didn't have them sell it, did you? Oh no, Franky. If I was a betting girl, which I'm sorry to say I am, I'd say you killed the dog yourself. You killed the dog, under the supervision of your grandfather, and then you buried it there beneath the stones. A constant reminder of your achievements and a permanent warning to Carson."

"Franky!" Charlotte said, and she seemed genuinely surprised to hear such a thing. "You? And Grandad?"

"He loved that dog," Franky said. "He had to be warned off."

"But a warning from a young teenager wouldn't really cut it with a man like John Carson, would it, Franky? That's why you had to enlist the help of your grandfather, and his grubby little friend."

"Andrew is not grubby," Franky hissed.

"Ah. You have a soft spot for him," Freya said, allowing a grin to spread across her face like the petals of a Peony opening for the morning sun. "We'll come back to him, don't worry. I don't want to lose my train of thought. You see, the affair continued. John Carson didn't pay heed to the warning, did he?"

This question was aimed at Charlotte, whose eyes rolled to the floor, then to her hands and her fumbling fingers.

"I thought so," Freya said. "Sometime in the last week, Franky, your father learned of the affair. I don't know how it was kept a secret for so long, and quite frankly that's neither here nor there. But the fact remains that the news sent your father over the edge. Perhaps your parents argued? Perhaps not? Perhaps you came home and discovered your dad barely conscious. Your mother wasn't around. No, of course not. So, you had to do something, didn't you? Any other kid would have called someone for help. An ambulance, maybe?"

"I am not a kid–"

"But you drove him. You can drive, can't you? Good old Grandad taught you on his farm. You swiped the pills down the back of the bedside table so your mother wouldn't see them. Then you helped your father to his car, and you drove him to the hospital."

Franky's glare was unwavering. She locked stares with Freya with more confidence than many adults have.

"Meanwhile, your mother returned home. She found the house empty. And what does a cheating wife do when presented with such an opportunity?"

"An opportunity?" Charlotte said.

"To leave," Freya explained. "To make plans."

"What plans?"

"Your plans to meet your lover, of course," Freya said. "Sadly, I know first-hand what goes on in the mind of a cheat. You saw a chance to escape."

"This is all lies," Charlotte said. "I told you Theo was missing for days before..."

"Before?" Freya said, and Charlotte bit her lip.

"Before it happened," Charlotte said softly.

I think Theo had been missing. But you know what? I think he came back. I think he came back to fix things. I imagine he came back ready to talk to you. Ready to make amends, to apologise. But all he found was an empty house and a missing pair of walking boots from the pile beside the back door. You pushed him over the edge. But you didn't give him a second thought, did you? You couldn't have cared less how he was feeling."

"That's not true," she sobbed, and then stiffened when Franky reminded her of her precarious position with a prod of the knife.

"The bond between you and your father, Franky, is admirable. I wish I was as close to my own father as you are to yours. You'd do anything for him, wouldn't you?"

Franky stared at her, making no attempt to hide the truth.

"He's a Wood. He's my father."

"And you killed for him," Freya whispered. "You drove back from the hospital so upset that you clipped the kerb in the car park. You knew where your mother would be. You took your father's car to the ruins and that's when you saw them again. You ran to your grandfather's for help. But he wasn't there, was he? So, you took the first knife you could find. A fillet knife with the same handle as the one you're holding now. The type of knife set a couple might get handed down to get them started in life, with a few missing perhaps. And then you ran. You ran as fast as you could. I imagine tears running down your face as you did. Tears of bitter hatred, and tears of revenge. You walked up to them as they lay on the blanket, and you didn't even hesitate. You plunged the knife into his back."

Recalling the events had touched something inside the girl. Her eyes reddened; it was the first true sign of emotion she had displayed.

"If he didn't die, my dad would have. If not last week, then someday soon. John Carson deserved it," the young girl said, her tone soft with a hint of regret or doubt.

"But you hadn't finished," Freya said, and the words seemed even to silence the bird noise from the garden, as if the entrance to hell had opened. "You went after your mother. They both had to die."

"No. It was me," Charlotte said. "You're wrong. I told you it was me. Leave her out of this. It was all me."

"I think we're way past that now, Charlotte," Freya said. "You knew this was coming. You've been running from your daughter ever since, haven't you? You're petrified of her and your father-in-law, and his grubby little friend. You couldn't bring yourself to see her imprisoned for what she'd done, but you couldn't live with her. With the fear of waking up finding her standing over you with a knife to your throat. The only way out was suicide or prison. So, you made an anonymous call to the police to start the investigation. Then you confessed. If you hadn't have made that call, your lover's body could have been up there at the ruins for days. You didn't have the luxury of time, did you? You see, when Franky killed John Carson, she came after you. You ran, of course. It was Franky that moved John Carson's body. Her and her grandfather, who arrived an hour or so later and found Franky in his house, but it was you, Charlotte, who tossed the knife in the grass. I can only imagine it was you who later returned to plant a pair of your daughter's underwear there too. To complete the story. To make us believe John Carson had assaulted your daughter. But you missed one vital point. We found no DNA on John Carson's body, and Franky showed no signs of interference. That struck me as odd. Then there was your confession, which was far too fast, Charlotte. Nobody gives up that easily. Not unless they have something larger to hide."

"You're wrong," Franky said. "The underwear was my idea. And I didn't chase after her. I wouldn't kill *my own mum*." She spoke the words as if the idea was ludicrous, despite standing there with a carving knife pressed into her mother's back.

"Wouldn't, or couldn't?" Freya said, and Franky looked away for long enough to know that Freya had struck a chord. "You couldn't, could you? So, you blackmailed her? That makes sense. Your mother would take the blame for the murder."

"I took my underwear off. Me. It was me who threw the knife in the grass, and it was me who dragged his body to the rocks. I stripped him. I wanted them to know who he was. I wanted them to hate him like I did. His family. I wanted them all to know what he'd done to me."

'What he'd done to you?" Charlotte said, and she turned to stare at her daughter, who for some reason allowed the move, though held the knife ready to strike. "Did John...?"

"Twice," Franky said. "I tried to tell you. But you were so smitten. You dismissed it. You said I was lying because of what you and he had done. Nobody believed me. Not even Grandad."

"Oh, Franky..."

But the young girl pressed the tip of the blade into her mother's chest, silencing the sympathy and regret that, instead, rolled down Charlotte's face.

"I wanted everyone to know. I wanted everyone to listen to me for once. Now they'll listen. Now they'll realise I hadn't made it all up."

She spoke with pride and without fear of consequence. Freya had seen hundreds of adults with less courage, and more than twice her years.

"So, when I set your mum free, you had no other option," Freya said. "She had to pay somehow. The Woods always take care of their own problems. Am I right?"

Franky nodded, and her nostrils flared in time with her heaving chest. Freya was running out of time.

"There are two ways we can go forward now," Freya said. "Franky, you can do what you've been planning to do, and my colleague here will arrest you. You'll spend the next twenty years or so in prison. Or you can put the knife down. You'll both go to prison, but for much shorter terms. You could even have a life ahead of you when you get out."

Freya placed her hands on the table, palms down, mirroring Charlotte.

"Which will it be?"

"There's a third option," a voice said, as the back door slowly creaked open to reveal Leigh Carson raising a shotgun to her shoulder. "You can both go to hell."

There were two screams in quick succession. The first was the chair legs sliding across the tiled floor as Charlotte shoved the chair back and stood, putting herself between the gun and her murderous daughter. The second was the sound Charlotte emitted as Leigh pulled the trigger, and it was cancelled out by the blast of the shotgun.

The whole event had taken less than three seconds and seemed to play out in slow motion, until the moment the tiny pellets hit Charlotte's chest, and then, in an instant, she slammed into the range, landing in a twisted heap, still and silent.

Ben was the first to move. He bounded across the room, tackled Leigh to the floor, and wrestled the weapon from her grip. Leigh Carson offered no resistance. She neither smiled nor grimaced. She was, Freya thought, in a state of fulfilled revenge. The consequences of her actions no longer mattered to her.

Ben tossed the gun to one side. It was an old Remington. Freya recognised it from the days spent on shoots with her father and his old cronies, when she would be confined to the back of the Land Rover, cold and numbed at the sight of the growing pile of pheasants. She recalled Ben's description of the weapon Solomon Yates had carried when they had first met.

Franky, meanwhile, was dumbstruck. Blood spatter streaked across her face and it seemed an age until she blinked. Slowly, she turned to stare down at her mother's body, emotionless.

"It's over, Franky," Freya said.

The girl took a few moments longer to stare at her mother's body. Freya was unsure if there was any remorse at all. Perhaps the final actions of her mother's life had somehow swayed her opinion of the woman. As if the move to save her daughter had shone a new light on who she really was. Or perhaps, Freya thought, Franky was simply savouring the moment. Taking in every detail to recall during the lonely nights and long years ahead of her.

She turned to look at Freya. Her eyes were dark and cold, and her shoulders square, not hunched like so many suspects Freya had carted away.

"Yes," she said, her voice unwavering. "Yes, it's over now."

CHAPTER SIXTY

THE AMBULANCE WAS PULLING AWAY FROM THE WOODS' HOUSE JUST as Gillespie arrived with two transporters in tow. Cruz was in the passenger seat of Gillespie's car, and beside the large Glaswegian, he looked like a schoolboy riding up front with his father.

"What the bloody hell happened here?" Gillespie asked, as he was climbing from the car. A few curtains twitched in neighbouring houses, and the more brazen watched from their doorsteps with their arms folded, gossiping with their neighbours about what might have happened. There was, in Freya's opinion, very little they could have done to hide the fact that a body had been removed from the house. A body bag is a body bag, and has just one purpose. "It's like a bloody circus."

"No. Circuses make people laugh, Gillespie," Ben said. "This is horrific."

The uniforms from the transporters led both Franky and Leigh away from the house. Neither uttered a word, and the older of the two was the only one who showed any kind of remorse, with tears streaming down her face, and her eyes wide with post-adrenalin shock. Franky was, as ever, cold and sullen.

"That's Leigh Carson," Gillespie said, as Gold's car pulled up behind Gillespie's. "Why's she been arrested?"

"I'm afraid I'm tired of going through it all," Freya said. "Perhaps you could read the report when it's finally typed up."

He looked at Ben for an answer, who simply shrugged, then nodded a greeting to Gold who was a picture of guilt with her hunched shoulders and sorrowful, big eyes.

"I'm sorry. I didn't know she'd left the house," she said. "I thought she was upstairs having a bath."

Ben shook his head and waved the apology off, then returned his attention to Gillespie.

"I've no words to describe it, Jim. I didn't see it coming."

"Nobody did," Freya said, to Gold more than anybody else. "As far as I'm concerned, everyone on this team did their best. Let's get back to the station. We can let CSI do what they need to do. Ben, you and I will need to submit statements."

"Shouldn't we wait for the others?" Cruz said.

"The others?"

"Yeah. Nillson, Chapman, and the new girl."

"Anderson," Freya said.

"Yeah, her. They're all on their way here."

"On their way here? Why? I didn't tell them to."

"It's not every day we get a report of a gunshot, boss. Everyone was worried sick. Especially the new girl."

"Anderson?" Freya said.

"Yeah, her. She was up and out of the door before anyone. We thought you'd been hurt, boss."

Freya cocked her head, warmed that the team would care so much for her wellbeing.

"What about me?" Ben asked.

"What about you?" Cruz said.

"*I* could have been hurt."

"Well, yeah. I suppose you could have," Cruz said, and looked to Gillespie for support.

"I didn't hear about you all dropping everything and rushing to the scene when I *was* actually hurt a couple of months ago."

"Yeah, but it's you, isn't it?" Cruz said. He was about to dig himself an even deeper hole when Anderson's car came to a screeching halt behind Gold's. Three doors opened, three women climbed out, and their three faces seemed to be in sync when they saw Freya and relief washed over them.

"Thank God," Chapman said, as they drew close to where Freya, Ben, Gold, Gillespie, and Cruz were standing. "Sergeant Priest told us about the gunshot. He said it was a middle-aged female. We all thought the worst."

"Well, you should know better than to make assumptions," Freya said, trying to ignore the reference to her age. Although it stung a little. "But this is a shocking ending to a complex murder investigation. It's one that I will find it difficult to forget. Of that I'm certain."

She glanced across at Franky who peered through the rear doors of a transporter, emotionless sneer etched onto her face.

"Aye," Gillespie added. "Shocking. I would never have thought she was capable of that."

While all of this was taking place, Freya caught sight of Anderson, who remained at the gates of the property, looking on as an envious child might study a group of her peers.

"Anderson," Freya called. "Aren't you going to join us?"

"Am I welcome?" she said, after a moment of thought.

"You're part of the team now," Freya replied.

"Aye. Come on, Anderson. It's not often we get to stand around and chew the fat."

"What do you mean?" Ben said. "That's pretty much all you ever do."

"Aye, well. You know what I mean. I'm just trying to give the wee lass a bit of encouragement."

Slowly, Anderson, shoved off the wall and sauntered over to them.

"Chapman, how did you get on with Sykes?" Freya asked.

Chapman inhaled while she thought about what to say. But it was Nillson who answered on her behalf, which was probably for the best, as Chapman would have downplayed the result with her usual modesty.

"She nailed him, boss," Nillson said. "Bang to rights. He admitted to the dognapping. He admitted to breaking and entering. And he admitted to his involvement in stealing and killing the Carsons' dog. She broke him, boss. It was amazing. I've never seen so much paperwork in an interview before. She laid everything out before him and gave him nowhere to turn."

"And the other offence?" Freya asked.

Chapman stared at her, closed her eyes for a few seconds, and swallowed hard.

Then she nodded.

"Full confession," she said, her voice a mere whisper compared to Nillson's proud outburst.

Smiles ran through the team, although they were muted. They all understood that a conviction would not heal Chapman, but it would help.

"How did you get him to confess to all that?" Freya asked.

"Simple," Chapman said. "I made a deal with him. I laid out all the evidence for the rape, such as his jacket, the piece of material Ben found at my house, and the photos of the footprints in the mud outside my window. Anderson contacted somebody in London and managed to get access to Sykes' phone movements. We could put him at my house at the time of the incident. I told him if he confessed to the rape, I'd see to it that he cooperated and I'd make sure it was known that this was a one-time offence. He'd get a shorter sentence and an easier time in prison. Nobody likes a serial rapist, ma'am. Especially convicted felons."

"You befriended him?" Freya said.

"Not befriended," Chapman explained. "But, with Anderson's help, I was able to approach the interview objectively. It seems I'm not alone in being the victim of assault or abuse."

"No. No, you certainly are not," Freya said. "Well, I'd say that's a result worth celebrating. The drinks are on DC Cruz tonight."

"Eh?" he said.

"You win," Freya said. "Which, by rights, means you buy the first round."

"Win what?"

She fished the roll of banknotes from her pocket and held it up for the team to see.

Gillespie rolled his eyes, while Nillson smiled away the defeat with practiced composure.

"I won?" Cruz said, as if he was expecting Freya to tell him it was all a joke at his expense.

"I told you all that whoever makes the biggest contribution to the investigation will win the money, and you made the biggest contribution."

"And I seem to remember I chipped your twenty in," Gillespie told him. "So, it's actually more like seventy-five for you. That'll help pay for my new car window."

"I saw that," Gold said. "What happened?"

"I gave him a lesson in manners," Nillson said.

"Aye. It's a lesson I won't forget. That's for sure," Gillespie said, before turning to face Nillson and Anderson. "I suppose there's no chance-.

"None at all," Nillson said, flatly.

"What's that?" Freya said, and Gillespie tried to move the conversation on with a wave of his hand.

"Ah, it's nothing," he muttered.

"Gillespie was hoping that Anderson and I would deliver on the promised goods. But he didn't win. So, that's something at least," Nillson said.

"Promised goods?" Cruz said, staring between then all as if they all knew something he didn't.

"A kiss," Anderson said.

"A what?"

"Ah, come on. It was just a game. I didn't really mean-."

"A kiss?" Freya said. "If you had won the bet, you thought that Nillson and Anderson would have kissed you?"

"Aye, well. I mean-."

Freya stared at him, from his boots to his reddening face, letting the silence deliver the message that she despised him.

"I want it to be known," Freya added, "that I will not tolerate gambling among the team. I'll let it go this time, but if I catch anybody betting for money, or anything else for that matter, I'll be forced to take action. Is that understood?"

"Ma'am," Gold said, although she hadn't been a part of the bet.

"Aye, boss," Gillespie said. "I'll not be betting with you lot again. You can be sure of that."

Freya tossed Cruz the roll of notes, which he unfurled, sniffing each one as if it was hot off the press.

"Reports, statements, and evidence," Freya said. "I want everything in tomorrow morning. So don't get drunk tonight."

"Aren't you coming down the pub?" Gillespie asked. "Cruz said he wants to buy everyone a drink with his winnings."

"Maybe later," Freya said, and she turned to Ben who was waiting to go. "DS Savage and I have another little wager to settle."

CHAPTER SIXTY-ONE

It was three days later when Ben and Freya entered Lincoln in Freya's Range Rover. Gone were the days when Ben did all the driving. He didn't really mind. Freya's car was far more comfortable than his old Ford, not to mention it was faster.

The Friday afternoon exodus from the city had busied the oncoming traffic, but their journey had been fast. Twenty-five minutes at the most.

"I can't help but feel a little conflicted about what you said the other day. When uniform were taking Franky Woods away."

"What did I say?" Freya asked.

"To the team," he said. "You know? About there being no tolerance on betting for money or otherwise. And here's me buying you dinner as a result of a lost bet."

"You said Theo was guilty."

"I was coerced into entering the bet," Ben said. "Lured, by your bloody charisma."

"Just my charisma?" Freya said, and she raised both eyebrows at him with that saucy expression she wore so well. "Besides, I think it's a lesson for us all. After this, there'll be no more bets."

"I bet there is."

"Oh really?" Freya said. "How much?"

It was a joke, and Ben knew it. He sighed at the thought of how much the lost bet was going to set him back, but a part of him wondered what she had in mind exactly.

"I keep thinking about Theodore Wood," Ben said, moving the topic along. "Imagine it. You come out of hospital after a suicide attempt and find your daughter is on remand for murder, your father is missing, and your wife is dead."

"He's not missing," Freya said. "Sorry, hadn't you heard?"

"No. Solomon Yates was found?"

"Uniform picked him up. He was never going to get very far with two bloody vicious dogs. And let's face it, he was never going to let them go."

"No, he wasn't. So where is he?"

"At his farm. If you can call it a farm, anyway. It's more like a graveyard for old kitchen appliances if you ask me."

"Do you think he'll go back to his old tricks?"

"No," Freya said. "His partner in crime won't be out for a very long time. No, I think he and his son will live out their days in Bardney. Theo can run the business now, too. He might even turn a profit now his wife isn't running it into the ground. That's what I hope anyway. That's what I imagine will happen, if the world is in balance in any way, shape, or form."

"Very poetic."

"I can be, you know?" Freya said. "Poetic. Justice is best served cold, and with the element of surprise."

"Where exactly are we going?" Ben asked, as they crossed Pelham Bridge. "And why have you made me bring an overnight bag?"

Freya grinned as she slowed the car, indicated, then turned off the main road and headed towards the train station.

"You'll see," she said. Then, using her usual diversion tactics, she changed the subject. "Good news about Anderson moving in with Chapman, don't you think?"

"I do, as it happens," he replied. "It makes perfect sense. Neither of them feel safe alone. It's like everything came together in the end."

"It did indeed."

"But it wasn't without its casualties, was it?" Ben said.

"Casualties?"

"Us," he replied. "Oh, come on. I was wondering if you'd ever treat me like a friend again."

"I'm offended, Ben," she said, as she reached the end of the road and turned right, then immediately pulled left, turning into the train station's long-stay car park.

"What the bloody hell are we doing here?" he said.

"We're having dinner," she replied.

"Where? In the sandwich shop on the platform?"

"Not quite," she said. "You should have realised by now that my taste is a little more refined than to have an egg and cress sandwich that's curling at the edges."

"Then why here?"

"Any restaurant. That's what we agreed," she said. "Where were you going to take me if you had won our little wager?"

He suddenly felt like a fool and was apprehensive about telling her. But she stared at him from across the car, eyebrows raised, fingers stroking the leather steering wheel.

"A pub in Coningsby," he muttered.

"A what?"

"A pub," he repeated. "In Coningsby. Gourmet food. Absolutely delicious. Costs a bloody arm and a leg too."

"Coningsby?" she said, clearly close to being offended.

"What's wrong with Coningsby?"

"There's nothing wrong with Coningsby. It's a lovely village. But not quite what I had in mind."

"And what do you have in mind?" he asked.

"A dinner, Ben. I keep telling you," she said, as she climbed from the car and retrieved her expensive-looking little case from the rear seat. "You'll have to wait and see."

Ben leaped from the car and snatched his bag, which was nothing more than an old sports holdall with a ripped side pocket. The front had a mud stain on it from where he'd chucked it into the back of his dad's pickup once and never bothered to wipe it off.

She was already halfway to the station by the time he'd gathered his belongings.

"Freya?" he said and pointed up the road to the high street. "Where are you going? The city centre is this way."

She entered the station, walked through to the platform, and he found her checking her wristwatch with her case by her feet.

"Are we getting a train?"

"It seems a likely prospect given the train tracks, Ben. Nice detective work."

"Are we going to Peterborough?"

"No, Ben. Although, I think we might be passing through."

"London?" he cried. "We're going to bloody London?"

"Again. We'll be passing through London," she said, then reached into her pocket. "Oh, I nearly forgot. You'll need this."

She handed him a brown envelope. He felt the contents and surmised it contained a small book. So, he peered inside out of curiosity.

"A passport?" he said.

"No. Not just any passport, Ben," she said. "*Your* passport. I had Anderson search for it in your house. I hear it on good authority that she's a dab hand at illegal searches."

She eyed him knowingly, and ordinarily he would have reddened or looked away. But the illegal search was nothing compared to the intrigue she had built up.

"Why do I need my bloody passport?"

"Oh, for crying out loud, Ben," she said. "We agreed that the loser would buy the other dinner in a restaurant of their choice and cover all expenses."

"Right?" he said.

"Well, it just so happens that my favourite restaurant is called the Restaurant Guy Savoy," she said, and he stared at her quizzically. "That's in Paris, in case you hadn't guessed."

"*Paris?*" he repeated, and a few people on the platform turned to stare at him. Calmly, Freya collected her case, handed it to him, and then stepped closer to the edge of the platform to greet the oncoming train.

"Come along, Ben. This is our train," she said, purposefully not meeting him eye to eye.

"And what do they serve in this Guy Savage place, then?"

"It's the Restaurant Guy Savoy, Ben. At least pretend to be a little cultured, for my sake. And they serve many things," she said, clearly growing exasperated at his persistence. "Justice is my favourite."

"Justice?" he said, noticing her wry expression. But then something dawned on him that he'd entirely overlooked before. "Hold on a minute. It was you who said Theo was the killer. I said he was the victim."

"Oh, did you?" she replied, her nonchalant tone drowned out by the grinding train brakes. "But he wasn't actually the victim, was he?"

"He wasn't the killer either."

The train stilled and doors hissed open along the platform.

"So we were both right," Freya said, with one foot on the step up to the train. "And well, we're here now, aren't we?"

Ben shook his head in utter astonishment, saying nothing as she climbed onto the train. She turned and stared back at him with that winning smile of hers.

"Do come along, Ben," she said, with a wink. "*Tout suite*."

The End.

DANCE WITH DEATH - PROLOGUE

The summer sun was a welcome treat that seemed to silence the world around Myra, save for the bird song, buzzing insects, and the crunch of dry grass beneath her boots as she turned off Dunston Fen Lane onto the single track with a destination in mind, and the promise of a warm hand to hold.

Warm air licked at Myra's bare legs as her feet kicked through the long grass surrounding the field. She held her phone to her ear with one hand, and in the other, a limp dog lead hung, knotted and worn from years of use. Jambo, her working cocker spaniel, darted through the grass somewhere far ahead. She couldn't see him. But every so often, a family of lapwings would scatter from their nests and he would leap up to catch one. Inevitably he would fail and disappear from sight again.

"Where are you?" her daughter said over the phone. "Are you out with Jambo?"

"You know I'm walking the dog, Claire. I always come home to walk the dog at midday," Myra said. "Besides, Vince next door always cuts the grass at lunch time, and you know I can't bear the noise. Honestly, sometimes I think he does it just to annoy me."

"I just wondered how far you were into the walk, Mum. That's all."

"Halfway," Myra replied. "So we've got ten minutes or so to speak. Tell me about Kevin. What's he doing?"

"Are you in your usual haunt?" Claire asked.

"Of course," Myra said. "I always come here. There are plenty of other dogs for Jambo to play with usually."

"That's nice."

"And Kevin? Or are you avoiding talking about him?"

"Mum, do we have to go through this?"

"I just asked what he was up to."

"You were hoping I'd tell you that we're separating. That's what you were hoping for."

"Now you're putting words into my mouth," Myra said. "So? What's he doing?"

"Oh, you know. Working, as usual, I suppose. I haven't seen him since yesterday."

"Left you to do the housework, no doubt," Myra said, glancing out across the freshly harvested fields and using the break in conversation to listen and appreciate the silence.

"He does what he can," Claire replied. "He needs space to do what he can."

"It's not enough. He should be helping you more," Myra said, making her way towards the raised riverbank at the far end of the field, which was easily twenty feet high and stretched as far as the eye could see.

"He works, Mum."

"He sits in his study doing what he loves to do, while you have to clean that house all by yourself. I'm telling you, Claire, if you don't put a stop to it now, he'll walk all over you for the rest of your life."

"A rod for my own back. Yes, you've said that before."

"Is he listening? Is that why you're speaking quietly? Did you show him what I sent you?"

"No, Mum. He's not listening. He's gone away for a few days. Can you just leave him to me?"

"Gone away for a few days? After what he did? You should have kicked him out."

"Mum!"

"Leaving you to look after the house, no doubt?"

"Listen, Mum. We've been over this," Claire said. "I can't keep talking about it."

Myra stepped off the track and into the long grass beside the field, making her way towards the riverbank.

"Where are you anyway?" Myra said. "I can hear birds. Are you in the garden?"

"I'm just keeping on top of it," Claire said after a pause. "What about you anyway? Have you given your fancy man his marching orders?"

"He's not my fancy man. And yes, I have. Not that it's any of your business."

They shared a moment of silence, as they often did. Sometimes Myra just enjoyed having her on the end of the phone; it gave her a connection.

"Mum?" Claire said, her voice calm and thoughtful. "Mum, you wouldn't lie to me, would you?"

"Lie to you? No, dear. Why? Why would I lie?"

"It's just..." Claire started, then stopped. "Sometimes I think you twist the truth to get your own way, that's all. Like the whole thing with Kevin, and I just think that..."

"Think what, Claire?"

"Well, if you'd lie about that, what else would you lie about?"

"I am not twisting the truth," Myra said. "I would never lie to you. You're all I have."

"And you won't meet him again? Your fancy man, that is."

"For goodness sake, Claire. I promise, hand on heart, that I will not see him anymore. Why can't you just leave my private life alone?"

"Because he's married, Mum. You know it's not just your lives you're affecting?"

"I read his last book, you know?" Myra said, knowing it would tease her daughter back into a more amenable conversation.

Claire took a long breath. "You changed the subject," she said with a sigh. "And did you enjoy it?"

"Well, I say I read it. I skim-read it."

"You mean you read the last chapter to see who the killer was, then flicked through looking for mistakes?"

"You know I don't like surprises," Myra said.

"Then why read a murder mystery?" Claire said. "Why not read a romance or something, where you know the lovers will end up together?"

"I'm just showing an interest, that's all. It gives me something to talk to him about. Lord knows we have nothing else in common, him and I. I doubt I shall ever be able to look him in the eye again after what he did to you."

"You both have me," Claire suggested.

"We do, yes. But regardless of what he says, dear, you know that no man could ever love you like I do. Remember that, will you? There's no greater love than a mother's love."

"Yeah, I know," Claire said, although her voice was tinged with doubt.

"You *should* know, too. You need to stand on your own two feet more. Be independent. Show him you don't need him."

"I am standing on my own two feet, Mum."

"Well, stand taller. I shouldn't have to clean your house when I visit–"

"You don't have to–"

"There's dust everywhere I look. I wouldn't do it if I didn't love you. The bathrooms too. It's a shame that husband of yours can't put his books down for long enough to clean them. Although, I dare say he'd cut corners. Men just don't clean as well as women. It's a fact."

"Mum!" Claire said, and Myra sighed as she entered the shade of a large oak.

"I just want you to be happy, that's all," Myra said. "I won't always be around to watch out for you. I mean it, Claire. Just have strength. Stand up for what you believe in and be the best person you can be. Remember that and you won't go far wrong."

"The best person I can be?" Claire said.

"Just…" Myra began, and she stifled a tear, controlling her breathing and quelling the whimper in her voice. "I love you, Claire. That's all."

"Goodbye, Mum," Claire said, at last, her voice a faint whisper over the line.

"Goodbye," Myra said, hearing a footstep behind her in the grass. She inhaled, long and deep and found the smile she had buried somewhere inside of her.

"I didn't think you'd come," she called out, as she pocketed her phone, then turned to face him.

But instead of being met with a kiss, a strong hand clamped over her mouth and another gripped her throat before she was pulled to the ground.

The scent was familiar. The heavy breathing, even more so. But the strength was beyond what Myra had thought them capable of.

The last memory that passed through her mind as her world turned black was the day Claire had been born.

It was a beautiful memory. It had been a wonderful life.

And given the chance, she wouldn't change a single thing.

ALSO BY JACK CARTWRIGHT

The DCI Cook Murder Mysteries

A Winter of Blood

A Secret to Die For

The Wild Fens Murder Mysteries

Secrets In Blood

One For Sorrow

In Cold Blood

Suffer In Silence

Dying To Tell

Never To Return

Lie Beside Me

Dance With Death

In Dead Water

One Deadly Night

Her Dying Mind

Into Death's Arms

Join my VIP reader group to be among the first to hear about new release dates, discounts, and get a free Wild Fens novella.

Visit www.jackcartwrightbooks.com for details.

VIP READER CLUB

Your FREE ebook is waiting for you now.

Get your FREE copy of the prequel story to the Wild Fens Murder Mystery series, and learn how DI Freya Bloom came to give up everything she had, to start a new life in Lincolnshire.

Visit www.jackcartwrightbooks.com to join the VIP Reader Club.

I'll see you there.

Jack Cartwright

AFTERWORD

Because reviews are critical to an author's career, if you have enjoyed this novel, you could do me a huge favour by leaving a review on Amazon.

Reviews allow other readers to find my books. Your help in leaving one would make a big difference to this author.

Thank you for taking the time to read *Lie Beside Me*.

COPYRIGHT

Copyright © 2022 by JackCartwright

All rights reserved.

The moral right of Jack Cartwright to be identified as the author of this work has been asserted by him in accordance with the Copyright, Designs and Patents act 1988.

All the characters in this book are fictitious, and any resemblance to actual persons living or dead is purely coincidental.

All rights reserved. No part of this publication may be reproduced, stored in a retrieval system or transmitted in any form or by any means, without the prior permission in writing of the publisher, nor to be otherwise circulated in any form of binding or cover other than that in which it is published without a similar condition, including this condition, being imposed on the subsequent purchaser.

Milton Keynes UK
Ingram Content Group UK Ltd.
UKHW030639191124
451300UK00014B/345/J